Praise for the novels of Jane Myers Perrine

THE WELCOME COMMITTEE OF BUTTERNUT CREEK

"[G]entle, funny, romantic, and honest new series...This is a delightful first volume in what promises to be a wonderful series." —*Publishers Weekly*

"A warm, witty, wonderful book. I loved it, and you will too." —Susan Mallery, *New York Times* and *USA Today* bestselling author

"[W]ill definitely appeal to fans of Jan Karon's Mitford series." —*Library Journal*

"Fun characters and a storyline that will hit close to home for a number of readers make this novel appealing to a wide variety of people." —*RT Book Reviews*

"Wow! Jane Myers Perrine has penned an amazing story with heart, hope, and humor...you can't help but fall in love with the people and the place." —Christie Craig, author of *Hotter in Texas*

"Heartwarming and hilarious, *The Welcome Committee of Butternut Creek* offers a touching, small-town view of the ties that bind." —Award-winning author Colleen Thompson

THE MATCHMAKERS OF
BUTTERNUT CREEK

"I did not want to put this book down. The characters and Jane Myers Perrine's storytelling gift captured my heart on page one and held on to the satisfying end. This is truly a special story." —Laurie Alice Eakes, award-winning author of *A Flight of Fancy*

"Fans of Jan Karon will feel right at home in Butternut Creek." —*San Francisco Book Review*

"With small-town charm and the perfect amount of humor, Perrine's second novel set in Butternut Creek is sweet and engaging." —*Romantic Times*

THE WEDDING PLANNERS OF
BUTTERNUT CREEK

"Perrine offers a pleasant, meandering glimpse at love and courtship in Butternut Creek...An affable and entertaining romance." —*Kirkus Reviews*

The Welcome Committee of
BUTTERNUT CREEK

Also by Jane Myers Perrine

The Matchmakers of Butternut Creek
The Wedding Planners of Butternut Creek

The Welcome Committee of
BUTTERNUT CREEK

A Novel

Jane Myers Perrine

Faith
Words®

New York Boston Nashville

FaithWords
Hachette Book Group
237 Park Avenue
New York, NY 10017

www.faithwords.com

Printed in the United States of America

RRD-C

First trade edition: April 2012
First special trade edition: April 2014

10 9 8 7 6 5 4 3 2 1

FaithWords is a division of Hachette Book Group, Inc.

The FaithWords name and logo are trademarks of Hachette Book Group, Inc.

The Hachette Speakers Bureau provides a wide range of authors for speaking events. To find out more, go to www.hachettespeakersbureau.com or call (866) 376-6591.

The publisher is not responsible for websites (or their content) that are not owned by the publisher.

The Library of Congress Cataloging-in-Publication Data

Perrine, Jane Myers.
  The welcome committee of Butternut Creek / Jane Myers Perrine.—1st ed.
    p. cm.
  ISBN 978-0-89296-921-0
  I. Title.
  PS3616.E79W45 2012
  813'.6—dc22
                                                        2011015395

ISBN 978-1-4555-5699-1 (spec. ed. pbk.)

Acknowledgments

My deepest gratitude and love go to my husband, whom I have followed to small-town churches from Dixon, Missouri, to Burnet, Texas. Without him, I wouldn't have had the experience to write this novel or the confidence to keep going.

To all of the kind people in the churches George and I have served, many thanks. You have taught me so much and shared your lives and your stories with me. Mary Alice, no one in this book is based on you.

I appreciate Tim Tutt and Priscilla Holt for sharing several anecdotes and Jessica Scott, a fellow writer, soldier, and friend, for sharing her expertise. Any errors are mine.

Many thanks to my wonderful editor Christina Boys and the terrific people at FaithWords/Hachette Book Group who have faith in Butternut Creek, its inhabitants, and the author.

Finally, I cannot thank my agent, Pam Strickler, enough for her guidance and belief in me. Truly, without her, this novel would not have been written.

*This novel is dedicated to Cheyenne Steve,
my dear friend.*

Prologue

From the desk of
Adam Joseph Jordan, MDiv.

I'm a sad burden for Birdie MacDowell.

Over the years, she's often told me that.

Miss Birdie has been a member of Butternut Creek Christian Church since—well, as long as anyone can remember. Certainly long before I showed up. I'm not sure at what age one becomes a pillar of the church, but Miss Birdie has been one for at least forty years. I think she probably took over running the church while she was on the cradle roll. For that reason, I often think of her as both Miss Birdie and, in my mind only, the pillar.

The cause of her distress is and always has been my ministry, plagued by what she calls my sad ways and errors as well as what she describes as either disastrous decisions or, less catastrophically, the poor choices on my part. She tells me at least once a day, and several times on Sunday, that her ability to put up with all my failings plus my inclination to use incomplete and run-on sentences have equipped her for sainthood.

Not that Miss Birdie hasn't attempted to change me since the day I arrived ten years ago, to—in her words—help me avoid mistakes, both spiritual and social and, I'm sure she'd add, physical. Probably grammatical as well. She believes, she says, that this is her mission, the reason God placed her in Butternut Creek at this time: to train this imperfect fellow God has left in her care. Miss Birdie takes that responsibility seriously.

Two or three times a week she drops in to see what I'm doing, to give me excellent words of advice, which I promptly either reject or forget. Not that it makes any difference which. If I could remember her advice, I'd reject it, and vice versa because it doesn't meld with my beliefs about what is best for the church and best for the congregation.

That propensity to think for myself is what makes her unhappy, makes her long for the imminent arrival of her crown and halo instead of the eternal martyrdom of having to put up with a young and still—in her opinion—very inexperienced minister.

She often bemoans the fact that the elders didn't heed her exhortation and call a man far more experienced and godly than I. Instead they called me, inexperienced and impulsive as I am, because I was all they could afford. A more experienced minister would be called to a larger church in the city. A married minister would expect to be able to feed his family on his salary.

And so I then became the thorn in Miss Birdie's side, her cross to bear, and her hope for everlasting salvation.

That relationship, in great part, is what this book is about. But it's also about what happened during my first year in Butternut Creek: the people in town, their joys and burdens and everyday dilemmas, death and sorrow and love, the stories my friends and members of the congregation have told me and even the gossip I've heard, as much as I attempt to avoid it.

I dedicate this book to the wonderful people of Butternut Creek with my love and admiration, and in the desperate hope that someday Miss Birdie will forgive me for my many errors.

Chapter One

On a blazing-hot June afternoon in the middle of a clogged US 183 in Austin, Texas, Adam Jordan clenched his hands on the steering wheel of the stalled car and considered the situation. As a newly ordained minister, he probably should pray, but he felt certain the drivers of the vehicles backed up behind him would prefer him to do something less spiritual.

The day before, he'd headed west from Lexington, Kentucky, toward Central Texas, a twenty-hour, thousand-mile trip, in a car held together by his little bit of mechanical skill and a lot of prayer. Sadly, on Tuesday, the Lord looked away for a moment as Adam attempted to navigate the crowded tangle of highways that is Austin. The radiator coughed steam as the old vehicle stopped in the center lane of more traffic than he'd ever seen gathered together in midafternoon. Did rush hour start at three o'clock here? He soon learned that rush hour on US 183 could last all day and much of the night, because the city grew faster than its highway system.

He got out of the car and began pushing what had once been a brilliantly blue Honda across two lanes of barely moving traffic and onto the shoulder amid the honks and the screeches of highway noise and curses of angry drivers. If his defective directional skills hadn't led him on a fifty-mile detour into South Austin, the pitiful old vehicle might have made it to Butternut Creek—but they had and the car hadn't.

As happens to everyone and everything over the years, the Honda had faded and frayed until no one could tell what it once had been. The identifying hood ornament had long since fallen off, and the paint was a crackled and blistered gray. And white. With rust peering through it. But it usually ran.

Adam's first thought was to abandon the heap right there, but he'd heard Texas had laws against that. Instead, he called Howard Crampton, an elder of the church and the chair of the search committee that had called Adam.

"Hey, Howard," he said when the elder picked up the phone. "I'm stuck in Austin on 183."

For a moment, Howard said nothing. Finally he asked, "Who is this?"

So much for believing the church breathlessly awaited his arrival. "Adam Jordan." When silence greeted that, Adam added, "The new minister."

"Hey, Adam. Good to hear from you. Sorry I didn't recognize you at first. I'm in the middle of a bank audit and my brain's filled with numbers. What can I do you for?"

"My car broke down on 183, north of something called the Mopac."

"Know exactly where that is. I'll send a tow truck to pick you up."

"All the way from Butternut Creek?"

"Not too far. Sit tight."

As if he could do anything else.

And that's how Adam entered Butternut Creek: sitting in

the cab of the tow truck, chatting with Rex, the driver, about fishing and hunting, neither of which he did back then, with his car rattling on the flatbed behind the two men. Although his disreputable arrival didn't signal a propitious beginning, he fell in love with the town immediately.

They entered on Farm-to-Market—FM—road 1212A, which passed between the Whataburger and the H-E-B. Rex pointed out the football stadium and high school about a hundred yards to the north and up the hill. Then the residential section began, big Victorians shoved jowl-to-jowl with bungalows and ranch houses, split levels alongside columned Colonials, interspersed with apartments and motels. Here and there, large, beautifully manicured lawns stretched out, some decorated with a gazebo or fountain while in a yard next to them appeared an occasional pink flamingo or enormous live oak trees dripping with Spanish moss.

Everyone waved as Rex chugged along Main Street. Adam waved back, instantly charmed by the town, by the people who smiled a greeting, by the sturdy brick buildings with Victorian trim and enormous old trees standing tall and full and casting shade and shadows across the lawns and the streets.

"Town square just over on the other side of the courthouse, that way, Padre." Rex nodded to the right. "I'm fixin' to leave you and your car at the church. I'll help unload it. Don't look like you've got a lot of stuff."

As Rex turned the steering wheel, the truck lumbered into the church parking lot. "You leave your keys in the car and I'll pick it up later."

Adam swiveled to look at the driver. "Leave the keys in my car?"

"Padre, you're in Butternut Creek. No one steals cars here."

He glanced back into the rearview mirror. "Especially not that one."

While Rex lowered the car onto the asphalt, the new minister turned to study the parsonage.

His eyes lifted, up and up. He'd seen Victorians but never one quite so big. When the pulpit committee had come to Lexington to interview him, they'd described the house, but he hadn't realized the massive size of the pale yellow edifice: three stories, each six or eight windows across, doors and shutters of a dark green, every inch of surface covered with painted wooden curlicues of a dark purplish color—maroon?— plus newel posts and bric-a-brac and, bringing it all together, gingerbread. What in the world would he do with all that space?

As he studied the turret and the bay windows and everything else on the house, he felt sure the parishioners expected him to multiply and be fruitful, producing enough babies to fill every bedroom and all the children's Sunday school classes. He shook his head. Bad planning not to have brought a wife with him.

Sadly for the hopes of the congregation and all those empty rooms, no prospect for a bride had presented herself over the last few years, not since his fiancée Laurel dumped him after she decided she didn't want to marry a minister. The teas and worship services and good works, she'd said, weren't really her thing.

The church management professor at the seminary had warned the newly minted and still-single ministers not to date a young woman in the congregation. It could cause jealousy. It would cause discomfort if they parted. Gossip could ruin a minister's reputation.

Although warned by the professor, Adam had ignored the

problem being a single minister presented several months ago. He'd known a few women interested in marrying a preacher, but they were in Kentucky. Even they wouldn't covet that position enough to follow him to Texas. Besides, he'd always felt a little uncomfortable with the forward women who made their determination to marry a minister clear. Not that he felt comfortable with any young woman. That personality flaw probably doomed the possibility of, like Abraham, his fathering a multitude of nations or even two or three children to fill those rooms.

Maybe the extra space could be used as classrooms for Sunday school? A library? A boardinghouse to bring in a little additional income for the church?

Adam reached forward to try the front door. It opened right up. Getting used to all this trust in small-town Texas was going to be hard. Would he insult someone if he locked the door?

Inside, his footsteps echoed. As he walked, he looked around the great expanse of hardwood floor, the huge and beautifully curved staircase leading up to a second story, the empty parlors on each side of a hallway that led back and back into unknown areas he'd explore later. The silence crushed in on him, and he felt even more alone than he had when his parents left him at boarding school years earlier.

"Grab a box, Padre," Rex shouted from outside, interrupting his reflections.

"Coming." Adam ran back out to the car and flipped the trunk open. Within a few minutes, the two men had unloaded the car and lugged everything inside.

When Rex left, the sound of his work boots thudding across the polished floor, Adam glanced at the tiny heap of his possessions in the middle of what looked like a family room or maybe a dining area, and then began to explore. First he ambled back to the front porch, which looked as if it surrounded the entire house. His neighbors to the right and across the street lived in similarly huge Victorians. Then he turned to the left to study the beautiful brick church just north across the parking lot. Huge live oaks dripping with Spanish moss shaded the green lawn. Strength and love and serenity seemed to flow from the steepled roof and huge white columns. How could he have been so blessed to do the Lord's work here, in this perfect place?

Of course, he hadn't met Miss Birdie yet.

Adam's college days and nights had been spent in a dorm room. During seminary, he occupied the furnished parsonage of his student church up near Maysville, Kentucky, a town founded by Daniel Boone and famous as the birthplace of Rosemary Clooney. Because, as an adult, he'd lived in furnished spaces, he possessed no furniture: not a card table, not a desk chair, not a bed. Oh, he did have a sleeping bag from the youth retreats and church camp, a television that he hoped to hook up to cable soon, and a computer with the sermons he'd preached over the past three years. He'd shipped all his books ahead. All those boxes should be stacked in the minister's study at the church. Other than that, all his earthly possessions were in a couple of boxes and two ancient suitcases.

He studied the pile of his things and shook his head. This little bit to fill a huge parsonage.

Miss Birdie was horrified when she brought him dinner that evening.

"You're Adam Joseph Jordan?" Without identifying herself, she strutted into the barren desolation of the parsonage like a five-star general inspecting her troops. The fact that only one slightly terrified man stood before her didn't lessen her resolve.

"Yes, Miss Birdie." Adam knew who she was. Howard had warned him, told him how to address her and how to act in her presence. In that moment, he realized Howard's words of caution, the admonitions Adam had laughed off, were disturbingly true.

"Well, I swan." She looked way up at Adam. "You are a tall, skinny boy, aren't you?"

At six-four and 160, Adam had been tall and skinny as long as he could remember. Most people didn't comment on it.

She studied his face and height for a few more seconds. "With a name like Adam Joseph Jordan, guess you didn't have much choice but to become a minister." Then she took off across the entry hall. Her tiny feet, shod in tie-up shoes with fat rubber soles, squished across the hardwood floor before she stopped and stood between what Adam had labeled as two large parlors.

She wore her white hair in a no-nonsense, almost military style: short and parted on the right. No curls, no waves. Straight with a hint of bangs brushed to the left. Her chest held as high as a proud robin's, she turned to look at the empty space. Every inch of her body showed disdain as she inspected the area. How could such a tiny, thin woman give off such as air of authority, control, and doom?

How could she intimidate a man more than a foot taller than she? But she did. Adam cringed inside.

Chagrin oozed across her features. "Tut, tut, tut." She made a quick turn in the middle of the room to glare at the new preacher, then closed her eyes and shook her head. When she finally opened her eyes, she glared at him again.

"What kind of minister…what kind of person has no furniture at all?"

Adam smiled at her in an effort to ingratiate himself. She didn't smile back. He'd disappointed her, as he figured he would many more times.

Did she expect Adam to be ashamed of his lack of furnishings? To look mortified? He didn't because he wasn't, but Miss Birdie wouldn't understand. Generations separated them. She'd probably never heard of a futon. When he didn't flinch—at least, not outwardly—or apologize for his shortcomings, she said, "Hmph."

He'd rapidly learn that she expressed some of her most powerful comments with sounds.

With a quick turn, she marched down the short hallway and into the room where his few possessions resided. She glared at the pile of stuff.

"What's this?" She pointed at his pitiful collection of belongings. "You really don't have any furniture? None?"

"I have a television and a computer and a…that's about it." Instantly recognizing that his words didn't satisfy her a bit, Adam added, "I'll have to work on that." He again attempted to disarm her with a smile but learned in a moment that Miss Birdie was not disarmable, especially when the truth lay so heavily on her side. "Treasure in heaven, you know," he added.

Ignoring the biblical reference, she said, "Where am I supposed to put this?" She nodded toward the quilted tote that dangled from her arm and emitted a mouthwatering aroma. "Where are you going to eat it?" She tilted her head and squinted at him. "Are you the kind of man who stands at the kitchen counter to eat?"

Yes, Adam was, although he hadn't realized it qualified him

as part of a decadent class of humanity. After disappointing her about the furniture, he couldn't confess he was guilty of what she so clearly considered a lack of proper etiquette, of gentility and acceptable rearing. She would have turned, he feared, and taken that dish away. The aroma of what she'd prepared called to him, made his stomach growl after a ten-hour drive without stopping for meals because he'd been afraid the old car would conk out if it got a rest and a chance to think about how much farther it had to go.

"Oh, no. I plan to get some furniture and sit at the table. For the moment, I'll have to stand at the kitchen counter to eat." He nodded his head, then shook it, not sure which action was required to respond to her question. "Only for a few days."

"Don't suppose you have a bed?"

"Sleeping bag."

"Sofa? Chair?"

He shook his head.

She took a step forward and scrutinized him. Adam felt judged and found wanting. No hope of redemption existed. Miss Birdie's expression didn't even hold out the promise of grace. "Do you have a towel? A bar of soap?"

"Soap. Yes, I have soap." Glad to have finally passed one of her tests, he pointed toward a box and a small suitcase. "And probably a couple of towels." He waved at a tattered suitcase held together with a belt. "Somewhere."

With a deep sigh—one that Adam felt came from the very depths of her soul and left no doubt what she thought about this feckless young man who stood to eat and yet had the audacity to undertake the task of becoming her spiritual adviser—she placed the dish on the kitchen counter, turned, and squish-squished out of the house. Without a *Good-bye* or a *Blessings* or a *Welcome to Butternut Creek*, she left.

After she slammed the front door, Adam discovered a spoon and plastic tumbler in one of his boxes and was able to eat some of the delicious chicken spaghetti right out of the dish. Still, he kept checking the entrance hall in case Miss Birdie might fling the front door open and shout *Aha!* when she found out he hadn't even bothered to find a plate because he was a rude and boorish young man, as most twenty-five-year-old bachelors he knew were. The fear of her appearance made locking the door seem like a good idea.

He put the leftovers away in the refrigerator provided by the church. Inside were a carton of milk, another of orange juice, butter, and a dozen eggs, all left by some helpful person. If he could find a frying pan, he could fix breakfast in the morning.

Over the next few hours, more members of the congregation stopped by. They smiled and welcomed Adam and brought cakes and bread and vegetables and fried chicken and a brisket.

Once that slowed down, Adam considered unpacking, but he had no hangers and none had been left in the tiny coat closet. Probably some hung in the huge number of closets upstairs, but he didn't feel the call to explore tonight. All those large empty rooms would probably depress him. He left everything in the suitcases, boxes, and plastic bags. Surely everyone—except Miss Birdie—would understand.

Next he called his parents, who'd retired to London after his father sold his company for gazillions of dollars. It was very early morning there, but his mother was glad to hear he'd arrived safely and promised they'd visit soon. His father expressed amazement that Butternut Creek had telephone service.

Tomorrow he'd email his sister in Kenya. Not that she'd

worry. Traveling between refugee camps as she did was a lot more dangerous than the trip through Tennessee and Arkansas he'd just made.

Having completed everything he needed to take care of right away, at nine thirty he rolled out the sleeping bag, plugged in the television, and searched for a baseball game. Unfortunately, only one station came in, a feed from Austin transmitted from Llano. The picture was snowy, and the sound faded in and out. The problem constituted another introduction to the difference between city and rural life, but he didn't mind. He listened to the local news and watched the blurry rerun of a sitcom before deciding to go to bed. Or, to be more exact, to go to sleeping bag.

Filled with gratitude to be here, he said his prayers and dozed off as soon as he finished.

After the long, exhausting trip, he slept well.

❧

The insistent ringing of the doorbell started at nine o'clock. Adam shook his head in a futile effort to clear it, slipped into jeans and pulled on a T-shirt. When he opened the door, two muscular men stood there, carrying a sofa between them. Adam stepped back and watched as they brought it in without a word. They settled it against the wall of the room where he'd slept, then headed back out to a large truck with HILTON FURNITURE painted on the side.

"What are you doing?" he asked as the furniture came inside. "This isn't mine. I didn't order it and I can't pay for this," Adam attempted to explain as they carried in a large dining room table. They didn't stop.

Like a yappy little dog, he ran after them asking where all this had come from.

"You're in the wrong house," he said but the men continued to ignore him. Taciturn and focused, they kept unloading and placing the furniture where they thought it appropriate: a recliner, a coffee table, that dining room table with six hefty chairs, a queen-size bed—well, almost everything a bachelor minister needed to set up housekeeping except, of course, that big bed they'd taken upstairs, which suggested marriage at some time down the road.

During this entire time, the men didn't pay the slightest bit of attention to him. When they had finished, Rodolfo—the name embroidered on his shirt—handed Adam a clipboard and pen. "Please sign, Pastor."

He took the invoice and read it, attempting to find out the source of the furniture and where it should have been delivered. There was nothing on that page except the word WIDOWS and his address. Well, not the real address because, as he later learned, no one knew one another's numerical addresses. This house was described as "the parsonage next to the Christian Church."

"I can't pay for this."

"It's taken care of."

"Everything's been paid for?"

"Uh-huh." Rodolfo took the page Adam had signed, then tore off and handed the minister a copy. Followed by his crew, he left.

"Who paid for it?" Adam ran along behind the crew.

"Don't know."

"You're sure you're in the right place?"

"This is the parsonage, right? Next to the Christian Church?" He turned back and pointed at both. At Adam's nod, he and the other men got into the truck.

"Who are the widows?" Adam shouted as they drove away.

When the truck disappeared down the highway, he wandered inside to look around the newly furnished rooms.

Where had all this come from?

The only person he could think of who knew he didn't have furniture was Miss Birdie. Well, the other church members who'd dropped by must have noticed the lack, but they hadn't seemed to mind. Perhaps they believed the rest of his stuff would be delivered later. Or they might have realized that young ministers seldom had money and wouldn't have a great number of worldly goods.

But Miss Birdie had cared deeply about the inadequacy. She'd taken it almost like an insult to her personally and to the church that had called him. As he walked through the parsonage on the hardwood floors he bet the ladies had buffed earlier in the week, he remembered her deep disappointment in his lack of possessions and her sharp words.

Now a sofa sat against the north wall of the larger parlor, a great green-plaid beast with soft pillows. He'd have a place to sit and watch television. He sat down. Comfortable and exactly long enough to take a nap during a slow ball game.

Miss Birdie wore comfortable shoes and inexpensive clothing. Surely she didn't have enough money to buy all this. Was Adam wrong about that, too?

Only a few minutes later while he admired the rest of the furnishings, the doorbell sounded again. When he opened it, a white-haired gentleman stood there.

"Jesse Hardin." He grasped Adam's hand in a huge hand. "Got a card table for you." As he dragged the table inside, Jesse said, "My wife and I own a farm outside town. Do you like to ride horses?"

"Well, I'm from Kentucky so I should," Adam began. "But I don't."

"Well, if you want to give it a try, give me a call."

A few minutes after Jesse left, Howard Crampton dropped by with two folding chairs and put them in the breakfast nook with the card table.

"Great cowboy hat," Adam said, noticing the wide-brimmed hat the elder wore.

"Son." Howard's expression was someplace between a smile and a frown. "I'm going to teach you a little something about Texas. Don't ever call this a cowboy hat. You could insult some good ol' boy who might take exception, physically, to your sentiments. This"—he pointed to his head—"is my Stetson. Some men prefer a Resistol, but real Texans wear Stetsons."

Adam nodded. "Thank you, sir." He dropped his gaze. When he did, he noticed Howard wore cowboy boots, too, with intricate tooling on the toe, but Adam sure wasn't going to ask about those. Instead he asked a completely different question, the one that really bothered him. "Howard, who are the widows?"

"Don't worry about that." The elder shook his head. "You'll find out soon enough. Relax today, get settled."

Before he could ask more, Howard sprinted out.

Now Adam really worried.

After Maudie Adams left, a set of towels hung over the bars in both upstairs bathrooms, the bed was made, and more linens were folded in a closet. Later that afternoon, two high school football players lugged in an enormous rustic oak armoire, which they settled against the wall opposite the sofa. Adam's little portable television sat in splendor inside.

He had furniture. An abundance of furniture. More than he'd ever owned or thought he'd possess. The sight of his parlor and the new furniture filled him with a feeling of comfort, security, and joy. Even if they were temporary, even if the furnishings belonged here, stayed in the parsonage for the next minister of Butternut Creek, the sight of this plenty and a self-indulgent pride of ownership filled Adam with such an agreeable warmth that he struggled to force back that unholy and impious sentiment and attempted to refocus on the spiritual.

That not quite accomplished, he wandered onto the front porch and settled on the swing, pushing back with his feet a couple of times until the movement became established. A soft breeze dried the perspiration he'd worked up from watching those fine new belongings being brought in.

He looked out across the wide green yard he'd need to mow soon. Then his gaze again turned toward the church with the tall pillars in front, two on each side of the massive front door that looked as if it could have been part of the Arc of the Covenant. His eyes climbed the spire to the cross atop the steeple.

On that lovely, gentle evening, he whispered a verse from Psalms: "I give thanks to You, O Lord my God, with my whole heart, and I will glorify Your name forever."

The beautiful town wrapped itself around Adam, enveloped him in peace while the pale blue of the sky relaxed and refreshed him as the last rays of the sun warmed the air. The wonders of creation filled Adam with awe as day became night.

"All is right with Your world, dear Lord."

And it was.

Yes, it was and it still is.

Chapter Two

Birdie's feet hurt.

But pain wasn't the worst of her worries. Neither was the certainty that the new minister was a disaster. No, her biggest concern was money. Actually the lack of it.

She glared at the back of the last customer as he strolled out of the diner. He'd left her a quarter and a dime. Thirty-five cents on a seven-dollar order. She shoved the tip in her pocket and balanced his dirty dishes on her arm.

The lunch crowd was getting stingier and stingier. Due to the uncertainty at the asphalt plant, the town's biggest employer, fewer people ate out and those who did left smaller tips. With two teenage granddaughters to raise on her salary and tips and the payments from her husband's Social Security, eking by was difficult. Sadly, *eking* was the best she could do. She needed new shoes if she continued to spend six hours a day on her feet, but couldn't buy them now, not with school starting in a couple of months, not with the girls' expenses.

She dumped the dishes in the plastic bin and rolled it into

the kitchen, then returned to wipe down all the counters and tables. That finished, she pulled out her cell to call Mercedes Rivera, her lifelong friend, who had a break at work now.

"The new minister is a disaster." Birdie spoke into the cell as she settled in one of the booths. "I don't know what to think of the man. He's so darned young." She knew her friend would disagree. That's what she always did, but Mercedes disagreed courteously.

"Now, now, we all have to start someplace. He'll learn through experience."

"I don't want a minister to learn his job by practicing on me. I want a minister with an established connection with God."

"Stop complaining, Bird. I swan, you're getting so grumpy."

Birdie didn't respond. If she said what she wanted to, she'd just prove Mercedes right, again, so she didn't say a word.

"Think of him as a novice," Mercedes said. "Someone who will benefit from your influence."

Birdie snorted. Mercedes had learned years earlier—back in the toddlers' class at church when she'd attempted to use the purple crayon Birdie wanted—not to confront her directly. Now Mercedes attempted to lead Birdie.

"We're not Catholic," Birdie snapped. "We don't deal with novices."

"Then an apprentice. You'll get him in shape. You know you will."

Birdie leaned back against the high back of the booth and sighed. "I've got a lot going on with the girls and work. You know, I'm not a spring chick. I may be too old to train him."

She knew Mercedes struggled not to laugh—or be heard laughing over the phone—at the statement. Her friend was always polite.

After a pause, Mercedes said, "Bird, Bird, Bird, as if you'd allow something as insignificant as being busy or growing old to turn you away from your duty."

The problem with a lifelong friend was that she knew Birdie far too well.

"Rodolfo told me the preacher was really pleased with the new furniture." Mercedes changed the subject as she always did when Birdie was upset. "Nice of you to bull...to persuade people to donate."

Birdie harrumphed.

"I know you don't like to be thanked for good works, but it *was* nice of you."

"Hated to see the house bare," Birdie explained. "He didn't have a thing, not a stick of furniture, nothing worthy of that beautiful old parsonage. I couldn't stand it."

"All right. You got the community together to provide furniture only to preserve the architectural integrity of the house." Mercedes didn't contain the laugh this time. "I should know better than to compliment you for doing something nice."

Birdie glanced at the clock. Nearly two thirty. She needed to get home if she wanted to see the girls. "Talk to you later." She folded the phone and stuck it in her pocket.

As usual during the summer, the girls had slept in this morning. Bree, a junior, had volleyball practice until six and Mac, a sophomore, would be marching with the band until five thirty. If she hurried home, she could see them before they took off.

Her daughter had given the girls silly names: MacKenzee and Bre'ana. Whoever heard of putting an apostrophe in the middle of a name or identical vowels at the end? Birdie had given her daughter a sensible name. Martha. Martha Patricia. Had Martha lived up to such an honest, trustworthy name? No, at seventeen and without finishing school, she'd run off with a no-good man who'd deserted her when she got pregnant the second time. Everyone had told her he was all hat and no cattle, but Martha wouldn't listen.

Martha, irresponsible Martha who'd always needed a man to take care of her and couldn't take care of anyone else, spoiled by her father and disciplined by her mother, had come home to have the baby. She'd disappeared only weeks after MacKenzee's birth, as Birdie had suspected she would. Birdie had ended up raising two girls when she was looking to retire, but what else could she do?

The community had shortened the girls' names to Bree and Mac. With that, every trace of Martha disappeared from Butternut Creek except the memories of her miserable mistakes and her terrible grades in the permanent record of the school district.

All that had happened a few months after Elmer's death. The double loss about killed her. Not that she let anyone know, but inside, deep inside, she'd felt as if she didn't have anything left but a future of pain, exhaustion, and sorrow. But the girls, they'd pulled her out of that. They'd brought new meaning to her life, as well as worry and fatigue.

After she finished wiping down the last table, Birdie shouted, "Bye, Roy," to the manager as she left the diner. He waved, then went back to separating the checks and credit card receipts.

After the two-block walk to the bungalow she and Elmer had bought forty years earlier, she entered and shouted, "I'm home, girls."

"Hey, Grandma." Mac came down the stairs to hug her. The child had curly brown hair, matching brown eyes, and the sweetest smile in the world. "Gotta go. Band practice starts in fifteen minutes and I need to get my trumpet out of the music room."

"Did you eat lunch?" Birdie shouted as the girl ran out the door.

Then Bree, always in motion, dashed across the room, her long, straight dark hair swirling behind her. Everything about this older grandchild snapped with energy. She made Birdie tired just watching her. With a quick wave, she passed her grandmother and shouted as the screen door snapped shut behind her, "Love ya. See you tonight."

At least she'd seen them. Birdie grinned for a second. They were good girls, turned out well. If she weren't so worried and weary, she'd admit she loved them more than anything. They'd been the joy and center of her life since she'd first held them, but Birdie'd never tell them. Well, maybe on her deathbed. They'd get swelled heads if she got all sentimental. Besides, she wasn't real good about expressing feelings. They'd all feel uncomfortable, her most of all.

Stepping out of her shoes, she headed toward the laundry room and tossed a load into the washer. Within two hours, she dropped folded towels on a spot she'd cleared on Bree's unmade bed by shoving several stuffed animals on the floor. She hoped the child could find the pile when she needed them.

She rotated her left shoulder. Impingement. That's what the doctor had said a month ago, then sent her to physical therapy. When her shoulder started hurting, Birdie quit picking clothes up and straightening the girls' room. They were old enough to do that. If Bree couldn't find a clean uniform because they were all in her athletic locker or Mac complained the jeans she'd planned to wear that day were dirty, Birdie just shrugged. Amazing how quickly the girls discovered the location of the dirty clothes hamper and learned to use the washing machine.

For a moment she paused, considered her thoughts, and shook her head. She had become a crabby old lady, exactly like Mercedes had told her, politely and as only a friend of long standing could. The realization had surprised her a little, but this was not the time or place for self-examination. She had plenty to do and no time to find a new attitude.

On Bree's side of the bedroom hung posters of men and women with tattoos. She called them tats and wanted a rose on her back. What did she call it? A "tramp stamp"? If that didn't beat all. Birdie'd never allow that. At times, the girl acted a lot like her mother, except that Bree made fair grades and didn't get in trouble, and had the possibility of a college scholarship in either volleyball or basketball.

Birdie smiled. A MacDowell in college. Every member of Mercedes's family had gone to college, most to graduate school, but Bree would be the first MacDowell.

In contrast with her sister's, Mac's side of the room looked spare. Desk with a lamp on it, desk chair, dresser, and bed. One of the posters on her wall showed some scientist from England with numbers floating over his head. Stephen Hawking, Mac had told her. Why would anyone have a poster of a physicist—that's what Mac said he was—on the wall?

The other poster showed Wynton Marsalis playing a trumpet, the instrument Mac played. The portraits of the two men faced each other across the bedroom, precisely hung and as straight as if they'd been lined up with a ruler. Birdie felt as if she should straighten the stack of clean towels to conform to the rigid angles of the room.

Forget it. Little Miss Perfect—Bree's name for her younger sister—could refold them if they didn't please her.

In her own bedroom, Birdie padded barefoot across the scuffed hardwood to put her shoes in the closet and slide into a worn pair of slippers. On the way, Carlos the Cat attacked her ankles before he ran under the bed.

Lord, she was tired. She leaned against the wall. For a moment, she felt dizzy from exhaustion, but she shoved the feeling aside. She couldn't get sick. What would happen to her granddaughters if she did? How would the church survive this new minister without her guidance? She attempted to pray for strength but it took too much effort and never seemed to help much anyway.

Or maybe it did. Maybe she'd be in an even worse state if she didn't pray.

She needed to sit down for a minute, rest. After pausing in the kitchen to pour herself a glass of tea, she went out to the front porch of the small house and settled into one of the Adirondack chairs. Elmer had built them so he and Birdie could sit on the porch and wave to neighbors. He'd died only a year after that and she no longer had the time or the desire to sit there. She hadn't when Elmer had placed them there, but he'd enjoyed that hour together even if it made Birdie want to leap up and start sweeping the steps or pull a few weeds.

Early evening was surprisingly cool for June, although the weather was never really cool in Texas during the summer. Long hot, at maybe eighty-five degrees. The big maple she and Elmer had planted years ago shaded the area. A nice breeze cooled the porch as peace and quiet overcame her. She took a deep breath and leaned back, closing her eyes to breathe in the warm Texas air laden with the scent of gardenias.

The calm lasted five minutes before she got antsy. She hated peace and quiet. Too much to do. She wouldn't relax until they put her in the casket, if then. She pulled the phone out of her pocket to call Pansy about the food pantry. The woman would destroy the entire effort if Birdie didn't step in and set her straight.

When Adam explored the entire house the next morning, the sheer size again overwhelmed him. Downstairs, the tiny basement had a dirt floor. Spiderwebs hung from supports and a twenty-watt lightbulb illuminated a small circle, but a washer and dryer sat in the corner so he didn't mind the primitive surroundings.

The second floor had five bedrooms, each larger than both the bedrooms together in the Kentucky parsonage, and two bathrooms. The space on the third floor stretched across the entire house with storage closets built into the eaves. It seemed like a huge playroom for all those children he didn't have.

He strode up and down staircases and across halls and into bedrooms, his footsteps resonating loudly on the hardwood floors. Last night, his sleeping bag had felt warm and familiar. Tonight he'd haul his things upstairs, and approach the nuptial bed.

Before he could decide which to do—to laugh at or worry about that thought—he checked his watch. It was after nine o'clock, the time he'd decided a *real* minister started the day. He'd dressed like a real minister in a pair of black slacks and a white shirt with one of his two ties: a red one and a ministerial one with black and gold stripes. He also had a Christmas tie his best friend had given him. Red with elves on it that played "Santa Claus Is Coming to Town." He doubted he'd have many chances to wear that one, now he was a real minister.

Because he was already running late, Adam hurried, descending the steps from the second floor two-by-two. Reaching the first floor, he grabbed a file folder and his Bible and headed out the door toward the church.

"Hello, Preacher," a woman called from behind him as he headed north across the lawn.

When he turned, Adam saw a smiling blonde coming down the steps of the even larger Victorian next door, a plate in one hand and a little girl grasping the other.

"I'm Ouida Kowalski." She nodded at the child. "This is Gretchen."

"Weed-a?" he said.

"Yes, that's how it's pronounced. It's spelled O-u-i-d-a. A Southern name and a family name. Most people who aren't from here don't know it." She smiled and held the plate out. "I heard you're young and single so I brought you some sweet rolls for breakfast."

He took the offering and couldn't help but smile back. "Thank you. Are you a member of the church?" he asked, completely ignorant of who was and who wasn't.

"No, not of any church." Her smile didn't diminish. "George, my husband, says we're missing the spiritual gene. I don't know." She shrugged before leaning toward him. "But even if we're heathens, we're good neighbors and are delighted you're here. That parsonage has been empty for too long. I hope you don't mind, but the kids have been playing on the swing set in your yard."

Other than noting the existence of grass, he hadn't studied the back lawn in detail. "No problem. Glad someone can use it."

"Mama." Gretchen tugged on her mother's hand.

"Better go," Ouida said. "Again, welcome."

The sun shone and the birds sang and his neighbors had brought him breakfast. There could be no better place to be in the entire world.

When he entered his office, an immediate problem confronted him: sixteen boxes of books and only two small bookcases, already filled with dusty tomes that he felt sure no one had perused in years. Maybe centuries.

"Excuse me."

He turned to see a plump dark-haired woman.

"I'm the part-time secretary, Maggie Bachelor." She held out a hand and gave him a hearty handshake. "Good to meet you. I just got here, running a little late. I work from nine to eleven four days a week. I answer the phone, type the newsletter, and print the bulletin." She ticked off each duty on her fingers. "I'll need everything written out and on time so I can get the bulletin and the newsletter done." She put a sheet of paper on his desk. "Here are the deadlines."

She reminded him of a hummingbird. She talked fast—not that hummingbirds talk—but she also flitted from place to place.

"Do you have your sermon title, scripture, and hymns?"

Fortunately, he'd realized that his first week would be busy and had worked on the sermon last week. "It's from the tenth chapter of..."

She pointed at a pad and pen on the desk. "Write it down."

"Do you have a hymnal handy?" Adam had imprudently neglected to memorize the page numbers of the hymns. Actually, he'd neglected to choose any but wasn't willing to confess that failing.

"On your desk, too." She fluttered her fingers toward him and left.

Following her instructions, Adam jotted down his sermon title and scripture, then hunted through the hymnal. Finished, he stood and walked the information out to Maggie.

She glanced at the hymns he'd chosen then glanced up at

him. "Oh, dear, Pastor, the congregation doesn't know the last two."

"Won't it be fun to learn them?" he asked.

Her expression assured him it wouldn't. She picked up a pen. "I'll choose a couple we know."

"I'd like for the congregation to sing the ones I picked. They go with the theme of the morning."

"Well, if that's your choice, but…" Her words, expression, and shrug warned of dire consequences. "Well, then, here's your visitation and hospital call list for today." She handed him several note cards.

At eleven thirty, half an hour after Maggie left, Adam heard a knock at the office door. Just outside, he saw a large man wearing enormous paint-stained overalls with an orange-and-yellow Hawaiian shirt underneath.

"Ralph Foxx." The visitor stretched out a meaty hand. "Two x's on the end, like that old baseball player, Jimmie double-x Foxx. Played for the Philadelphia A's."

Adam didn't know about the baseball player and hadn't realized the A's had ever been in Philly, but he still shook his visitor's hand and gestured toward chairs covered with books. "Please sit if you can find a place."

"Don't mind if I do." Pulling a chair in from the office, Ralph settled down and made himself comfortable. Adam later discovered settling down comfortably was one of his greatest talents. Talking was another. Within minutes Adam had learned about Ralph's sciatica, his wife's hysterectomy, and much more. He didn't know how to shut off this font of information, but what else did Adam have to do this morning except pick up his car, which Rex had called to tell him was ready?

Adam discovered within a week that the retired men of the

church felt it was their duty to keep the minister company, especially a single young man like him who obviously had nothing else to do and needed to be amused.

"Are you working today?" Adam successfully interrupted after five minutes.

Obviously disappointed the minister had gotten a word in, Ralph shook his head. "I'm a painter. Seasonal work. Not much business today. That's why I'm retired *this* week."

"Then maybe you can help me."

The two men spent the next hour moving the church's books to the library and putting the new minister's on the shelves as Ralph talked on and on. Finally, Ralph said he couldn't work anymore, because of that sciatica. When he left, Adam knew more about the Foxx family and its far-flung branches all over the country than he'd wanted, but he'd also learned a few things about church members. Not a wasted morning.

❦

"Getting old isn't for sissies," Birdie mumbled to herself. Stiff and straight in the chair of the physical therapy waiting room at the hospital, she flipped through a magazine. Old Elgin Crump who lived down on Highway 28 slumped in his wheelchair. Must be at least eighty-five. Next to him sat Susan Pfannenstiel, her walker pulled up next to the chair.

Two younger patients waited alone, reading magazines. One was a cheerleader, a friend of Bree's, who'd fallen from the top of a pyramid during halftime at a basketball game. Those stunts should be outlawed. What had happened to the cheerleaders of her time, back when they wore uniforms that covered their navels and reached to their knees? Back then, they just jumped up and down and shouted. Now they jiggled their bodies and built towers the girls toppled off.

Birdie didn't recognize the young man. Maybe six feet tall but she couldn't tell. He slumped. His dark hair fell almost to his shoulders, rumpled but clean, like a man who cared about hygiene but had no interest in his appearance. She'd noticed when he came in that his jeans and khaki-colored T-shirt hung straight from his broad shoulders like he'd lost weight and hadn't bothered to buy clothes that fit.

Mostly she'd noticed his stumbling gait on the crutches when he entered, the lines of pain etched on his face, and the missing right leg. And yet, with the stubble on his world-weary face, he was handsome in a lost-soul way, in the dangerous and slightly disreputable manner many young women would find intriguing.

Was he Effie Peterson's nephew? Couldn't be too many amputees in the area, but he didn't look a bit like the happy kid who used to visit his aunt—no, his great-aunt—years ago. She'd heard Sam'd come back and was living in Effie's house. No one had been inside since Mercedes and Birdie and her granddaughters had cleaned it after the funeral. Probably covered with dust now and smelled musty.

She should go say hello to the young man, even if he wasn't Sam Peterson. Wouldn't hurt. Might be the only time anyone from the church could get in touch with him, but she hated to step up. No one would ever guess Birdie MacDowell hesitated to do anything. She usually didn't, but speaking to anyone about her church never felt comfortable, not in the least, especially if she had to approach a man who looked so unwelcoming, and do that out here in the middle of a waiting room with people watching.

But doggone it, she had to. God would expect it.

To protect her left shoulder, she pushed herself up with her right hand and briskly walked to his chair.

"Hello." She stretched out her hand. "I'm Birdie Mac-Dowell."

He ignored her hand but made brief contact with eyes that held no emotion.

"Are you Effie Peterson's nephew Sam?"

He dropped his gaze to the magazine.

"I'm a member of the Christian Church on the highway, the one your aunt attended. We'd surely like to see you there sometime."

He didn't say a word, didn't nod or lift his eyes or change expression.

She'd tried, which was all anyone could expect her to do. "We're a friendly church," she said to the top of his head. "Give Pastor Adam a call if you need anything." She took a few steps backward, almost tripped over the footrests on Elgin Crump's wheelchair, then turned and headed for her chair.

As she settled back in her seat, she noticed everyone staring at her before their gazes fell back on what they were reading. She didn't care. She was supposed to welcome people to town, invite them to church. She'd done her duty.

When she considered the problems and pain that plagued the others in the waiting room, she guessed she was pretty lucky to have only this shoulder acting up. Not good at all for a waitress to have a bad shoulder but better than a bad back or a bad knee.

"Mrs. MacDowell," the physical therapy clerk, a flighty teenager named Trixie, called from the doorway.

Inwardly cursing the weakness she hated to display, Birdie again pushed herself up with her right hand and straightened to walk into the therapy area. Curtains covered the treatment area in the back while other clients walked or pushed and tugged on the machines and weights on the main floor. Birdie stepped on a stool to pull herself onto a high table. Across the room, a pretty redheaded woman watched another patient for a few seconds before turning and approaching Birdie.

"I'm Willow Thomas, the new physical therapist." She held out her hand.

Birdie took it, noticing the woman's gentle grip. She figured the dead-fish handshake wasn't a sign of weak character but an effort not to crush anyone's arthritic joints.

"Welcome home, Willow. We're all glad to see you back. I remember you from way back when you sang in the Cherub Choir at church." She smiled in as friendly a way as she could muster with the darned pain. "Won't ever forget when you and your friends used to come into the diner after football games when you were in high school."

How old was Willow? A little younger than Martha's age, she guessed. Thirty-two or thirty-three. Probably she'd been too old to have met Sam when he visited Effie during the summer, too wide an age difference.

The young woman smiled, a lovely expression that made her features glow. "I didn't know if you'd remember me. It's good to be home."

"You're still one of our kids. Hope to see you in church again Sunday."

"My sons and I plan to be there."

Birdie swelled with a sense of accomplishment. Someone had accepted her invitation, even appeared pleased to get it.

"I'm not going to work with you today because I have a few folks to evaluate," Willow said. "But I wanted to introduce myself. Christine will oversee your exercises."

"As usual," Birdie grumbled to herself. Christine, a PT aide, was sweet but so young she didn't know anything. Birdie had attempted to talk to her about the Beatles and the first Gulf

War, but she had to explain history and culture before 1990 to Christine. It was a whole heck of a lot easier to count the exercises out loud than attempt conversation with the child. Christine placed the cane in Birdie's upraised hands and watched Birdie move it slowly forward and back over her head.

In a few minutes, Birdie heard the clerk call Sam Peterson.

"How's the pain been?" the aide asked Birdie.

Obviously Christine hadn't seen Sam yet or the young woman wouldn't be paying attention to her.

"Fine, just fine," Birdie lied. She couldn't let on she was getting too old to carry heavy trays. If she did and lost her job, how would she support her granddaughters? If she didn't tell anyone, if she gritted her teeth, she could push through exactly like she always had.

"Well, that's good. Willow wants me to teach you another exercise to loosen up your shoulder and increase your range of motion."

Then Christine glanced away from Birdie and her eyes grew enormous. Birdie lifted her head to see Sam limp into the therapy room and watched the reaction of the females. It was as entertaining as she'd expected. Trixie could barely take her gaze off him and tripped over Angus's wheelchair while Christine just stood mouth open and outright gawked at the man. The cheerleader, who had been absorbed by her magazine back in the waiting room, followed his unsteady progress with wide eyes.

Sam didn't notice. He barely lifted his gaze as he manipulated around the obstacles. When he did glance up, his eyes landed on Willow, who was talking to the cheerleader and hadn't seen him yet. His reaction stunned Birdie. He stopped still, completely motionless, and gaped at Willow. Birdie bet she was the only one who had a handle on the meaning of his expression because the others were too busy watching other parts of the man, but she recognized it. Right there between the therapy table and the exercise ramp, he fell in love. At least, that was the way Birdie saw it. She was seldom wrong.

For barely a second, his expression was unguarded and vulnerable. Almost immediately, so quickly she might have thought it hadn't happened, his features became sullen again as he looked at his foot and swung himself forward.

Back before his leg was blown off, Sam had appreciated women. He liked how they smelled, flowery and sweet. He liked their soft roundness, which made him feel even tougher and stronger in comparison. As a marine, he loved the way their pink and pale blue and mint-green clothing floated and swirled like pastel butterflies around his drab camo or dress blues.

He appreciated their soft spirits, their generous gestures, their winks and smiles. He never had trouble attracting any of them.

So why did the sight of this woman hit Sam so hard? She didn't look soft and sweet. She wore tailored black slacks and a crisply starched white shirt, buttoned almost to the top. The combination didn't make her look anything like a butterfly. He doubted she'd ever swirl around him.

For whatever reason, his reaction to her hit him hard, like the kickback of a rocket launcher, with a shock that shook his world.

Red hair and, he guessed, green eyes. Since her beautifully rounded backside was all he could see, he didn't know.

When she turned to pick up a file, she glanced at him and smiled absently before returning her attention to the patient.

Yeah, green eyes and dimples and long lashes and a slender,

slightly tilted-up nose. Her smile seemed cursory, as if she'd barely noticed him while she concentrated on her other patient. Not a usual female reaction to him.

But even her perfunctory smile made him feel like a man for the first time in months. Probably because the greeting came from rounded lips on the more-than-pretty face that topped her great body. He guessed she thought the severe hairstyle made her look more professional, but it didn't. The sleekness emphasized her cheekbones and eyes and skin, almost everything about her. He bet she dressed like that to look strong and in-charge, but a woman who looked like her could never hide behind a starched shirt.

For a moment he swayed on the crutches as he checked her out. How old was she? Thirty-something? She didn't look like it, but there were a few—he didn't know what to call them. Not wrinkles because they didn't make her look old. Maybe brackets or creases? No, she had a couple of *grooves* around her eyes, and frown marks between her eyebrows that emphasized dark circles under her eyes. A year ago, he would've thought he was just the man to cheer her up, but his confidence had ebbed considerably since the injury. As much as he liked them, his interest in women had lessened, too, until now.

"Excuse me, Mr. Peterson." Trixie stepped in front of him, grinning and fluttering her eyelashes at him.

He hated women's reactions to him now. His looks had been inherited from the general and generations of military men going back centuries. He had nothing to do with his appearance, plus he didn't really want anyone noticing him for any reason. Right now, he didn't feel too good about himself and was hardly a great choice for anything, not even a date. He had more problems than he could handle himself, let alone burden anyone else with.

Unfortunately, the longer he allowed his hair to grow, the scruffier his whiskers, and the deeper his frown, the more women fell at his feet. Most of them didn't mind the fact he was missing a limb and lost his balance more times than he could count, but *he* did. Most of the females wanted to rescue him, to take care of him, to fall in love. He didn't want to be taken care of or rescued. Didn't need to be fixed and refused to fall in love.

He didn't want romance. He didn't want a relationship. Right now, he didn't even want to pick up a woman, not with the stump at the end of his leg guaranteed to scare her off. With that and the pain any kind of movement caused, celibacy seemed pretty much his only choice these days.

But still Trixie stood in front of him, smiling and winking and flipping her hair while he swayed on the crutches.

Willow Thomas sighed. Whenever a good-looking guy arrived in PT, Trixie lost every bit of her nearly invisible veneer of professionalism. More good-looking guys than Willow had thought came here: college kids with broken bones and high school football players with bad knees, all far too young for Willow. But this one looked about Willow's age if she discounted the deep lines of pain and the snarl Trixie's attention brought forth.

Flirting was like breathing for Trixie. Willow had counseled the young woman, attempted to explain, then finally lectured her on the difference between their clients in PT and possible dates for the weekend. Trixie's efforts at professionalism lasted until the next good-looking guy entered the room. Now she was nearly drooling.

Even displaying depression and anger like most of the vets she worked with, the new patient was hot. Willow had to admit that. This patient—she glanced down at the schedule—Captain Samuel Daniel Peterson looked so fine, even Willow felt an instant attraction. Hard for any man to make her feel that way.

But she ignored it. She was a therapist who treated all patients the same: professionally.

"Captain," she said as she approached him. "I'm Willow Thomas, one of the physical therapists here." She reached her hand out. When he glared at it, she drew it back. "I'll be doing an intake at your next appointment. Today Trixie, our PT aide, is going to check your range of movement and degree of strength to get a baseline."

Willow smiled. He didn't.

"Please let me know what I can do to help."

He glanced up at her, making eye contact for a second. He had beautiful blue eyes, but they were red with broken veins. She knew well what that meant, had seen it often before. Seemed sad that this man should let himself go, drink so much it showed.

Then he dropped his gaze again, an admission that he really didn't care where she went or what she did as long as she left him alone. So she did, but not before she glanced at his reflection in the mirror that covered the entire west wall. As she moved away, he'd again lifted his eyes and watched her.

Chapter Three

That evening, Adam looked out the kitchen window while he rinsed the plate off. He had a dishwasher that would take him days to fill, so he washed his one dish and a fork to use at the next meal.

Outside, Ouida watched her girls—Gretchen and the other one whose name he couldn't remember. It was still light although the sun headed rapidly to the west. His evening chore completed, he walked outside to join them.

"How did your day go?" Ouida asked.

"Hospital visits went well. My car made it to Llano and back, which is always a relief."

"Are you unpacked and completely moved in?"

There were still ten unpacked boxes in his study and huge piles of books that overflowed onto the chairs and formed heaps on every surface. "Pretty much," he said.

The AME church a block away had evening services. Over the sounds of crickets and children playing, he could hear the music and harmonies: "Amazing Grace," "Sweet House of

Prayer," and several that he couldn't place but lifted his heart and calmed his soul.

Within five minutes, Gretchen had curled up on her mother's lap and Carol—aah, yes, that was her name—yawned, struggling to keep hold on the chain of the swing.

"Okay, girls." Ouida got to her feet and shifted Gretchen to her shoulder. "Let's go home and get ready for bed."

The three left through a gate in the fence, overgrown with the beautiful orange flowers that Ouida had identified as trumpet vines. Once their voices faded, Adam was left alone with the breeze and the succulent scent of a Texas evening floating on the sweet notes of a spiritual.

Sunday morning dawned warm and bright, the normal state for summer mornings in Texas. After a final read-through of his sermon, Adam ate breakfast and showered. While he shaved, he studied himself in the mirror. His hair touched his collar, and, he realized, he did look young, really young. Had he expected a few days in ministry would age him? Well, yes. Unrealistic but he still looked too young to preach, as young as Miss Birdie had proclaimed, eight years younger than his twenty-five years. Would growing a mustache help? Maybe a beard?

He shouldn't start that today. Miss Birdie probably wouldn't approve of facial hair. She wouldn't consider her minister standing in the pulpit with a light stubble to be at all professional. Not a good impression for his first Sunday here. From the nearly bare closet, he pulled a suit—his only suit, a ministerial black that served as both his marrying and burying suit. Once dressed, he headed out. That walk across the parking lot was his last moment of peace for the rest of the day.

"Hear you're not married." Jesse Hardin leaned against the

doorjamb of the minister's church office with a mug in his hand, ready for a chat.

What single female relative did Jesse have he'd like to introduce Adam to?

"I've got a niece. Lives in Llano. Nice girl."

"I'm sure she is. Thanks. I'm not looking at the moment."

When Jesse nodded and started toward the chair in front of the desk, Adam said, "I'm going to wander through the building, greet anyone who comes in." Ignoring Jesse's obvious disappointment, Adam left.

With a smile and a firm handshake and feeling very ministerial, Adam greeted everyone as they entered the church. Several children waved and headed toward their Sunday school class.

"In a church this small, Pastor, we don't have many kids," Miss Birdie said. "Most of them come with their grandparents." She gestured toward a hallway. "That used to be the elementary wing, classrooms filled with kids. Now they're all in one class and we take turns leading it." She headed off toward a classroom. "I'm teaching the children today."

If they knew what was good for them, they'd behave.

At eleven, when he heard the playing of the chimes, Adam entered the church through the door between the study and the chancel area. About forty-five people gathered in groups of three to five, scattered through a sanctuary built to hold two hundred. Maggie sat next to an aisle. Some huddled in the back row with the intention, perhaps, of leaving early. Nearly every one of them had white or graying hair and wore glasses except the two girls sitting with Miss Birdie and a few kids with their grandparents. As he had been told but now realized, this was an old and dying church.

As the service began, Adam asked the congregation to stand

for the first hymn, stated the page number, and nodded toward the organist. He expected they'd all start singing together. Didn't happen. As Adam began in his wavering and consistently off-key tenor, he noticed everyone stared at him, mouths firmly closed. Behind him, Adam heard the voices of the three women in the choir. It was as if the four were a gospel music group, perhaps Adam and the Eves or the Pastor and the Pips. Somehow Adam, the most pitiful of vocalists, sang lead while the choir acted as backup. Fortunately, the organist played so loudly, no one could hear him anyway.

After communion and the reading of the scripture, Adam stood to preach. Within ten minutes, he noticed a restlessness in the congregation. Men checked their watches and women set their purses on their laps. Was the sermon that bad? He hadn't thought so. He'd worked very hard at polishing up one of the favorites from his student church, but everyone seemed ready to leave. Not only ready, but determined. One child began sobbing until his grandmother handed him a cookie. A timer went off on someone's watch.

Realizing he'd lost the congregation, Adam hurried to finish, dropping the last two points and heading fast and straight for the end. When he'd written it, he'd thought the words were such a clear, uplifting statement of shared convictions it would turn the entire church around, the triumph of faith calling the congregation to action.

Unfortunately, as soon as he said, "And in conclusion," people put the hymnals in the racks, dropped their bulletins on the pews, and sat forward, ready to bolt. Adam stopped midsentence, came down from the chancel, raised his hand, and pronounced the benediction. Even before he said "Amen," people tumbled from the pews and rushed down the aisle and out.

Disappointment filled him. He'd hoped to meet more people, to get feedback on how he'd done, how much he'd inspired them, how they looked forward to a future together. Had his sermon been so terrible they all needed to leave without talking to him? He hurried toward the door at the back of the sanctuary with the hope of greeting someone, anyone, but only one person remained.

"You did a good job," Howard said, his voice and expression filled with relief. The elder must feel vindicated that Adam hadn't fallen down the chancel steps or dropped the offering. The fact that the minister he'd called could preach a passable sermon must take a lot of heat off him.

"But I should have warned you about something," the elder continued. "We have to get out of church by eleven fifty or the Methodists will beat us to the Subway for lunch."

Adam checked his watch. Noon.

Howard nodded. "There's going to be a long line today."

Seminary didn't give students the most practical information. Why hadn't they taught him the importance of getting out of church before the Methodists?

"Cut your sermon a few minutes and don't sing so many verses of each hymn. Should take care of things." Howard grabbed Adam's hand and shook it. "You'll have it down in no time." He hurried off.

Adam had hospital calls to make but decided to pick up a sandwich at the Subway, to see what the place was like and meet the congregation.

"Pastor Adam?"

He glanced up from the sermon he'd been working on to see Miss Birdie striding through the door.

"Come on in," he said although the invitation didn't seem

necessary as she was halfway across the office and followed by another woman he recognized from the previous day. He stood.

"Hello, Preacher." She glared at him. "You know me. This is Mercedes Rivera." She waved toward the other woman before she said, "They call us the Widows."

They Call Us the Widows. Sounded like a great name for a movie, a Western maybe.

Then he remembered: WIDOWS was the word written on the delivery form from the furniture store. He started to ask about that, but before he could, Miss Birdie spoke.

"Mercedes is the town librarian." She motioned toward the attractive Latina again. "You need any information on anything or about anyone in town, she's the one to call."

"Birdie just finished her breakfast shift and I took a break from the library," Mercedes explained. "She wanted to come see you."

"I have a bone to pick with you," Miss Birdie said.

Not a surprise. She'd probably picked a couple of carcass-fuls of bones with quite a few ministers.

"Won't you sit down?" he asked cordially.

Miss Birdie stretched her arm out and waved it around the room, where piles of books still filled every surface and boxes covered much of the floor.

"Sorry about the mess in here. I'm attempting to bring order to my books. Didn't realize I had so many."

"Well, you'd better hurry, because people are going to want to sit in these chairs," Miss Birdie stated firmly.

"Bird means *she* wants to sit down now," Mercedes explained in a whisper, as if Miss Birdie couldn't hear.

With alacrity, Adam picked the stack of books from a chair and looked for a place to put them. Finding none, he placed them on the floor beside the chair, then cleared another for Mercedes. Both women sat. That completed, he hurried to sit—to hide—behind the desk. Didn't actually hide, but he appreciated the separation provided by the broad surface and the tower of books between them.

"Pastor, we dropped in to welcome you on your first official day in the office." Mercedes smiled at Adam, then flicked a nervous glance at her friend.

"Yes, and then I have a bone to pick with you," Miss Birdie repeated.

He didn't doubt that.

"I don't want to coddle you. Mercedes thinks I should give you a little more time…"

"Yes, I do—" Mercedes began.

"But you have to know what people are saying."

"Birdie feels it's our duty to tell you what *she* says people are saying, although I believe we should give you a chance to settle in first before we make suggestions."

Miss Birdie glared at the other woman. "Pastor, Mercedes and I've been friends for more than sixty years. Occasionally we don't agree. I say strike while the iron is hot."

For a moment, Adam smiled—inside—at the difference between the women. Mercedes looked a bit uncomfortable, a slight flush on her light brown skin, but attractive with her black hair, beginning to gray at the temples, pulled back into a neat French braid. In contrast, Miss Birdie's short hair meant quick and easy preparation. Wash and comb. No fuss.

Mercedes wore a nice navy dress with matching pumps while Birdie wore a pink uniform. Aah, yes. Now Adam remembered. She was a waitress.

"In the first place," Miss Birdie continued, "you don't look like a minister at all, not in my opinion."

"Her opinion counts for a lot here," Mercedes said with an apologetic smile.

"You're too tall, too young, your hair's too long. You're almost handsome, if you weren't so skinny and didn't have all that hair." She leaned forward and fixed her eyes on him. "That means some of the younger women and a few of the widows might covet what isn't theirs to claim. After all, you're a man of God."

She kept her eyes on Adam as if he planned to seduce the younger women right here, right now, and right in front of her. He didn't know where to find any gullible young women and wouldn't know how to seduce one if he could find her. Besides, he didn't plan to start doing that, certainly not in front of the Widows.

But he knew Miss Birdie expected an answer.

"Thank you for the information." Then he added, "I'll get a haircut as soon as I can." First, he needed a salary check because he had about twenty dollars in his billfold, which he planned to use for food and gas.

Miss Birdie's glare told Adam he'd better do her bidding and soon.

Before he could explain the cash-flow problem, Mercedes said, "But you have a humble charm." She warned her friend with a glance before facing the minister again. "We can work with you, help you. Bird—that's what I call her—can steer you in the right direction."

Whether Adam wanted to go that way or not.

"What we're here about—"

"What *you* are here about." Mercedes broke in.

"It's those songs you chose for Sunday," Birdie said before Mercedes could interrupt again. "Nobody knows them." She pursed her lips before saying, "Did you notice no one was singing? We want the old favorites back."

"Very nice sermon, Pastor," Mercedes said. "One of the best we've had in years."

Miss Birdie didn't agree or disagree with her friend's compliment. From their short acquaintance, he felt as if the pillar might believe no one should praise a young minister before she had him properly trained.

"All right," Miss Birdie grudgingly conceded. "A nice sermon but terrible hymns. People have been telling me they don't like those new ones."

The church management professor at the seminary had told his class to be careful when the word *people* was used because that usually meant the speaker and a few others he or she'd been able to browbeat into agreeing. He smiled in an effort to look cooperative and appreciative.

"A nice smile," Miss Birdie said. "But I don't care about nice smiles at the moment. I expect results."

"I wanted all parts of the service to fit a theme, the idea of a new beginning for the church. I chose the hymns for that reason."

"A bunch of people mumbling or not singing at all can hardly add to any theme." She fixed him with a glare that let Adam know she expected him to pay attention to her every word. "We like the familiar songs."

"That's a very good point. You know what I believe I'm going to like best about you, Miss Birdie? You always state your opinions so clearly."

Mercedes said, "That's true, but no one has ever complimented Bird on that before."

Miss Birdie glowered at her friend, then turned to study Adam's face. He had no idea what opinion she reached about his sincerity. He attempted to look exceptionally earnest.

"Do you ladies mind if we pray together?" he asked.

Without waiting for a response, Adam began, "Loving God, we gather here in Your name, to listen and do Your will. Open us to work together to Your glory, we ask in the name of Your son. Amen."

"*Open us to work together?*" Miss Birdie asked. "Pastor, after sixty-plus years of church attendance, I've learned to interpret ministerial prayers, to translate the words preachers use." She scrutinized Adam. "Sometimes I'm a little wary. What do you want to say with those words?"

"Bird, why do you always question?" Mercedes said. "*All of us together* sounds nice. We should all work together in the church."

Not one to be deterred by a prayer, Miss Birdie repeated. "About those hymns, Pastor Adam."

His lips quivered. He found her determination amusing. If he didn't, she'd probably drive him nuts. Unfortunately, she caught that quick expression before he was able to wipe it away.

"It's not funny, Preacher." She kept her eyes on him as if daring his wayward expression to return. "I brought a list of songs we like to sing." She handed him a sheet of paper. "And the page numbers."

"Very thorough." He glanced at the paper and recognized many of the old hymns popular in the Kentucky churches. "Thank you."

"And you'll use them? During the service?" She continued to study his expression.

Adam could only hope she had a little trouble deciphering it because, as young and inexperienced as he was, he had no idea how to react to her demands. No, to her *suggestions*.

"I promise you at least one a Sunday, and I'll work with the choir on the new hymns."

"Oh, Pastor, you surely noticed our choir isn't very big. Just three sopranos and Ralph, who can't really sing anymore," Mercedes explained. "Good view of the congregation from up there. Ralph likes to sit in the choir so he can see what everyone in the sanctuary is doing during the service."

"But still, they can lead you in learning some new hymns," Adam suggested.

"We like the old ones," Birdie said clearly. "None of us wants to change."

"How are you going to learn new hymns?"

"We don't want to." She bit the words off slowly and precisely. "We are happy with the ones we know."

"Oh, don't be so old-fashioned." Mercedes smiled at Birdie, then at Adam. "I liked some of them. We sing several of the spirit songs at the women's retreats but never have here."

Traitor, Miss Birdie's frown said.

"I'm surprised you're working today," Mercedes observed.

Adam had noticed that Mercedes always attempted to change the subject when Miss Birdie scowled.

"Most of our ministers take Mondays off," the librarian said.

"I don't know what day I'll take off, but I just got here and there's so much to do to get settled. I do have a question for you ladies."

"Pastor Adam, I've learned a smiling minister often means he's fixin' to make an unwanted suggestion," Miss Birdie stated.

"Oh, not at all. This isn't difficult. Wonder if you ladies could tell me about the Widows."

"Oh, that's us." Mercedes grinned and pointed at Miss Birdie then at herself. "We're the Widows. We put together the sympathy dinners and take food to the sick and watch over the fellowship dinners, whatever service is needed here at the church and in town."

"You sound like real treasures." Adam considered carefully how to ask the next question. "I wonder if you know anything about the furniture that Rodolfo from Hilton's delivered to the parsonage."

They glanced at each other. "Pastor, this is a small town," Mercedes said. "In a small town, we look after each other. Don't you worry. It's taken care of."

"Would you please thank the group for this gift? I appreciate the generosity."

"You just did." Mercedes pointed at Miss Birdie and herself. "We're the only two Widows left. We ordered the furniture, but lots of people donated. We'll pass that on."

Miss Birdie nodded but obviously didn't want to talk about this subject anymore. He guessed discussing her good deeds made her uncomfortable.

"One more thing, Pastor Adam," Mercedes said. "There's a young vet, an amputee in town. Sam Peterson. His great-aunt Effie died and left her house to him. He's here for rehabilitation at the hospital."

Adam jotted the name on a note card. "I should visit him."

"Yes, you should." Miss Birdie nodded vigorously. "We've tried several times but he won't open the door. He lives in a little green house on Pine Street."

"You'll recognize it because it looks empty and has a dozen old newspapers on the lawn."

Adam nodded and stood, feeling the visit was over. The Widows didn't move, which meant, obviously, it wasn't. He guessed that decision was up to them. He sat back down.

"Tell us a little about yourself, Pastor Adam," Mercedes said. "We know you're from Kentucky." She edged forward in her chair. "How old are you?"

He sat back down. "Twenty-five."

"You don't look twenty-five," Miss Birdie said. "You don't even look eighteen. How can we trust someone as young as you...," the pillar said through pursed lips.

Mercedes shushed her friend, quickly changing the subject. Adam admired how well she could redirect the pillar. "Tell us about your call to become a minister," she said. "I always like to know."

"Grew up in Kentucky where my father had a business. As a kid, I always went to church. After I graduated from the University of Louisville, I taught high school for a year."

"And the call to ministry?" Mercedes prompted.

"I heard the call one day while I was standing in front of a class of thirty-five ninth-grade English students who had no desire to read *Julius Caesar*." That sounded shallow. The reason went much deeper, but that had always been his story because it was short and because the actual Damascus road experience really had taken place right there, in class. It came not only in the voice of God but also in the sullen silence of the students.

With a sweet smile and ignoring a glare from Miss Birdie, who obviously still had a few more bones to pick with him, Mercedes said, "I hear you're single. Have you heard that Birdie and I are matchmakers?"

He felt sure that a look of pure terror washed over his face, because he could feel panic rising inside. Adam pulled himself together and said, "Do a lot of single women live in town?"

Mercedes sighed. "Not as many as we'd like. Most of our young people go off to college and stay in the big cities, so matchmaking's an enormous challenge nowadays."

"But working with what we have, we've been very successful," Miss Birdie added. "We're resourceful and motivated."

Both Widows nodded. The gesture chilled him.

"Yes, we've been very successful." Mercedes tilted her head. "Would you like us to try for you? We've noticed you aren't keeping company with anyone here in Butternut Creek."

"I've only been here a week."

"Perhaps you have a young lady back in Kentucky?"

Adam held up his hand and considered what to say to let them know—politely but firmly—he didn't require their services. "No thank you. I'm a hardened case, ladies. No woman wants to put up with a man married to his vocation." Adam shook his head and added, "I'm not good with women. I'd be too much of a challenge."

He knew immediately he'd made a big mistake. Miss Birdie shared a quick, amused glance with Mercedes.

"We enjoy nothing as much as a challenge," Miss Birdie said.

All hope died within him. As he'd begun to suspect and was borne out over the next years, the Widows loved a dare, rejoiced in achieving the impossible.

Only a few minutes after the Widows left, Adam wondered about Miss Birdie. Mercedes presented herself as she was: friendly and easy to get along with.

But he hadn't met anyone like Miss Birdie before. Oh, every church had a kitchen lady, the woman in charge of nearly everything including meal preparation and service and keeping the congregation in line. Miss Birdie was different, though, stronger than most but also caring and concerned about the flock. How did a person combine her judgmental personality with a heart that had organized the furniture purchase and sent her minister to call on an amputee?

He wished he understood her better. *How can I minister to her if I don't know her?* he reflected.

Of course it could be she didn't care if he ministered to her or not, as long as he did what she expected.

The church administration professor at the seminary had told the class there were members of a congregation, often a clan, who wanted to own the minister, who hoped to be the only family he ate Christmas dinner with, who expected the minister to attend every family gathering including the birth of a nephew or grandchild. Adam didn't think Miss Birdie fell into that category.

The professor had explained there was a second group who wanted to be the only ones the minister listened to, to control the church by controlling the pastor. He'd said ministers should do everything possible to avoid that situation.

The professor had never met Miss Birdie.

Chapter Four

Rockets exploded around Sam Peterson. Amid the screams of the wounded, officers barked directions as mortar shells screamed toward them. Over the rocky landscape hung the acrid smell of ammo and war and the coppery stench of blood. Gunfire rained down on them from the surrounding hills.

He wished the Taliban didn't love hanging out in obscure caves.

"Incoming," Gunny shouted.

"Gunny, we need suppressive fire." Sam pointed west. "Where the hell is the second squad?"

Reacting with the instinct of long training and months in Afghanistan, Sam lifted his M4 to answer the barrage. As the suppressive fire began, he shouted to his radio operator, "We need close air support now and—"

Before he could finish the sentence, a second mortar impacted, driving Sam's face into the dirt. A blast of pain punched him, burning through flesh and bones and nerves.

He reached for his leg. It wasn't there.

His leg had been blown off and he lay alone and bleeding

out on the hard surface made slick with his blood. He shouted
to his best friend Morty for help, but Morty stretched out next
to him, motionless, blood pooling around his head and his eyes
staring into the darkness as the battle continued to rage.

"Medic!" Sam yelled, but no one came. Despite pain that
nearly knocked him out, he reached for his first-aid kit and
grabbed a tourniquet. Fighting against the throbbing and a
darkness that threatened to envelop him, he wrapped the
nylon strip around his thigh and tightened it with clumsy fingers slick with blood, turning the plastic grip until the flow
stopped.

That finished, he clenched his fists and forced himself to
breathe, to pull air in and out of gasping lungs. He lay alone
in the dark and the throbbing anguish, waiting for death in a
foreign country. With the last bit of strength he possessed, he
reached out and put his hand on Morty's shoulder.

When the din grew louder, his eyes flew open. For a moment, he floated, caught between the pandemonium of war
and the pounding noise of wherever he'd awakened. Above
him, Sam saw not a black sky pierced with the flashes and
trails of rockets and mortar fire but a ceiling covered with
that ugly white popcorn stuff. He took a deep breath. Fresh,
clean air. He'd had that nightmare again and hoped Morty
didn't die at the end. He always did. It destroyed Sam every
time.

He wasn't in Afghanistan. He'd been airlifted out six or
seven months earlier. Now he lay in his aunt Effie's bed in
Butternut Creek, Texas, in the house he'd inherited from her
when she died. Even here, he was alone and in pain and isolated.

Butternut Creek. A stupid place for a marine. He should be
in battle at the head of his division, leading his platoons in-

stead of lying in a pale pink room in a cottage. What kind of marine ended up in a place called Butternut Creek?

This one, obviously.

Finally awake, he shook his head to clear it. A mistake. The motion made his head throb.

He shouldn't drink so much. But it had felt so good at the time.

After nearly a minute, he realized the uproar that awakened him came not from a battle in Afghanistan but from the backyard. Sounded like a couple of platoons fighting off insurgents out there. Either that or a bunch of very loud kids. He assumed the latter only because he couldn't figure out how that many marines could fit in his yard or why they'd be there.

He didn't need the noise, not when he'd drunk a fifth of whiskey last night in an attempt to overcome pain and insomnia and memories. He glanced at the clock. Nine thirty on Wednesday, no Tuesday, morning. Maybe Monday.

Who cared? For a moment, Sam considered the pros of getting up. Deciding to try for a few more hours of sleep, he put a pillow over his head. At the same time, a loud crack came from inside the house. As much as he'd like to ignore what sounded like a broken window, he couldn't. Someone could be robbing Aunt Effie's house.

No, it was his house now, his responsibility.

After a few seconds of silence, he heard a knock on the slider. Very polite burglars.

With a struggle, he sat up and slipped on the bottom of a sweat suit but didn't bother to cover the T-shirt he slept in. Then he turned in the bed, put his left foot on the floor and into a slipper, grabbed the crutches, and shoved them under his arms.

The knock came again.

Once the crutches were in position, he struggled to swing what remained of his right leg around, then stood and steadied himself before he hobbled across the thick shag carpet. If he decided to stay in the house for longer than a few more months, the fiend of a rug that grabbed his crutches with every step would be the first thing to go.

Then came still another knock on the slider. "Hold your pants on," he shouted, then cursed. He'd hoped they'd left by now and he could go back to bed.

He avoided the pile of trash on the floor, bottles and old newspapers and boxes from microwave dinners. He should pick those up someday. Noxious fumes made up of the odor of trash and spilled booze, mixed with the smell of an old house left shut up for all the months after his aunt died, filled the room.

When he reached the slider in the dining room, he pulled the lacy curtains back to see a large hole in the middle of the right panel. He tried to open the door, but with the broken glass, it stopped after only a few inches. Two boys stood in front of him with expressions of fear and remorse on their freckled faces.

"We're sorry, sir," said the taller kid. Then he gulped.

Two pairs of round, green, guileless eyes stared at him. He'd heard someone, probably them, fooling around in the backyard for several days, but this was the first time he'd seen the perpetrators. Amazing only two boys made so much racket.

But he didn't fall for those eyes. He knew how easy innocence was to assume, although the apology had sounded fairly sincere. In his youth, he'd had to apologize plenty of times and knew exactly how to seem earnest and repentant. He'd fooled everyone but his father the general.

"Don't know how that happened, sir." The younger boy pointed toward the broken slider. "One moment it was fine and the next, it wasn't."

The older kid scowled at him.

They were cute kids with spiked red hair and burnt orange University of Texas T-shirts worn with jeans and athletic shoes. They had to be brothers. But at that moment, Sam didn't care if they were good guys or gangbangers. His missing foot had started to throb again, something the VA medical staff called phantom limb pain but felt excruciatingly genuine to him. The raw agony made him want to scream, except he was a marine. Marines didn't scream.

On top of everything, he was here and his troops were… how many thousands of miles away? The fact he wasn't with them tore at him so badly he hurt inside almost as much as in the missing limb.

And Morty was dead. He died every night.

Gritting his teeth, Sam turned, balanced himself on the right crutch, and leaned over to pick up a fist-size rock. Shards of glass covered the floor and stuck to the curtain. By the time he'd struggled to stand back up, he saw the boys squeezing through the narrow opening and inside.

"Don't suppose this"—he tossed the rock into the air several times and looked through the broken pane—"had anything to do with the broken window."

The eyes of the shorter boy grew even rounder. "No, sir," he said.

The older brother shushed him and said, "Yes, sir. Sorry, sir."

The kid was either very polite or he knew Sam was military. Probably because of his camo sleeveless T-shirt.

"Names."

"I'm Leo." The older boy straightened his thin shoulders

and stood at attention. "He's Nick. Thomas. Our last name is Thomas."

If anything could, the sight of Leo's posture would have made Sam laugh. "How old are you?"

"I'm ten." Leo pointed at himself. "My brother's eight."

"When does school start?" The pain began to move up from the missing foot through his absent shin and settled in his shattered knee. He didn't feel like chatting but couldn't figure out how to get the two to leave. He could shout at them, curse at them, but even he had his limits. He couldn't do that to kids.

"In August," Leo said.

"Where's your mother?"

"She works, sir." Leo pulled his hands out of his pockets and held them straight and flat against his side.

"At the hospital, sir." Nick squared his shoulders, mimicking his brother.

Aha. If he didn't hurt so much, he'd have figured out much earlier that these two redheads must belong to the luscious PT he'd met at the hospital. He grinned, inside.

"And your father?" Might as well collect all the information he could.

He hadn't thought the boys' eyes could look any sadder, but they did.

Leo lowered his gaze. "Back in Chicago."

"With his stupid new wife Tiffany," the younger kid muttered.

Leo gave Nick an elbow to his ribs.

"When my folks split up, we came back here." Leo grimaced. "Is Butternut Creek the stupidest name you've ever heard of for a town, sir? All my friends back home—" He swallowed hard. "All the guys laughed at me when I told them we were moving to Butternut Creek, Texas." His voice dripped with disgust.

"Yeah, mine, too," Nick added.

"Shut up," Leo said. "Your friends didn't even—"

"Yeah, they did. And I have as many friends as you."

"Do not." Leo turned toward his younger brother and glared at him.

"Stop." The sound of squabbling made Sam's head pound harder, in time with the throbbing of his leg. "Let's get back to basics. One of you broke my window, but you both were playing in my yard where you shouldn't be. Stop arguing and man up."

"Wow. He said *man up*." Nick's voice filled with wonder.

"Okay, man up, squirt," Leo said to his brother, then turned to Sam. "Nick broke the window."

"Did not."

"He was pretending to toss a grenade into the guardhouse to save me. He didn't mean to hit the glass, but he did throw the rock."

"It was an accident," Nick whispered. "It sort of slipped out of my hand."

Sam glared at the boys for a few seconds and wondered what he was getting into by talking to them, by allowing them to enter the silence he surrounded himself with. Nothing good. Nothing he wanted to get involved in. "What are you going to do about it?" he demanded because he couldn't think of any other way to respond and he guessed it would kill their self-esteem if he mocked them or sent them away. Not that he had reason to care about their self-esteem.

Why was he acting like such a nice guy when he did not care about people and pain throbbed through his missing leg? The brothers looked at him then at each other. They shrugged.

"Don't know," Leo said.

The tendrils of the headache had started to move down Sam's neck. He had to get the boys outside so he could close the drapes, settle on the sofa, and do his exercises. He needed darkness, not sunshine. For a moment, he tried to gather his thoughts and consider how he could get them out of there. He turned away from the slider and leaned against the table.

"Look," the younger one whispered. "He's got tattoos."

"Tats, idiot," the older brother said. "He's got barbed wire on his right arm."

"And something marine-y on the other," the younger one said. "Look at those muscles." A note of awe filled the whispered comment. Sam would have laughed but that would hurt his head. Instead he glared at them and said, "Have your mom call me."

"Oh, no, sir. Please don't make us tell her." Leo's voice quivered. He cleared his throat. "We'll do anything if you won't tell my mother."

"She gets sad and *really* disappointed in us." Nick's lips trembled.

"Have her call me," Sam said in his command voice. "Seven-one-four-four." In Butternut Creek, everyone shared the same prefix so he didn't bother with it.

"Seven-one-four four," they repeated simultaneously

"If you don't tell her, I'll call her. You won't like what happens after that." With those words, he pointed toward the slider. "Now. Go!" As they dashed out, Sam slid the door shut as far as he could and closed the curtain. Then he steadied himself on the crutches as he stumbled toward the sofa in the living room with glass crunching beneath his shoe. Once there, he fell on the cushions and took a bottle of pills from the end table. He popped three in his mouth and swallowed them dry, in too much pain to stand and get water.

He leaned his head against the back of the sofa, closed his eyes to relax, and began to imagine himself going down in an elevator while he read the floors. "Ten," he said. "Nine, eight..." The pain lessened with each number.

As the muscles of his neck loosened, the phone rang. The jangle made his shoulders tense up and increased the pounding of his headache. Hadn't thought it could hurt more.

Probably the general or a wrong number. No one else knew where he was. He'd let it ring, because he didn't want to talk to the general. Actually, he didn't want to talk to anyone but most of all, not to the general.

As much as he liked the solitude, Sam hadn't planned to be alone here. The general had meant to be here when Sam arrived in town, but he'd had a mild heart attack. At the time, Sam had felt relief not to have the general close. Not that he could imagine the old warhorse fussing as he took care of his only and deeply disappointing son, but he hadn't wanted him there at all. Ever. His presence would have intruded on Sam's privacy.

The general had improved greatly, but the cardiologist refused to release him from his care for another month. Good old Dad always followed rules and commands, usually at the expense of his family.

Sam knew he should have outgrown that bitterness years ago.

He closed his eyes and started counting down again. "Ten...nine..."

When he felt better, he'd call the insurance agent about replacing the glass in the slider. The number should be somewhere, maybe in the box of stuff his aunt's lawyer had left.

Then he'd call the liquor store and arrange for another delivery.

❦

"Preacher?"

Adam looked up from his Bible, attempting to bring himself back to the present from the time of David. Maggie stood at the door. "Yes?"

"I need the hymns for Sunday."

He picked a piece of paper from the printer tray, glanced at it, then grabbed the list of Miss Birdie–approved hymns and a pen. With that, he crossed out his choices and changed every hymn to one of Miss Birdie's choosing.

That should make her believe she'd broken him in, which should make his life easier. His plan was, little by little, to slip in some of the newer hymns and drop most of the Fanny Crosby hymns and several of the old favorites she enjoyed. "Jesus Is Tenderly Calling Me Home" had always made him feel as if he were at a funeral. However, allowing Miss Birdie to win the first skirmish seemed like an excellent strategy.

Finished, he handed the list to Maggie and headed out to call on Sam Peterson. Easily finding the right house, Adam picked up all the papers—two weeks' worth—and placed them on the porch next to the front door, then rang the bell.

He didn't hear the sound of the chime inside, so he knocked. And knocked again. No one came, and it seemed as if no one would. If Captain Peterson didn't want visitors, Adam had to respect that. Besides, even a minister could hardly force himself on the man. Adam backed away from the door and turned to step off the porch.

He'd keep trying. He wanted to meet this man and he knew Miss Birdie wouldn't let him forget his duty.

Chapter Five

Friday evening Adam lay half-on-half-off the sofa, watching some action program he couldn't concentrate on.

The time since his arrival had gone well. Most of the congregation liked his preaching, although the pillar—Miss Birdie—made several suggestions. He'd made a number of much-appreciated hospital and nursing home visits and met the ministers of the Lutheran and Episcopal churches, spent a few hours at the food pantry every week, had coffee with Father Joe, and done a lot of ministerial stuff. But books and boxes still covered the surfaces and floors of the office. Someday he'd get to them.

As busy as he'd been with all those activities and events and meetings and services to fill time, Adam felt on edge. For the past few days, he hadn't been able to sit still. In the parsonage, he'd paced through the parlors and up and down the hall several times, even up the stairs to wander into empty bedrooms and the attic, then back down, over and over. None of that movement brought relief.

Adam stood and moved to stare out the front window.

Somewhere out there lay what he needed. Could he find it tonight? How would he be able to locate his fix in a new town? Where to start?

He didn't know, but he had to find something to get him through the night, to allow him to sleep, to take the edge off.

He had to find a pickup game of roundball.

After changing into athletic shoes and sweats, he found his basketball and dribbled it down the stairs, across the hall, and outside.

During Daylight Saving Time, sunlight in Central Texas lasted until nine thirty. If he could find a court, he'd have about an hour to shoot hoops.

Some people ran. Others walked or swam. Adam played basketball. He'd always needed the physical demands of the game to release all the pent-up tension and nervous energy his body built up with inactivity. Add to that the stress accumulated over the days without exercise, the jitters of being a new minister, the strain of knowing Miss Birdie watched his every move. His body screamed for a hard game of basketball.

He missed the competition, the moves, the jukes, and the almost chess-like thinking that took place in nearly every game, even pickup games.

Easy to find a game in Kentucky where basketball was pretty much another religion. If no one at the seminary was playing, he'd cross the street to the university or to Prall Town, a nearby neighborhood.

He jogged down streets lined by crepe myrtle. Heavy with flowers, their branches stretched up and up before crashing down in cascades of pink or purple or cottony white. Every now and then, a dog came to the fence and sniffed or growled. Several barked loudly enough to be called back by waving neighbors.

"Good evening, Preacher," a man called from his yard.

Recognizing the voice and face of a church member but not remembering his name, Adam wandered over to the fence.

The member of the congregation glanced at the ball Adam carried. "Looking for a game?" He pointed. "Over yonder. A block south and a couple more east. Goliad Park. Always a game going on."

Adam followed the directions. As he got closer, the noise and the glow of lights blazing through trees drew his attention.

On the court, two teams, players of different sizes and colors, worked hard, sweat dripping down their faces and bodies causing dark skin to glow like ebony. Near the fence stood several more guys and a couple of girls, all watching and cheering. On a court farther south, young women played.

If this had been a party or social hour, Adam would have walked away, uncomfortable because he didn't know anyone. But this was *ball*. He didn't lack confidence here. "I've got next," he yelled. Did the rules and phrases from Kentucky work here?

The games stopped. Everyone—those on both courts and those watching—turned toward him. Adam knew exactly what they saw: a newcomer, a tall, skinny old guy carrying a ball. Most of the players outweighed him by thirty pounds, and Adam had at least five or ten years on them. A few snickered. Others grinned and laughed.

"I've got next," he repeated, undaunted.

They nodded before resuming their games.

While they played, Adam dribbled toward one of the baskets outside the court and tossed up a few shots, then moved farther away and put several more in.

"You shoot like that when you're guarded?"

Slowly and deliberately, Adam took another shot, missed,

rebounded, and put it in before glancing at the speaker. The kid outweighed him and was stronger but Adam had more experience, a few inches' advantage in height, and longer arms.

Sweat glistened on the player's dark skin, which meant he must have warmed up and been playing already. Should be good competition.

"Try me." Adam tossed the ball to him.

Expressionless, the kid watched him for a second, then put the ball on the cracked asphalt and dribbled, glancing left, then right, and from Adam's feet to his eyes, watching and judging his movements. With a fake to the left and a drive to the right, the other player broke toward the basket. Like a hustler, Adam gave him that one. An early score made the other guy overconfident and cockier.

The kid turned with a big grin. With swagger and attitude, he tossed Adam the ball. The preacher had the guy exactly where he wanted him. Before he could react, Adam put the ball in the air for a long shot. The ball didn't make a sound as it passed through the metal chain of the basket. All that swagger and attitude disappeared, and the two got down to playing ball.

For the next thirty minutes, they fought. Despite the breeze, sweat poured down them both. They threw elbows, tripped each other, shoved and talked trash. Adam's trash talk consisted of "Oh, yeah?" and "Who's your daddy?" among other tame taunts, but it worked okay for him. The kid used tougher phrases filled with words the preacher hadn't used in years, but they didn't bother him. He didn't really hear them. All he cared about was the game, the competition. When he played ball, Adam wasn't clumsy or uncertain or too young and inexperienced. He was in the zone.

Within a few minutes, a small crowd had gathered, including the guys who'd been playing when he arrived. After a hard-fought game, Adam won thirty to twenty-six.

"Hey, Pops, you play pretty well for a skinny guy," his opponent said.

Adam read the subtext: *pretty good for a skinny white guy.* The nickname showed the kid recognized the preacher as being older, but he didn't care. He'd more than held his own against the youngster. That felt good.

The other guy spun the ball on his finger and studied Adam. "I'm Hector Firestone."

"Hector." Adam nodded but didn't say more for a few seconds. He was so winded he could barely talk, but darned if he'd let Hector know that. "Just call me Pops."

As he walked home that night, dribbling the ball in front of him and making moves toward phantom baskets, Adam cooled off and considered the next day.

Sam Peterson. He had to visit him again. Or try to.

❦

Sam groaned, inside. He didn't want to face intake with a PT who had read his eyes and understood what the redness meant. But here he sat, in her office, waiting for an interview and for the therapist to lay out a program to fix him. He looked out the window between her office and the treatment room.

As if feeling his gaze on her, Willow glanced at him, then away as she chatted with a patient. He grinned as he considered what he'd say to her. He noticed again the brackets between her eyes and understood them better. Moving to Texas, a cheating husband, and two active boys, as well as a new job, could wear a woman out. Maybe a year ago, he'd have sympathized, but compassion no longer made his top twenty list. In fact, compassion came well below "attempt to function" and "could care less."

As she entered the office, Willow Thomas turned a friendly smile at him but still didn't react like other women. Her lack of response probably was good but still odd in a *life-is-pain* sort of way. The only woman he'd seen in months whom he *might* like to attract didn't respond to his charms. Not at all. Not that he wanted to attract her, not now, but a positive response, the usual *my-my-my-aren't-you-hot* reaction, would feel good.

With another surreptitious glance at the redhead, he realized what a bunch of bull his desire *not* to attract her was. He'd like her to find him attractive and not only for the ego boost.

Once in her office, he'd shoved the crutches against the wall and settled into the chair, glad to take the weight off his shoulders. Aware of the warning from his doctor and the PTs in other hospitals not to cross his legs, he did exactly that, right over left, to see if he could get a rise from the professional and gorgeous therapist.

Before her death, his mother would've said he was acting out. He didn't care; he wanted to see the woman's response. Most likely, her dimples and honeyed smile would disappear.

Leaning back, he attempted to use the biofeedback exercise again. His leg hurt, but he found it difficult to relax in this chair with the commotion outside and the proximity of the redhead.

"Hello, Captain Peterson." She stood in front of him. "Make yourself comfortable," she said.

Yeah, fat chance.

"As you know, I'm Willow Thomas, one of the two PTs in the department. I'd like to review the notes Trixie made the other day and conduct an intake interview with you."

As Willow closed the door, he saw her eyeing his crossed leg, but she didn't say a word about it. Choosing her battles, he guessed.

"How are you doing today?"

"Peachy."

She nodded like she believed him, settled at her desk, and brought a file up on her screen. She perused the information for a moment before turning in the chair to look at him. "Why don't you tell me about your injury?" She picked up a clipboard. "You served in Afghanistan? A marine?"

He nodded.

"Your records say you were stabilized in Hawaii then transferred to Walter Reed in DC?" At his nod, she continued, "A transtibial amputation. That's fortunate."

"Oh, yeah, losing your leg is always lucky. All of us amputees celebrate it every glorious day."

She blinked. "I apologize. I can't believe I said that." She bit her lower lip. "I shouldn't have used those words. What I meant is a transtibial amputation is easier to treat, easier to find a prosthesis that fits, one that will be comfortable. The loss of part of your leg certainly is not a lucky event." She attempted a smile but it came off more worn-out than cheerful. "An unfortunate choice of words. I'm sorry."

He nodded again.

She studied the screen. "I see you already have your initial prosthesis." She glanced at the leg, which obviously didn't have one. "Do you have it with you?"

He'd have to use a few more words to explain. "It's at home. It's not comfortable."

She nodded, with sympathy. He hated sympathy and the sweet smiles and pitying glances that came with it. He slid down farther in the chair. He knew he was behaving like a butthead, but he figured if he was drowning, why should he go alone?

"We'll see what we can do to alleviate the pain, maybe add some cushioning. You're going to have to get used to the prosthesis you have before the prosthetist can fit you for a new one."

Like the new one would be better.

She glanced at his records again. "All right, let me check your file. I have copies of your initial intake from Hawaii and another from DC." She looked up with green eyes as clear as a high mountain spring, exactly the same color as her sons'. On them they looked full of spirit and mischief. On her, they promised healing.

He'd rather they promised something else.

She turned away from the screen to face him. "How did you happen to end up in Butternut Creek when you could have rehabbed at Walter Reed or other large facilities?"

He'd have to speak or he'd look like even more of a jerk than he was. "Didn't want to stay in DC so the general— that's my father—pulled a few strings. He was a marine, too. My aunt died a while back and left me a house over on Pine Street."

"On Pine Street?" She smiled at him. "I live close to that, in the new apartments on Eleventh."

"Oh?" He nodded as if the information were new.

"Why don't you tell me about your daily schedule," she asked. "What's your level of activity? What kind of physical activity do you take part in?"

He narrowed his eyes and grinned—inside. "I do a lot of elbow bending, ma'am." He mimed the actions of pouring from a bottle to a glass, then drinking. With a slow, mocking grin, he added, "I do it very well. No pain. No problems."

He had to hand it to her. A complete professional, she allowed not one sign of judgment or disgust to cross her face, to give away her opinion of a man who spent his day filling himself with booze to smooth off the ragged edges of pain and splinters of loss. She must have interviewed a lot of angry, depressed wounded vets.

"But you're a physical therapist," he said to the top of her head as she made notes. "Why are you asking me questions about occupational therapy?" He knew the difference. He'd been interrogated by dozens of people in many different departments since the injury.

"This is an intake session that covers all areas, to make sure you receive optimal care. Also, many of our services overlap."

He nodded and enjoyed the view of her beautiful hair.

"You drink a great deal?" she asked without a trace of emotion. "How much would you say you drink a day?"

"As much as necessary. I drink until I feel better, pass out, or can't feel anything."

She studied him for a moment, her face expressionless. "You do know alcohol can change the effect of or weaken some of the medications you're taking?"

Too stupid a question to answer. Of course he knew. He didn't care. No drinker would, but at least she didn't give him the lecture about how he was ruining his life.

She scribbled a few notes before asking, "Do you live alone?"

He nodded.

"How did you get to the hospital today?"

"The community bus for cripples."

When her gaze flew to his face, he felt a spark of contrary pleasure. He'd gotten to her, but not for long. She looked back to her page, cool as ever.

"Tell me about how you handle the chores of daily living."

"Chores of daily living?" He laughed without one note of humor. "They don't get done."

"We offer in-home services like housekeeping, a medication aide, help with bathing."

"No," he said. When she glanced up he added, "Thank you," but didn't mean it.

"Are you aware of the veterans' support groups in the area? One meets at—"

He snorted.

"I take it you're not interested." When he didn't respond, she said, "When you're ready, if you're ever interested, I can give you some information. One meets at the Christian Church." She jotted more notes. "How well do you sleep?"

"Have trouble nodding off."

"Pain?"

He nodded. "But once I have a couple of nightcaps to blunt the pain and fall asleep, I don't want to wake up. Could probably stay in bed all day." He paused. "If it weren't for the kids."

She glanced up at him quickly, a touch of confusion in her eyes. "Kids?"

"Yeah, sounds like a dozen but I've only seen two boys About this high, and this high." He used his hand to indicate their heights.

"Two boys? In your neighborhood?" The confusion had changed to concern.

"In my backyard."

She blinked. He was getting to her. Good. She looked nervous.

"Yeah, redheaded little fiends, make more noise than you could imagine. Running around in my backyard."

"Redheaded little fiends?" She closed the file with a slap

and leaned forward. "In your yard?" Her voice remained even but her eyes flashed.

He'd pierced her calm facade. Could he tell her she was beautiful when she was angry? No, too clichéd and too forward. Rudeness didn't bother him these days, but he hated clichés. He nodded and hid a grin of triumph.

"They broke my slider yesterday. Threw a rock through it."

She glared—only a bit—but emotion in those eyes was much more interesting than her cool, professional demeanor. Obviously the kids hadn't told her. Of course, it had only happened the day before. Probably hadn't gotten up their courage yet.

"Yes, the little scamps did. Took me forever to clean the glass off the floor. Talk about chores of daily living. Using a broom and dustpan is difficult for a guy with one leg."

She swallowed and attempted to mask her response. Cool on the outside but obviously upset inside. "Has the glass been fixed?"

"I took care of it right away but it cost more than I had in the budget."

The therapist's beautiful green eyes grew large.

"Funny thing." He paused. "I gave them my phone number, to have their mother call me. No one did." He shook his head. "Guess she doesn't care. Guess she can't control them."

She took a deep breath. A determined look covered her face, and her eyes showed a resolute glint. She glared over his head, her lips narrowed to almost nothing. An amazing transformation from compassionate professional to troubled mother.

"As you have probably guessed, those two were my sons. Your expenditure will be taken care of and the nuisance addressed." She stood. "If you will excuse me." She headed toward the door and opened it. "I'm going to ask Mike to work with you on strengthening your leg and core muscles and on improving your balance. We'll complete the intake during your next appointment."

He watched her walk out the door.

He didn't get as much pleasure out of ticking people off as he used to, but, as long as he got a reaction, he wasn't about to stop. What else did he have to do, other than watch the great parts of Willow Thomas as she moved away from him? He figured she'd refuse to add that means of entertainment to his treatment plan.

The occupational therapist would expect him to find a wheelchair basketball league or learn to whittle, but neither of those interested him nearly as much as Willow Thomas and the way her eyes flashed when she became upset.

Nothing scared him more than the attraction toward this woman. He was a mess and so was his life. He knew what a bargain he was *not*. She had too much on her plate now without taking on a bitter cripple.

Besides, his interest was completely physical. The woman had a great body, and she was nice enough. But he had no interest in an emotional entanglement with a single mother of two rambunctious boys, or any woman for that matter.

Watching her didn't commit him to anything, however, and it gave him more pleasure than anything had in a long time.

Chapter Six

Willow pulled into the parking lot of her apartment complex, parked, and turned off the ignition. Her husband had bought her this very expensive car two years ago, back when he was seeing Tiffany but still felt guilty about it. The insurance payments took a big hunk of her paycheck. Her lawyer should have done a better job on that. Also, the backseat was tiny and the gas mileage was terrible, but it looked great and went very fast on the highway.

As she tapped her fingers against the steering wheel, she knew she was delaying entering the apartment, postponing the discussion with the boys. What was she going to do with them? What should she do about them? They were young boys who'd lost their father, friends, and home to come to a small town hundreds of miles away from Chicago with a completely different culture and climate.

Knowing they'd want to be active, she'd enrolled them in a day camp until school started, but not enough had signed up so the last session was canceled. By that time, it was too late to enroll them in the summer soccer league. She could hardly take them to work, but she thought they'd be safe playing in the park, walking to the library, and wandering over to the box store on the edge of town. After all, they were eight and ten. Never had she thought they'd trespass and break a window.

She shouldn't have allowed the captain's revelation to bother her so much. For heaven's sake, she'd run out on a patient during the intake sessions. How incompetent did that appear? But she'd felt overwhelmed by life, and breaking down in tears in front of the captain wouldn't seem professional to him or to anyone. Certainly not to her.

Exactly what she needed: to have Leo and Nick running wild and to have a patient think she was a terrible, uncaring mother. That would hardly justify his having confidence in any area.

Would it have mattered if the patient hadn't been Captain Peterson? As much as she tried to ignore it, the question wiggled into her brain. Yes, he was handsome and charismatic. His eyes smoldered. Wasn't that the word they used in romance novels? Didn't the hero always have smoldering eyes that burned into the soul of the heroine? But this wasn't a book and he wasn't the hero and she shouldn't care about the opinion of a patient more than that of anyone else.

Nor was this about her. This was about Leo and Nick and how she could guide them without making them more unhappy about their situation.

But as hard as she attempted to ignore this—she certainly was deep in denial this afternoon—she had to admit she liked how the captain had looked at her, as if he found her an attractive woman, maybe even sexy. Her self-esteem had suffered when she first found out about Tiffany, but the captain seemed to…

"Mom?"

She glanced up to see Nick standing at her window.

"Is there something wrong?" He frowned a little as if wondering why she was still in the car in the parking lot. "Are you sick?"

"No." She smiled at him. Plenty of time to talk about that broken slider once she was inside with both boys. "Just thinking. But I do want to talk to you and Leo."

"Oh."

That one syllable, spoken in the high, shaky voice Nick used when he was worried or frightened, tipped her off. He and his brother *had* broken the slider and hadn't told her. Not that she'd doubt the captain, who had no reason to make the story up, but she'd wanted to ask the boys first. Now she knew.

"Let's go inside." She opened the door and handed the sack of hamburgers to him. Probably shouldn't buy their favorite fast food when she was going to have to punish them, but after a long day of work, she couldn't face cooking. "Where's your brother?"

Nick gulped as he took the bag. "Watching television," he said, his voice still wavering.

When she unlocked the apartment and Nick shoved the door open, he said, "Mom wants to talk to us."

If she hadn't already known what had happened, the sight of Leo leaping to his feet and glancing at his brother in silent communication would have tipped her off. She closed the door, walked toward the window, and opened the blinds. That completed, she turned back to face the boys. "Boys, does either of you want to tell me about Captain Peterson?"

"Mom, he's the coolest man," Nick said. "He has tattoos—I mean tats—and he's a marine."

"He was wounded," Leo added, his voice filled with admiration.

She could tell by his face that her eldest had just realized a wounded marine might end up at physical therapy. "Have you met him?" he asked.

She nodded.

Nick and Leo exchanged glances again.

"Guess we'd better tell you what happened," Leo said.

"Yes, and after you do that, explain why you didn't tell me about it and what you're going to do to repay the captain." She'd have to be tough because she didn't want anyone—not only the captain—to think she let the boys get away with anything.

But making the boys compensate him for the broken door meant she'd have to see him again. She didn't want to, not outside the secure walls of the hospital, the safe haven of the physical therapy department where she could hide behind her professional demeanor. He and his scrutiny made her feel attractive, like a woman again, as her husband had done for years. But Grant taught her not to trust men, and she'd learned that lesson well. With two sons, she didn't dare make another mistake.

Adam hurried across the parking lot toward the church, carrying the plate of warm muffins Ouida had handed him on his way out of the parsonage.

Surely there could be no better place for a bachelor than living next to a friendly neighbor who baked. He whistled as he entered the church. When he spotted the frown on Maggie's face, the whistling stopped.

"You have a guest." She continued to type the bulletin, but

her tone and lack of eye contact suggested he might not be pleased with the identity of the visitor.

Guessing who it was, Adam attempted to recapture his exhilaration. It eluded him. He hadn't seen Miss Birdie's old van outside, but she could have walked. No destination in town was too far to walk.

"Who is it?" he whispered.

Maggie kept her eye on the screen and didn't answer. Surely setting the margin couldn't demand so much attention.

Squaring his shoulders, Adam pushed the door open and walked into the minister's study. He knew he should call this his study, but he worried about acting too possessive, as if claiming this as his might make the extraordinary place disappear. Magical and un-Christian thinking, he knew.

Yes, Miss Birdie stood next to the desk. She hadn't heard him enter and rubbed her shoulder as if... Well, for a moment, she looked vulnerable. Like a real person, like a church member whose minister should comfort her instead of wanting to run and hide every time he saw her.

When she heard him come in, the pillar dropped her hands and turned toward him. Her lips curved, an expression he couldn't read but made him suspicious. She looked almost friendly.

He had to quit judging Miss Birdie. She was a member of the congregation, a child of God who deserved to be loved and accepted by her minister. Adam smiled back. "What can I do for you?"

"Well, first you need to do something about these books all over the place."

"I agree, but..." He realized as he began to defend the mess that the books weren't the real reason for her visit. Oddly, instead of appearing confident, she looked almost uncertain about her purpose. Adam guessed the hesitation would disappear as soon as the reason for her presence emerged. Miss Birdie wasn't one to hem and haw.

The minister gestured toward the two chairs he'd cleared after her first visit and walked to the desk. Piles of books and tottering stacks of paper littered the surface. As if he'd always meant to do exactly that, Adam opened the large bottom drawer, swept the mess inside, and closed it. "Won't you have a seat?"

"No, I need to get some things done before the lunch crowd comes in." She paused. "Preacher, I'd like you to be my guest for breakfast in the morning."

Now Adam felt incredibly foolish. He'd misjudged Miss Birdie again and should look out for that tendency. He needed to be more accepting. "How nice of you. Thank you. Eight o'clock at the diner?"

"No, no, no. A little earlier. Maybe seven fifteen? Before the crowd gets there."

Why so early? Had she said *before the crowd*? Although Adam hadn't eaten there yet, he thought most people who had to get to work would arrive about seven. And if she wanted to discuss something important, why would the restaurant be a better place to converse than the church office?

There he went again, trying to explain and understand her invitation instead of accepting it gratefully. "Seven fifteen. Thank you. I'll be there."

She walked to the door before turning and looking a little uncertain. "Oh, and wear a tie, please. Don't suppose you could get a haircut?"

Odd.

"I…aah…want to show my minister off to all my customers."

"I'll try." But before he could complete those two syllables, she'd disappeared, again without a good-bye.

That night, as Adam walked home after a tough game of three-on-three with Hector and his friends, two questions repeated through his brain. First, considering the aches and pains he suffered from the blocks and shoves, should he play ball with kids ten years younger? Without resolving that concern, because he knew he'd never give the game up as long as he could still dribble, he pondered Miss Birdie's odd invitation to breakfast. Attempting to understand the twists and turns of the pillar's brain baffled Adam, and yet hadn't he promised himself not to always believe she had ulterior motives? Hadn't he decided to trust Miss Birdie? He gave up trying to figure her out as he approached the front steps of the parsonage.

❦

As Adam contemplated himself in the mirror at six forty-five Thursday morning, he knew he had to get a haircut. Most of the first check had paid for repairs on the car. He'd set the rest aside for food because he'd run out of the goodies people had brought those first weeks. Surely he could scrape together enough to get a haircut soon. At least he was wearing a tie, he thought as he straightened it.

Adam left the house at 7:05, plenty of time to walk to the diner. When he entered the restaurant, he looked around. All the booths lining the walls plus the five or six tables in the center of the room and every stool at the counter were occupied, mostly by men drinking coffee and talking. He spotted a few members of the congregation and was headed in the direction of Howard's booth when Miss Birdie intercepted him. Her plastic nametag said only BIRDIE. If he wanted to escape her wrath, he figured he should never call her that.

"Good morning, Pastor Adam. We're busy this morning so you're going to have to share a booth."

Odd. He thought she wanted to share breakfast with him, to talk to him about something personal, a problem or concern, but how did she expect to do that here? The place was packed. People held up cups for refills all over the room. She obviously had to work.

And this was *before the crowd*?

Adam pointed toward the booth where the elders sat. "I'll join them."

"No, no, I have a place set and ready for you." She grabbed his arm with her free hand and gestured toward the corner with the coffeepot she held in the other.

Adam had made it a rule never to oppose a woman armed with a hot carafe. However, when the two got within six feet of the booth, he realized a young woman sat there, her back to them as she read the paper. He stopped.

"Someone's already there," he said although he knew full well why someone was already there. The matchmaker had roped him in, set him up. He'd been dumb enough to believe her sincerity, accept her invitation, and walk into her trap.

When would he learn?

With a quick glance at the woman in the booth—who, fortunately, hadn't noticed that he and his captor stood only a few feet away—then another peek at the door, Adam calculated his chance of escape. Could he run fast enough to get out of the diner before the woman in the booth could lift her eyes from the opinion page of the *Austin American-Statesman*?

Foolishly he hadn't figured Miss Birdie in his calculations. The pillar motioned toward Adam with that pot of hot coffee.

Once she ascertained he wouldn't attempt to run, she said to the young woman, "We're full today. Do you mind sharing the booth?"

Miss Birdie continued to wave Adam forward and, unwilling and suspicious but not wanting to insult the young woman, he followed. Besides, he couldn't run without causing a scene and infuriating Miss Birdie. Neither seemed wise, and he was hungry.

"Hello." Adam nodded as the woman glanced up.

A lovely smile, he noted, dimples showing on a round, sweet face. Her dark hair was pulled back with one of those plastic styling things he'd seen advertised on television and wondered both how they worked and if anyone bought and used them. At least this woman had.

"Hi." She gestured at the red upholstered seat across from her. "Please join me."

Adam slid in before glancing at Miss Birdie, whose smile stretched bright and broad and triumphant across her face. What next? A victory dance?

No, she simply turned a cup over and filled it. "Your breakfast will be right out. I ordered for you, Preacher," she said. "Pastor, this is Reverend Patillo, the minister at the Presbyterian church. Why don't you two get acquainted? As ministers, I imagine you have a lot in common." She dashed off, leaving them alone and looking as proud as if she'd posted a MISSION COMPLETE banner.

Not that Adam felt particularly alone with fifty to sixty people crowded into the café. The eyes of every one of them studied the two in the booth surreptitiously. Was the entire town in on Miss Birdie's matchmaking scheme?

"I'm Mattie. Have we been set up?" She chuckled, a warm, friendly sound but hardly the siren's call of immediate chemistry. "You must be Adam Jordan from the Christian Church. I'd heard a single minister was coming to town and figured it was only a matter of time before someone tried to get us together. How long have you been here?"

"A few weeks."

"I'm surprised this hasn't happened earlier." Mattie took another sip of her coffee. "I want to..."

"Sorry to interrupt, but here're your breakfasts." On her right arm, Miss Birdie carried a platter holding two large plates and two small ones. "Toast and half a grapefruit for Reverend Patillo." She placed them in front of Mattie. "The rest for Pastor Adam. Hope you enjoy this, Preacher."

With those words, she set down a platter in front of Adam with a stack of pancakes topped with whipped cream and strawberries and syrup and another with four pieces of bacon, a small steak, three sausage links, a couple of biscuits, an enormous mound of scrambled eggs, grits with oceans of melted butter on top, and hash browns. It took up nearly the entire table. That finished, she folded her hands in front of her and smiled, her glance shifting from minister to minister. "Isn't she just about the prettiest thing you've ever seen?"

He responded, "I can't eat all this."

"Course you can. Wouldn't hurt you to put a little meat on those bones. Take the leftovers home for breakfast tomorrow."

Adam studied the amazing amount of food. Except for the grits, the food would last for a week. Even though he'd lived in Kentucky for years, he'd never learned to like grits. They must be a taste acquired immediately after weaning. To him, grits tasted like ground Styrofoam. It wasn't that he disliked them; he just saw no reason to expend the effort to swallow something so tasteless.

"Now, you two enjoy. Take your time." She patted his arm,

friendlier than she'd ever behaved. "No reason for you to hurry. We have plenty of room." With that, she rushed to another booth.

Adam glanced at the packed room and the line out the door. Oh, sure, plenty of room. Within minutes he discovered that even if he were interested in Mattie, it wasn't conducive to romance to have half the town watching while the other half wished they'd stop eating and leave, giving up a booth big enough for four or five of them.

"You don't think she's too obvious, do you?" He attacked the pancakes.

"She's sweet." Mattie picked up a packet of jelly, tore it open, and spread the contents on her toast.

"No, she's not. She's controlling and has to be right."

"And she thinks every minister should be married, even women pastors. I've heard she's not too certain women should be in ministry unless we work with children, but if we are she wants us married." She grinned. "Right?"

He smiled back. "But only because she cares."

"You two are getting along well." Miss Birdie appeared with her ubiquitous coffeepot and topped off their nearly full cups.

Adam noticed she looked very pleased, probably sure her plan to marry off two ministers was going well.

The pillar wandered off but kept her eyes turned toward them. He should tell her that if she wanted to play matchmaker, she shouldn't hover or gawk. Instead, he took a bite of sausage. After a few bites, he studied the plates again. "Mattie, can I interest you in a piece of bacon? Sausage? Steak?"

"No, thanks. I'm fine." After taking a sip of coffee, she asked, "What are you preaching on Sunday?"

"I'm planning to use the lectionary text from the gospel. What about you?"

"Me, too. How are you going to approach it?"

For a few minutes the ministers discussed the meaning of the verses and their structure and historical background as well as examples they could use in a sermon. As they exchanged opinions, Adam noted and ignored Miss Birdie's fluttering around the table. He hadn't thought the pillar could do fluttering. She filled their cups, removed plates, even dropped ice in the overflowing glasses and brought more orange juice. Inside Adam laughed because he knew hearing them talk about the interpretation of biblical texts must make Miss Birdie crazy.

Besides, he was having fun. He liked discussing sermons with another minister, and he felt more comfortable with a woman than he had for years because he didn't think of Mattie as a woman—not that he'd tell her or Miss Birdie that. She seemed like another minister, a colleague but not a possible wife or a woman to impress or date. He felt at ease with her, and the constant surveillance of Miss Birdie amused him.

"I need to tell you something," Mattie said after Miss Birdie had run out of things to bring or empty or pick up or wipe down and had left several huge take-home boxes, which Adam filled with enough food for breakfasts for the next week. Before Mattie said more, she searched until she spotted Miss Birdie waiting on a table on the other side of the diner. "You are the nicest single man I've met in Butternut Creek."

"Oh? Are there many of us?"

"Actually, you're the only one I've met under fifty." She grinned. "Right now, I have no desire for a relationship. I broke my engagement before I came here and am not interested in anything, not for years."

"Pretty bad, huh?"

She nodded.

"Fine with me. I'm not interested in dating now, either. New job, new life." Adam leaned forward and spoke softly. Miss Birdie would probably believe that those heads close together meant something romantic. "How would you like to go to a movie every now and then or go out for lunch? Maybe discuss the lectionary once a week. That should throw the town matchmakers off."

"I'd like to. I could use a friend." She picked up her check. "Give me a call."

❦

At nine, after the preachers and most of the morning crowd had left, Birdie pulled out her cell phone and punched speed dial. She'd always thought they were a stupid expense until the girls became teenagers. Then they'd become necessities.

"A total waste of time. Not a spark between them," she said as soon as Mercedes answered. "They spent most of the time discussing the lectionary. What's the lectionary?"

"Someone divided up the Bible into verses to use in sermons."

"Why would anyone do that? What's wrong with the way the Bible was written, all those books. All together."

"The lectionary covers most of the Bible in a couple of years so you have an idea of the complete Bible instead of just sections."

"Sounds too complicated." Let down and disappointed, she shook her head, as if Mercedes could hear that. "Well, that's what they discussed. For nearly an hour. Hmph. Didn't work at all."

"It could," Mercedes answered. "After all, sometimes it takes a while for the seed to take root. They have something in common. Don't be so impatient."

"Bah, I'm not impatient."

"I'm not going to debate that with you because I have to get back to work. Bye."

After Mercedes disconnected, Birdie stared at the phone and wondered about her minister. Why hadn't he found a wife on his own? He was an attractive young man even though his hair was a lot longer than she felt a Christian young man should wear. Of course, Jesus wore his hair long, but Pastor Adam wasn't Jesus.

"Miss." One of her customers waved his hand and held up his cup. "Coffee."

She shoved the phone in her pocket and hurried toward him.

This matchmaking stuff was a lot harder than she'd remembered. Was there another single woman in town she could fix the man up with? Willow Thomas was her only thought, but she was saving her for Effie's nephew.

Which pretty much left her baffled, not her normal state and very uncomfortable.

Chapter Seven

Noise from outside once again jerked Sam awake far earlier than he wanted to be conscious.

This time the commotion didn't come from the exploding mortars or flashes of rockets that tormented his nightmares. No, someone was knocking on the front door. They did it again, with at least two sets of knuckles. And then again. Someone he didn't want to talk to—which included about everyone in the world—waited outside. The sound made waves of pain bounce against his skull from the inside.

He groaned. Although he didn't hear voices, he had an idea of exactly who stood outside and had changed to even more insistent hammering. He had learned that people in this town didn't leave when he ignored them, but he was still willing to try.

He squashed the pillow over his head so the streak of sunshine didn't hit him right in the eyes and tried to fall back asleep. If changing position didn't hurt so much, he'd turn over and bury his face in the mattress.

"Captain Peterson, it's Willow Thomas, the physical therapist from the hospital."

Exactly what he feared.

He squeezed his eyes shut, turned one ear against the mattress, and put the pillow over the other. Didn't work. He still heard the knocking and the shouting. It wasn't going to stop. The look in the PT's eyes yesterday had revealed a determined woman who didn't act like she'd turn aside from her duty because of a locked door or being ignored by the person inside.

He hated tenacity in a woman.

"I have my sons with me. They want to talk to you."

Oh, sure. He'd wager chatting with a worn-out, crippled shell of a man who'd yelled at them was exactly what those two kids wanted to do.

His head throbbed. With the pounding and shouting, the pain reached a higher level. Why wouldn't she go away? Didn't she have work?

"Captain, the boys have all day free and I'm staying here, with them, until noon. We're not leaving until you come out even if we have to knock on your door for the next three or four hours."

He couldn't escape. After all, the woman worked with amputees all the time. Probably understood them very well, knew their reactions. She probably believed that before they were wounded and became so angry and frustrated and rude, wounded veterans *had* been nice guys. She probably thought he was a nice guy, deep inside. He could easily prove her wrong, only not right now and not from his bedroom. He'd have to get up to show her what a jerk he could be.

He tossed the pillow aside, turned in bed, pushed himself to his foot, and shoved the crutches under his arms. He glanced at himself in the mirror. He looked like he'd come off a five-day binge. Maybe he should quit drinking so much. He considered that for a second before he decided it would be easier to take down the mirror instead.

"Hold on," he shouted. Last night he'd fallen asleep in his camo cutoffs and T-shirt. Wrinkled and scruffy but fairly clean, they covered most of him. Attempting to go around the worst of the trash, he caught a crutch on the carpet and with a loud expletive nearly collapsed in a heap. He regained his balance and shoved away from the wall, then hobbled across the living room to the front door. Once there, he glared at the three members of the Thomas family through the glass panel.

"Yeah?" he mumbled.

"Captain, the boys have something they want to say. Can we come in and talk to you?"

He looked behind him at the squalor of his house.

He hadn't minded the mess when the window man was here the other day—the repairman was a guy—but allowing these three in? Two kids and his PT? Besides, he wasn't sure what else lay under the mess. Probably mice and cockroaches. As far as he knew or cared, there could be wild boars or feral cats under it all.

The stench had begun to bother him yesterday but not enough to do anything about it. Now company waited. Maybe they'd leave as soon as they came in and the miasma nearly asphyxiated them. Of course, he didn't plan to let them in. He could stick his head outside, hear the apologies, and shut the door, coming back in alone.

When she saw the conditions, if she didn't run, Willow Thomas's eyes would be filled with sympathy, which he didn't need, or with disgust, which might be a good thing. Right now, he could see they sparkled with determination, which signaled she was not going away. Why fight the eventual outcome?

He flicked his glance toward the boys. Even with the

spiked hair, they looked innocent but frightened. Shame filled him as he realized he couldn't let them see what he was really like.

When they'd been in before, the boys had entered the dining room—which he seldom used and was fairly uncontaminated. If he let them in, they'd see everything. Everything.

No, he didn't want them back inside, in the part of the house he used and trashed. Didn't want them to know what a slob he was or how much he drank or how little he cared about anything and certainly not how little he cared about himself or his future.

"Captain Peterson?" Willow repeated from outside. The determination in her voice convinced him even more she wouldn't be content to stay outside.

In an effort to make an inroad in the mess, he tried to kick bottles out of the way. Hard to do with only one leg. Sam took a few steps away from the door and used a crutch in an effort to shove a few under the sofa. He nearly fell between the cluttered end table and the pink velvet love seat.

Finally, he gave up with a curse, deciding he wouldn't feel ashamed. This chaos stated clearly who he was. He manipulated himself back to the door, opened it at the same time she pushed on it, then moved away so they could enter.

Willow didn't flinch when she and the boys entered. Probably had visited a few wounded vets in her time and knew what to expect, but the boys stood still, just inside the door, and studied the mess with wide eyes.

"Look at all the bottles," Nick said in a voice filled with awe.

"Do you recycle?" Leo asked.

He'd been wrong. The fact that kids had been exposed to his excesses made him feel more ashamed than he thought possible.

"Any pizza left?" Leo scampered toward a box.

"You wouldn't want it if there were," Sam said. "It's really old." He shoved an empty fried-chicken bucket off a chair and onto the floor, then lowered himself onto the sofa between a couple of Chinese delivery sacks and dropped his crutches on the floor before he asked, "To what do I owe this visit?"

"Boys, come here," she said to her sons. The boys' heads turned back and forth as they admired the jumble and heaps of trash. Finally, her words brought them back to reality and, he supposed, the reason they stood in the middle of his living room.

The two moved a few steps to stand next to their mother, reluctance showing in every step. The journey seemed as tortured and protracted as a trek through deep snow in weighted combat boots.

"Leo and Nick have something to tell you." When they didn't say a word, she nudged Leo.

"We're sorry, Captain Peterson," the older brother said. "We shouldn't have been playing in your backyard without your permission."

Nick nodded. "And I shouldn't have been throwing rocks. I'm sorry about your window."

Sam didn't say a word, just watched the trio and waited.

"The boys apologize for causing trouble and that you had to buy a new window. Unfortunately…" She paused, took a deep breath, and exhaled through her lips.

Beautiful, sensual lips that promised more than he wanted to consider now. Not that she actually *offered* anything other than the apology, but he wasn't too wounded to fantasize.

"Unfortunately," she repeated, "with our move and my starting a new job, money is a little short right now. The boys will work off their debt." She glanced at the boys, then toward him, uncertain for a moment. "If that would be convenient for you."

He couldn't imagine anything less convenient than having two kids around the house unless it would be the presence of these two kids and their mother.

The two boys nodded, looking as solemn as imps with spiked red hair and freckles could.

"No." Sam waved the offer away. "Not necessary."

"Yes, it is, Captain Peterson." Her chin jutted out a bit, only enough to show her determination. "They need to learn that bad behavior has consequences."

And *he* was the consequence? He grinned a little, inside. Being the consequence not the instigator of bad behavior was a first. It amused him. At the same time, he had no interest in actually being the consequence, and had to get the idea out of her determined, redheaded mind. He sat forward and clasped his hands in front of him. "The boys tell me that your husband ran off with a younger woman."

At his statement, she paled. For a moment, he regretted the words even though he'd meant to hurt her. But his inability to behave in a civilized manner should make her gather her sons and make a dignified, if quick, departure. Actually, he'd prefer an undignified departure—he'd like to see her scramble out.

He'd obviously underestimated the character of Willow Thomas.

She lifted that chin a fraction of an inch more and stared at him. "That does not mean that Leo and Nick can get away with breaking a window and not taking responsibility for the damage. Although it may not appear that way to you now"— she glared at each son—"they were raised to behave better."

She looked so brave and the boys so solemn that he had to steel himself. These were exactly the kind of people he'd have enjoyed before...All the more reason to beat her off with words and attitude.

"Ms. Thomas, I'm not going to take care of your sons because you can't control them."

That should do it.

She took another deep breath, but before she could say anything, Leo stepped forward. "Sir, Mom expects us to behave ourselves. We were wrong to play in your yard without your permission and really wrong to break your window. Now we have to man up."

The old Sam, the pre-injury Sam, would've laughed to have his words used against him. This Sam shook his head. "You can't shame me into this."

"Please, Mister...um, Captain." Leo took another step toward Sam and swallowed. "Please. We're good kids and we won't bother you, but we can"—he looked at the mess—"we *can* clean this place. We're good at that. We know how to vacuum and dust. Mom's taught us a lot of stuff."

"Please?" The younger brother used every bit of his body to express his contrition: quivering lips, sad eyes, and bowed posture. Sam thought even the spikes in his hair bent in shame.

He thought he'd discarded compassion for others in the strife of the last few months, but the remorse of these two kids was more than he could handle. He recognized it as emotional blackmail. It worked.

"All right." He gave up, amazed at how easily the family had defeated him. "You can police the area."

"Yes, sir," Leo said. "Thank you."

At the same time Nick said, "Wow! We get to police the area."

Willow nodded. "Thank you. How much did the window and the installation cost?"

"Four hundred dollars."

The boys gasped.

"That means each of the boys owes you two hundred dollars' worth of work. At five dollars an hour, that means forty hours of work each. Does that seem fair?"

"Too much."

She glared at him, and he found himself nodding. He could shut himself in his bedroom if he had to and drink himself under the bed.

"Was there any other damage?" She looked at Sam, then at the boys.

"No, that's all," Sam answered. "Forty hours of work from each." Would he survive it?

"When can they start?" She glanced at her watch.

"What day is it?" Didn't really make a difference. Every day seemed the same to him. He only remembered appointments because someone called him the day before to remind him.

"Thursday."

"Next week," he said. Maybe they'd forget by then.

"We can start right now, Captain," Leo said.

Sam shook his head to clear it, but it didn't help. He'd planned to sleep until noon at least, but before he could suggest next week again, Willow spoke.

"I have cleaning supplies in the car. Boys, go get them."

As the two ran out, he glared at her. "Don't you think I have cleaning supplies?"

In fact, he didn't. He'd used up the bits left in his aunt's pantry and hadn't bought more because it was hard enough just to carry food home. Besides, he'd had no desire to clean. Living like this had seemed right, but still, her assumption was insulting.

"Of course you do, but you shouldn't have to pay for them. Not when my sons did the damage."

He nodded.

"I brought some work to do," she said.

Sam noticed the laptop hanging from her shoulder. He hadn't noticed that when she came in. What man would when a woman looked like her?

"I have a lot of paperwork to catch up on." She checked her watch. "I'll stay until noon and fix you all lunch before I leave."

"Ma'am, despite the fact that I'm disabled, I'm perfectly capable of supervising two kids."

"Of course you are."

He could read the implication. Although she'd read his file and knew his background, she was careful with her sons except when they ran around on their own. He admired that.

"You don't want to leave them alone with a stranger, especially one whose house is filled with bottles and trash," he said. "I have a lot of bad habits, but I don't hurt kids."

She didn't agree or argue or deign to answer but turned toward the dining room, picking up bottles as she went. As she moved away, she left a view of that great derriere and a trail of perfume that floated behind her and smelled so sweet it masked the odor of the room for a second or two.

The boys came loudly back into the house, loaded with supplies. To make sure they understood his reluctance, he frowned.

Didn't faze them.

"We'll start by picking up the cans and bottles," Nick said.

"No, leave that for me," Sam said. He didn't want these two picking up beer cans and drained tequila and bourbon bottles.

"I'll take care of the bottles," Willow said.

He nodded. "Okay, you guys shovel up the other trash while I take a shower and get dressed."

"Go ahead." Leo waved him away. "We'll be fine. We know how to do this."

"Yeah, we're good at it." Nick dropped his bucket on the floor. "We clean for Mom all the time."

No matter what they did, it couldn't get any worse. Not even a herd of goats could make this any worse.

"You sure have ugly furniture," Nick said.

"Remember your manners," his mother said.

"Shut up," Leo whispered.

Sam bet the older brother had just given the younger an elbow to the ribs, but he hadn't seen it. He turned toward the bathroom and longed to shut himself inside while these two fought it out and while the luscious Willow Thomas leaned down to pick up trash. Because he hated to miss a single second of her efforts, he delayed the shower for a few minutes, until she finished.

Chapter Eight

Before lunch a few weeks later, Adam wandered over to the square, not a place he frequented. In the middle of a green lawn and big trees sat the courthouse, an ornate brick edifice built in 1865 with a tower and cupolas on each corner. A street wrapped around it with several gift shops, a tearoom, and an antiques mall facing the turreted brick building. Butternut Creek even had a small country music venue across from the courthouse, a site that must have once housed a movie theater.

Benson's Barbershop was between a tanning salon and the library and looked a lot like the shop his father had taken him to as a kid. Adam entered and sat down to wait because the barber stood at a huge chair, cutting the hair of an elderly man. On the counter were a couple of jars filled with combs and a blue liquid, a germicide, Adam guessed. Hunting and fishing magazines covered a table.

"There you go, Roscoe," the barber said finishing up with the elderly man. He opened a bottle of something red that smelled like roses and rubbing alcohol, patted it on Roscoe's neck, then lowered the chair and said, "I'm Joe Bob. What can I do for you, young man?"

When Roscoe departed, Adam climbed into the chair. The barber tied a cape on him and raised the chair. "I like my hair long on the top and shorter than it is around the ears and in the back," he explained. In the mirror, he watched Joe Bob nod.

The barber picked up a clipper, turned it on, and started in. Before Adam could say *That's too short*, the man had nearly skinned him. Adam could feel his head growing larger—at least, that's how it looked in the mirror—as his hair got shorter.

Then Joe Bob put the clippers back on the counter, took a pair of scissors and a comb from the disinfectant, and started trimming. Adam sat mute, because he couldn't think of anything to say. Besides, the damage had been done with the first pruning. After three minutes, the barber dropped the tools onto the counter and opened that bottle of red liquid.

"No, thank you," Adam said quickly. He didn't want to smell like roses on top of having no hair left.

"Eight dollars."

Adam took out his wallet, handed the barber a ten, and glanced at himself in the mirror. He had whitewalls an inch wide over both ears—and, he imagined, in the back, but he refused to use the mirror to check on that. The top measured a quarter inch if stretched. He looked like a new marine recruit. On marines, the shearing looked macho, but Adam looked like a hayseed, like Oliver Hardy. Like…he didn't know like what, but not himself.

After five seconds of observing the scalping, he couldn't take it. He turned and ran, leaving the barber a two-dollar tip he couldn't afford because he couldn't watch his reflection long enough for Joe Bob to hand him change. On the other hand, this was a bargain. For ten dollars, he wouldn't need to pay for a haircut for months.

"Pastor Jordan?" Birdie MacDowell tapped gently on the carved door of the pastor's study. Adam knew it was Miss Birdie because Maggie had shouted the information when Miss Birdie's ancient van pulled into the parking lot.

The pillar, not usually so meek, didn't come in. Had a summons directly from her minister filled her with dread?

Adam should have known better. When he got to it, he discovered the door was locked. He opened it and the pillar shoved the door wide to dash inside, followed, of course, by Mercedes.

"Why did you call us? Has someone died?" Miss Birdie glanced around her as if expecting a grieving family in the study. "Was there an accident? I know a tree didn't fall on the church because I didn't see any damage."

Frightened the summons would give her a heart attack, Adam hurried to say, "No, nothing like that." The words didn't calm her.

"A fire in the kitchen?"

"Bird, calm down." Mercedes patted her friend's back, then turned toward Adam. He could tell the exact moment she noticed the haircut. She stopped talking, her eyes grew larger, and her mouth dropped open. Quickly recovering, she said, "Every time Bird's called to the preacher's study, she worries. She's certain something terrible has happened to someone in the church."

"Oh, my Lord." The pillar stopped glaring at the chaos of the minister's study and scrutinized him. Then she stalked toward him, keeping her eyes on his newly visible ears. "You got a haircut." Her voice filled with awe.

"As ordered," he said.

"Look, Mercedes." Miss Birdie pointed at Adam as if her friend couldn't figure this out on her own.

"I noticed, Pastor." Mercedes put her hand over her mouth—probably hiding a smile or perhaps stifling a giggle.

He couldn't blame her.

"You must have gone to Benson's on the square, didn't you?" the pillar asked. "They cater to the old men and the ranchers." She shook her head. "Good thing your ears aren't too big or you'd look like a jug."

Having Miss Birdie notice that his ears didn't stick out didn't make him feel a bit better.

"You might should go to Marble Falls, next time, Preacher," Mercedes suggested. "You know, the best thing about hair is it grows."

The pillar continued to stare, her glance falling to his newly naked neck. "Terrible cut. Your neck's long and bare, like a giraffe's."

Exactly what he wanted to hear.

"No, it's not, Bird. You know giraffes have fur," Mercedes said.

As if that helped.

"But all in all, you do look better," Miss Birdie added.

"Don't worry, Preacher," Mercedes added. "It looks…" Adam thought she wanted to say more, but he was learning she had a complete inability to lie. She didn't utter another word.

In an effort to change the subject, Adam waved toward the cleared chairs. He now had much smaller piles of books and papers *beside* each chair. A great improvement in his opinion, but he could tell by her posture Miss Birdie didn't share that view. "Please make yourselves comfortable, ladies."

"Comfortable would be in the kitchen where we have pie and coffee," Miss Birdie grumbled.

"Now, Bird," Mercedes chided. "Preacher, she doesn't always realize how crabby she sounds."

Miss Birdie straightened and turned regally toward her friend. "Yes, Mercedes, I do. I sound the way I want to sound."

Before the two could argue more—an event that probably happened fairly often—Adam said, "But there's no privacy in the kitchen and I need to talk to you about something confidential."

The Widows exchanged a satisfied glance when they heard the word *confidential.*

"After all," he added, reeling them in, "anyone might walk into the kitchen or overhear our conversation from the fellowship hall. If I had important, private, hush-hush information to share with the two of you, I wouldn't want anyone to overhear."

Her attention grabbed, Miss Birdie seated herself and asked, "What is it, Pastor?"

As Mercedes settled in another chair, the pillar studied Adam. As much as Adam had rehearsed what he planned to say, speaking and looking at Miss Birdie at the same time made him more than nervous. She'd pick up on that uncertainty and exploit it.

So he looked at Mercedes instead and took a deep breath in an effort to calm himself. "I'm not sure exactly how to phrase this."

"Should've thought about that before you invited us to your office," Miss Birdie stated.

Adam could feel his lips quiver. Her predictability amused

him, but only for a second or two. When she noticed his expression, she glared. Had she thought he was laughing at her? He hoped not. He bet no one laughed at Birdie MacDowell.

He continued solemnly. "You're right as usual, but the matter is a little sticky."

"Has Harvey Wallace finally run off with his receptionist?" Mercedes asked.

"Did the bank turn the church down for the loan for the new air-conditioning unit?" Miss Birdie said at the same time.

"No, no." He gave them a quick update on the lack of action on the air-conditioning before, smiling at both of them, he returned to the subject at hand. "You know how much I appreciate everything the Widows have done for our church."

Miss Birdie nodded. "We're still doing it, Pastor. We aren't done yet." She spoke forcefully, as if warning him of the consequences should he dare to stick his nose in the business of the Widows.

"Of course not. Everyone tells me you're miracle workers. I know that from how you welcomed me—you're practically the welcome committee of Butternut Creek. And you do so much for the congregation and the town. Truly, you are the heart of the church."

Both Widows smiled proudly.

"Yes, we know, but it's pleasant to have it confirmed." Miss Birdie nodded with the grace of royalty.

"Howard tells me there were six of you only two years ago." He pretended to study the list on the desk. "Now there are only two Widows."

"Oh, yes." Mercedes sat forward in her chair. "Effie Bannister died and Blanche Moore went to live in a nursing home in Cedar Park. Emilia Post moved to Atlanta to stay with her daughter."

"And Jenny Dunn married her no-good second cousin and went to live with him in Conway," Miss Birdie finished.

"With only two of you left, I'm concerned." Adam shook his head in an effort to show sympathy and worry. "How can you do all the good works the Widows have always done? Strong and willing and committed as you are, the two of you cannot do *everything*."

"We don't do everything," Mercedes said. "As much as we try. Pansy Martin helps a lot."

"But she's not a widow, you know," Birdie said, watching Adam closely as if she'd picked up on his purpose.

"No, her husband is amazingly healthy for a man his age," Mercedes added. "Will probably live for years."

Before either woman could say more, Adam continued, keeping his voice clear and pastoral. "The Widows are a living treasure. We don't want to wear the two of you out."

Mercedes preened at his words. Miss Birdie looked skeptical.

"Are you setting us up for something?" the pillar asked. Her expression said that whatever it was, she would not like it.

"Mercedes." He leaned toward her and smiled. "You keep the town library working wonderfully and keep up with your big family."

He turned his gaze toward Miss Birdie. "And you're so busy with your job and taking care of your granddaughters. With everything else you do, I don't want to take advantage."

He attempted to color the words with both admiration and concern, but Miss Birdie wasn't buying a word of it.

"My job's just not hard, Pastor, and my granddaughters don't take a lot of care. I can handle it all."

"Never thought you couldn't, but I don't want to take advantage of your good nature."

When Mercedes laughed, Miss Birdie glared at her. He'd probably gone too far with that last remark. Possibly no one in Butternut Creek would describe the pillar as *good-natured*. Adam hurried to distract them.

"Do you mind if we have a word of prayer?" Without waiting for an answer, he bowed his head. "Mighty and most merciful God, we come before You with praise for these women and their service." He glanced up to see Miss Birdie frowning, as if attempting to discover where the prayer was leading. He quickly lowered his gaze. "We ask, most loving God, that You will find others to share their good works and that You strengthen all who serve You. Amen."

Finished and feeling fortified, Adam said, "I have a few pastoral concerns to share with you."

He picked up several index cards from his desk. "Sam Peterson," Adam read, then glanced at the women. "I still haven't been able to get in touch with him."

"Such a sad thing." Mercedes shook her head. "He used to visit Effie during the summer, played baseball with my son. Now he's lost his leg. I hear he lives like a hermit."

With an echoing shake of her head, Miss Birdie added, "We set up a schedule to make sure he has enough to eat. When I call him, he doesn't answer the phone. I saw him at the hospital and invited him to church, but he wouldn't talk to me."

"Guess the best we can do is keep him in our prayers and keep trying." He dropped the card on the desk and looked at the next. "Willow Thomas has come back to town."

"Yes," Mercedes said. "I knew her back when she was Willow Brubaker, kin to the Brubakers down on Lampasas Road." She pointed east. "The Brubakers lived in the big yellow house next to where the post office used to be. Willow went off to school, married a man from Chicago about ten or twelve years ago, here in the sanctuary."

"I saw her at the hospital, too," Miss Birdie added. "She said she'd be coming to church."

"As usual, you ladies already know more than I do."

He picked up another card and gazed at it. "Winnie Jenkins gave me the information on the woman they hired as the new CEO of the asphalt company. She's very new to town."

Mercedes reached for the card. "I'll call her."

Adam handed her the card. "Winnie recommends you give her another week or two to get settled, both in her apartment and the company."

"Oh, Winnie did, did she?" Miss Birdie said, then made a low *grumph* sound. "Who is she to make suggestions? The nerve."

Adam had no idea what to say to diffuse the unexpected.

Fortunately, Mercedes ignored her friend and slid the information into a zippered pocket of her purse. "I'll handle this," she said evenly.

Before continuing, Adam took a deep breath. A mistake. The pillar's expression showed she'd noted the hesitation and didn't think she'd like the next suggestion.

"As I said, I talked to Winnie Jenkins lately."

"Bossiest woman I've ever met," Miss Birdie mumbled.

"Hush, Bird," Mercedes hissed.

Adam kept going, hardly skipping a beat, afraid the pillar would interrupt if he did. Not that anything he said or did would waylay a determined Miss Birdie. "She's at loose ends now. Since she retired from the plant, she doesn't have anything to do."

"I understand. The business was her whole life, Pastor,"

Mercedes said. "Except for coming to church, I don't think she had another interest but work."

"Difficult to be a woman in a man's business," he added.

Miss Birdie sniffed. "An asphalt company. How in the world did a woman get into the asphalt business?"

"A lot of hard work," Adam said, attempting to sound more like a minister than he felt at the moment. "I know both you ladies understand and respect hard work and dedication." He ran his thumb across the corner of the cards.

"Preacher, you seem nervous," Mercedes said. Then her expression changed, as if she'd suddenly understood his nervousness, the *real* reason he'd asked them to his office. When she glanced at her friend, Adam's eyes followed hers.

"Winnie's not a widow, you know," Miss Birdie said, biting her words off clearly so any idiot—even her young, inexperienced minister—could understand exactly what she meant. "She's never been married."

"Yes, I know. That's why I hesitate to ask."

The pillar's eyes narrowed. "Ask us what, Pastor?"

Adam took another deep breath. "If you could find it in your hearts, I wonder if you could make her an honorary Widow. She's looking for a place to serve."

Miss Birdie raised an eyebrow and said, "An honorary Widow?"

"She's an intelligent, active woman who suddenly doesn't have a thing in the world to do. In my opinion, she'd be a big help with the important jobs you do."

For a moment, Miss Birdie studied her minister as if she couldn't believe he'd asked this seriously.

"I don't believe you know who the Widows are, not completely," Mercedes said with a slight edge to her usually soft voice. "You want us to invite an old...umm...an unmarried woman to become one of the *Widows*?"

"Preacher, you've started meddling." For a moment, Miss Birdie closed her eyes. "Although it may be I don't know everything."

His mouth almost dropped open.

"Those last few words, Preach, those are Bird trying to sound less grumpy," Mercedes explained.

Miss Birdie turned toward her friend and glared. "You don't have to blurt out everything you think."

That reaction pretty much destroyed the idea of the pillar's being less irritable.

Then, looking like the voice of reason and acceptance, Miss Birdie turned back to Adam and smiled, one of the affable smiles he'd begun to distrust. "But she's an old maid," she clarified. "A spinster as my mother used to say."

"Perhaps a bachelor or a single lady," he suggested.

Miss Birdie nodded. "Possibly, but *we* are called the Widows for a reason. She is not a widow. However," she said magnanimously, "we'll consider it."

Mercedes nodded as well. "We'll get back to you."

Probably the best outcome he could hope for.

❦

"I heard—" Hector's voice was tinged with disbelief and betrayal as he approached Adam. "We've all heard you're a minister." He looked back at the other guys, who shook their heads. They had just finished a game, and Hector and Adam and a team of three of Hector's friends had lost. "Say it isn't true. Are you a preacher, Pops?"

"Is that so terrible?"

"Oh, yeah," Hector said. "Why didn't you tell us?"

"Why should I? When I tell people I'm a minister, they change. They don't feel comfortable. I just want to play ball."

"But how can we…cuss and push and all with a minister around?"

"That's what I mean." Adam took the ball, dribbled down the court, and put up a shot like the one that had been blocked. It went in. "I'm just like you but older and with a cleaner vocabulary. Don't worry." He tossed the ball back to Hector.

"But Pops…"

"Maybe I'll see you in church some Sunday morning. Christian Church on the highway. Service starts at ten thirty." He smiled. The guys didn't.

As Adam walked away, he could feel eighteen eyes watching his progress. He turned back. "You'd better get used to who I am because I'm coming back."

※

"Bye, Roy," Birdie called to the manager as she left the diner between her shifts. She'd stop at Busch's Bakery. Always good food there. As she pulled her tips out and counted them, she entered the store.

"I'd like that dobos torte." She gulped as she saw the price. It would take most of her tip money, but she had to buy it. She was on a mission.

Butch Busch—how could a parent give a child such a terrible nickname?—studied her for a second. "I could cut the torte in half. That would be exactly the right size for a small family."

"But no one would want the other half of a torte."

"Sure they will. I do this all the time." He took a knife, sliced the pastry in half, and placed the larger section in a box.

She knew he didn't. Everyone in town knew about everyone else's struggles. With the worry about jobs, she bet not all that many people bought pastry items. Butch's were expensive because he used real butter and pure imported vanilla. Worth every penny, but Butch knew she couldn't afford the entire thing.

After she counted out the coins, he handed her a little box he'd tied with a lovely blue ribbon bow.

"Thanks, Butch."

"You're welcome. It feels good to know someone's going to enjoy that."

She hoped the recipient would. Heading down the street, her steps grew slower the closer she got to Effie Bannister's house. Remembering the conversation at the hospital, she knew she wouldn't be welcome, but maybe this gift from the bakery would help. If he opened the door, she might could slip around him and get inside the house for a short chat. Surely he couldn't push an old lady out.

Surprised, she paused on the sidewalk in front of the house. The old newspapers that had dotted the yard had disappeared. She strolled up the walk, now swept clean, and noticed a lovely red geranium on the porch. The window of the front door sparkled. It looked almost as nice as it had before Effie passed, before it stood empty for months. The porch swing still looked a little rickety but, on the whole, certainly better than it had since Effie's nephew moved in.

What had happened? Maybe he hired a service, but she didn't think so. No use speculating. She climbed the steps to the porch and knocked. No one came.

She knocked again. Over and over, for nearly three minutes until she heard cursing coming from inside. The young man certainly sounded like a marine, but even that experience couldn't have prepared him for how stubborn she could be.

He tossed the door open and leaned against the jamb. "What's wrong with you people?" He glared at her. "Haven't you learned to go away when someone doesn't answer your knock?"

"I'm Birdie MacDowell. We met at the hospital."

He nodded.

"I was a friend of your aunt."

He nodded again.

"May I come in?"

She could tell from his scowl he didn't want her inside so she squeezed between his broad shoulders, the crutch, and the doorjamb. Once inside, she walked to Effie's pink floral sofa before she turned to watch him. He looked flummoxed. People often responded to her like that.

"Thank you," she said. "Are you going to stay in Butternut Creek for a while?" She placed the box on the coffee table and sat on a chair upholstered in floral brocade. Although the decorating had obviously been done by a woman and years earlier, the place looked better than she'd expected for a bachelor's place. Tidy.

He balanced on the crutches and moved toward her, then dropped onto the sofa. "Don't know."

"If you do, you might want to paint." She looked at the wallpaper with roses climbing trellises. "Effie sure did like pink."

He didn't say a word.

"And fix that porch swing. Someone could get hurt."

He didn't look as if he cared.

With a gentle shove, she pushed the bakery box toward him. "I remember how much you used to like dobos tortes when you spent your summers here."

He stared at the box before he lifted his gaze to her. He

smiled and almost ten years fell from his face. He looked like the happy, carefree teenager she'd known. Oh, it wasn't a big smile, but it was worth every penny she'd paid for the pastry.

"You remembered?" he said in a soft, disbelieving voice. "You brought me a dobos torte?" He untied the bow and looked inside the box. "Aunt Effie made these every time I visited."

"She said you could eat more than any boy she ever saw."

For a moment he looked at the torte hungrily, as if he wanted to drag a finger through the caramel topping, down through the chocolate buttercream, and lick it clean.

Instead, he looked up at her. "Would you like a piece?" he asked politely.

"Thank you, but there's just enough for you. Now"—she shook her finger at him, then pointed toward the kitchen—"you'll want to refrigerate that."

"Yes, ma'am, but I don't think it's going to last that long." He smiled—a big smile this time—and put the box back on the table. "Thank you."

"We'd like you to come to church someday."

He shrugged but didn't say no.

"I'm glad you're back. We all are." She stood. "I'm sorry about the injury."

His face contracted into the furrows and lines of pain.

"How old are you?" she asked. "I remember you played baseball with Mercedes's nephew Felipe. He's twenty-seven or -eight."

He nodded but didn't say anything, so she kept prodding. "He's married, two kids. Are you married?"

When he didn't answer and she couldn't think of anything to say that didn't sound even ruder than she usually allowed herself to be, she said, "Hope you enjoy that torte. I'll let myself out."

She walked toward the door, but before she could open it he said from the sofa, "Thank you, Miss Birdie." He cleared his throat. "You'll never know how much I appreciate this."

Once she'd closed the door and stood on the porch, she congratulated herself. She'd made an inroad. Now she'd have to tell Mercedes. They'd work on getting inside again and bringing him food, make him feel like part of the town, maybe get him to church. Exactly what the boy needed. Later, they could attempt a little matchmaking. She feared working something romantic out between two people with problems like Willow Thomas and Sam would take a lot of effort, but she knew where his interest lay. Only meant they had to set up opportunities between the two and push Willow a little.

On top of that, they still had to find a woman for the preacher to fall in love with. The Reverend Patillo seemed real nice, but Birdie hadn't seen a single spark between them.

No, Birdie was fresh out of ideas. She'd considered everyone she knew, people at church and at the diner. Granddaughters' friends were all too young. Mercedes might have some suggestions. And yet with everything on Birdie's plate and all Mercedes did with her family and with only two Widows left to carry the load—well, it wore her out.

Maybe they could use some help, like the preacher had suggested. She had her job and the girls plus all the time she spent to keep the church headed in the right direction. This matchmaking might could take a lot of planning and work. She had no idea how to start. Life and love had changed a lot since she'd married her Elmer—bless his soul—over forty years earlier.

All right, they could use help. Not that the preacher's suggestion would work. Even if he'd suggested different words to describe her situation, Winnie Jenkins was still an old maid. Although Birdie's love life was long behind her, at least she'd had one. What did an old maid know about romance?

On top of that, Winnie Jenkins was the bossiest woman Birdie had ever known.

Chapter Nine

After lunch on Monday, Willow dropped the boys off in front of Captain Peterson's house. Her first impulse, once the boys were out of the car, was to drive away immediately, not even waiting to make sure they got inside okay. She knew why. Oh, yes, she did. The sight of the man filled her with the most unprofessional thoughts: longing and even— doggone it!—desire. She could feel the draw of the man out here, fifty feet away from him, separated by the wall of the house. What an absurd reaction for a woman with two children and very little trust in men.

What a coward she'd become, to refuse to approach the captain. What a terrible mother. She forced herself to wait, to make sure her sons got inside safely, as if there were danger that the boys would be captured or attacked on the short sidewalk between her car and the front door in a residential neighborhood in Butternut Creek.

Forcing herself not to take off as if the Indy 500 had begun and she was the lead car, she waved to the boys when they reached the porch, watched them knock and enter the house. Sam waved back at her, then closed the door.

She had to face facts. The sight of the man gave her a pleasant rush. For a moment she remembered herself as the high school junior who used to drive past Stephen Nielson's house in the hope of catching a glimpse of him. She'd had such a crush on him. One day he'd been in his yard when she drove by. The sight of him had so unnerved her she'd stopped the car with a squeal of tires, thrown it into reverse, and backed down the street at fifty miles an hour so he wouldn't see her. As if everyone in town didn't know her mother's old red convertible. How cool had she been?

Obviously, age plus all her education and marriage and the birth of two sons hadn't elevated her level of coolness. She wanted to catch a glimpse of the captain nearly as much as, paradoxically, she didn't.

She attributed this need to her wounded ego and her low libido, severely damaged by her husband's defection to Barbie-doll Tiffany who had no sags or stretch marks.

Then her cell rang. She grabbed it and flipped it open.

"Willow, where are you?" Trixie said. "You have a patient waiting."

"Be right there." She glanced at her watch. For heaven's sake, she'd sat there for several minutes mooning about the man. How completely unprofessional. How immature.

Before she could consider at length what an idiot she'd become, she put the car in gear and took off, forcing her mind back to the business at hand and away from her foolish yearning.

❧

"Oo-rah," Sam shouted. A trickle of sweat eased down his back. Little shade in his backyard. The only tree had lost its leaves already, which didn't seem right. Not that he knew anything about trees, but it seemed too early for that. Maybe he could get Leo and Nick to research the problem—which would give him a little peace, use up a few of their hours, and maybe save the tree.

The boys threw their thin shoulders back and echoed his words. "Oo-rah."

"Semper fi, men," Sam said.

"Semper fi," the boys repeated. Their lips twitched a little as if they were attempting to hide grins.

"No smiles, Gyrenes." Sam had about reached the end of his marine vocabulary, at least the words he could use in front of kids.

"Sir, no, sir." They stood straight, kept their expressions serious, and watched every move Sam made.

Which presented a problem. Sam had no idea what to do next. On top of that, the prosthesis Willow had cushioned had begun to hurt a little. Oh, it felt a lot better, but still didn't feel like a real leg.

Since noon, the boys had cleared the yard, a patch so small it had taken only an hour to pull weeds and pick up a few pieces of trash. They'd cut the grass using an old push mower Sam showed them how to oil. Not that there was much grass. Aunt Effie hadn't been any better a gardener than he was and probably hadn't watered the lawn when she was so ill. Here and there a few clumps of grass and weeds huddled together, shorter now but dry and close to death.

The brothers watched him with what looked like admiration. A heady experience for him but not an emotion anyone should feel toward him.

Of course, with his eyes slightly clearer—he'd finished off only a few longnecks the previous evening, placed the bottles in the trash, and actually fallen asleep at a normalish hour—

he didn't look like quite as much of a wreck as that first day. He'd shaved this morning, nicking himself a couple of times. Even with those wounds, he didn't look completely disreputable.

"Gyrenes, how many hours have you worked today?"

"Six, sir."

They knew they hadn't worked forty hours. His reckoning said they'd worked thirty-one each. He could tell them they were finished, that they'd earned all the money they owed him, but he knew they wouldn't accept his ignoring the remaining hours of work. They didn't want to disappoint their mother. Besides, he enjoyed having them here, though he'd never admit it.

"Sir, I looked in the shed and carport. You don't have a hose," Leo said. "And you don't have a sprinkler."

"I found a spigot on the side of the house," Nick added. "It works. You have water."

"We can go to the hardware store on the highway. It's only two blocks away." Leo pointed vaguely to the south. "Mom lets us walk there by ourselves."

He knew she did because she'd given them money to buy him a dipped cone from the Dairy Queen next to the hardware store. They'd walked from there to here with only a few licks missing, because they'd had to stop the dripping.

Reaching in a pocket, he pulled out his wallet and handed them some bills. "Get what you think we need, but stay within budget, okay?"

They took off running. Sam walked to the small patio, poured himself a glass of water, and waited.

Last week, the junior marines had swept and wiped and vacuumed and cleaned. He'd documented the hours each boy had worked inside. He even counted the time spent eating the lunches their mother had brought or prepared, but he was running out of chores.

Yesterday they'd sprayed and squeegeed windows, cleaned out the kitchen cabinets. They'd packed up some of Aunt Effie's dishes and clothing and possessions like the lacy tablecloth and fluffy mint-green bedspread he'd never use. The boys stacked the bags and boxes on the front steps.

When their mother brought lunch, they'd stuffed several bags in her car. She'd promised to drop them off at the community thrift shop, then left them alone to eat and work. Her attitude had seemed very professional, like he was her patient, but he'd seen her studying him once or twice with what he thought was a spark of interest. Could he fan it into an ember? Maybe a fire? Did he still know how to do that?

Not that he wanted to. Not that he needed anyone now, and he felt certain she didn't, either.

So why did he keep thinking about her and their being together?

Whenever he got the chance, he watched her leave, had even dragged himself to the front door so he could observe her. Today she didn't get out of the car. Disappointing. Just that little bounce in her step and wiggle in her hips made the day worthwhile.

Stupid to feel this way, dumb to want what he couldn't and shouldn't have. What in the world would a woman like her, educated and gorgeous and the mother of two great kids, find attractive about a worn-out loser like him?

With her professional training and experience, Willow Thomas—unlike most women—knew what lay beneath the face that attracted other women, knew about the pit that existed in his soul, was aware it drew in anything positive and hurled it into the dark chaos inside him. And yet, once she'd vetted him, she'd left her children with him. Maybe she didn't think he was as bad as he knew he was. Not that he'd ever hurt the boys, but he was hardly the ideal example for them.

Within twenty minutes, the boys were back with a long hose, a receipt, and his change, plus the biggest, most gimmicky sprinkler he could imagine.

"See, this part goes around in circles," Nick demonstrated, "to get the grass around the sprinkler, and the top part spurts water like a fountain to really soak the ground."

"And there's a button on the bottom so you can change the pattern from a square to a circle." Leo showed him how to do exactly that.

"I think that is one of the most amazing inventions I've seen in years." He bet it wouldn't last a week, but the kids were so proud and excited about it, he didn't say that.

"They had one that you could program to roll across the lawn," Leo said.

"But it cost too much." Nick added.

"This one looks terrific. Good job, Gyrenes."

"Thank you, sir." Nick saluted.

"We'll hook it up now." Leo ran off.

Within five minutes, the sprinkler was pumping out water and spraying and making loud hissing sounds. Might not last, but he had to admire the creativity of the person who'd designed this incredibly complicated and shiny piece of equipment that threw out torrents of water in all directions and sounded as if there were an angry cat inside.

The boys were delighted with themselves and the purchase.

"We have to show that to Mom," Nick said.

Sam doubted she'd be deeply interested in the contraption but knew she'd come to the backyard, *ooh* and *aah*, because her sons purchased and set it up. He really admired how much she cared about the boys.

He grinned. They were great kids. He'd like them around even if they didn't have a gorgeous, intriguing mother. He'd miss them when they finished their hours. Oh, yeah, he wouldn't mind sleeping late or not picking up after himself before they came, struggling to wipe off the kitchen counters, but he'd miss the companionship and the way they seemed to look up to him. A balm to his scarred soul.

What had happened to the man he'd been a few weeks ago?

"What's inside that door inside?" Nick asked. "You know, the one you never open."

Leo elbowed his brother in the ribs and muttered, "Shut up."

After he glared at his brother, Nick continued, "You know, the other door off the living room. One goes to the bathroom. One goes to your bedroom. What's behind the third door?"

"Oh, yeah." Sam dropped onto the sofa. "That's the extra bedroom. For my father."

"Your father?" Nick looked at Sam with huge eyes. "You have a father?"

"Everybody's got a father." Leo scoffed. "Someplace." Then he turned to Sam. "Where's yours? Is he coming to visit?"

"The general's in DC now. He'll be here in a few weeks, maybe."

"We should make sure his bedroom's clean," Leo said.

They were right. When Sam arrived, he'd taken the first bedroom he came to because he'd been exhausted after the trip. His father would sleep in the other bedroom when he arrived. Sam hadn't opened that door because he didn't want to think about that ever happening. Still, he'd have to face his father's presence someday, and now seemed like a good time, with the boys here. "All right, marines, let's police these quarters."

"Sir, yes, sir." The boys ran inside ahead of him and opened the door to the unused bedroom.

"It doesn't smell good, Captain," Nick said.

"Probably need to air it out. Can I open a window, sir?" Leo added.

By the time Sam arrived at the door, Leo had thrown the window open. A breeze blew through and ruffled the feminine white lace curtains. Sam had sneaked out that window as a kid to wander through the neighborhood. Once he'd met up with Annie Morgan in the park for his first make-out session. Probably shouldn't share those memories with the boys.

Nick had pulled the bedspread back. "No sheets."

"Get some from the linen closet in the bathroom."

"We need to check in the closet and dresser, sir, to see if there's anything inside to clear out," Leo said.

Sam nodded. "Take the closet and I'll go through the dresser."

In less than an hour they'd finished. The room smelled better after Nick bombed it with air freshener, which caused a five-minute evacuation. Once back in the room, they made the bed and put together a small bag of stored clothing and knick-knacks for Willow to take to the thrift store. Leo had insisted they hang a framed photo of bluebonnets found in the closet, to brighten the room. It took another ten minutes to decide where to put it, measure, and pound a hanger into the wall.

What next? Sam wondered as he considered the bright room and the punch of color from the bluebonnets. Nothing left to do in here. Maybe if they went outside, he could think of something.

"All right, you jarheads, this afternoon we're—" He had no

idea what they were going to do. Fortunately, almost as soon as they'd re-formed in the backyard, a woman's voice drifted over the rickety fence.

"Captain," she shouted.

He turned to look at a tall attractive woman in her sixties, he guessed. White hair swept back, a nice smile.

"I'm Winnie Jenkins." When he didn't recognize the name, she added, "From the church. Glad I found you home. The ladies have prepared some food. I'm parked in front of your house. "

He hoped she'd brought a dobos torte.

"I could use help."

"All right, Gyrenes," Sam said, and the boys stood at attention. "Marines always assist women unloading their cars."

"Sir, yes, sir."

"Fall out."

The boys zoomed past him—not difficult—through the house and out the front door before he made it inside. Within seconds, they came back carrying pans covered with aluminum foil and Tupperware bowls. Plastic cake carriers dangled from both of Nick's wrists.

"Where do you want these, Captain?" Winnie said.

By this time, he'd finally arrived in the kitchen. Fortunately, earlier this morning the boys had cleared off and scoured the small, round breakfast table and the counters. He hadn't had time to mess them up again.

"Anywhere you find room. I'll—we'll put them away later."

"This one"—she held up the pan she had in her hands—"is a very nice brisket Pansy Martin made for you. Over there are two chocolate cakes." She turned toward him. "I didn't realize the duplication. I hope you like chocolate."

"Yes, ma'am," Nick and Leo said in unison. "We do."

She smiled at them. "Are you going to help the captain eat all this?"

Because the boys looked at him with bright, hopeful eyes, Sam had to say, "At least the desserts."

"The ladies made some vegetable casseroles." She turned a serious gaze on him. "We really want you to get healthy, young man. You're far too skinny. That's why we used a lot of cheese and butter in all our dishes."

The *fatten-you-up* result of their concern sat all over the kitchen surfaces and he'd enjoy every bite of it.

"Thank you, Miss Winnie," he said. Yeah, he really had become a wimp who could be bought with lots of cheese, extra butter, and brisket.

"This is my specialty." She patted a covered bowl. "It's my orange gelatin and carrot salad."

His stomach clenched at the memory of gelatin salads at church dinners, but he smiled. "Your salad takes me back to when I was a kid." Which was the truth. He'd hated it then and bet it tasted just as bad as he remembered.

She beamed. "Someone's bringing a ham tomorrow. All this"—she waved her hand—"and the ham should hold you for a week."

"Miss Winnie, this should feed me for the rest of my life. Thank you." He leaned over—almost falling but steadied himself on the table—and kissed her on the cheek. An odd reaction he couldn't really explain but he knew if he tried to say something, emotion would overwhelm him.

"Oh, my, young man." She put her hand to her face and held it there. "How sweet of you." Then she picked up the basket she'd brought in. "When you're through with the dishes, I'll pick them up and take them back to church. Or *you* could bring them back," she added. "We'd love to see you."

Not committing himself, Sam said. "Please thank everyone."

When she left, the boys gazed at him with that hopeful expression that usually got them whatever they wanted. "Okay, guys, but if you tell your mother I let you eat chocolate cake this close to dinner, we're in big trouble. All three of us."

Fortunately, they'd finished the cake, rinsed the plates and forks, and headed for the backyard by the time Willow showed up. Was he happy to see her only because he always liked to see her or because he had no idea what to do with the guys next?

He'd have to think of some odd jobs before they came again. Shampoo the furniture? Paint the house? No, repairing the rickety fence would probably work best. For now, he'd enjoy her presence and consider the chores later.

"Hello, boys." Willow hugged each son before they wiggled away. "I see you're wearing the prosthetic device, Captain. How does it feel?"

He shrugged. "Fine."

"How did the day go?"

"Fine." He nodded. For some reason, he lost the ability to communicate when she stood too close. What an idiot he was, a marine who shot macho weapons in war, who'd faced incredible odds and death, but who couldn't carry on a conversation with a fragile-looking redhead.

"Captain, I didn't drive today. The boys and I are going to walk home. Would you like to go with us?"

Her smile was friendly but not particularly inviting, the expression of a mother asking the boys' little friend to join them.

Nevertheless, he wanted to kiss those gorgeous lips and pull her next to him, to cover himself with her long hair, to touch her and...He refused to complete the thought. After all, her sons were only a few feet away.

"No thanks," he said.

"Oh, please, sir," Nick begged.

This time, he didn't give in to their expressions. And Willow Thomas was much more inviting than chocolate cake and one hundred times more delicious.

"Good exercise," Leo said.

"You guys give me more than enough exercise," he said.

She smiled, almost in relief he thought. "Don't forget your next appointments," she said. Then the three left, the boys hopping down the porch steps and along the sidewalk with her.

He longed to join them, be a part of that group. To be carefree as he'd been when he visited Aunt Effie, back when he ran along the sidewalk with his friends looking for a pickup game of basketball or riding bikes to the lake.

Instead, he watched her walk away.

❦

They were getting too close, Sam realized as he got ready for bed that night. He hit the counter in the bathroom with his fist.

It hurt.

He remembered the laughter of the three as they walked away from the house. He smashed his hand against the counter again. Hurt even more.

He could feel the town and the people and the boys and their mother all sneaking inside his carefully constructed barrier. He didn't want them inside. He did *not* want to care about anyone or anything. All he wanted was to be left alone in this mess of a house. He couldn't take *feeling* again, didn't want to, refused to.

Now the house was clean and people walked in and out.

He cursed as he hit the counter again but not as hard because, although depressed, he wasn't stupid.

What should he do if she and her sons and the insufferably friendly people of Butternut Creek persisted in trying to tear his defenses down? These people needed to leave him alone, stop bringing food and tortes and dropping in. He wanted to be dead inside. He wanted to stay that way, had no desire to join the happy throng parading through his house. Why had he let them inside? He should've guessed the cheerful name of the town described exactly the positive attitude of the people who inhabited it.

He cursed Butternut Creek.

For a moment, tears gathered in his eyes, but he refused to let go. He had to be tough, had to remember who he was and what he'd left behind, the parts of himself he'd abandoned in Afghanistan, one visible from the outside, the other losses hidden inside.

He lifted his gaze to the mirror. A useless man looked back at him. If he forgot Afghanistan, he'd forget Morty and the others who'd died there and those who still fought. He'd start agreeing with people who said he was lucky to get out alive, even if he had lost a leg, and he couldn't do that. Morty had died on an isolated mountainside, killed by an enemy they hadn't even seen. Losing his best friend while he still lived didn't feel a bit lucky.

He scrubbed any trace of grief away, then hardened his expression. He was a marine, not a pansy. Not a rainbow of peace and light.

❦

Once the sanctuary emptied on Sunday morning, Adam wandered back down the central aisle, unzipping his robe as he walked. Hot to wear on an August morning with the air-conditioning spitting very little cool air into the sanctuary. Another repair. The crack in the wall from the corner of the baptistery to the ceiling and the peeling paint on the windowsills also needed to be fixed. He and the church members could repair and paint the walls themselves, but the air-conditioning would cost.

The bank had turned down their loan request. Where would the money come from?

Adam hadn't seen Captain Peterson in church. Not that he'd expected to. He'd gone by Sam's house two more times, left notes in the door, and telephoned twice, but no one answered. So he'd written a letter.

"Dear Lord," Adam whispered. "Please help me reach him."

It was the first Sunday of the month, which meant it was time for the fellowship dinner. As in all churches and as he'd learned with dishes people dropped off at the parsonage, the food was great. He hurried to his study, hung up the robe, and studied the jacket that lay across a chair. Too hot. He checked his tie in the mirror and wished he could leave that in the office as well, but a new minister without his suit coat and his tie would probably cause Miss Birdie to hyperventilate. At least his hair was not "too long" anymore. It had grown a little, enough so his scalp didn't show around his ears quite as much. Nearly enough that people didn't stop on the sidewalks and snicker, although Hector and his buddies hadn't let Adam forget.

Once in the fellowship hall, Adam said grace. He'd learned the minister's trick of saying the blessing only a foot away from the serving table. When he said "Amen," he moved quickly into the head of the line and arrived at the counter spread with dishes of so many kinds he hardly knew where to start. He piled on the sauerkraut and sausage, the pickled beets—which he seldom had—the chicken and dumplings, the beans, and more.

"We'll fix you a plate to take home," Pansy said. "You can make a couple more meals out of it."

Adam was beginning to enjoy being spoiled.

After about two months here, he knew almost half of the people gathered by name. Willow Thomas sat with two kids. He waved but steered clear of her. If he sat next to her, tongues would wag. He chose a chair across from two couples—all four with white hair—he barely knew and talked with them for a few minutes.

At least until Ralph approached, dragging a young blond woman behind him. Adam wanted to slip under the table, but people found such behavior by ministers unseemly. Unfortunately. Because she looked nearly as uncomfortable as he felt, Adam smiled and hoped someone would take the chair next to him before she got there.

No one did.

"Hey, Preacher. Want you to meet my niece Nancy from San Saba." Ralph pulled out the chair and shoved the reluctant young woman in it. "She's visiting today."

Nancy glared at Adam, uncomfortable and rebellious, as if her presence were his fault. He smiled but had no idea what to say to a female who obviously wished she were anyplace other than sitting next to him.

❦

"That's not the way to handle it." Birdie watched from the long serving counter between the fellowship hall and the kitchen as the preacher politely attempted to engage Ralph's relative in conversation. "Too obvious."

"Neither of them looks happy," Mercedes observed. "How old is Nancy?"

"Don't know. Hear she has a boyfriend the family doesn't like, but forcing her on the preacher isn't going to work." Birdie could hear a note of satisfaction in her own voice. Why? Shouldn't she rejoice if anyone found a good match for the preacher? Of course, but this woman didn't look like "the one."

"We have to keep looking," Mercedes said.

With a nod, Birdie checked out the crowd in the fellowship hall. About half of the diners had filled their plates and another half stood in line. Of all those people, she couldn't see another single woman in the place younger than sixty. Well, except Willow Thomas, but Birdie had plans for her.

"We have a problem," Winnie whispered, pointing toward a platter on the counter.

"Heavens preserve us," Birdie whispered. They were out of fried chicken. How could such a thing have happened? Distracted by the preacher's love life, she hadn't noticed. How could she have acted so irresponsibly?

"What do we do now?" Mercedes picked up an empty plate while Birdie shoved a casserole of Pansy's delicious chicken spaghetti into the space left on the counter.

"I'll run down to the H-E-B and pick up more," Winnie suggested. She pulled her keys from her purse and studied Birdie, a question so obvious in her eyes even Birdie couldn't ignore it.

Mercedes watched both women and waited.

Birdie knew what Winnie's words and actions meant: a test of Birdie's leadership, a day of reckoning, Armageddon in the kitchen of the Christian Church. If she took Winnie up on her offer, there was no retreat, no going back. Winnie would be a Widow against all the rules of widowdom.

Birdie sensed that everyone in the fellowship hall froze, as if time had stopped. Every eye in the hall lifted to the two women. Those in line stared, their gazes hopping back and forth between Birdie and Winnie as if they were watching a tennis match. Birdie saw that the preacher—poor young man, he should be spared a scene like this—had been attempting to chat with the blond visitor. His efforts at conversation stopped as his glance leaped toward the Widows and the wannabe.

The moment immobilized those at the tables with their forks halfway to their mouths, but their stares glued to Birdie's face.

The time had come.

How should she answer the challenge?

Not a sound came from the room, but it seemed as if Winnie's words and the jingling of her keys still echoed around them.

Then Birdie nodded. "Get two large buckets."

With that, everyone went back to eating or talking or picking up food from the dishes scattered across the counter while Winnie hurried out the side door and into the parking lot.

Mercedes said, "She did a good job in rounding up and delivering the food to Sam Peterson."

Birdie knew exactly what her friend meant. She'd done the right thing to add one more Widow to the group, but she had needed an excuse, like fried chicken.

"Hey, Grandma." Bree stood in front of her, piling her plate with more food than a girl should have been able to put away without gaining at least a pound or two—no matter how tall and thin she was. Bree had her mother's eyes but her height came from her father. Dad gum man.

"Hello, dear." Birdie patted her granddaughter's hand. "Where's your sister?"

"Over there with Willy Marti, Jesse's grandson." Bree rolled her eyes. "Grandma, she's too young to have a boyfriend."

Before Birdie could answer—she agreed but now wasn't the time to discuss the fact—Bree hurried over to the dessert table and grabbed the last piece of Pansy's better-than-sex cake.

"They're good kids." Mercedes picked up a pile of empty dishes and put them in the sink to soak. "You know they are. You worry too much."

"Their mother was into drugs at fifteen. That could happen to them also. No one's immune." Birdie joined her friend to clear the counter as the last few members filled their plates. "Could end up like their mother." She hated to even consider that, but they could, either one. The possibility broke her heart.

"Do you see any signs they're doing drugs?"

No, she hadn't, and she knew what to look for. She'd watched her daughter's slide and been powerless to stop it. Even now, tears clouded her eyes as she thought of that precious child and how she'd destroyed her own life.

When Birdie didn't answer, Mercedes said, "I haven't heard anything bad about them, and you know I hear everything. They're good kids. They make good grades."

"Lots of things to worry about with kids today." Birdie picked up a sponge and wrung it out in the sink. "Pregnancy. You know how many girls don't finish school." She'd spoken to each granddaughter often to warn them of the dangers of unprotected sex, to beg them to abstain until they were old enough to handle the responsibility involved. How likely was it they'd remember that when one of them was out in a car with a pushy teenage boy whose testosterone levels were through the roof—the usual status for a high school boy—and the moon shone romantically and love songs played on the radio?

Just then, Winnie hurried in with the chicken, which started a rush on the counter.

"They're good girls," Mercedes said as she picked up a few serving spoons.

Yes, they were good girls, Mac and Bree, but a lot of unknowns awaited them outside the walls of this church and the little house they shared, temptations that could lead them astray, exactly as they had dear Martha. She had no idea how to keep the girls safe without tying them to the sofa.

And she didn't know any knots that would keep them there.

Chapter Ten

Hey, Captain," Nick shouted. "Did you realize there's a chocolate cake all wrapped up in foil in the freezer?"

Sam eyed the bundle as he spread mustard on three pieces of bread. "How do you know it's chocolate cake?"

"I peeked." Nick paused. "You know, only to make sure it...umm...wasn't something that might spoil." He fingered the foil. "I think if we unwrap it while it's still frozen, the frosting won't come off." Nick put the lumpy package on the counter and carefully stripped off the covering.

"Looks good." Leo snapped off a small chunk of frozen icing and chewed, his head to the side as if considering the flavor. "And it tastes good. No freezer burn."

Sam picked up the note wrapped inside and read it. "It's from Farley Masterson."

"He doesn't like us," Nick mumbled from a mouth full of frozen cake.

"You know Farley Masterson?" Sam asked.

Sam did. Deputy Masterson had given him a hard time when he visited his aunt. Not that he didn't deserve some of it, but Masterson was a hard man who didn't like boys. The guy must have mellowed a bit. Nice of him to bake Sam a cake.

"Yeah." Leo nodded. "He doesn't like us."

"He said we're loud and have bad manners. He upset Mom." He shook his head. "We hate it when that happens."

"He's the reason we started playing in your yard. We didn't think anyone lived here, not at first. 'Cause you didn't yet, not when we first came around."

"It worked out okay." Sam glanced at both boys, who looked at him with wide, admiring eyes. He was getting deeper into the lives of these kids than he should, liked them more than was wise, but he couldn't ignore them the way that jerk of a father did. "You might want to let it thaw."

Before he finished the sentence, the boys had used a sharp knife and a lot of force to cut the cake into large slices, placed them on napkins, and began to wrap it up in foil again.

"Don't forget your mother, men."

Looking guilty, they cut a small piece for their mother.

"Mom's not a big eater," Leo said. "Always watching her weight."

"Eat your sandwiches first," Sam warned with a grin. He figured these two devoured everything that wasn't locked away before she had a chance.

He picked up the small piece of cake, covered it with foil, and handed it to Nick. "Put this in the refrigerator. Don't eat it."

"Sir, yes, sir."

After they finished lunch, including the still-icy cake, Sam picked up the clipboard and totaled the boys' hours. "That does it," he said. "You guys are finished. You've paid off the four hundred dollars." He glanced up expecting to see smiles. Instead, the boys studied him with the sad, puppy-dog expressions that broke the small section of his heart he allowed the brothers to touch. The part that expanded every day, whether he liked it or not.

"Don't you have more work we can do?" Nick asked.

"You guys are good workers. I can't think of anything more and I don't have the money right now to pay you."

"You don't have to. Maybe... maybe we could just hang out with you." Leo stood and came to attention. "For free, sir."

"Hang out?" Sam said.

"You know. Do stuff together." Nick followed his brother's example and stood. "Sir."

"I know what *hang out* means, Nick. You guys want to hang out here?"

The surprise in his voice must have wounded the boys. Did they think he didn't want them around? They nodded, their expressions even more vulnerable. Crap. He couldn't hurt them. "Okay, but doing what?"

"Well," Nick said in an uncertain voice. "Could you... could you..."

"What?"

"He wants you to take him to the first day of school. He's afraid to go alone," Leo said. "Sir."

Double crap.

"Am not *afraid*." Nick glared at his brother but knew better than to punch him, not in Sam's house. Instead, he thrust his lower lip out as if daring him to disagree. "I'm not afraid." Then he turned to Sam. "Sir, Mom wants to take me, but I'm too *old* for my mother to take me to school."

"Are you enrolled?"

"Sir, yes, sir," Leo said. "I'd like you to go with me, too. We're both at the elementary school, so you'd only have to go one place."

"Won't your mother want to take you and meet your teachers?"

"Sir, yes, sir." Nick made a disgusted face by stretching his lips out and frowning. "But we're not little kids. We don't want the other guys to make fun of us."

"How does your mother feel about this?" Sam guessed she'd be hurt, but what did he know about this woman's feelings?

"She won't care," Nick said.

"It's going to hurt her," Leo corrected. "But we're men now. Gyrenes."

"Gyrenes honor all women and care about their mothers," Sam said. "Gyrenes don't hurt their mothers' feelings. That's not being a man. That's being a grunt. Do you want to be a grunt?"

"Sir! No, sir," they shouted in unison as they stood at attention.

"And I don't have a way to get you to school. Have you noticed that, marines?"

Nick said, "Sir, no, sir," at the same time Leo said, "Sir, yes, sir."

"Sir," said Nick, his thin shoulders held straight and high, his narrow chest thrust forward. "My mother can pick you up. You could go with us."

"Why would I want to do that, marine?"

Neither boy had an answer. Their silence and the solemn entreaty in their eyes made him feel like a heartless, selfish jerk. They were kids, just kids.

"What day?" Sam asked.

"Tuesday after Labor Day, sir," the boys said in unison.

Had they practiced this?

He had several handy and completely believable excuses,

good excuses. His leg hurt. Even after having more cushioning and doing exercises in PT with the prosthesis, he couldn't walk for long. He didn't have a car and he didn't like getting into a car because he looked so clumsy and Willow's car was really low. He could tell them he had no interest in their lives. But he couldn't lie. And he couldn't hurt them.

He wasn't their father. He wasn't even related. He had no responsibility here. Still, he knew exactly what was going to happen next.

"Sir, please?" The last word ended with a quaver in Nick's voice that made the kid swallow hard and glance, embarrassed, at his older brother.

Sam could tell them no if real Gyrenes stood in front of him, but not these two. They needed a man in their lives, even a half-used-up man like him.

In his head he cursed. They were opening him up like a trout being gutted. It hurt.

"Then, sir, yes, sir, I will come to school with you next week."

The boys looked at each other and laughed and shouted, then started toward him.

"Do not break formation, marines."

They stopped, completely still, and came to attention. "Sir, no, sir," they said.

"Sir, will you wear your uniform?" Leo asked.

Where had he put his uniform? Had the general taken it back to Ohio with him? It wasn't in his closet. Other than jeans and T-shirts, nothing was. "No, but I will wear my marine T-shirt."

"Cool," they said, still at attention but smiling happily.

He'd never seen such happy marines. No, kids. He couldn't make these guys into fantasy. They were kids. He was a washed up ex-marine with only one leg. In his fantasy, these boys had become his men, his troops. Pitiful.

Even worse, every time they were here, he hoped their mother would drop by, so he could catch an eyeful of her. Even more pathetic.

Okay, if the boys wanted to hang, he had to come up with something for them to do. If they had the material, they could start on that fence, but they didn't. They'd already measured but the lumberyard couldn't deliver until next week. Neither he nor their mother wanted them to just sit around and watch him sleep. He had allowed them to spend a little time watching DVDs of old war movies with him, and that would eat up thirty minutes before they became restless. What could they do the rest of the time?

Maybe he could teach them manners. A couple of weeks earlier, the general had sent him stationery in case he felt like writing anyone. Oh, sure. The box lay in the bottom drawer of his dresser, still sealed in cellophane or whatever that plastic stuff was.

"Marines, time to write a thank-you note to Mr. Masterson for that great cake."

After Leo completed that chore and Sam found a stamp in the package of stationery, the boys ran to the corner and mailed it while Sam watched from the porch.

He was becoming a mother hen, but if anything happened to those kids, their real mother would kill him. Or shout at him. Or give him that disappointed look her sons had described. Sam didn't think he could take that.

"What are you guys doing?"

His attention had been so focused on the boys he hadn't realized Willow had approached the house, even climbed the steps of the porch, and stood only five feet from him.

What kind of marine allowed an incursion like that? What kind of *man* didn't notice a woman like Willow standing that close?

"Mom." Nick bounced up the steps. "We saved you a piece of cake."

"Chocolate cake," Leo added.

"Where did it come from? Did you bake it, Captain?"

"I'm not much of a cook, ma'am."

"There was a note from Mr. Masterson with it," Leo said.

"He must have donated it when Miss Pansy brought me food."

"Because we ate so much, Sam made us write a letter to thank him," Nick said, then gulped when Leo glared at him for giving away the fact they'd eaten chocolate cake, not exactly a health food.

"Thank you for helping the boys with their manners." She smiled at Sam. "I've tried. It's not easy."

"Come on inside, Mom. The cake's in the refrigerator." Leo opened the front door for her.

"Do you mind?" She glanced at Sam, oddly uncomfortable; he noticed.

"No, ma'am." He liked calling her "ma'am." It put a little distance between them. Probably why she called him "Captain." "You'd better hurry before your sons eat the whole thing themselves."

Nick took her hand. "Come into the kitchen."

She glanced over her shoulder and caught him watching her. He lifted his eyes to her face. Had she noticed? Probably didn't matter. Most likely she was accustomed to guys checking her out.

"Have a seat." He remembered as he spoke that there were only two chairs at the kitchen table and the stepstool the boys dragged in so the three of them could all sit there. She took one chair and he took the other.

Nick took a fork from the drawer, placed it on the table in front of his mother, then stood at attention next to her while Leo brought her the piece of cake.

"Looks lovely." She looked at the sliver and grinned.

"It's not very big, is it?" Leo said. "We should have cut you more."

"This is exactly the right amount. Thank you."

"We asked the captain to take us to school," Leo said. "Along with you. Is that okay?"

"Oh?" She glanced at Sam, but he couldn't read the expression. Was she hurt that they wanted him along? No, he thought she looked more nervous than displeased.

"Is that all right?" he asked.

"Of course. I'll have the boys give you the information when we know more."

She cut the tip of the cake, placed it on her tongue, and closed her mouth to chew.

Oh, Mama. He could watch her do that all day.

It only took her a few seconds to finish the small piece. Then she glanced at Sam. Obviously he hadn't hidden the emotion that had flooded him as he'd watched her savor the cake.

"Gyrenes, pick up the equipment in the backyard." With a quick movement of his head, Sam signaled for the boys to leave. As they ran out to obey his orders, he put his hand on hers.

She glanced down at their hands, then lifted her eyes to his. "Captain, this is a very bad idea." She stood but he held her hand in place so she couldn't move away. She didn't struggle but she didn't sit, either. "Captain..."

"Sam," he said.

"I need to go. It's not a bit professional for me to be here." She nodded toward his hand. "Like this. Alone."

"You're not my only physical therapist. What's-his-name works with me, too."

"Yes, but I do work with you and will supervise the fit of your prosthesis."

He grinned. Although he didn't know why, the expression was usually very successful with women.

"Oh." She blinked.

Obviously the grin worked on her, too, because she sat back down slowly, as if she'd lost the strength in both of her legs and the will to resist. He could only hope.

He was glad she'd settled in the chair next to him because standing, balancing on one good leg and a prosthesis wasn't easy. Even seated, he couldn't keep his feet steady on the floor. Sure that falling out of the chair wouldn't show his macho-ness, Sam kept his right elbow on the table to stabilize himself. Feeling secure enough to make a move, he leaned forward to run his thumb down her cheek. He hadn't flirted with or attempted to seduce a woman in forever. Had he forgotten how to do it?

She blinked again and swallowed, but she didn't say anything. Then she shivered a little. He grinned, inside. He still had it.

Slipping his hand behind her neck, he pulled her forward gently and leaned in enough—keeping himself balanced—to touch her lips with his. Then he pulled her even closer until their mouths met, hard against each other. He nibbled her lower lip. For a moment she relaxed and opened her mouth a little, but when he started to slip his tongue inside, she pulled away and leaped to her feet.

"No fair," he said. "I can't stand up that fast."

"I...I...have to see how my sons are doing." But she didn't move, just stood still and studied him.

"Coward," he whispered.

"No, I'm not."

"Then what?"

She shook her head. "I don't know. I...my husband..."

"Must have been a complete idiot."

For a moment she stared at him. Then she grinned. "Yes, he was, but Tiffany's a young and gorgeous creature. One day he's going to realize she has no brain, but right now he doesn't care."

Pushing on the table, he stood. "Don't run away."

"I wasn't." She looked down for a moment before meeting his eyes. "Okay, I was. And I am, but..."

"You felt something."

"Oh, my, yes. Only the dead wouldn't have, but I don't think I'm...I mean, it was...but I'm not ready."

"If you weren't ready, you wouldn't have felt it."

She glared at him. "A fine argument. I bet it works with some women, but I know that sometimes the body acts before the brain can kick in."

"Maybe the brain should stay out of this."

"Oh, like with my husband and Tiffany!"

Not what he meant at all, but he'd stupidly reminded her of the general treachery of men. From the flash in her eyes, he could tell he'd blown any chance he had, at least for a while.

"Sir, we put everything in the shed." Leo clattered through the slider, across the dining room, and into the kitchen with Nick following.

"Are you guys finished?" Willow asked.

"Yes, ma'am," they said together.

"Then we need to go, Captain." Willow grabbed Leo and started toward the front door, holding her son like a shield.

"Just a minute, Mom. I've got to police the kitchen." Nick glanced at Sam as he picked up her plate and fork to take them to the sink. "Sir, you have something pink on your mouth," he said.

Twirling, Willow dropped Leo's hand, took the plate from Nick, and shoved him toward the door, then turned on the hot water and squirted dishwashing liquid. "Go on outside, to the front porch. Now! I'll be right there."

"Did you cut yourself?" Nick asked Sam. "Are you bleeding?"

Leo's thoughtful gaze leaped back and forth between Sam's face and Willow's.

"Shoo." Willow waved her hands at her sons while Sam burst out laughing. "This is not funny, Captain."

But it was. He laughed harder than he could remember laughing for months.

"Go on out to the car, boys," she said and waved them out the door.

When they left, he said, "I'm going to kiss you again." He watched her scrub the plate so hard she might remove the pattern from its surface. "Someday."

"Don't count on that." She twisted the dishcloth as if she wished she could wring his neck. Then she turned and glared at him. "You have a very high opinion of yourself." Before he could answer, she tossed the dishrag on the counter and hustled out after the boys.

He stopped smiling. Okay, so he'd kissed her and he wanted to do it again. But after that, what? Going after a woman with two kids counted as serious business. He didn't want to hurt any of them, but he sure wasn't ready for commitment, exactly like Willow.

What was he doing?

❦

The Thomases walked down the sidewalk and got in the car. In the rearview mirror, Willow could see the boys whispering. She put the keys in the ignition but kept her eyes on her sons.

After several seconds of Leo giving information, Nick said, "You're kidding?" Then he glanced up at her, eyes wide.

She dreaded considering what her sons might be saying. Actually, she had a pretty good idea, and she knew Nick, her lovable but bigmouthed child, would blurt it out as soon as he heard it all.

With the boys settled in the backseat, she put the car in gear and pulled onto the street. As she did, Nick said, "Mom, Leo said you kissed the captain. Did you?"

"Shut up," Leo whispered. "I told you not to say anything."

"Okay, okay," Nick said. After only a few seconds, he added, "Mom, do you like the captain?"

From the muttered "ouch" she heard, she bet Leo pinched his brother. "Of course. He's a very nice man. I really appreciate the amount of time he takes with you guys."

"No…ouch, stop it," Nick began before, she guessed, Leo elbowed him. "Do you *really* like him? More than you liked Dad?"

Of course her sons would wonder. They liked Sam. They knew he'd kissed her and wondered about the entire situation. "It's not like that."

"Then what's it like?" Nick persisted.

This time there was no *ouch* from the backseat.

"Yeah, what is it like?" Leo said.

"He's an attractive man, but I'm his physical therapist. It wouldn't be professional for me to like a patient, someone from work."

"That's dumb," Nick muttered. "Dad did."

"It's still not appropriate. Hard to understand, but that's how it is."

She'd pulled into the parking lot behind the apartments, found a place, and shut the car off. Was she safe?

As she opened the car door, Nick said, "But when he's better and you aren't his therapist anymore, then you could like him more, right? Kiss him again?"

"I don't know."

Before she could step out, Leo asked, "How could you not know? He's great, he likes us, and he likes you. Why wouldn't you like him back?"

She stood and watched the boys pile out of the back, then closed the door and hit the lock button. "It's more complicated than that."

"Wasn't complicated for Dad," Nick said. "He and Tiffany..."

"Shut up, squirt." Leo gave his brother another jab.

"Don't hurt your brother," she said, leaping on the opportunity to change the subject. "Just because you're the big brother doesn't give you the right to..."

"Yeah, just because you're the big brother," Nick said, "you're not the boss of me."

She sighed, deeply grateful for the interruption of the quarrel. *Not* that a good mother would encourage bickering, but she preferred that to their curiosity and the uncomfortable questions. Someday, of course, she'd have to face their inquiries honestly and work through her feelings, because whatever might or might not happen with Captain Peterson affected her sons as well.

As she listened to Leo and Nick argue, she knew the reprieve was temporary. Nick never let go of anything until the answers completely satisfied him.

❧

The next day, Willow considered herself in the full-length mirror in the PT department. Everyone had cleared out and she'd grabbed her purse and her laptop to head for the door when her reflection caught her attention.

She wasn't the type of woman men fell in love with immediately. Despite her fragile exterior, inside she was too pushy, too cold, too in-charge and controlling, not a bit girlie and flirty. The traits made her a great physical therapist, but not, as Grant had often said, a great wife.

The jerk. Fortunately, she hadn't listened to him. Much.

For example, her hair, which he'd mentioned more than occasionally. She'd never been able to do anything with it so she pulled the unruly red tresses back and forgot about them except when wisps escaped and refused to be pulled back.

Tiffany had gorgeous blond curls and waves, artfully shaped and colored and pampered by an expensive hairdresser. Willow had considered such spending unnecessary. No, she shook her head. She wasn't a bit girlie.

She turned sideways. She did have a great figure, through no effort of her own. Men liked that. Grant had. Sam did.

White shirt and navy slacks. Comfortable, flat shoes that didn't make her legs look yards long, like Tiffany's. Hers were actually longer than Grant's third and present wife's. She'd just never showed them off. Although very effective for stealing husbands, short skirts and strappy sandals on three-inch heels didn't work in the PT department or as the mother of two active boys.

Why after all these months did she continue to compare herself with that woman? Certainly she was better than that. If not better, at least different. She'd always accepted herself, always had pretty healthy self-esteem until Grant chose the über-feminine Tiffany.

All of which brought her back to the original question: Why did Sam find her attractive? He could have his pick of women, and yet he'd settled on her, at least for now. Maybe because she was handy? Propinquity?

Doggone, there she went again, unable to even think a man could find *her* attractive. Grant had done a job on her, ruined her self-esteem and trust—but she'd allowed that. Why? She had great kids, was terrific at her job, and had started a new life for herself and the boys.

Doggone number two, she sounded exactly like her mother comforting her back when Willow didn't have a date for the prom.

But she couldn't stop wondering. Why, after all this time, did she allow her cheating husband and his third wife to control her life and her thoughts? Habit? Guilt? She bet neither of them ever thought about her. What had she gotten for remembering the hurt? She leaned closer to the mirror and noticed two thin grooves between her eyes. Then she wiggled her jaw, an action that hurt because she clenched her teeth too much. All she'd gotten was wrinkles and painful muscles.

"Mizz Thomas?" The janitor stuck his head inside the door. "Are you still working?"

"No, Ralph, come on in and clean." She glanced at the clock. "Five thirty. I didn't realize I was so late." The boys would be wondering where she was.

As Ralph rolled the cleaning cart inside, Willow turned slowly to study the department. She'd done a great job here in the few months since she arrived. The number of patient hours had increased significantly. Although the hospital hadn't purchased as much new equipment as she wanted, she'd added a lot and requisitioned more.

"Mizz Thomas?"

"I know. You need to get to work." She grabbed her lunch bag and remembered the brownie Nick had placed inside, saved from dinner with Sam the previous evening. Not a complete brownie. There was a corner nibbled off, but he'd given her most of it. Yes, she had great kids who loved her. She didn't need a man to make her feel whole.

On the other hand, why not? Having Sam around added zing to her life. Captain Peterson's interest and her response made her reluctance to become involved with him seem ridiculous. She liked men, especially this man.

She wasn't ready to consider kicking over the traces just yet, but she would be someday. As her grandmother Brubaker used to say, God willing and the creek don't rise, she'd do exactly that. Just not this week.

❦

Wednesday afternoon, Sam headed down the hospital corridor toward the physical therapy department. She'd have to see him today. Willow could run away from his house, but she couldn't run away from the physical therapy department.

Maybe not quite true. His glance flew around the PT room. All the other staff members helped patients, but he couldn't see Willow.

"Come on over, Captain." Mike stood at the parallel bars. "Willow's seeing hospital patients this afternoon. She wanted me to work with you and to tell you the prosthetist will be here in September to fit you."

Sam handed a PT aide his cane and grabbed hold of the bars.

"How is the one you're wearing now?" Mike asked.

"Okay. Slips a little. I'll be glad to get the new one."

"Once you're warmed up, let's practice balance."

After twenty minutes, Mike glanced at the clock. "Thought Willow'd be back by now, but sometimes it takes longer depending on patients' needs. When she gets back, I'll tell her how much progress you've made. Good job."

Willow had gone to see some of the hospital patients. Made sense. All of them shared that duty, but why now? Why at the time of his appointment? Did it mean anything? Was she trying to avoid him?

He didn't know, but next week when they took the boys to school, she couldn't pretend the kiss hadn't happened. She couldn't ignore or avoid him.

Chapter Eleven

Adam stood at the door of Sam Peterson's house and knocked again. Inside, the television blasted. From the gunshots, he guessed it was a cop show. Outside, the breeze blew across the porch. "Captain, I'm Adam Jordan." He spoke clearly and loudly enough to be heard over the sounds from inside, he hoped. "I'd like to visit with you for a minute."

Still no one came to the door.

Pleasant out here, he thought as he turned to study the neighborhood. Small houses but all neat and tidy, well kept.

The sun had begun to head west, huge and orange and brilliant. He'd been up since sunrise to pray with a member of the congregation having surgery and was tired. Surely the captain wouldn't mind if he sat down on the ancient swing at the end of the porch to rest, if he swung for a couple of minutes to cool off. After Sam had ignored Adam several times when he called or came by, the minister felt fairly certain he wouldn't answer the door now. If the marine ran out here and screamed at the preacher for sitting on his swing, Adam would still be ahead. He would have met the elusive man.

Adam settled onto the swing and shoved with his feet to get it moving. After only seconds, the swing supports gave a screeching groan. He quickly and with a good amount of trepidation lifted his eyes to the ceiling of the porch. Well-warranted trepidation, he realized. As if in slow motion, the wood in the ceiling began to splinter around the hooks. Then time sped up. Before he could stand, the swing dropped onto the porch with a deafening crash and a crack that knocked his breath out. It felt like he'd broken every bone in his butt.

The sound of the falling swing and shouts of pain had to drown out the television. Adam would probably get to meet the captain soon.

As he sat groaning and gasping in the wreckage of the swing, his knees bumping against his ears, the front door opened. A man Adam guessed with fair certainty to be Captain Peterson launched himself out faster than the minister thought a guy on a cane could move.

"What the hell?" the marine shouted. A normal response in the situation.

Because the swing had broken into small pieces, Adam had nothing to hold on to that would help him get to his feet. To tell the truth, he didn't want to stand and still could barely breathe. There was no way something like this could be handled with dignity. If he could have, Adam would have rolled off the porch and hidden in the scraggly shrubs surrounding it.

But a minister couldn't do that. A minister had to be made of sterner stuff, aware of his mission and ministry. In an effort to gain an iota of composure, Adam forced his aching legs to straighten and stand, stifled a moan as he realized how much his body hurt, smiled, and reached out his right hand.

"Hello, Captain Peterson," he said on a gasp for air. "I'm Adam Jordan, the minister of the Christian Church."

The captain watched him, his gaze moving from the broken swing to Adam's feet, then slowly up the length of the minister's body, pausing to glance at the outstretched hand, and up to Adam's face before he burst out laughing. He leaned against the wall to stay upright.

Again, a normal response. The preacher looked down to find his feet covered in the bits of the ruined swing. He looked up to see two holes the size of CDs with splintered wood around them. After several seconds and despite the pain, he broke into laughter as well.

"So, you're the minister who's been bugging me," Sam said between guffaws.

Adam nodded.

"Well, come inside before you break something else."

The house looked nearly spotless except for the coffee cups and empty glasses on the end table and the newspaper on the floor.

"I have help," Sam said following his gaze. "That's why it doesn't look like a bachelor lives here. Willow Thomas and her two sons go to your church. The two boys…well, it's hard to explain, but they've been cleaning and picking up for me."

"I know them. Nice people."

"The kids broke the glass in my slider. Seems the only way I meet people is when they attempt to destroy my house."

"I'm sorry. I shouldn't have," Adam babbled. "The swing looked so inviting. We'll fix it. I'll get some of the men from church. We'll get you a new one."

Sam waved the offer away as he fell into the sofa and dropped the cane on the floor. "My father's coming in a few weeks. He'll need something to keep him busy."

"Then I'll pay…"

"No need. Sit, please." He watched as Adam took the

chair across from him, then said, "You look young to be a preacher."

Adam nodded. "You look young to be a war hero."

An expression of utter despair covered Sam's face, wiping away any trace of the laughter that had been there, reaching deep in his eyes. "I'm no kind of hero, Preacher."

"We have a vets' group at church…"

"Don't try to fix me."

"I'd never do that. I just…" But Adam didn't complete the thought. He probably had been. That's what people like him did. "I won't do that again."

After Sam nodded, the two men sat in silence. Getting inside should make Adam feel good but it didn't. He'd immediately stuck his foot—big as it was—into his mouth.

"So," Adam tried again. "What do you like to do?"

Sam shook his head. "You said you wouldn't try to fix me again."

"Didn't mean to. I was trying to start a conversation."

Sam leaned back and glared at the minister. "Preacher, I'm not fit for company, much less a chat." Brackets around Sam's mouth and between his eyes suggested he was in pain. "Why don't you come back another day?" he said. "If you bring pizza, I promise I'll let you in."

"Why don't I order delivery now?" Once inside, even dirty and hurting all over, Adam refused to let go of this moment of contact. He didn't wait for an answer before pulling his cell, punching it on, and asking, "Pepperoni okay?"

Sam watched Adam for a few seconds, then, finally, smiled. "Okay, Pastor, you win. Anchovies, pineapple, and roasted"— he paused and looked toward the ceiling—"eggplant." He lowered his eyes to scrutinize the minister. "You're going to order that?"

Adam nodded. "I figure this is a test of some kind. You want to let me in on what it is?"

"Are you really going to let the pitiable amputee guilt you into ordering a pizza with roasted eggplant?"

Adam shrugged. "In the first place, I was going to have that stuff put only on your half. In the second, the pizza places in small towns like this don't put roasted eggplant on pizzas. The ingredients at the Pizza Palacio are pretty basic." He punched a button.

"I like you," he said. "I like a man who has a pizza place on speed dial." He laughed, actually laughed. "Don't ask for the pineapple or eggplant. Marines don't eat pineapple on pizzas."

When Adam finished the order, Sam didn't look as if he were in any hurry to begin a conversation so Adam jumped in again. "Your father's coming soon?"

Sam nodded again, the smile gone. This man presented a challenge—not in the same way as Miss Birdie but definitely a test of a minister's pastoral skills. Not that Adam had developed many of those yet.

"How did you happen to come down here by yourself? Why didn't you wait until he came, too?" Adam realized as the words came out that they sounded as if he didn't believe Sam could take care of himself. "I mean..."

Before he could make another mistake, Sam said, "Because I wanted to be alone." His glare reminded Adam he wasn't alone, that the man who sat across from him had invaded his isolation.

After another few minutes of silence—little by little Adam was realizing Sam didn't plan to make this easy—he said, "You know, I did call you. Several times."

"People in this town are odd like that. You'd think if a person didn't answer his phone or the door unless pushed to it by

someone invading his porch and destroying his property..."
He stopped and glared at Adam. "Where was I? Oh, yes, you'd
think those people would leave you alone."

"If you had an answering machine," the preacher suggested, "you wouldn't have to talk to people but you'd know
if there were any important calls."

"I don't have an answering machine," Sam explained as if
talking to a slow child with only a tenuous grasp of the English
language, "because I want to be left alone."

They spent a few more minutes staring at each other until
Sam picked up the remote and turned on the news. Fifteen
minutes of silence later, the doorbell rang. Adam leaped to his
feet. A stab of pain in his hip reminded him of the earlier accident.

"Get me a beer while you're up," Sam said obviously willing to take advantage of the preacher's service while not wanting much to do with the preacher.

But at least he was inside. A small success but a success.
He couldn't wait to tell Miss Birdie. Or maybe he wouldn't.
Maybe he'd let her ask him about it.

Birdie hated Fridays. Each waitress had one day she had to
come in early and set up: Check the salt, pepper, and sugar,
fill them if necessary. Make sure the napkin holders were full
and that, overnight, nothing disgusting had entered the diner or
plopped itself down on one of the tables. Start the coffee—although she'd always asked Roy, the manager, why they couldn't
buy timers for that and why the late-duty waitresses couldn't
check the tables. He ignored her first suggestion and told her
the waitresses who worked until nine were too tired. If she
didn't need to keep her job, she would have pushed, but she

did. She'd shut up. That's why, still half-asleep, she stumbled past the tables until she reached the switch to turn on the lights.

Outside the front window, it was still dark. One streetlight glowed half a block away. No one wandered along the street yet. Customers would show up at six, the same time the cook ran into the restaurant and turned on the grill.

But someone stood out there, or something. Birdie couldn't tell what. At the bottom of the window, just above the frame, the top of something white showed against the gloom. Maybe a large dog. Could be a cougar. Someone had said they'd seen one out by the lake the other day, but she doubted they'd come this far in, this close to people.

She blinked. Her sight had become cloudy—probably needed cataract surgery—but when she opened her eyes and focused them, the blob was still there.

Curious, she walked to the window and attempted to make out the form.

Oh, my Lord, it was a child. What was a child doing out there at this hour? And alone? She hurried to the front door, unlocked it, and looked out at the child, then swept the street with a glance, expecting to see an adult nearby. No one out there but this little creature.

Birdie took a step toward the child but it—or he or she—moved away and huddled in a small ball as if trying to disappear, to hide in a tiny, invulnerable package. The sight squeezed Birdie's heart, an organ many thought she didn't possess.

"Are you hungry?" Birdie asked.

The little girl didn't move. If anything, she shrank even smaller. Then her stomach growled.

"Let's go inside and get you something to eat." Birdie held out her hand.

The child studied her, glancing first at her face, then dropping her eyes to study Birdie's uniform before moving back up to her face. A quick peek through the window seemed to convince her that Birdie and this place were safe. She stood and followed Birdie.

Once inside, Birdie locked the door and turned to speak. She stopped as she realized how dirty the child was. She leaned forward to scrutinize her, but when an odor reached Birdie, she leaped back. Soiled lace on the child's socks confirmed that it was in fact a girl—and one who wasn't just grubby but indecently so: snot-nosed, black-fingernailed, sooty-faced, torn-shirt, and muddy-trouser filthy. Far more dirt covered the little one than she could have picked up in a few hours or overnight.

Tears ran down the girl's face, leaving pink trails on grimy cheeks. She lifted her arm to wipe them away and left a trail of mucus across her face as well as the sleeve of her ragged shirt. How old was she? Four or five?

"Let's wash you up before you get breakfast."

The girl nodded.

"I'm Birdie—Miss Birdie. What's your name?"

"Missy," she said in a wavering voice.

"Where's your mother?"

Tears filled Missy's eyes again. "Don't know. Lost." Sobs shook the child's entire body, and she buried her face in her hands.

"Where's your daddy?"

"Gone," the child whispered. Then her stomach started to growl again, not dainty *grrs* but reverberations so loud it sounded as if her insides contained a ravenous lion.

Birdie glanced at the clock. If she worked really fast, she could give the child a quick cleanup and get her breakfast before people started to arrive. If the girl's mother hadn't showed up by the time the crowd thinned, she'd do *something* about it. She had no idea what.

"How old are you, Missy?"

She held up four fingers.

"What's your last name?"

"Last name?" Missy thought for a moment before getting to her feet. "Mommy calls me 'Missy' or sometimes 'sweetheart.' Is sweetheart my last name?"

If the mother didn't show up, Missy'd given little information that would help find her. Birdie tried again.

"One more question, Missy Sweetheart. Where did you sleep last night?"

"Outside," she whispered. Her voice shook.

Birdie shut her mouth. The questions didn't help any and drove the child to tears.

"Okay, let's go." Birdie took the girl's tiny, grubby hand and led her toward the restroom. She tried to wipe away whatever grime she could, including washing Missy's face and hands with paper towels. All the task accomplished was to make the child look a bit less like a hobo and more like a girl. Birdie then took Missy back into the dining area and settled her at a booth facing the front window. Her mother could see Missy through the window if she was looking for her. Why wouldn't she be?

In the light, she could see Missy's freckles across pale skin and her dark eyes filled with sadness. "You look outside and tell me if your mother comes by." Missy nodded.

Birdie set a glass of milk and another of orange juice on the table before she went back to making sure they were ready for the morning crowd. Another waitress and the cashier arrived a few minutes before six. They each asked for an explanation of the waif at the front table as they prepared for their jobs. The cook arrived just as Birdie opened the front door and the early customers crowded in.

When Birdie picked up Missy's breakfast ten minutes later and took it to the booth, both glasses were empty but the child lay on the red plastic seat and slept. Birdie was a sucker for a sleeping child. She watched her for a few seconds before she took off her sweater and placed it over the girl. After that, she took a few steps and placed Missy's breakfast in front of Howard Crampton.

"Not what I ordered," he objected.

"That's okay. You'll like it. It's hot."

By nine, the breakfast bunch had mostly left and Birdie had time to check on Missy again. The child was waking up.

"Hungry?"

When Missy nodded, Birdie put another order in. "More milk?" she asked.

Missy used her fists to wipe the sleep from her eyes and nodded.

What was she going to do with the child now? She didn't want to turn her over to foster care, not when the girl looked so pitiful and small and sad and lonely. Why had Birdie allowed herself to get caught up in the situation when she already had plenty on her plate? She couldn't take on the care of a four-year-old.

Of course, the mother would probably show up soon, probably in a few minutes, explain what had happened, and everything would be fine. No problem. For that reason, Birdie went to the door and looked up and down the street again. All she saw was a normal morning in Butternut Creek: stores opening, people parking and walking toward the courthouse, a few men playing chess under the branches of the live oaks around the square. She recognized almost everyone, and those she didn't know didn't look a bit like a hysterical mom searching for her lost daughter.

So where in the world—or in the state of Texas—was the girl's mother? Why had she left her daughter alone for so long? A mother doesn't just misplace her child. Even the worst mother would certainly realize she was gone by now.

Birdie had a lot of questions about Missy she needed answers to but didn't feel many answers would be forthcoming from Missy. She took out her cell phone, punched a number, and waited for Mercedes to answer. "Meet me at the church ASAP," she said and hung up without waiting for a response. Mercedes would be there.

"Judy, cover for me. I'll be back for lunch," Birdie told the other waitress. "Come on, Missy." She held out her hand.

On the way to the church, Birdie used her key to open the door of the thrift shop run by many of the churches. Not all the churches because there were some groups that refused to cooperate, not even to feed the hungry or to help a pitiful, lost little girl. She pulled out a change of clothes and underwear for the child, taped a note to the cash register—"Please charge $10.58 to the account of the Christian Church"—and headed over to the church office.

❦

Adam looked up from his notes to see Miss Birdie stride into the study holding the hand of a very dirty child.

"Didn't expect you to be here," the pillar said as she stopped and glared at him for being in his own office. He guessed he'd never please her.

"Awfully early for you," she added.

Glancing at the clock, he nodded. "I had some things to finish up. I could leave if it's inconvenient to have me here."

She didn't, of course, get the joke. Instead she said, "You can stay. You might have some ideas." Her voice suggested she doubted that.

He stood and walked around the desk to kneel in front of the little girl. "I'm Adam. Who are you?"

"This is the Reverend Jordan," the pillar explained with a glare toward him. "Sometimes you're too informal, Preacher."

"I'm Missy," the child said. "I lost my mommy."

"When was that?"

She shook her head.

"Losing your mother can't feel good. Where did you put her?"

Missy shrugged. "I don't know." Her voice quivered.

"Do you live in Butternut Creek?"

The girl smiled. "What a funny name."

"Guess not," he said to Miss Birdie. He picked Missy up and sat on one of the cleared chairs with her on his lap. The child patted him on the cheek.

"What do you know about this lovely young lady?" he asked the pillar while bouncing Missy up and down.

"Nothing. She was alone outside the diner when I opened up this morning." The pillar went on to tell the story. "When her mother didn't show up, I brought her over here to give her a shower and talk to Mercedes about what to do now."

"How nice of you," he said. "Most people would have left her there, ignored her, decided she was someone else's problem."

The pillar said nothing, embarrassed to be called a good person.

Adam smiled at Missy again. "Missy, do you know where your daddy is?"

"Away," she said with no particular emotion.

"Your grandmother or grandfather?"

"Grandpa's with Jesus." Missy nodded confidently.

"Someone's taken her to church." He glanced up at Birdie before looking back at Missy.

"And your grandmother?"

"Virginia," she said which didn't help a whole lot. Was that a name or a location?

Before he could seek clarification, the child said, "I want my mommy." Tears clouded her eyes.

"Of course you do, and we're having people look all over for her." Adam reached to the desk and got a tissue to wipe her eyes. "Can you tell me anything you remember?"

"I was cold." She shivered. "And scared." She began to sob.

"Why don't we take a walk and see if you remember anyplace," Adam said.

But a fifteen-minute walk during which Adam carried Missy didn't jog her memory.

Once they got back to the church and his study, Adam joggled Missy on his lap.

Miss Birdie said, "I called DPS—protective services. They're sending a social worker."

Adam felt a great sense of relief. Someone who knew how to handle this would take over.

"Sweetheart, a nice lady will be coming to take you someplace to wait for your mommy."

"Take me someplace?" Fear tinged Missy's voice. "What nice lady?" She looked at the pillar, her eyes wide again. "Are you the nice lady?"

"No, another lady will find a place for you to stay," he said. "A very nice lady. She'll be here soon."

Missy hopped off his lap, ran the short distance to Miss Birdie, and grasped the pillar's hand. "Want to stay with you."

Because she'd taken in her two granddaughters, Adam

knew a soft place for abandoned little girls existed in the pillar's heart, as much as she attempted to hide it. From her expression, he could also tell the conflicting emotions that raged inside her: fear and consternation but also duty and compassion. Miss Birdie possessed an easy-to-read face, though usually it showed only frustration with her pastor. The range of her feelings at this moment intrigued him.

"She won't be lost very long," Miss Birdie said as if considering the addition of one more to her family. "The police should find her mother right away. I bet she's looking for Missy as we speak. But she really needs a shower."

"Why don't you take her to the gym and wash her up." Years ago, the church had had an active recreation program with great facilities. Someday, he hoped to start that again, but the entire area needed a lot of work and the church barely had enough money to keep the main building functioning. "I'll wait for Mercedes and children's services and call the police."

When they returned twenty minutes later, he'd finished the calls. Missy's brown hair stood up in wisps from being towel-dried and her freckles showed against clean, pale skin.

"I got her a change of clothes at the thrift shop but put the dirty clothes in this." She held up a plastic sack. "Too dirty and ragged to wear again, but I thought maybe the police could find something on them if it comes to that. Nothing in her pockets, no identification. Of course, I'm sure someone is looking for her."

Adam nodded but added nothing to the conversation Miss Birdie carried on with herself.

"You know, I have two girls I'm already taking care of," she said. "You know my plate is full now."

Yes, he did, but he didn't dare insult her by suggesting she couldn't do everything.

When he didn't say a word, the pillar said to the little girl, "Missy, when the nice lady gets here, she'll find you a place to stay until they find your mother."

"Please," Missy said in a trembling voice and with a beseeching expression only the hardest of hearts could resist, then she climbed on to Miss Birdie's lap and put her arms around the elder's neck.

A sudden rush of tenderness covered Miss Birdie's face before she again donned her no-nonsense, pillar-of-the-church expression. "All right." She nodded. "Bree and Mac will help and she'll be with us for such a short time."

"You can use the Presbyterians' day care," Adam suggested. "The ministerial benevolence fund can cover that."

Seconds later Mercedes walked into the room. "Sorry, I got held up at the library." After listening to how Missy had ended up in the pillar's lap, the Widow made more calls to check on legalities with her various relatives and make sure Miss Birdie would be immediately approved for foster care if necessary.

Twenty minutes later, the police arrived. They found out little from Missy but took her picture, clothes, and fingerprints. They also noticed smudges on the child's shoes they thought might be her mother's fingerprints. Or maybe not, but they'd send them to the lab in Austin. They'd check the hospitals in Austin and the morgue and put out a bulletin about the girl covering a hundred-mile radius. With so little to go on, they couldn't do more.

The two Widows left with a little girl between them.

"I'm sure she won't be with me for long," Miss Birdie said as she closed the door. She'd looked more worried and uncertain than Adam had seen her during their short acquaintance.

He vowed to help her as much as possible, but he wouldn't

insult her by letting her know he was looking out for her as much as for Missy.

❧

Sam would never have opened the door if he hadn't looked out the window and seen two horses standing in his front lawn. A man stood with them, a man he recognized. Sam's mind associated the man with horses, but how hard was that connection when the man stood with two horses? Still, Sam thought it was an important link, something from those years he'd visited here.

Oddly, today he was up, showered, and dressed earlier than usual, but after fixing his own breakfast, he had no idea what to do next. Probably the reason he didn't usually get up so early.

"You don't remember me," the man began as Sam stepped out on the porch.

Not true. Sam could remember him, but he couldn't remember how.

"I'm Jesse Hardin from the Christian Church."

Sam took the man's callused hand and shook it before a memory surfaced. "Hey, I do remember you. You're the horse man. Aunt Effie used to take me to your place to ride." Sam grinned. "Those are some of the best memories of my life."

But he still didn't understand why these two horses—the gray with a saddle and the Appaloosa with only a blanket across her back—stood there, munching on the sparse grass of what he and the boys laughingly referred to as the front lawn.

"Thought you might like to take a ride this morning." Jesse jerked his head toward the animals.

"This morning? A ride?" He grinned. "In town? Is it legal?"

"Sure. I called Mercedes the other day. Her sister the judge approved the ride as a medical treatment for a vet, one of our boys."

"Medical treatment?" Sam stepped onto the porch, closed the door behind him, and studied the animals.

"Saw a program on the TV about amputees, vets who've lost their legs. Seems that if they ride a horse, it helps build up muscles and gets them used to a prosthesis better. Cheers 'em up, too."

"Really?" Sam turned to study Jesse. Was the man kidding him?

"Yup. Figure if it's on the TV, it must be true. Want to try it?"

Oh, yeah. Much better than walking between parallel bars.

"Supposed to also help with your balance and build your core, whatever that is." Jesse pointed. "You get the horse with the pad, Captain, because that's supposed to allow you to feel the horse better. That's what the guy on the TV said."

For a few seconds, Sam studied the horse. Tall creatures. "How do I get on?"

Jesse smiled. "Figured that out before I got here. You go to the edge of the porch and put your leg—the right one—over the back of the horse. I'll stand down there and give you a hand if you need it."

Sam had visions of himself rolling over the horse, ending up sprawled on the ground. But marines didn't mind falling on the ground. Marines were tough. He could handle this. "Okay. Let's go."

Jesse ran down the steps, pulled the Appaloosa toward the porch. He angled the horse so she straddled the steps, pushing her a little sideways and closer. The horse obeyed calmly, an action that made Sam feel more confident. This didn't seem like a creature who'd run away with him or buck him off.

"Gracie's a gentle old lady." Jesse stood on the other side of her and held out his hand. "You're perfectly safe."

With a nod, Sam approached the horse, leaned over to put his hand on her neck, and shifted his weight before raising his right leg to mount Gracie. When he settled on her broad back, she shifted a little but stayed still enough for him to relax, regain his balance, and pick up the reins. Jesse stood, unobtrusively, next to Gracie but didn't offer assistance.

When Sam felt secure, Jesse said, "Stay right there," as if Sam planned to gallop off.

The older man took the reins of his horse, got on, then reached for Gracie's reins. "The program showed the horse being led. Don't know why."

"If the program said that, go ahead."

It was fun, sitting on Gracie's back, her gait rocking him. Keeping his balance was harder than he'd thought but truly much more enjoyable than the parallel bars. He could feel strain in the muscles of his leg and other parts he hadn't worked on in PT. He didn't care. He was on a horse, ambling along the street and out to the countryside northwest of town. He felt great.

After fifteen minutes, Jesse turned the horses around. "Don't want to wear you out the first time," he said. "The program said once a week so I'll be back next Friday, if that works for you."

"Thanks, Jesse. That works great for me." He'd clear the entire day, the entire week, if he needed to.

They headed back toward town, through the rolling scenery and the green grass of the Hill Country.

"Next spring the bluebonnets will cover all this." Jesse waved at the fields. "Ever seen the wildflowers?"

Sam shook his head. "I always visited in the summer."

Would he be here next spring to see them? He had no idea. Right now, he looked only far enough ahead to riding Gracie again, to ambling along the farm-to-market road toward Llano on her back.

On the way home, his thighs cramped and his back began to hurt from holding his posture. It felt like a good kind of hurt, the kind that came from exercise, not injury. The lethargy that filled him was just plain old exhaustion. He should sleep well tonight.

Odd how he'd begun to care about this community and the nice people. Jesse didn't have to do this, but he rode in front of Sam, perfectly happy to be ambling along the road, spending his time doing something for Sam. And the ladies had brought him so much food, he seldom had to microwave a frozen dinner. Because of them, he'd started to feel positive emotions, to be thankful, to feel alive—almost happy.

And he regretted every one of those feelings.

Chapter Twelve

Birdie stepped out of her shoes and wiggled her toes before she slipped on a pair of soft slippers. She closed her eyes for a moment—only a few seconds because she'd fall asleep if she stopped moving. Lord, she was plum wore out. Seemed she was always tired. And now what had she done on top of everything else? Taken this child in.

The child was sleeping so maybe Birdie'd take a nap. Yes, she would, later, after she put the groceries away and thawed something for dinner and...well, a few other things. After she finished all that, she'd take a nap. Of course, by that time, Missy'd probably be awake. She sighed as she rotated her shoulder to relieve the stiffness and headed into the kitchen.

She had to take care of herself. The girls couldn't get along without her and she'd just added one more child. All right, Missy was temporary and didn't really count on Birdie, but others did.

If she did too much and got sick, what would the church do without her? Everyone would leave things to this young minister, who might begin a guitar service, or use PowerPoint to

display praise songs on the wall, or introduce all kinds of fool-
ishness without her supervision. Not that he'd showed that
inclination yet, but she needed to be here in case the tendency
broke out unexpectedly.

No, she couldn't get old. She refused to get sick. Probably
she should pray about it, tell God to either give her more
strength or chip off a few layers of responsibility, but she didn't
have the time or energy to instruct God about how to run the
universe, not right now.

The girls would be home soon. They'd figure out how to
watch Missy. First they'd...

A knock came on the front door. She glanced down at the
sofa where Missy slept with Carlos the Cat curled up happily
next to her. Don't that beat all? Carlos was usually an attack
cat, but there he lay, snuggled against Missy. Then she opened
the door as she moved her shoulder to get that final kink out.

❦

Adam watched as Miss Birdie again rotated her shoulder and
grimaced. The pillar did have a breaking point, was actually
human. He had to remind himself that she was nearing sev-
enty and had the aches and pains of an elderly person—not
that he'd ever call her that when she could hear—and the
responsibilities of a much younger woman. As her minister,
Adam had to remember she was a beloved child of God and
treat her as such, even during the times she acted so determined and in charge—and scheming.

"I didn't know if you had a bed for Missy," he said. "I went
over to the thrift shop and got a blow-up mattress and a night-
gown and some clothing for her." He held out a large box and
a small package. "Hope everything fits."

"Thanks, Pastor." She actually smiled at him, as if her minister had done something right, finally, but the smile didn't change the fact that she looked exhausted.

"Do you need anything else? Toys? More clothing?"

She shook her head. "Missy won't be here long. Maybe tonight. Maybe not. Her mother's looking for this little one. She has good manners and has gone to church. Someone has taken good care of Missy, taught her well, and must be worried."

The two both looked at Missy.

"Let me know if I can do anything," Adam said.

"Think I can't handle this?" Before Adam could answer, she plowed on, "Like a bachelor knows anything about children." She snorted.

The truce was over. Of course Miss Birdie would fight anyone who tried to shoulder part of her burden, but he'd do what he could even if he had to conceal his actions.

"My neighbor does. Ouida said she'd watch her in the evening, when you want to do something with your granddaughters. And I can take Missy to day care and bring her back. Besides, I do have a sister. There are things I can do."

Her glance showed she didn't accept that. "How old is your sister?"

Two years older than he, but Adam didn't say that. She'd just point out that he'd been too young to take care of a sister that close in age.

It didn't matter. He could allow her to win this one. Victory always cheered her up, and she deserved that.

Much earlier than Sam wanted to be out of bed, he studied his reflection and thought what an idiot he was.

To look almost civilized, he'd chosen his one dress shirt,

white and fairly presentable. Because he had no iron, he'd steamed it in the shower. He tightened the belt on khakis that hung on him. Add to that fairly new athletic shoes he'd found in the box of stuff the general had sent to him. He hadn't opened the carton until late last night after he'd had a couple of drinks. Only a few because he wanted to be able to function at the same time as he buffered himself from any memories rattling around loose inside, any reminders of activities he'd participated in back when he had two legs. Fortunately he'd found nothing but clothes and shoes.

He looked at himself in the mirror again. Over the last few days, he'd changed: better-looking clothes, shaved, and not hungover. What would he do next? Get a haircut? Not likely, but this "presentable" stuff seemed to be creeping up on him.

Who was he trying to kid with the white shirt and new shoes? He wasn't normal, lovable ex-marine amputee Sam Peterson, not inside or out, so why was he attempting to *look* like that? The kids didn't care about his appearance, which left only Willow Thomas to impress and she...she...Well, he didn't know about her but he did know about himself. He had no business dressing up to...what? To attract her? To date her?

To marry her?

Crap. What a load of crap.

He put the comb down, shook his head so the clean hair looked unkempt, and pulled off the shirt. With the prosthesis, changing shoes and trousers was more of a hassle than he wanted to face. He grabbed the cane and hobbled back into the bedroom.

In the corner, Aunt Effie's chair was piled with dirty clothes. On top of the dresser sat a pile of clean clothes he hadn't shoved into a drawer. Folding and putting clean clothing away was a hassle he'd learned not to bother with. A pile on the dresser worked fine and let him know when he needed to do the wash again. No one in this house cared if his T-shirts were wrinkled or not. He grabbed his marine T-shirt, the one the kids wanted him to wear, and tugged it on.

He'd have to wash clothes soon, not one of his favorite chores. Manipulating out to the washer and dryer in the back of the narrow carport with a load of clothing under his arm stretched his ability. After a few attempts, he'd learned to put the laundry in a dirty clothes bag and drag it behind him.

Dumb stuff to be considering. For a treacherous minute, he wanted to check himself in the mirror again, but he didn't. He didn't care how he looked. He was clean and that was all Nick and Leo cared about, if they even cared about that.

Seven o'clock. Ready and waiting. They'd pick him up in fifteen minutes. He grabbed his cane and headed toward the living room. He needed a drink. He functioned better dead to feeling of any kind.

Vodka? Did he have any vodka? No one would smell it on his breath. No one would notice if he were unsteady, not that he could get that drunk in fifteen minutes. A drink or two would take the edge off. He headed toward the kitchen exactly as a knock sounded on the door. Too late. He should've known the boys would keep on their mother until she gave up and headed over here early.

Why had he agreed to this?

"Just a minute." Sam forced himself to close the world out and quiet his thoughts.

"D'ya need some help, sir?" Leo shouted through the door.

"No," he called back. "Be right there."

For a moment, Sam hyperventilated, dragging in huge gulps of air while his heart pounded in his chest and sweat dripped down his face, all signs of an impending panic attack. "I'm doing fine," he said to himself in a low voice, attempting to calm his breathing and slow the heart. He hadn't had a panic attack since shortly after he got here. Why had one hit him now?

"I'm fine," he repeated quietly. As the VA counselor had coached him, Sam pursed his lips and pretended to blow an imaginary candle out to decrease the amount of oxygen he took in. His heart began to slow.

"Captain?" Willow called.

Oh, great, exactly what he needed, an anxious professional like Willow wondering what was happening.

"I'm fine," he said, loudly this time. And he was. His breathing had slowed and his heart no longer thudded as hard in his chest.

"I'll be right out," he shouted as he limped into the kitchen, got a glass of water, and drank it slowly. After that, he splashed cool water on his face and wiped it off, glad he'd caught it in time, before he went into full anxiety mode. He felt a little wobbly, but that would clear up soon.

He shuffled back through the living room and opened the door. "You're a little early," he said.

Willow scrutinized his face. She could probably read the physical signs of distress but didn't mention it, quickly turning her gaze away.

Couldn't she meet his eyes? Did she still feel a little uncomfortable about that kiss?

Or maybe it wasn't that kiss at all. Maybe as a professional she recognized the signs of a recent anxiety attack but didn't want to address it now. He didn't, either.

The boys wore jeans so new and stiff they crunched a little as they walked, with new burnt orange T-shirts and matching athletic shoes. All ready for the first day of school. Their mother wore slacks and a nice shirt, her usual dress, almost like a uniform for work. She'd changed from her professional shoes to some with a thin heel—what were they called? Kitten heels? Why did he know that? Probably from watching that late-night program with Stacy and Clifford when he couldn't get to sleep. Or was he named Clinton? He didn't know and didn't really care, but the shoes looked great on Willow.

"Cool," Nick said. "You're wearing your marine T-shirt. Sir."

"Come on, sir." Leo leaped down the steps and ran to open the car door.

"Mom says you get the front seat because it'll be easier for you to get in." Nick danced next to the car and watched Sam. "She knows stuff like that."

"It's a really low car," Willow apologized.

"We can help if you need us to hold your elbow or anything." Nick held out an arm.

"Get in, goofball." Leo dragged his brother to the driver's side of the car, pushed him into the back, and followed.

With the car door open, Sam sat on the edge of the seat, then turned as he picked up his right leg and placed it inside the car. In a car like this, it was a little awkward but not a difficult task. He grabbed the armrest and closed the door while Willow got in the other side.

"Sorry," Sam said. "I should've opened the door for you." He'd forgotten a lot about how to treat a woman.

"Thank you, Captain, but I'm perfectly capable of getting in the car by myself."

"I know that. That doesn't mean a gentleman should allow you to."

As she turned the key and started the engine, she glanced at him, then quickly away, concentrating carefully on the nonexistent traffic as she pulled onto the street. He grinned. She still couldn't look at him, which suggested... well, he didn't know what but *not* indifference.

"It's a short ride, sir," Nick said.

"He knows that. He used to live here," Leo said in an older-brother voice.

"I don't remember much about town." Sam looked over his shoulder at the boys. "I haven't been here for..." He paused to consider. "...for about fifteen years, and I haven't gone anyplace but to the hospital and the grocery store since I got back. Is the junior high still next to the H-E-B?"

"Did it used to be?" Nick said. "No, it's that way." He pointed vaguely to the east.

The boys attempted to explain where everything else in town was located and how the old IGA had become a department store and where the new post office was, as if he remembered where the old one had been. While they chattered, Willow kept her eyes on the road with so much attention she could've been driving at the Indy. After a few blocks of a carefully navigated route, she pulled into the driveway of the school, found a parking space close to the front door, and let out a deep sigh.

Sam would have laughed at her relief, but that would probably spook her more. To spook or not to spook? The question made him feel somewhat Shakespearean but didn't solve the dilemma that was Willow Thomas.

After their mother stopped the engine, the boys pushed out of the backseat and ran to his door to pull it open.

"Sir, we're here, sir," Nick and Leo said in unison.

As were a lot of other parents, all headed toward the building with their children. People might think they were a family, too. He'd never been a part of this kind of a family, not with the general always away or busy. Not that the four of them were family. Fantasy. When would he learn fantasy was not his friend?

He turned in the car, picked up his leg, and placed it on the ground before pushing himself to his feet and picking up his cane.

"Sir, take my hand." Nick stretched his arm out.

"No, lean on me, sir." Leo shoved his younger brother aside.

"Thanks, guys, I can make it. However, I think your mother is closer in height to me. If she could just give me a hand to get over the curb."

An expression of doom flashed across Willow's face, but, like a professional, she reached out, took his hand, and placed it on her arm. Although she attempted to hide it, she shivered, only a bit. Fortunately, he knew exactly what that meant.

He grinned. She kept her gaze at the ground as if it were filled with craters that presented insurmountable obstacles for an amputee, as if there were an IED buried nearby that she needed to guide him around.

It wouldn't hurt to allow himself this fantasy for an hour or two. Maybe it wouldn't hurt to feel nearly normal, pretend he was like those dads with kids running ahead of them and with a pretty woman by his side, even if only for a short time.

Chapter Thirteen

The fantasy collapsed an hour later, as soon as Sam got home. Once inside, the solitude hit him like the thick humidity of the Texas coast on an August afternoon.

He was alone. No family, no redheaded sons, no wife. Alone.

What irony. For months he'd wanted to be alone. He must be doing better if he'd started wanting people near, but it didn't *feel* better.

He took a step toward the kitchen. If he couldn't find vodka, he'd call the liquor store. They were always happy to deliver. But he stopped himself. He didn't want liquor and numbness. At least, not complete oblivion, not like he used to.

He wanted someone with him. He wanted to hear the boys in the backyard, but that wouldn't happen, not with school starting. And as skittishly as she behaved, their mother didn't seem likely to drop by for a visit just because he was such a nice guy.

He took a few steps toward the phone, picked it up, and

hit the quick dial. "Hey," he said when the general picked up. "When will you get here?"

He'd become really desperate if he wanted to talk to his father and actually looked forward to the general's arrival.

Willow breathed a sigh of relief when the captain got out of the car. She hadn't thought he could leverage himself up, not from this low car. He'd refused to allow her to give him a hand up or a shove in the back but struggled to get out on his own. *Men!* she thought, then changed her generalization to *Marines*. Stubborn and independent but admirable and inspirational— and the boys adored him.

Not that she wanted to consider those positive qualities because she didn't want to care about the captain as a person, as the man who'd pretty much adopted her children or, at least, had provided day care. That couldn't be fun for a single man like him.

Then she realized she'd spent the last few minutes watching him move up the walk and take the steps one at a time. She'd noticed again how fine he looked from every direction, front, back, and sides. What an idiot. She put the car in gear, checked behind her, and pulled out. Unfortunately, she had never become accustomed to the power of the engine. It sounded like a race car: *vroom*.

Was he dating? Surely, having grown up here, he knew people, probably families with women his age unless, of course, they'd all moved to the big city. The fact that he wasn't driving yet would cut down on that. The places to take a date in Butternut Creek were limited.

She shouldn't be considering either the captain's love life or his body. With a glance at the clock, she turned her mind back to her schedule for the day. Nearly eight thirty. She'd arrive early for her first appointment. After that, she'd go onto the floors to evaluate several patients.

But no matter how hard she attempted to concentrate on work, a corner of her brain kept bringing her back to that moment in the hallway at school, when Sam had put a hand on the shoulder of each son and smiled down at them. Leo and Nick looked up at him in such awe and, well, yes, love that the air around them seemed to sparkle.

No matter what he said or did, Captain Peterson was a good man, a man who cared about her sons. That scared her a lot, because she could fall for a man who spent time with the boys. Grant seldom did. She could care for a man who—oh, who was she kidding. She was already incredibly attracted to this man for reasons that had nothing to do with his relationship to her sons. She was attracted because, despite his attitude, he was smart and handsome and sexy. She'd begun to think no man could make her catch her breath, make her peek out the window of her office just to see him exercising.

For heaven's sake, she sounded like a lovesick schoolgirl. No, not true. He made her feel like a desirable woman. She hadn't felt that way since she'd found out about Tiffany.

❦

"Reverend Jordan," Maggie shouted from her office. "Phone."

He picked up the receiver. "Adam Jordan."

"This is Detective Somerville calling. Want to fill you in on the investigation about the child's family."

He grabbed a pen and a sheet of paper. "Go ahead."

"We identified her mother through fingerprints as Deanne Smith, lives in San Saba."

"Melissa Smith. So we know her last name. Have they located any relatives? Friends?"

"The local cops went by the house, but no one's home. Looks as if someone lived there until a few days ago. Newspapers in the front yard and mail in the box, but only junk mail. Nothing personal." He paused to clear his throat. "Mrs. Smith teaches third grade at the elementary school. She didn't show up for teacher training last week. The police checked at the school board office, but the emergency contact in Virginia doesn't answer."

"Missy said *Virginia* when we asked about her grandmother," Adam interjected, though the detective knew that from when they spoke earlier.

Somerville continued, "We ran down the references but none of the people listed have talked to her recently. That's about it."

"A dead end, huh?" Disappointed, he sat back in the chair.

"Sir, we'll keep investigating. Hard to believe she could just disappear without a trace."

"What about Missy's father?"

"No information and not a trace of men's possessions in the house. Also not listed on Mrs. Smith's job or rent applications." He paused. "The police have Mrs. Smith's fingerprints from her background investigation, which is how they were able to match the ones the lab found on the child's shoes. They'll put the prints in the system to see if anything shows up."

"You mean like a body?"

"Yes, but also could be a Jane Doe in a hospital. I'll let you know if I hear anything."

❧

Bree'd be home in an hour from volleyball practice and Mac was studying upstairs. As she cuddled the child who'd fallen asleep in her lap, Birdie enjoyed the soft, sweetly scented warmth of a little girl. At the same time, she realized her shoulder ached and she was simply too old for this.

The preacher had called her earlier about Missy but had no helpful information. "Dear Lord," she whispered, "You need to have Missy's mother turn up soon. I'm worn out."

Too tired to carry the child upstairs to the blow-up mattress they'd put in Birdie's bedroom, Birdie carefully placed her on the sofa and made sure the blanket covered her. Then she headed into the kitchen to see what she could thaw and heat up for dinner.

The previous night, Missy'd fallen asleep at ten thirty after Mac had spent nearly an hour rocking and calming the child. Birdie'd been asleep for only a few minutes when Missy's sobs awakened her. She stumbled across her bedroom to the corner where Missy slept and picked the girl up.

"Mommy. I want my mommy."

"I know, sweetheart, I know." She sat on the edge of her bed and rocked Missy until she quieted.

When she got back in bed, Birdie pulled the sheet over her shoulders and attempted to fall back to sleep but two questions haunted her:

When was Missy's mother going to show up?

And why had she, an old lady feeling older each day, taken the child in?

🐦

Sam had gone off the wagon last night. Not that he'd been securely on it. At least, not completely, but the pain and the isolation and the longing...

What kind of a wimp had he become? Why had he turned to alcohol again when he knew it didn't help? He knew the emptiness and the ache would still be there long after the fleeting surcease of tequila...well...ceased.

He was supposed to be at the hospital in an hour. The van would be here in forty-five minutes. He pushed himself up to a sitting position, knowing no amount of counting backward would make him feel better. Even the idea of walking up and down between the railings in PT intensified the pain.

And he'd have to see her again. Willow Thomas, who'd been avoiding him for nearly a week. The boys had come over after school a couple of afternoons. Like he wanted that or needed them.

Yeah, he did. He might try but couldn't lie to himself how much he enjoyed the kids. With the start of school, Willow had given them permission to visit him but they had to leave here at five, walk home for dinner, and do their homework. Because he'd taught them discipline, expected them to honor women, they didn't dare leave a second late.

He thought karma meant if he did good, he'd get good back. In his case, karma should mean if he followed the rules and got the boys ready to go home on time, he'd see Willow once in a while. Obviously it didn't work that way for him. Sometimes life came back to bite you. No good deed goes unpunished.

What other clichés could he think of to put off getting up?

He now had thirty-five minutes to get dressed and eat and be ready for the van.

The short period of preparation explained—mostly—why he looked scruffy. Not enough time to shave made his beard show dark. With only a few minutes to take a shower and no time to blow-dry his hair, it still dripped when he ambled into the therapy room on his cane. Clean, of course. Dirty wasn't an option. Sadly, arriving hungover with a pounding headache and queasy stomach seemed to be.

While several clients pulled on bands attached to hooks or lay on treatment beds lifting canes over their heads, he stood alone by the parallel bars.

"You don't look well, Captain."

Willow had appeared in front of him looking bright, smiling in her best professional manner. Her perkiness made his head hurt even more.

"Tough night?" she asked.

He'd shake his head if the movement didn't cause pain to shoot up his neck and scramble his brain. "I'm fine."

"I need to observe you today." She picked up a clipboard. "After that, I have to make some notes and do a few measurements for the prosthetist. I'll send him a report today because he's coming here to see you next week."

Sam pulled himself between the rails and attempted to walk as well as possible. Dumb. Not as if he needed to impress her with how little he limped.

"Captain," she said. "You're slouching." She placed her hand on the small of his back and pressed. "Straighten here." Keeping the pressure on, she watched him take several steps. "Does that feel better?"

It did. Took some strain off his leg, but he wondered how long he could maintain that position. He'd been surprised how much strength and muscle he'd lost over the months before he started rehab.

She watched him, evaluating every movement. "Try not to swing your right leg so much. That's hard on your hip. Use your muscles, not that rocking motion."

"Easy for you to say," he mumbled.

"Probably so, but if you over-rotate any part of your body,

you'll have trouble later." She smiled, again professionally, as if he were a pitiful wretch she had to rehabilitate—which he was, of course.

Women were seldom attracted to a pathetic shell of a man.

After a few repetitions of the exercises, she said, "Captain, please come with me so I can take a few measurements." She turned precisely and strode toward her office. Her posture cried, *I'm a professional and not the least bit interested in you.*

If she wasn't attracted, why the statement? Why the attitude?

The tension in his neck decreased as he followed her, gorgeous even under the lab coat. He grinned and his headache lessened a little.

"Please sit down, Captain." She gestured to a chair as she settled behind her desk.

With his cane, he pushed the door shut. Then he shoved the chair closer to her. She pushed it back and moved hers in the opposite direction. Unexpected. He'd never had a woman react like that.

"Captain," she said in an unruffled voice.

One more thing he'd lost: his touch with women. The always successful Sam Peterson charm didn't affect this woman, at least not now, not in *her* department. He knew it had a couple of times, but today Willow looked cheery and chipper, spunky and totally, obnoxiously in charge.

She watched him coolly. "I need to make some measurements, but you'll need to remove your prosthesis."

Another problem: Sam didn't feel toward her as he should with a professional.

"That means I'm going to have to take off my jeans," he said stupidly. Obviously he'd have to unless she'd developed X-ray vision, a superpower he hadn't noticed she possessed.

As for taking off his jeans, he didn't think that was a good idea. Although she didn't seem to think of him as a man, he couldn't forget she was a woman. Panic spread through him. "Why don't you have Mike measure?"

"Because, Captain, this is my job."

Her voice firm, she glared at him. Though he didn't think it was possible, her posture became straighter and even more professional. He didn't know how she did that because she'd sounded like a real medical badass only seconds earlier.

"I'm the PT who works with the prosthetist, Captain. That's my job, my specialty."

Great. He'd insulted Willow. Her words made him feel like a complete jerk. No, as the man who'd tried to be his counselor at the VA had told him a million times, he'd decided to act like a jerk. She'd just caught him at it.

Why did *this* woman attract him? His usual choice in women was pretty and petite and adoring, cute and compliant. Those women didn't glare at him, and they didn't act like *any* kind of badass.

No matter how educated and trained and competent she was, he wasn't feeling patient-like enough toward her to drop his pants.

She stood, opened a cabinet, and pulled out a gown. "Put this on." She placed it on her desk only inches from him. "Take off your trousers. Now. I'll be back to measure."

He hesitated.

"Suck it up, Captain." She glared at him. "If you want to get rid of the clunky old prosthesis, the one you hate, the one that rubs and doesn't fit well, do this. I have to send Leland the information." Then she raised one eyebrow. "I'm a trained professional."

He'd had measurements taken and been examined, prodded, and photographed by nurses and doctors and PTs in Hawaii and DC. It never bothered him before, but this...

"Next time, wear shorts so you don't have to change." She swirled and stalked out of the office, closing the door behind her.

He picked up the gown and studied it. A marine wouldn't wear something like this. But he couldn't have worn shorts, either. Everyone would see he was missing a leg. Everyone could see the prosthesis, if he wore shorts.

Was he ashamed? No, but it was unsightly. He'd have to expose that ugliness and loss to the world, at least to the part of the world that lived in Butternut Creek.

Why? Why should he feel that way? He'd lost that part of his leg when fighting for his country. It should be a badge of honor.

It *was* a badge of honor, of service, not a disability to hide.

That decided, he reached toward a pencil holder on Willow's desk and pulled out a pair of scissors. With his thumb, he measured a few inches above his knee before he began to cut the leg of his jeans off.

Finished, he examined his new semi-shorts. The right leg of the trousers hit mid-thigh. A little uneven but, all in all, it worked. He tossed the gown back on the desk, removed the prosthesis, and leaned back in the chair.

Willow tapped on the door. "Ready?"

"Come in."

She opened the door and stopped, looking not at his missing leg but at the new semi-shorts. "Very clever," she said with a smile.

He felt pretty proud.

The measurements completed, she said, "Leland will be coming next week with a new prosthesis. You're going to be surprised by how comfortable this one will be, how much you can do with it after you get used to it."

"Like playing basketball? Running?"

"Don't see why not."

"Dancing?"

"Of course."

"Good, because I never could dance before."

She smiled. Nice of her because he bet she'd heard that joke a thousand times. Her expression encouraged him to add, "I'm no prize, an amputee who drinks too much. I don't have the slightest idea what I'm going to do when PT is over and I'm completely rehabilitated, at least physically."

"Perhaps—" She turned toward him with an expression of…well, interest. Not interest in him as a man but as her patient. "Perhaps I should set you up for vocational counseling."

"What I mean is that I find you very attractive but I don't have much to offer."

"You sell yourself short, Captain. I'm sure many people find you personable." She made a few more notes on his chart, added something on the computer, and kept busy for a few minutes.

While she did, he watched her and mulled over the statement. Personable. Exactly what he'd been looking for. What did that word mean, really? Almost any other adjective, perhaps *charming* or *handsome* or *sexy*, would've made him happy. But *personable*?

"Do you?" he asked. "Find me personable?"

"Of course. What woman wouldn't?" She turned toward him. In that softer voice, she added, "Captain, please remember, I am a professional, at least trying to be. For a moment I forgot that. I should never have kissed you." She shook her head. "Never. As your therapist, I can't let that happen again." Her expression softened and she looked a little bit regretful.

With that small amount of encouragement, he attempted to take her hand.

Did he never learn?

"Don't you listen to anything I say?" She scooted away from him.

From her determined expression—eyes narrowed and chin forward—he knew she wanted him to leave. She was on the job so she didn't feel open to a bit of flirting. He had to remind himself she was like no other woman he'd dated, pursued, flirted with, or lusted after. He had to learn to back off, to give her room. He had no experience doing that. Until his leg was blown off, he'd always gone straight forward, regardless of the torpedoes.

Now he had to adjust to too many things in his life, and changing in any way had become harder than he'd ever thought. Nevertheless, with Willow he had to rein himself in. He forced himself to change the subject.

"Tomorrow night the boys are staying for dinner. Pizza. Join them?"

"Oh, that's right. They did mention that. I'd forgotten."

"Would you like to join us?" he repeated courteously, in a friendly way, not a bit pushy.

"Captain, I can't."

With tremendous effort not to crowd her, he didn't say a word, but he worried. She wouldn't take the boys away from him and his evil influence, would she? Stupid thought. The boys weren't his but he had to know. "Can Leo and Nick still come?" He pushed himself to his feet as he waited for her answer.

"Of course. They'd be really disappointed if they couldn't."

She smiled—slightly—at him. "They look up to you. I'd never interfere with that. I'll pick them up at seven. They have some chores to do at home."

As he opened the door, she added, "You'll be sober."

He turned to face her. "Of course I will. I'd never hurt them." No, he wouldn't—except, of course, wanting to have a couple of shots of vodka before he took the kids to school, but she didn't know about that and he hadn't done it.

"Wait, we—" she began at exactly the same time the phone rang.

Christine knocked on the door and shouted, "Willow, we need you."

He opened the door and pushed past the aide.

"Captain, we need to talk," Willow said as Christine entered.

He left the department, walked down the corridor and outside, where he settled on the bench to wait for his ride home.

As he sat there, he worried. The *you'll-be-sober* question hurt, but the *we-need-to-talk* statement scared the crap out of him.

Chapter Fourteen

Nervous didn't even begin to describe how Sam felt that Saturday night. He'd enjoyed the ladies but had never found one he couldn't easily replace with another.

Until now. That scared him.

He'd thought Willow felt the chemistry, too, but if she had she was ignoring it. Oh, sure, she'd agreed to let the boys come for dinner. She'd pick them up in a few minutes. He might not even see her. She might honk and the two would run out.

He checked the kitchen clock. A few minutes before seven. While they waited for their mother, Nick and Leo had run out to the backyard to look at the rickety fence that was their next project together. The dirty forks and glasses sat in the sink, and the boys had torn up the pizza box and put it in the recycle bin. He looked at his watch, then remembered he didn't wear it anymore because Morty had given it to him. It hurt too much to wear it.

Besides, he bet the time hadn't changed since he'd looked at the clock only seconds earlier.

To waste a few minutes, he went into the bathroom, moving

smoothly and without a cane. He still had one but seldom used it. The PT had helped incredibly; the Thomas family, even more.

Once there, he picked up a comb and pulled it through his hair. It was getting too long. Too much bother to wash and dry, but he had to keep it, at least until the general arrived. The man hated long hair. A lot.

Wasn't he too old to enjoy tweaking the general? He considered the subject. No, he wasn't. It was still fun.

When the doorbell rang, he turned and hurried down the hall. Opening the door, he saw Willow holding a pitcher.

"I brought you something." She smiled.

A smile and a gift—that was good, right?

"The boys are in the backyard." He walked toward the slider and pulled it open. "Nick, Leo, your mother's here."

"Mom, we saved you dessert," Nick said. He ran in and, after a glance at Sam, took the pitcher from his mother.

"The pizza came with brownies," Leo chimed in. "We know how you like them."

As the boys raced into the kitchen, Willow glanced at him.

"Your sons tell me you love chocolate." He held his hands up in front of him and shook his head. "This was all their idea, not mine. You are my PT and a professional who isn't interested in kissing me ever again. I'd never attempt to bribe a professional with chocolate. *They* insisted on saving the brownies until you got here."

She looked perplexed, as if she had no idea how to answer.

"Mom, come on," Leo shouted.

"Sir, what would you like to drink?" Nick asked as the adults entered the kitchen. "Mom makes the best peach tea in the world." He paused to consider that statement. "You know, if tea was really important to us men."

"Tea sounds great," he said. "You guys know where the ice is. I hide it in the freezer."

Sam lifted his gaze to Willow but she seemed busy, intent on taking glasses from the cupboard. He leaned against the doorjamb and, with pleasure, watched her move through the small area with such purpose.

Maybe they'd leave after they finished. He hoped so because the thought of the little talk Willow had mentioned terrified him more than facing a dozen rocket launchers aimed straight at him.

Willow studied the table but not the captain. No, she kept her gaze away from him, as if she didn't notice him sitting there. She attempted not to act really obvious in her effort to pretend he didn't exist.

With the glasses filled, napkins on the table, and the tiny box of brownies set in the middle, they all settled in. The boys chattered and asked questions about the marines, which Sam answered. Other than "Do you need more tea?" Willow said nothing.

When Sam glanced at her, she thought he looked perfectly friendly but, perhaps, a little worried. Why had she mentioned she wanted to talk to him? Guilt, of course.

When they were finished, Willow had the boys clear and wipe down the table while she started to wash the dishes. Considering they'd used three forks for dinner and a total of seven glasses, it wouldn't take long.

"I can do that later." Sam stood before he added in a casual voice, "Did you want to talk about something?"

She turned toward him, but her eyes shifted, not making contact with his because she really didn't want to talk to him. Why had she said she needed to? "I'm afraid we can't, Captain. We have to leave. We're going to church in the morning."

"It's not even eight o'clock yet. Do you think thirteen hours is enough time to get ready for church?" he said, his voice dripping with sarcasm. He grinned because now he was enjoying her obvious discomfort. "Or have you lost your nerve? About our chat?"

Well, she wasn't going to let him get by with that implication.

"Boys," she said, "I need to talk to the captain. Go in the living room and watch television for a few minutes."

Aware of the no-nonsense tone of her voice, the boys ran from the kitchen.

"Guys, I have a new war movie on the DVR," Sam called after them. "Go ahead and watch it."

"Thank you, sir," they said in unison.

"What's up?" He leaned against the counter only a few feet from the sink.

"I sometimes overthink things, Sam…Captain." Was that ever an understatement, she thought as she put the last glass in the drainer.

Sam waited for her to go on.

"Yesterday, as you were leaving my office, I realized I had to clarify that terrible question I asked." She glanced up, her voice sincere and urgent. "I took additional training in prosthetics. That's why I was hired here. I'm the person, the best person, in the department to help you with your rehabilitation."

"Okay." He shrugged. "I'm good with that. In fact, I'm grateful that you have that training and expertise. I understood that before I left."

"I know. I probably don't need to reiterate that."

"You can iterate and reiterate all you want, but I did catch your meaning."

"I know." She paused and cleared her throat. "I also need to apologize for my rudeness, for telling you not to drink. That's none of my business. I was flustered and confused." She grimaced. "You do that to me. I wish you didn't because I hate to feel uncertain and fluttery."

He grinned.

Darn, he was nearly irresistible when he grinned. Of course, listing the times that he *wasn't* nearly irresistible would take up very little time or space.

"I want you to know how much I appreciate all you've done with my sons. I know you wouldn't do anything to harm or endanger them."

"Okay." He nodded.

"I should never have implied..."

"You didn't imply. You stated."

She nodded. "I should never have said that. I'm sorry."

"Okay."

She should stop. Certainly she'd expressed enough regret for tonight, but she couldn't. "One more thing."

"You're in a real orgy of apologies, aren't you? Bet you'd prefer not to talk about orgies with me."

She glared at him before saying, "Just one more. I messed up by kissing you. I'm sorry about that, too."

"That's what you've said, but I wouldn't say you messed it up. It was a very nice kiss. You do that well. I enjoyed it and thought you did, too. I wouldn't mind doing it again." Before she could interrupt, he held his hand up. "But I'm going to leave that up to you. If you want to kiss me"—he pointed toward his mouth—"you know exactly where to find my lips."

She tossed the dishcloth in the water, hard enough that it splashed up into her face. "That's not what I had in mind when I started this apology."

"Okay, but kissing's mostly what I have in mind when I'm with you."

"Forget that." She glared. "The kiss."

"You really mean what you're saying? Forget that kiss?"

She nodded.

He shook his head. "I'd prefer to *remember* that kiss and try a few more, just as an experiment, to see if we really like them."

"We both liked that one. That isn't the problem."

"Seems to be with you."

He grinned as she felt herself becoming angrier—but at herself, not him. She yearned to say something clever and sophisticated, a few biting words to shut him up, but she couldn't think of words of any kind. Besides, she'd probably sputter if she tried.

"Okay, okay," he said. "As hard as it is for me, I'll behave. And just so we'll both be more comfortable, I'll wear shorts to the hospital. Then you won't have to tell me to drop my jeans."

"Mom?" Leo asked, his voice high and puzzled.

They turned to find the boys staring at them from the dining room.

"Why do you want Sam to drop his pants?" Nick asked.

She blinked several times as her cheeks reddened. Then she picked up the dishcloth and wiped the counter with quick, nervous strokes, ignoring the question.

"Nothing," Sam said. "She's giving me instructions on measuring for my new leg."

"You're getting a new leg?" Nick's eyes dropped to Sam's knee. "Cool. Can we see it?"

"Sure. Your mom's going to make sure it fits right."

"Awesome, Mom." Leo smiled at her, but his gaze fell to Sam's knee, too.

"When?" Nick asked.

"Soon," Willow said as she emptied the sink and rinsed it. "Let's go. You have to clean your bedrooms." When both sons groaned, she tilted her head and gave them *the look*. "You have to take care of your own home, not just the captain's."

"Yes, ma'am," they said in unison, obviously not daring to give her lip both because of her expression and because Sam watched them carefully.

"A marine respects women," Nick and Leo said together.

"Bye, Sam," Leo said. "Thanks for the pizza."

Willow left with a wave. "And the brownie."

As she drove away, she wondered where this thing, whatever it was, with Sam—with the captain—was going.

With a shake of her head she pulled her thoughts back to reality. There was no "thing" with Sam. Her husband had left her barely a year earlier. In no way did she feel strong enough, trusting enough, to enter any relationship with a man, especially a man who had no idea what he wanted or where he was going, a man who'd even called himself a bad bargain.

❧

Sam watched the three head toward the car. He didn't hold the boys' sudden departure against them. The look their mother had given them had scared him, too.

So, other than being terrified by her glower, what was going on between him and Willow? The feelings bouncing back and forth between them seemed both better and worse.

Wait. Did he want things to get better or to get worse between them? Kissing was good, but *better* scared him; *worse* depressed him.

He watched as the car drove off, the two boys waving back at him. With an answering wave, he turned the porch light off.

At that moment, the idiocy of the situation hit him. He was deeply attracted to a woman who thought he was personable. Personable. The facts: She smiled at him, seemed to enjoy his company although she didn't fall all over herself to be with him—all of that very low level of attraction showed how desperate he was for her attention. These were not the signals given off by a woman who wanted him. Right now, he didn't mind the barely noticeable signs because the entire situation was ambiguous.

For him, ambiguous was a good first step. It was certainly a lot more positive than hating everyone and drinking himself into an anger-fueled stupor.

He should accept all this, the ambiguity and uncertainty, sit back and see where it led them, not bug her too much.

Oh, sure. Relaxing and allowing life to flow by sounded a lot like Sam Peterson.

As she greeted members of the congregation and handed out bulletins, Birdie felt a glow of pride in the interior of the sanctuary. She'd worked hard to remodel the area a few years earlier. Colonial architecture with white columns on each side of the platform—what was the correct word for the platform? Wine-colored carpet covered the three steps. A lectern jutted out on one side of the chancel—that was the word! *chancel*—with a pulpit on the other. The covers of a few of the pew cushions showed wear, but the rest looked good. She had no idea why some were worn; not that many people sat there.

Not that she could enjoy the view as much as usual. On the back pew, Missy ran back and forth, occasionally stopping to clap her hands and dance. Her behavior completely baffled Bree, who sat on the bench next to the child.

"New dress," Missy said to Susan Pfannenstiel, who'd just started down the center aisle. "And new socks. With flowers."

"Very pretty," Susan said.

As the child showed off her new clothing, the organist played softly. Supposed to be a time for meditation but never was. People chatted and greeted one another instead of praying. That was a fight she'd given up on. Guessed fellowship was important. Besides, contemplating the Almighty didn't mesh well with entertaining a four-year-old.

"How's she doing?" Susan whispered.

"She's had a tough time," Birdie said. "She cries a lot, doesn't understand why her mother isn't here. I have no answer."

Behind the communion table was an old-fashioned baptistery. It consisted of an opening the size of a large window with burgundy velvet curtains on each side and a painting of the Jordan River on the wall. Beautiful, one of the best parts of the church in Birdie's opinion.

When she saw it, Missy straightened, obviously intrigued. After studying the scene for nearly a minute, the child stood up on the pew and pointed. "Look," she crowed, "a puppet show." Missy clapped her hands, obviously expecting an imminent theatrical performance.

The congregation burst into laughter.

"That's not for a puppet show," Bree explained in a low voice. "That's the baptistery."

Missy frowned. "What's a baptry?" she whispered back.

Birdie took a few steps toward her and whispered to the child, "That's where people become members of the church."

"Aah." Missy nodded. "Do they get to play with the puppets?"

Fortunately at that moment, Jesse Hardin headed down the aisle.

"Horse man!" Missy shouted.

Jesse grinned at her and reached in his pocket. He pulled out a peppermint candy and handed it to the child, which distracted her nicely.

Then the organist began to play more loudly while the minister and the tiny choir processed down the aisle singing the opening hymn. The congregation rose and joined in, mumbling the words in rhythm with the organ.

Pastor Adam looked nice in his robe, mature and almost spiritual. His hair had grown so his scalp didn't shine through as much. His sermons were pretty good. She'd keep working with him, send him a few emails every now and then about how he could improve. Obviously he'd taken her advice because he showed great progress under her guidance.

Ten minutes into the service, she sat next to Bree and Missy. She'd forgotten how distracting a child could be. Oh, she'd prepared. On the pew between them were a doll with several outfits and accessories, four or five coloring books and a box of crayons, and a few little books. Missy wanted each of them at the same time. A few minutes later, none of them interested her.

Obviously the child had attended church regularly. Missy knew about prayers, closing her eyes and folding her hands piously—for all of ten seconds until she was ready to do something else.

When in the world would Mrs. Smith ever show up? Birdie needed her nearly as much as Missy did.

❧

"Why don't we have a children's sermon?" Adam asked Maggie.

The part-time secretary had just pulled her chair up to the

desk and picked up her cup of coffee. She blinked. "I don't know, Pastor. We haven't had kids for so long, I guess it looked foolish for one or two children to sit up in the front with the preacher. Or no one, most mornings."

"How are we going to appeal to families if we don't have something for their kids? Do we have children's church or a nursery?"

"We haven't needed them since the last minister left. He had five kids."

"But the two Thomas boys were in church, and so was Missy."

Perhaps he could borrow Carol and Gretchen for Sunday morning if only for children's sermon, to swell the crowd. Oh, not only for his evangelistic purposes, but exposure to religion and the kids at church wouldn't hurt them much.

"How many of them are going to stay in town? As soon as they find a relative for Missy, she'll be gone."

A fact he knew well. Adam had called the police a couple of times, but they hadn't found out more. The emergency phone still didn't answer. Although obviously well cared for, Missy had not been reported as missing. The child seemed to be alone in the world, but both he and Miss Birdie knew she had, or at least used to have, a mother who loved her and who'd taken her to church and hugged her and bought her new clothes.

Where could she be?

At least she probably hadn't died. The police had sent the fingerprints all over the country; they didn't match those of any Jane Does they had in the morgue.

After nearly an hour of sermon preparation, the phone rang. Adam answered, again forgetting he had a secretary for two hours a morning. Would he ever get used to that? "This is Adam Jordan."

"Good morning, Reverend Jordan. This is Detective Somerville from the police department."

"Glad to hear from you. I've been thinking a lot about Missy. I hope you have good news."

"We found Missy's mother."

"Terrific."

"St. Michael's Hospital in Austin called. Fingerprints match a Deanne Smith who's been in a coma since August nineteenth. Airlifted from Butternut Creek. Hit by a car a few blocks from where the little girl was found."

"Great." Adam jumped to his feet, happy for the match although sorry for the injuries to the mother. "Sounds as if you found her. What took so long?"

"Snafu on that end. They identified her through a purse found near her but didn't send the prints until yesterday."

"How is she? What do we do next?"

"As I said, she's in a coma. You have all the information we know. Maybe you could visit her, see if you can find out anything."

"Glad to." After he hung up and jotted down the information, he wondered what to do next. Should he take Missy to see her mother? Probably not, at least not today. He should investigate a little, find out if this Deanne really was her mother and see if her condition might frighten the child.

"Maggie." He hurried through the reception area. "I have to go to Austin. Be back in a couple of hours."

The old car made it to Austin with no trouble. Rex had performed mechanical miracles with the ancient vehicle. When he got to St. Michael's Hospital, Adam checked in at the ICU and went to Mrs. Smith's bed.

Yes, this was Missy's mother. She had the same fly-away hair and freckles but her skin was pale, nearly gray. Her chest lifted rhythmically. The tubes and machines hooked up to her might scare Missy, as would her mother's stillness. He explained the situation to a nurse checking Mrs. Smith's vitals and asked her advice.

"Sometimes it's difficult for a very young child to see her mother like this, so quiet and on all the equipment," she said. "Maybe you could take a picture and talk to her about it before she came."

"But you do think I should bring her."

The nurse glanced at Mrs. Smith, then at him. "You'll have to decide, but often it's better for her to see that her mother is alive, even with all the machines. Otherwise, she might worry more."

"Will she be okay?"

"I really can't discuss the injuries without a family member. However there's a reasonable chance she will recover. It may be a slow process."

"Thank you."

With the nurse still hovering and taking care of Mrs. Smith, Adam pulled out his cell to snap a picture and attempted to find the best position that showed the fewest machines. Before he left, Adam stood next to the bed and picked up Mrs. Smith's hand. "Your daughter Missy is fine," he said. "She's being taken care of in Butternut Creek." He repeated the sentence several times, then gave a short prayer for healing before he lay her hand back on the bed.

The seminary's professor of pastoral care believed that people in a coma were able to hear. Adam hoped his words brought peace to Missy's mother.

When he got back to Butternut Creek, Adam headed for the diner where he knew Miss Birdie would be cleaning after departure of the lunch crowd.

"They found Missy's mother," he said as he approached the pillar.

"Praise the Lord!" She lifted her arms toward the sky. "Preacher, I love that little girl and I'm really happy for her and her mother. But"—she sighed and dropped into a chair— "I'm even happier for me. I'm pretty sure raising another child would be the death of me. Now." She pointed at the chair across from her. "You sit there. I'll get you a cup of cup of coffee, then you can tell me all about it."

"No, Miss Birdie, you sit down and I'll get coffee for both of us."

She didn't argue.

❧

On Thursday afternoon, Birdie settled in a chair with a clear view of the PT room. She felt a tiny bit of shame because she'd had to shove Susan Pfannenstiel and her walker out of the way with her hip. Not hard, but she had to get to that chair first. She needed to see what was happening inside.

In the center of the room, Sam swung his way across the parallel bars. A man—some kind of expert from Austin, she guessed—stood at the other end of the bars and watched.

Where was Willow? She couldn't see her anyplace. Just Sam and the man and that nitwitted, man-hungry Tixie.

When Sam reached the end of the bars, the man nodded. He reached down and patted Sam's thigh and knee. The captain had a new fake leg, Birdie guessed. Okay, the correct term was *prosthesis*. She hadn't seen the other one because Sam always wore trousers, but he had shorts on today. The artificial limb—that sounded like a good term—was shiny metal with all sorts of belts and hinges.

Then Willow wandered over. That's exactly what she did:

wandered. She didn't rush to see Sam, like she was really interested in him. Of course, Willow had never displayed the slightest bit of interest in Sam—a terrible failure for the Widows not to have worked on that, a loose end they should have tied up.

Birdie MacDowell, you are a foolish old lady, a dreamer, she lectured herself. Although she tried to hide it, she was a romantic, had been until Martha had run off with that no-good man. With that experience, Birdie felt ashamed to admit she still believed in true love and the dreams a mother has for her daughter's future.

Because she'd failed with Martha, perhaps she'd build up some treasure in heaven by bringing other people together, people who would be loving and faithful and responsible— and happy. Yes, she was a silly old woman, but how could matchmaking between two lonely people hurt anyone?

At least, that's what she thought until Sam looked up at Willow.

His expression was grim and his eyes bleak. Could it be pain from the new prosthesis? Birdie didn't think so, because almost immediately he smiled at Willow. Pleasantly. Yes, he wore a *pleasant* smile, not that amazed, love-shocked expression she'd seen that first day they met. He and Willow looked like patient and therapist. Where had the passion she'd seen in Sam's eyes gone? What had happened to the love-at-first-sight look that had burst across his face?

Bah. She'd let her matchmaking slide and look what had happened. Nothing. Actually, they'd moved backward. Not a bit of attraction showed between these two beautiful young people who were absolutely meant for each other. Not just because they seemed to fit but also because they were about the only single young people in town except for the preachers.

Pastor Adam and the Reverend Mattie had spent hours at the diner, drinking coffee. Often they were joined by ministers from the other churches and spent the time discussing sermons or planning upcoming church events. *Hrmp.* Hardly a romance blooming there despite the fact she'd heard the two single ministers went to Marble Falls to see a movie every now and then.

Perhaps she could salvage something from the rubble of her effort with Sam and Willow. If Willow was no longer interested in Sam, she and Pastor Adam could be a good match.

But what about Sam?

No, Sam and Willow were the couple they had to bring together now. Sam was obviously still in love with Willow. After the Widows completed that task—which had turned out to be much more difficult than she'd expected—they'd undertake finding a wife for the preacher again.

For now, she needed to meet with Mercedes and Winnie. They'd lost every bit of momentum and better get busy PDQ. She'd be jiggered if she couldn't make at least one match.

Chapter Fifteen

At nine o'clock, Maggie stuck her head into Adam's office. "Do you have your tickets, Preacher?"

His sermon for Sunday was in terrible shape and needed a significant amount of spiritual intervention to rescue it. Alas, that hadn't happened yet. For that reason, he welcomed Maggie's intrusion. He glanced up at her and asked, "Tickets for what?"

The question staggered her. She froze in shock, incredulity obvious in her expression. She held her hands over her heart as if she wasn't sure it was still beating. "For the football game." Her voice held the distress of a woman hearing her minister hadn't prepared for the second coming.

"Is that tonight?" he asked.

Obviously the wrong question. She gaped at him.

"It's the first home game of the season," she enunciated clearly so he could understand.

Texas football. Nothing like it, everyone told Adam—over and over and over. He'd thought the huge high school arenas where Kentuckians flocked for basketball were something, but high school football was even bigger in this state. In Texas, football was the number one sport and there wasn't a number two. Maybe way down the list at number five, basketball or baseball or volleyball would show up, but only as an afterthought.

He turned to look outside. "But it's hot, supposed to be ninety today."

She tilted her head. "So?"

"Who plays football when it's this hot?"

"Are you kidding, Preacher? This is Texas." She waved her hands around her, pointing at, he guessed, the entire state. "It's always hot here at the beginning of football season. The temperature drops a little after the sun goes down, and by October it's downright chilly."

Maggie wore a bright gold T-shirt with BCHS LIONS embroidered on it in black. The abbreviation made sense. BUTTERNUT CREEK HIGH SCHOOL would be hard to fit across anyone's chest. As a mascot, a lion sounded okay. The animal was, obviously, the color of butternuts.

He should've noticed Maggie's apparel when she'd entered the office. Blame that oversight on his surprise at her words. He'd been brought up to go to football games when the leaves changed and temperatures fell. By late October, Midwesterners didn't think they were having fun until snow covered them and they shivered in nearly zero weather, bundled up in blankets and heavy coats, knit caps, and electric socks. In fact, that was one of the reasons why Kentuckians all looked forward to basketball, a game played inside by people in shorts.

"Don't the players get sick in the heat?"

"Hydration," she explained as if he were a little slow or, maybe, some kind of an alien, which he believed anyone from outside the state was during the fall ritual called football season. This reaction showed that as much as people wanted to believe they were alike, deep down an enormous chasm existed between football people and basketball fans.

He'd have to adapt.

He'd also have to buy tickets. And a T-shirt. Probably a sweatshirt for those chilly October evenings.

Maggie left after giving him exhaustive instructions about how to accomplish all this, where to go and who to talk to and that the school board office where tickets were sold closed for an hour at noon. She drew a map and made him write everything down, clearly certain an outsider couldn't figure out how to undertake the mission by himself.

Not that the instructions were helpful. She said things like, "Next to where the post office used to be," and "Down the block from where Eddie and Susan Parker—you know, from the Methodist Church—lived before her mother died."

Shortly after Maggie left and before he could get back to performing CPR on that sermon, Miss Birdie called.

"Do you have your ticket for tonight?" she asked before he could even say *hello*.

"I'm fixin' to," Adam said, delighted he'd worked that Southern expression into the conversation.

"Because," she continued without waiting for a response, "my granddaughter Mac is going to lead the middle school band."

"That's terrific. I didn't realize she was a..." What did they call them? "...drum major."

"She's not. You know she plays in the high school band."

As if Miss Birdie hadn't told him several dozen times. "Yes, and you've also mentioned she's great on the trumpet."

"First chair." Adam could hear the pride in her voice. "Well," the pillar continued, more excited than he'd ever heard her, "one of the senior drum majors was going to lead the middle school but she got sick and the other one sprained his ankle so he's staying on the platform this evening, not marching." She took a breath. The torrent of words must have left her winded. "The director asked Mac to lead the middle school. He has a great deal of confidence in her."

"She must be really excited."

"Scared to death. She's never done this, but the director believes she can." Miss Birdie paused. "You'll be there." Not a question. A command.

"I'll be there."

"At halftime, after the high school band plays, the middle schoolers will march to the middle of the field and play the national anthem with the older kids. You'll be able to recognize Mac because she'll be out in front. And the band'll be wearing their summer uniforms—no hats—so you can see her face."

After he hung up, Adam realized how much he'd begun to feel like part of Butternut Creek. During halftime at the first home game of the long-awaited season, one of the church's kids would be leading the middle school band.

At one thirty, Adam grabbed Maggie's map—as if one could get lost in Butternut Creek—and made his way to the school board office to purchase season tickets. After that, he stopped by the sporting goods store to get a shirt. At six thirty, dressed like a proud BCHS Lions fan, he left home. Plenty of time to get to the stadium before the game started at seven thirty. Plenty of time to pick up a hamburger and fries at the band booster club's tent and find a seat.

By seven twenty-five, the stands were packed. After greeting more church members than usually attended the service on Sunday morning, Hector and some of the basketball players, and other ministers who attended the game, he started looking for a place to sit in general admission. Fortunately, the Kowalskis were there and called for him to sit with them about halfway up the twenty or thirty rows of bleachers.

Excitement and anticipation radiated from the crowd. Most fans wore gold or black and many waved pompoms or noise-makers or large foam-rubber hands. From the end of the stands, the high school band played "Wabash Cannonball" and the cheerleaders jumped and danced. Their long blond hair—yes, six of the eight had blond hair—swayed with the tempo as they ran toward a huge hoop in the middle of the field with HENSON TIRES ROLL WITH THE LIONS painted on the paper covering it.

Then thunderous shouts erupted from the crowd. The band began to play something peppy—the fight song, Adam guessed—when the team burst from the locker room. The players stopped for a moment to jump up and down together. He had no idea why they did that but everyone in the stadium greatly appreciated the action and shouted even more loudly. After all that exercise, the team broke through the paper on the hoop and ran down the field to nearly deafening cheering, the tooting of air horns, and the sound of feet stomping against the metal bleachers.

Aah, Texas football. A dizzying and deafening experience.

By halftime, the sun had set and the temperature dropped to seventy-five but the enthusiasm built every time the team scored. After the first half, the Lions led twenty to sixteen.

But nothing that had gone before prepared Adam for half-time. First, the band of the opposing team came onto the field and very nicely performed country music tunes. The band played and marched, the flag team waved their banners, and the drill team strutted out and performed.

Once the visitors marched off, the Lion band took the field

to the roar of the crowd. Here and there, Adam could make out a football player, without pads and jerseys, marching with the band.

Of course, in their cowgirl outfits and the hats they used as part of their dance, the BCHS drill team was definitely superior to the other one. And the banners of the flag team floated higher than those of the visitors had. Adam wasn't sure what banners had to do with football, but the BCHS young women twirled them remarkably well. Noisy applause and cheering swirled around the field and ascended into the darkening sky.

But he hadn't seen anything yet.

Marching in place as if waiting for a signal, the middle school band had assembled behind the goalpost at the north end of the field, to his right. In front of them, hands raised, stood Mac. When she turned toward the field, she blew three quick toots on her whistle and started marching, followed by about a dozen rows of musicians. Moving together, silently in step, they marched through the end zone and across the goal line. Everyone watched as they passed the ten-yard line, then crossed the twenty-, thirty-, forty-, and the fifty-yard lines. When they crossed midfield, Mac glanced over her shoulder for a second but kept moving.

Wasn't it about time to stop their progress? The band filled the area between the two forty-yard-line markers. But Mac didn't stop them. She tooted three times on her whistle, the same signal she'd given to start the band. The toots didn't change anything. The musicians all kept marching along in perfect rhythm behind her.

Mac turned toward the stands. He could read her expression: panic, pure terror, covered her face. When she reached the thirty-five-yard line, Mac stopped.

Unfortunately, the band didn't.

A large boy with a tuba bumped into her, almost knocking her down. The first two rows of musicians silently surged around and past her. Mac regained her balanced and ran down the field to get ahead of the band. Once there and marching briskly and smartly, the musicians followed her over the twenty-five-yard line and the twenty. As well as the confusion covering the faces of the junior high students marching along in silence with their instruments at their sides, he could see the increasing terror on Mac's.

A hush filled the stadium. Would they ever stop and lift their instruments to play? If they didn't stop soon, they'd push Mac against the chain-link fence at the end of the field, moving in perfect rhythm behind her, on and on until all were smashed against the fence, instruments crushed among them, still lifting their feet in perfect rhythm but going nowhere.

The crowd remained mute, watching the band march noise-lessly down the field, keeping exact distance in front of them, marching in unison.

In one last effort, Mac stopped, turned toward the band, and shouted, "Stop!" The first two rows nearly mowed her down. The boy with the tuba ran into her again, but this time she kept her balance. Nimbly, she returned to the front, leading the group toward the edge of the field. Like lemmings, they followed her.

Just before Mac stepped onto the track, the sound of a whistle split the air: One long and three short came from the platform where the injured drum major stood. The band members stopped. The whistle sounded again, two short tweets. The students lifted their instruments. Mac turned, stepped onto the curb on the edge of the field, raised her arms and dropped them. On the downbeat, the band—still at the edge of the field and facing the scoreboard—started playing the national anthem. The high school band joined them. Silently, the crowd stood. Some placed their hands over their hearts, others removed their hats, but all faced the flag. A few sang, their voices wavering above the stands.

As the last notes faded, Mac ran from the front to the back of the middle school band and blew the whistle again in a pattern that must have meant, "Turn around," because the band did. After her three toots, they marched toward the opposing goalposts with Mac leading to the wild applause of the crowd.

They had succeeded. They'd marched, they'd played, they'd departed.

Adam didn't hear one laugh or snicker, only pride bursting from the people for their kids. Sadly, he wasn't as respectful and had to struggle not to smile, but he, too, succeeded. After all, Mac was one of the church's kids, and all of the musicians belonged to the community. He clapped and shouted wildly with the rest of the Lion faithful.

An occasion the town would remember forever. Probably one Mac wanted to forget.

After the game, Mattie and Adam and the most of the other ministers met up for something called the Fifth Quarter, an effort to keep the young people off the highway and sober after a game.

This was the biggest gathering place in town that didn't charge a fee. Besides, the Presbyterians didn't mind dancing as long as it was in good taste. The Christian Church, fearing a fight and a split, refused to discuss the situation, and the Baptists condemned the sinful practice.

For that reason, they'd ended up in the fellowship hall of the Presbyterian Church, a separate building so dancing—that wicked and corrupting behavior—didn't actually take place *in* the church. Besides, with adult volunteers outnumbering the students two to one, any depraved acts would be quickly halted.

Miss Birdie stationed herself next to the punch bowl, daring any teenagers to attempt to spike the beverage. For a few minutes, Adam wandered through the room and greeted people. Hector introduced him to a couple of his friends. Looking a little shaken, Mac sat in the corner with a few girlfriends. She gave him a wavering smile. Bree danced with a young man he recognized from the band.

Before Adam could move any farther, Miss Birdie grabbed his arm and pulled him toward the refreshment table. The grabbing and pulling actions were clues that she wanted to talk to him.

"Do you know why we do this?" Before he could say a word, she hurried on, as usual. "You know, there's not much to do here in Butternut Creek. McDonald's closes at nine."

He nodded, then shook his head. As usual, he had no idea which response she wanted.

"The movie theater's way over in Marble Falls. Twenty-mile drive on a dark, winding road. There are volleyball and football games and school-sponsored events, but not every night. So they"—she nodded at the group of about one hundred teens—"are in danger. We have these parties to give them a better choice, to keep them safe and sober and off the road."

"Keg parties all over, nearly every night." Mattie placed a plate of cake slices on the table. "Not just beer but hard liquor, too. You'd be amazed how many kids get drunk four or five nights a week—then drive. They think they are immortal, but I know better. I performed the funeral for Randall Sacks in May."

"Had a basketball scholarship to Texas–El Paso." Miss Birdie sighed and shook her head. "Coming home from a party last spring, driving eighty miles an hour on a country road, his car hit a tree. Killed him instantly."

At that moment, they were diverted by the arrival of the football team. The crush of hungry players ate every bit of food in sight.

"I have a bone to pick with you," Miss Birdie said as the crowd thinned, turning away from the refreshment tables and toward their friends. She paused for a moment. The short silence struck fear into his very core. He never had any idea which of his weaknesses she'd attack next.

"Have you visited Sam Peterson?" She glared at Adam, certain he'd failed her again.

His spirit lifted. "Several times," he said. "I bring pizza, we watch sports and talk."

"Ummh," she grunted, as if in grudging appreciation that he'd finally, finally done something right. "Did he say anything about...anyone in town?"

"Like who?"

She fluttered her hands, an action that seemed completely out of character. "Oh, any woman in town."

"We don't talk about women."

"Pssh." She emitted a sound Adam hadn't heard from her before.

"His father's coming," he said, glad to have a morsel of information to impart. "Should be here by Wednesday."

She glanced at Adam, eyes wide. "Wednesday? Oh, my! We have to get cracking."

A wave of relief washed over him. Sounded as if the matchmakers were on the move for Sam and whoever the chosen woman was. Also sounded as if he was safe for the time being.

Adam hated to throw Sam to the Widows, but, because nothing he could say would stop them, he rejoiced at the reprieve.

"He says you brought him a dobos torte." Adam kept his eyes on her expression to see how she'd respond to the fact that he knew about her act of kindness. "He really appreciated that."

"Hrmph." She turned away, an action that signaled the end of the conversation on her part and also meant the end of the conversation on *anyone's* part.

Adam picked up a cup of punch, filled a plate with cookies, and wandered away, feeling liberated until her voice echoed through the area.

"Pastor Adam, why don't you dance with someone," the pillar shouted in a voice so loud and demanding that everyone froze and turned toward her, then followed her eyes to study Adam. She pointed at the Presbyterian minister, then nodded. "Ask the Reverend Patillo to dance."

Miss Birdie hadn't given up. Why had he thought she would? He'd never be safe.

Chapter Sixteen

Birdie stood over Mac's bed and searched for words of comfort. She couldn't find any.

Missy was spending Saturday at Ouida's, thank goodness. One worry taken care of. But Birdie had worried about her granddaughter ever since halftime at the football game and had come home to check on her after the breakfast crowd left. Once she talked to her younger granddaughter, she had to return to the diner to serve the lunch crowd. After that, she'd called a meeting with the other Widows. Lord, what a day. "Give me strength," she whispered. "And I'd really appreciate it if You'd make this shoulder stop hurting."

Mac slept, her face innocent and lovely, so much like Martha's. She had to stop worrying Mac would turn out like her mother.

"Mac," Birdie called. The girl didn't wake up, and she hated to disturb her. In a heap on the floor beside the bed were the clothes Mac had worn the night before. If the child's sloppiness didn't shout *trouble*, nothing did.

She didn't want to have this conversation. She wasn't the best person to console anyone, much less this child she loved so much.

"You're a coward, Birdie MacDowell," she muttered, having decided to let the girl sleep. She turned and attempted to tiptoe out. Unfortunately, tiptoeing across linoleum plus rubber soles didn't equal silence. As she squeaked across the floor, Mac woke up.

"Good morning, Grandma." She stretched and yawned.

"How are you?" Birdie turned and walked back toward her granddaughter's bed. "About last night, at the game?" Birdie settled on the side of the bed.

Before Birdie realized what her granddaughter had in mind, Mac sat up and put her arms around her.

"It's okay, Grandma." She squeezed Birdie. "Thanks for asking," she mumbled against Birdie's shoulder.

Birdie had no idea what to do, how to react to a sign of affection since they were very seldom shared. For a moment, tears stung her eyes, but she blinked them back before she patted her granddaughter on the back and whispered, "There, there." As if that helped.

Letting go of her grandmother, Mac said. "Hey, it really is okay. I was mortified, but I talked to Pastor Adam for a while last night at the Fifth Quarter. He helped me a lot."

"He did?"

"Why are you surprised?" Mac tilted her head. "He is our minister."

Birdie hadn't meant to sound amazed although the fact *had* astonished her. Why? He'd visited Sam Peterson and helped with Missy. She hadn't seen him chat with Mac, but that could've been when she'd gone to the kitchen to make more punch. Maybe she'd have to admit he did have some good material in that tall, skinny body. After all, he'd gotten a haircut like she'd told him.

"He said we all have to accept the fact we aren't perfect, that we all make mistakes. He said I'll be famous for years to come, that people will say, 'Do you remember the night Mac MacDowell marched the junior high band all the way down the field?'"

"That's good?" Birdie attempted to figure this out.

"We decided it's good. We'll all laugh together and I'll be a legend. He told me he'd once scored a basket for the other team in seventh grade. When he goes back, everyone still kids him about it."

Birdie nodded. "It's okay."

If Mac felt okay, her grandmother was fine. "I need to get off to work." She stood.

"Thanks, Grandma. I'm going to get up in a while." Within seconds she was asleep.

So, Birdie guessed, Mac's jeans on the floor didn't reveal a meltdown, only a tired teenager. She picked up the clothes and tossed them into the hamper because, as much as she didn't mind clearing up a little bit for an exhausted child, she would if she didn't wish.

She had something more important ahead. If this wasn't a time to call a meeting of the new and expanded Widows, Birdie didn't know when would be. The information the minister had given her about the arrival of Sam's father constituted an emergency. The entire matchmaking enterprise faced complete failure.

Oh, the preacher was a lost cause, she mused as she headed over to the diner. No need to even discuss him. Maybe later they'd try to get him married. If the preacher didn't approve of their machinations—sadly stalled at the moment—he could get busy finding a wife on his own.

For now, they'd have to write Pastor Adam off unless a new, single woman turned up, which seldom happened in a town this size, out here fifty miles from Austin. In fact, the appearance of two single women within a few months of each other constituted a minor miracle.

They could count on no help from the Methodist Church. It was too late for a female minister to show up there this year. They'd had that little musical-chairs dance the Methodists did when all their ministers changed churches a few months ago. Now the Methodists were stuck with a man with a solid marriage and three darling children.

They had to marshal their forces on only one front. The captain and Willow Thomas—*that* was the relationship they needed to work on. If she weren't so tired, Birdie'd come up with a really good scheme. Although she hated to admit defeat, she had to admit her usually top-notch matchmaking skills had stopped functioning. She hoped Winnie or Mercedes would have an idea.

❦

Winnie sat so straight, it looked as if she'd had recent back surgery. She also beamed, obviously delighted to be sitting with the Widows in public although only the three of them remained in the diner. Guess it had been a good idea to include her. New blood, fresh ideas, and she seemed proud to be part of the group, as she should be.

"I believe the preacher is a lost cause," Birdie said. The other Widows nodded. "I've tried, goodness knows, we've all tried. He's not interested. But"—she paused to emphasize her disappointment—"that Sam Peterson." She shook her head. "He seemed to be smitten with Willow Thomas. Don't know what changed. What do we do about him?"

"You're sure there was something between Willow and the captain?" Winnie asked.

For a moment, Birdie bristled. How dare anyone question her?

Mercedes put her hand on Birdie's arm. "Winnie wasn't here when we discussed this before, Bird," Mercedes interjected. "She's asking for confirmation and information. That's all."

"All right." Birdie nodded. "Oh, yes, I saw it. He fell in love with her right away, at first sight."

"Although Bird doesn't look very sensitive," Mercedes explained to Winnie, "she's very good about recognizing all sorts of emotions."

"I haven't seen that look in weeks," Birdie moaned.

"Then we have to bring them together somehow." Winnie nodded, as if she were the boss of the Widows.

If Winnie's only contribution was to state the obvious, what good was she? They needed ideas.

"Perhaps we could invite them someplace, then leave them alone," Winnie suggested.

Hmmm, that idea had possibilities.

"Where?" Mercedes asked. "You mean like a meeting?"

"Don't think we could get Sam to attend a meeting or even drag him out of his house," Birdie said. "He's a real hermit."

"Not even the church?" Mercedes asked.

"Don't think so. He hasn't been to church since he got here," Winnie said.

"Then they'll have to meet at Sam's house," Birdie stated with a decisive nod. All of her nods were decisive, but she put greater resolve into this one.

"We'll have to set something up there. How do we get the two of them together, alone, at Sam's house? Any thoughts?" Winnie asked.

Maybe Winnie would work out, but she had to stop acting like she was in charge.

Winnie opened her purse and pulled out a small notebook and a pen. "We have logistics to work out." She uncapped the pen, ready to write.

"We'll have to do that before his father arrives on Wednesday," Birdie said, proud to know something the others didn't.

"His father's coming Wednesday?" Mercedes asked. At Birdie's nod, she added, "We don't have much time."

"We'll have to get rid of the two boys somehow." Winnie noted that on her page.

"I'll ask my granddaughters to take care of them," Birdie volunteered. "But Bree has a volleyball game Monday night so it will have to be Sunday or Tuesday."

"Tomorrow's too soon to get everything together," Mercedes added.

"All right, Tuesday evening." Winnie wrote "Tuesday" on her pad. "What are we going to do?"

By the time they'd finished planning, they'd decided to invite Willow and the boys to dinner at Sam's house. They'd tell Sam they were bringing dinner for him, then—after the guests he didn't know about arrived—have Bree and Mac whisk the boys and Missy away. Once everyone else left, the Widows would serve the food, then take off, leaving Willow and Sam alone.

"I don't know what more we can do," Birdie said. "If that doesn't work, I'll wash my hands of those two." But she knew she wouldn't.

She glanced at the clock. "Now I need to pick up Missy. We've got a good plan. Should work. Let's meet in front of the captain's house at seven fifteen."

No matter how carefully events were planned they didn't always succeed, Birdie reflected on Tuesday evening.

Winnie had scrupulously charted out the entire time. She'd brought a boom box and romantic CDs by Barry White. Mercedes had chosen a lovely wine and made her delicious gazpacho while Birdie had brought a dobos torte and great vegetable dish. Winnie also contributed two lovely steaks, seasoned and ready to grill, and baked potatoes.

But when they rang the doorbell, a tall man with white hair opened the front door.

The three women nearly dropped their bundles.

"Hello, ladies. I'm Sam's father, Mitchell." He spoke in a voice filled with authority.

As if she couldn't have guessed that. The man looked exactly like Captain Perrson with twenty years added, the posture of a general, and an air of command.

"What are you doing here?" Birdie blurted sounding ruder than usual. Probably should have welcomed him but the words had jumped from her mouth because, doggone it, the man really upset their plans. "We weren't expecting you until tomorrow."

"Come in, ladies." He stepped back and gestured them inside. "I got here about an hour ago. The drive took less time than I anticipated. Sam tells me you're bringing dinner. Hope you don't mind an extra."

He smiled, a nice, friendly expression. Didn't look much like a general except for his straight back.

"My son says you're the best cooks in the state."

He included all the women in the compliment but seemed to pick Winnie out for special attention. Winnie must have noticed that, too. At the age of sixty-something, the woman's cheeks turned pink. Didn't that beat all?

When the three women bustled inside followed by Bree and Mac and little Missy, they caught sight of Sam and Willow in the living room with the two boys sitting on the floor.

"Look, we have more guests," Mitchell Peterson said, waving toward the Thomases.

It was that stupid corn pudding. It wouldn't set and had slowed them down. And finding Missy's bear. The child had refused to leave the house without it. Otherwise, they would have been here before the Thomas family arrived. What a fiasco—well, maybe not. Everyone was settled. If they could get rid of the general...

Willow stood and smiled at each Widow. "I must have made a mistake. Sam"—she gestured toward the captain—"seemed surprised when the boys and I showed up."

Sam gazed at Birdie. She hoped that was laughter in his eyes but didn't know. Surely he didn't mind seeing Willow, did he?

"Wish you'd have mentioned the Thomases would be here," he said. "I'd have been less confused and more welcoming."

Birdie turned toward Winnie and Mercedes. "Didn't you tell the captain what we had planned?"

"Oh, dear," Winnie mumbled as she attempted to cover. "I thought I had."

"But we weren't supposed to do that," Mercedes said. "You told me…"

Poor dear, she always told the truth, as inconvenient as it often was.

"I thought we'd told you," Birdie spoke over Mercedes's attempt to explain.

"I didn't realize there'd be eleven of us," Willow said. "Hope you have plenty of food."

Birdie hadn't realized that, either. Unless they planned to act out the miracle of the fishes and the loaves, they hadn't brought nearly enough food. Of course, they had plenty considering that five—the boys, Missy, and her granddaughters—would be leaving and the Widows weren't eating. The food would stretch to include the general, but they didn't want him here. How could they get rid of him?

"Hi, Mrs. Thomas," Bree said. "We thought the boys might not want to eat with the old folks."

Birdie glared at her granddaughter.

"With the adults," Bree corrected herself. "We thought we'd grab a hamburger, then go to the carnival at the middle school."

"Carnival," Missy added with a big smile.

"How nice," Willow said.

The boys looked disappointed, glancing at Sam with adoration. Then their eyes turned toward Sam's father and the three Widows and glazed over as if they realized what the evening with all these adults might be like.

"Okay," the older one said as the other nodded.

"Is that all right with you?" Bree asked Willow.

"Of course. I'm sure they'll enjoy that. Thank you." Willow waved at the boys as they ran out the door.

"Bye-bye." Missy followed the others outside.

As the door slammed shut, Birdie looked at the six still left. What in the world would they do with Sam's father?

"Dad, I want you to meet these nice ladies from the church." Sam introduced each. "Ladies, this is my father, General Mitchell Peterson."

"We met at the door," Birdie said. "And I remember you. Everyone called you Petey back then, when you were a kid."

"Back when you visited Effie, years ago," Mercedes added. "Before you were a marine."

"Of course, ladies. Good to see you again." His gaze returned to Winnie, who didn't say a word.

"We call ourselves the Widows. We like to serve people in the church, and"—she raised her voice to speak loudly and clearly—"none of us is married." She glanced at the general, then moved her gaze to Winnie. "No, we're all single ladies, all three of us.

"Ladies, let's go to the kitchen and put this meal together." With that, her chest held as high and proud as a woman as thin as she could manage, Birdie led the Widows through the swinging door and into the kitchen.

"What are we going to do with him?" Winnie whispered.

"It's what *you* are going to do, Winnie," Birdie said. "Not us."

Winnie frowned as she placed her dishes on the counter. "I don't understand."

"You're going to take the general off our hands," Mercedes said.

Winnie whirled around. "What do you mean?"

"You're going to have to lure him away," Birdie attempted to clarify.

With a gasp, Winnie said, "I can't...what do you mean? I don't have any experience in luring."

"Did you see how Sam's father watched you?" Birdie took a step closer when Winnie shook her head vigorously. "Did you?"

"You're going to have to flirt with him," Mercedes said.

"I'm a single woman, an old maid. I don't know how to flirt," Winnie protested. "I never learned."

"You're going to have to do it," Birdie commanded. "For the cause."

"You're going to get him to take you out to dinner so Sam and Willow can be alone." Mercedes spoke very slowly and clearly to get her point across.

Still Winnie shook her head.

"Okay, listen." Birdie pulled a chair out from the table and guided Winnie toward it. Once she shoved Winnie into the seat, she sat across from her and glared. "Do you remember the plan? *Your* plan? We get rid of the children, we serve Sam and Willow, then we leave them alone. Right?"

Winnie gulped, then nodded.

"What should we do with the general?" Mercedes asked.

"I don't know." Winnie shrugged.

Birdie stood and leaned over the newest Widow, who didn't look a bit happy to be part of the group at this precise moment. "The general's interested in you."

"He can't be. Men have never been interested in me."

"Well, the general is," Mercedes stated.

"As I said, I don't know how to flirt. I haven't tried since I was twenty and was not notably successful back then." Winnie glared at the others. "You may have noticed I'm not married. I'm not good or comfortable with single men." She paused. "Is he single?"

"Yes, his wife died years ago."

"Why doesn't one of you do it?"

"Because Mercedes is keeping company with Bill Jones down at the bank."

"Okay, but what about you?" Winnie glared at Birdie.

"I'm an old skinny woman who looks like a strip of beef jerky. He didn't even notice me, but you're pretty and feminine."

Winnie opened her mouth to object.

"And he likes you," Birdie added before the other woman could say a word. "He thinks you're attractive."

With a frown, Winnie considered this. "He does?" She looked from Mercedes to Birdie. "Do you really think he finds me attractive?"

"Why wouldn't he?" Birdie tugged the reluctant seductress to her feet and pulled her toward the swinging door between the kitchen and the dining room. "Go get him." She shoved Winnie out.

For a moment, Winnie froze as the other Widows stared through the little glass slit on the door a few inches below eye level. When the general looked up and smiled, Winnie started forward, walking in a bent-leg style, her hips swinging.

"She was right." Mercedes groaned. "She has no idea how to seduce a man."

"She's going to break something," Birdie whispered. "Her hip or her ankle."

When the three in the living room saw Winnie's posture, three mouths dropped open and six eyes opened wide.

"She's going to ruin our plan," Birdie whispered.

Fortunately, the general stood, approached Winnie, and gallantly held out his arm. She placed her hand on it. Actually, she grabbed it as if she were drowning and his arm were a life preserver swiftly floating past. He didn't seem to mind.

As Winnie turned coyly away from the general, Mercedes and Birdie could see her working very hard to flirt. Birdie wished she couldn't. It was too painful. Winnie batted her eyelashes as if they were butterflies preparing for flight, screwed up her mouth into an imitation of a Renée Zellweger pout—attractive on neither woman—and tilted her head as if her neck were broken. The final effort was a breathless, "Hello there," accompanied by a Groucho Marx twitching of her eyebrows.

All of which seemed to delight the general. Thank goodness.

"Why don't we leave these young folks alone and go out for a bite," he said. "Just the two of us."

Winnie looked terrified. Her eyes sought out the kitchen door. With the hand the general hadn't captured, she gave a wavering thumbs-up.

"We'll see you later," the general said. "You two have a good time." With that, he turned toward the front door with Winnie on his arm and hustled her outside.

"That was easy," Mercedes straightened. "And you don't look a bit like beef jerky." She grinned. "Well, only a little bit," she added with that infernal honesty. "You're attractive in sort of a dried-up way."

"Oh, just stop talking and fix the food," Birdie said.

Once the Widows served dinner, Sam stared at Willow across the table. He couldn't think of anything to say. He refused to talk about the weather or his prosthesis or the boys, which left little else.

"You know, we've never talked about Butternut Creek." Good topic. "I used to visit during the summer and you grew up here. Maybe we have mutual friends."

But after a few minutes, they discovered they didn't. Oh, she knew Mitzi Harris, whose younger brother had played baseball with Sam. She'd dated Matthew Morgan, older brother of Annie, Sam's make-out buddy, not that he mentioned *how* he knew Annie.

"Do you think we ever met back then?" Willow asked.

Neither could remember. After all, the last summer he'd spent here, he'd been a skinny fifteen-year-old and she'd been a sophisticated college student. They hardly ran in the same circles.

"Probably not," she said. "You visited in the summer and I spent most of my summers working at camp or picking up extra hours at college."

After exhausting that subject, they still didn't have anything to talk about, at least not as long as the Widows wandered in and out to clear the table and pour coffee.

"As much as I like it, I didn't have a thing to do with this," he murmured as the women disappeared into the kitchen. "With our being alone."

Willow smiled at him. Good. That was a start.

"I didn't think you did. You looked as if you didn't know we'd been invited."

"Miss Birdie is a devious and determined woman," Sam said as he noticed a pair of eyes peeking through the narrow slit in the kitchen door.

"She certainly is. And you looked as startled as I felt when Miss Jenkins hunted your father down."

"She did, didn't she." He grinned at the memory. "Sort of stalked him."

"I don't think he minded," she added.

"Guess their plan to get us alone hadn't taken the general's early arrival into consideration." The entire situation struck him as so funny, he started laughing. She joined but, when she stopped, he glanced at her. Her gaze wandered across his face, almost in surprise but also with interest and attraction.

She blinked—a little dazed, maybe? "I haven't seen you laugh before."

He bet she hadn't. Her reaction seemed like a good sign except she sat at the table on a chair and he sat across from her on another chair.

And that nice sofa stood empty in the living room.

Who was still in the house? He glanced at the slit again to see two pairs of eyes staring back. Not the time to make a move. He preferred to do his courting—if that was a viable option in this situation—without an audience.

Before he could say a word, the eyes disappeared. The sound of hushing and movement came from the kitchen followed by a loud "Good-bye," spoken in unison. The door from the kitchen to the carport slammed loudly.

With all the stuff they were carrying, he hoped the remaining Widows could get out that way. The general had brought Sam's car down, the classic Mustang. Before his injury, when he was home on leave he'd spent every free hour rebuilding it. With the Mustang there, the narrow carport was a tight fit. Still, the Widows either managed it or were going to spend the night there, because they didn't come back in.

Now he and Willow were alone. To make sure, he stood, walked to the swinging door, and pushed it open. "Miss Birdie?" he said. No one answered, but on the counter was a CD player with several discs. Who had left that?

"They're gone." He allowed the door to swing back.

Willow leaped to her feet. "Then I'd better go, too."

"What about your sons?" He walked toward her. "When Nick and Leo come back and you're not here, they'll worry."

"Nice try, Captain. You can tell them I went home."

"How will they get home? Do you want them walking in the dark, alone?"

"You make it sound as if danger lurks around every corner." She paused to consider that for a few seconds.

He wondered if she was trying to think of an excuse to leave and a time when she should come back for the boys. He waited.

"You're right," she said after a deep sigh. "I don't."

He took her hand. "Why don't we sit and talk? Get to know each other?" He attempted to make his voice sound casual and nonchalant, as if they were friends who wanted to chat and enjoy each other's company.

Didn't work. She tugged away and took a few steps to sit in one of the chairs, her hands folded primly on her lap.

But Willow Thomas could never look prim. Oh, she'd tried, pulling her hair back, but the soft brilliance of her red curls made him want to wrap a strand around his finger and... actually, everything about her made him want to touch her.

Sadly, she didn't look as if she felt the same way. But she might. He wouldn't know if he didn't try. "I thought maybe on the sofa?"

"I thought maybe facing each other." She pointed from her toward the sofa. "So we can see each other as we...um... chat."

Her eyes showed a note of panic. He grinned, inside.

"Do you think I'm going to attack you?" He colored his voice with a note of wounded sincerity.

Her eyes flew open and she glanced up at him, worried she'd hurt his feelings, he guessed. She was a very nice woman.

"Of course not."

Before she could figure out what he had in mind, he took her hand and pulled her to her feet, using the end table for balance and leverage. Ignoring her protest, he dropped her into the middle of the sofa and sat down next to her, his arm across her shoulders in case she tried to escape.

That didn't work, either. She slid away from his arm and to the other end of the sofa. "I went to the University of Texas," she said. "Finished my degree and got a master's in physical therapy. Married. Moved to Chicago where the boys were born," she concluded. "And you?"

"All over Europe and Asia with my parents. A&M, so I guess we're rivals. Marines," he said, matching her staccato delivery. "Iraq, then Afghanistan. Walter Reed. Here." He wanted to slide closer but he didn't have the smooth moves he used to. Lack of balance and lack of practice. Instead, he reached out to pick up her hand and used his thumb to rub circles on her soft palm.

At least he did until she pulled her hand away, stood, and sprinted to the other side of the room. Once there, she crossed her arms and glowered at him.

He'd blown it again. How many times did he have to remind himself that Willow didn't react like the women he'd flirted with before?

"Captain, what do you think you're doing?" she demanded.

Her voice sounded neither frightened nor wary but as if she'd pretty well tagged who he was and what he had planned.

"Why don't you tell me more about living in Chicago?" he asked in an even and—he hoped—fascinated voice.

"Because I don't believe learning all about the scintillating life of Willow Thomas is your ultimate objective."

"What do you believe that objective to be?"

"Oh, come on, Sam."

Why was he so fumblingly obvious with this woman?

"I *have* known a few men before you. I know your objective." She took a few steps back.

He had no idea where she planned to go. Outside? To the chair? Home? No, she began to tap her foot and continued to glare at him. Not a bit promising, but better than her leaving.

For only seconds, he considered playing the sympathy card, but he knew it wouldn't work, not with her. Besides, he didn't want to use it with her. He went for humor. "Maybe you could think of kissing me as therapy."

As he'd known it would, the suggestion fell flat. He groaned—inside. He'd always been much cooler with women, had seldom needed to make an effort. Willow was tough. With her, he sounded like a lecherous idiot.

She studied him. "Great line, Captain, does that ever work?"

Crap. She'd called him "Captain." "I liked it better when you called me 'Sam.'"

She didn't answer.

"And no, that never works because I've never used it." He

shrugged. Might as well be honest. "I've never used a line before."

"Aah, women just usually fall at your feet."

Could this get much worse?

Surprisingly, the situation improved. She sat down again. Sadly, she'd chosen the chair. "However, we could try a different kind of therapy."

He couldn't believe she'd agreed with him.

"You know, maybe more conversation."

Great. At least she hadn't suggested going home.

"Why don't you tell me about your father?" She relaxed back against the chair.

"My favorite topic."

She smiled. "You don't sound enthusiastic."

He didn't bother to answer.

"He's a handsome man, very military. I notice you call him 'General' instead of 'Dad.'"

"Doesn't take much insight to notice that." He spoke with withering condescension in his voice, but the tone didn't seem to bother her. She raised an eyebrow.

"That's basically who and what he is—a general, not a father." Not what he wanted to discuss so he said, "And your husband left you?"

Instead of the verbal slap he deserved, she said, "Aah, so we're getting into the *who-can-hit-whose hot buttons* section of the conversation. My, we've come a long way and quickly. I believe, Captain, you're hiding behind these attacks."

He should have remembered she was a professional, trained in counseling jerks like him as well as how to work with damaged muscles and frozen joints.

"My ex-husband is a doctor, ten years older than me, separated but not divorced from his first wife when we met. We were married for ten years, had two great children. He met Tiffany at the hospital two years ago. She's a drug rep. Imagine my surprise when I realized that, to feel manly and boost his ego, he needs a new, younger wife every ten years."

"Idiot."

"I agree." She shrugged. "It hurt me, but the boys…" She glanced at him, serious. "I hated how much the split hurt them. A few months after that, I got this great job offer. We moved because Butternut Creek's a great place for children to grow up." She took a deep breath before she said, "It has been, thanks to you, Captain. You've been wonderful for them. They need a man in their lives."

Great. She saw him as a good guy, a surrogate father, the man in the lives of her boys.

"But I don't. Need a man in my life, I mean."

He studied her. If she didn't need a man in her life, why was she so uncomfortable with him? "But you liked that kiss."

"Captain…"

She kept calling him that.

"I'm grateful to you…," she said.

Not what he'd hoped for. Grateful, personable—the words she chose made him feel pitiable.

"I went through a rough breakup, devastating because I didn't know it was coming. We've moved, I started a new job. I feel as if I'm juggling so much that if I add more, I'll drop everything."

"It's not like I'm looking for a relationship," he said before he realized what a mistake those words were. Willow was a relationship woman if he'd ever met one.

She glared at him. "Oh, a quick hookup?"

"No, not that." Sam shrugged. "I didn't mean to insult you. It's me. I'm no prize. I have no idea what my future's going to be."

"You've said that before, but I don't agree. You have a degree from A&M..."

"In military science, hardly useful now, but that's not the issue. I'm not interested in a relationship because I need to get some things straight before...before I can do anything with my life. I have to figure out what's in my future, if I have one."

As the words left his mouth, he knew he was lying. Yes, he needed to get his life back in order, but the rebuilding was happening, sort of on its own. It had started with the move here. He owed a lot to the friendliness of the Widows and the church, to Jesse and the weekly horseback rides, to Nick and Leo and Willow plus the staff in the PT department. He didn't know what was ahead but he suddenly recognized he looked forward to it, a little. He'd thought about teaching, maybe math or science to kids Nick's age. The idea had been nagging at him for weeks.

Not that he was ready to share any of that, certainly not with a woman who showed such a cold, aloof expression.

"Me, too," she said with that determined lifting of her chin. "Then do we understand each other completely."

No, they didn't. Not at all, but he felt pretty sure they should leave it alone.

"Captain, I find you a very attractive man."

A better word than *personable*. However, he knew there was a "but" coming.

"But..."

Yeah, there it was.

"I'm not ready. If I were..." She shrugged. "If I were and

I weren't your physical therapist, a relationship might be possible."

"I find *you* attractive." Hot, too, but this was *not* the time to mention that. Probably should stop now, but he'd never been good about recognizing that. "And you're grateful to me for being friends with the boys?"

She glared and leaped from the chair. "Not *that* grateful."

"Not what I meant." He pushed himself to his feet because he felt at a disadvantage sitting while she stood. Like a pitiful cripple.

She really was gorgeous. He wanted her, but he had no idea what to say next to communicate his feelings when she looked so unreceptive. He repeated, his voice steady and as sincere as he could make it, "That was not what I meant."

He'd really screwed this up.

❧

Willow glowered at Sam for a few seconds until she felt her expression slowly softening. Could she trust him? He hadn't made a move toward her. And yet, six feet away, she could feel his interest in her. No, more than that. He wanted her. His eyes blazed with desire that he did nothing to hide. The intensity of his need vibrated between them. Surprisingly for a woman who hadn't allowed herself to feel for two years, she responded to that need.

"That wasn't what I meant. Do you believe me?" he whispered, studying her as if searching for a hint of her feelings.

She nodded. "I believe you," she murmured into the simmering connection that stretched between them.

"Why do you keep pushing me away?" Sam said. "I can read your eyes. I know what that look means."

"Confusion, that's what you see." She had to gather herself together. She didn't want this, not at all.

She was, of course, lying to herself. "I have no idea where this…this *whatever* is going or even if it is going anyplace. I don't believe we can call what we share a relationship. Maybe lust or interest or two lonely people searching for companionship."

He gave a bark of a laugh. "Companionship?"

"I'm not ready for anything now. Nothing."

"Not what I'd hoped to hear, not how I feel or want, but…"

"But?" She pushed him to continue.

"But if I say anything more, I'll tick you off."

He took a step forward. From his grimace and his whispered curse, she could tell he realized the action had been a mistake.

"I'm pushing again." He stopped and shook his head in chagrin. "I can't seem to stop myself."

She took a step back, aware of how dangerous his proximity was to her peace of mind.

"I shouldn't have moved." He stood very still but still watched her.

With another step back, she ran into the wall. Unable to get farther away, she swallowed, lifted her gaze to his, and held her hand in front of her like a crossing guard.

Unfortunately—or perhaps fortunately because who knew what she might have said or done next—and before the silence lasted too long, the front door opened and the kids spilled into the house, Missy asleep in Mac's arms. Sam took a step backward to drop onto the sofa and Willow turned toward the children. The movement broke the contact with Sam, easily done because the connection had been tenuous at best. Relieved, she hugged her boys and thanked the girls.

The seven of them—well, five of them, because Sam didn't join in and Missy slept—chattered for a few minutes before the girls left. Willow hurried out with the boys before they could do much but wave toward the captain. The quick departure seemed unfair to the boys. Leo and Nick wanted to talk to Sam for a while, but Willow couldn't stay in that small living room any longer, not with Sam there filling the air with, oh, the *Samness* that had become so toxic for her peace of mind.

Hours later, with the boys bathed and sleeping, Willow turned over in bed again and punched her pillow while thoughts tumbled through her brain. Had she made a mistake? Should she have accepted Sam as he was? Didn't she deserve happiness?

That was, of course, pretty much the center of the problem. Could Sam bring anyone happiness in the shape he was in now? Could she accept it, as confused and broken as she felt? He wasn't the only one dragging baggage with him.

Another huge part of the equation was Willow herself and what she'd refused to face in months. She tossed the sheet aside, turned the reading lamp on, and opened the drawer on the night table. Inside, under a couple of books, a pair of scissors, and a package of emery boards, lay a professionally taken photo of her family, all four of them, taken over a year ago. In the photo, Willow sat on a bench with one boy on each side. Grant stood behind her, his hand on the shoulders of the boys. He looked distinguished—which he was; wealthy—his tailored suit and perfect haircut witness to that; and like a good father and loving father, protecting his sons and sheltering his wife. At some time, he'd meant to be all that, probably, but even at the time the portrait had been made, he'd been in the midst of his affair with Tiffany. Not a smudge of remorse or shame for the deception showed on his face.

How could she still allow the man who had so easily shoved her aside to reach into her brain and control her life after all this time?

Carefully, she pulled the picture out of the frame, then picked up the scissors and snipped Grant out of the photo. The disembodied hands on the boys' shoulders looked odd, but she felt better. Since she found out about Tiffany, she'd felt angry, both at herself for being so naive and at her ex for being who he was. With that action of removing Grant from the family circle, she realized anger no longer burned inside her and she no longer felt like a failure.

She had to admit she hadn't accomplished that reconciliation by herself. Thanks to Sam, she felt like a woman again. What in the world could she do about the sensations he'd awakened? The awareness that zinged back and forth between them?

After placing the butchered picture back into the frame and tossing Grant's head in the wastebasket, she stood and went to the dresser to pull her cell phone from the charger. She flicked through the pictures until she found the one she'd taken of Sam and the boys working in his yard. All three smiled. Nick and Leo looked up at Sam with admiration. Like Grant, he had a hand on each boy's shoulder. His smile showed how deeply he cared about her sons. She knew he'd never hurt them.

And, good Lord, he was so handsome, so good with her sons it made her ache.

Did she love him? She was incredibly attracted to him, but did she feel more? Did she even know the man, the real Sam Peterson?

Why all the questions? When had she become such a dithering idiot?

She'd become a dithering idiot when she realized how close she was to making a decision based on little more than chemistry, exactly as she had with Grant.

❦

An hour after everyone left, Sam put down his book and finished his beer, the only one he'd drunk that evening. The general still hadn't come home. Should he wait up for him? It was after ten. Pretty sure the general could take care of himself and that Winnie Jenkins wouldn't lead him astray, Sam headed back to his bedroom.

After washing up and getting in bed, he stared at the ceiling. For one of the few times in months, his thoughts didn't focus on war and bombs and Morty. No, instead he thought about his future. Did he want to teach? Did he really want to go back to school to pick up the necessary hours?

And why in the world did this bug him at *this* moment? Why should he consider change, any change, now? Wasn't getting used to the loss of his leg and the addition of the prosthesis and putting up with the general and being shot down by Willow enough stress for now? He picked up his book and immersed himself in a fantasy world of science fiction until he turned off the light at nearly midnight.

And the general still wasn't home.

Chapter Seventeen

Rockets exploded around Sam Peterson. The screams of the wounded reverberated through the narrow ravine. Gunfire rained down on them from the surrounding hills. He lifted his M4 to answer the barrage but a second mortar impacted, driving his face into the dirt. A blast of pain punched his leg, burning through flesh and bones and nerve. He reached for his foot. It wasn't there.

Sam knew this wasn't real, but he couldn't wake up. He lay in bed, covered with sweat, his missing leg hurting more than it had when the mortar fire tore it away. If he didn't wake up soon, he'd have to relive touching Morty's body. He hated that part, hated this endlessly repeating horror.

Even as he lay there, putting off the moment he dreaded, he sensed he wasn't alone. He fought his way through the fog of terror and sleep to open his eyes a slit.

"Son, wake up." The general sat on a chair next to the bed. His hand hovered over Sam's left shoulder.

Sam slowly regained consciousness. Probably had the nightmare because of the general's arrival. Change always brought it. He'd hoped he'd never have to experience it again.

In the glow of a night-light, he could see the general's face, drawn and white.

"You've had this dream before," the general stated.

Were there tears in the general's eyes? Of course not. If he'd taught Sam one thing, it was that men didn't cry. Of course, he'd also learned from the general that men didn't show emotion, men followed orders, men were always strong. Men were men, and marines were *real* men.

For a few more minutes, the general sat of the edge of the bed. Once he reached out to touch Sam on the shoulder but pulled his hand back. With that, Sam remembered another rule: Men didn't show sympathy.

Most of his life, Sam had believed that.

He struggled to think of something to say to the man who didn't look like the general, but they'd never talked. Why start now?

"Go to sleep. I'll stay," the general said. He pulled the chair from the corner and settled into it. "I'll be right here."

Sam quit struggling for words. Within seconds, peace enveloped him, almost as if the general's presence protected him. At least for now, Sam didn't have to worry about reliving that nightmare. The general was there. He'd wake Sam up again if it came back.

Then he remembered no more.

❧

When he woke up, Sam felt better than he had in months. Rested. Sunlight filtered through the blinds and shone in his eyes. The aroma of bacon coming from the kitchen had wakened him.

He hadn't had bacon for months, not since he left the hospital where it had been slimy and limp. He didn't even bother with the prosthesis, just grabbed his robe and crutches and hobbled toward the scent.

The general stood in front of the stove in a camo T-shirt and matching shorts. Around his waist, he'd tied a towel, an incongruously pink one Aunt Effie had left behind. "Hungry? Sit down, son." He waved toward the table. "Breakfast's almost ready. Do you still like your eggs sunny-side up and runny?"

"Yes, sir."

When silence fell, broken only by the sounds of cooking, Sam said, "Where'd you get the bacon?" He hated the heavy stillness that pressed down and nearly suffocated him around the general and had to punch holes in it with words, even if just a stupid question. "I don't think I have any."

"Son, all you had was a couple of six-packs of some Texas beer, half a loaf of moldy bread, peanut butter, and the leftovers from last night." He dumped the eggs on a plate and added the bacon. "Winnie—Miss Jenkins—and I went to Marble Falls last night after I was chased out."

Sam noticed a grin, barely perceptible to anyone but him. He'd trained himself to read the general's few facial clues

"Don't think we chased you out. Looked like you didn't mind all that much. Where'd you go?"

"Went to a movie, then decided to give you and Willow a little more time together and went to the H-E-B to stock up on food." He placed the plate on the table, poured two cups of coffee, put one in front of Sam, and sat down. "Eat."

Sam leaned against the table and swung into the chair. "Did you have fun on your date?"

The general drank from his cup, then smiled—really

smiled, not just a barely detectable curve of the lips. "Yes. And you?"

"It wasn't really a date."

"Winnie tells me she and the Widows want to get you and Willow together. How do you feel about that?" the general asked.

Sam took a bite of toast, not about ready to have a heart-to-heart about his feelings with the man.

"She seems like a lovely woman, but she's got those two boys." The general shook his head as if in regret.

Even knowing the man was playing him to get a reaction, Sam had to respond. "Great kids, sir."

"So you like them?"

"Great kids." He dug into his breakfast, aware that the general kept an eye on him. "Sir."

After nearly a minute of playing who'll-break-the-silence-first, the general said, "Wonder if you'd try calling me something other than 'sir' or 'General.'"

Sam's gaze jumped to the general's face. "Like what?"

"Like 'Dad'?"

Why would he ask that after all these years?

"I don't know if I could do that, sir."

"I really messed up, didn't I, son?" The general shook his head, but his expression wasn't the stony, disappointed one he usually turned on Sam. He looked sad and watched his son with such desperate longing and sorrow that Sam had no idea what to say or do.

Because he didn't want to respond, Sam took a bite of the crispy bacon and chewed. He wasn't ready to call the man "Dad," but it sure seemed like he'd hurt the old man's feelings. He'd never believed he could do that.

Was the old man getting soft?

Sometimes together, sometimes separately, Adam or Miss Birdie carried Missy to see her mother every day. Several of those days, Mrs. Smith had awakened when she heard Missy's voice but then fell back asleep without saying a word. The doctor said she was out of the coma but slept deeply as her body struggled to regain and build strength. The nurse said her vital signs always improved after the visits from her daughter.

As they drove to Austin, Adam glanced back to see Missy asleep in her car seat, then he looked at Miss Birdie.

"You look tired," he said before he considered the consequences of pointing that out. She must have been really exhausted because she didn't turn the killer glare on him.

"I am, Pastor." She sighed. "I love that little girl, but I didn't think Missy'd be here this long. Three weeks." She sighed again, which made him realize the toll this had taken on her.

"I didn't, either. I'm sorry so much has fallen on you." He turned off the highway and headed south on the Mopac.

"No, no, it was my idea. And everyone has helped. Jesse and Barb had Missy spend the weekend with them. She rode a pony and fed the ducks, had a great time. She likes to play with Ouida's girls. Even Willow and her sons have entertained Missy several Sunday afternoons."

"Good. I'm glad they've pitched in."

"She still cries at night."

"Which means you don't get much sleep."

Miss Birdie rushed on, ignoring his effort to sympathize. "She asks about her mother over and over. Pastor, it's heartbreaking. I try to answer her questions and comfort her, but I'm not the most comforting person in the world."

"Miss Birdie, you took her in when she had no place to go. You have been wonderful. You gave her a home, you hold her and care for her." He pulled onto the ramp leading to the hospital. "You allowed her to stay in one place, safe."

"You've helped, too. Thank you for picking her up from day care."

Feeling good after those unexpected words of appreciation, Adam pulled into a parking space and turned off the engine. Missy awoke, and he carried her into the hospital.

When they arrived in Mrs. Smith's hospital room, she was sitting up in bed. Most of the tubes and wires were gone and a tray with bowls of Jell-O and broth sat in front of her.

"Mama," Missy shouted as she ran toward her mother.

"Be careful," Miss Birdie said. "She's still not well. Just hold her hand."

"Hello, darling," Mrs. Smith croaked. She cleared her throat and looked up at Miss Birdie and Adam.

He introduced himself and the pillar and told her they'd been taking care of Missy.

"I remember your voices," she said. "Thank you."

"Your husband, Missy's father. Can you tell me where he is?" Adam asked.

"We've been divorced for years. I have no idea where he is." She patted Missy's hand. "We're pretty much alone here. I have family in Virginia. My mother has gone to Richmond to take care of my sister and her new baby."

Explained why no one could locate her.

"Do you want us to notify them?"

"No, thank you. I called my sister an hour ago. My mother's coming as soon as she can book a flight. But I worry about her. Mom has heart and health problems of her own. I can't dump mine on her."

"Can you remember what happened?" Adam asked. "How you and Missy got separated?"

"I'm not exactly sure. Missy and I took the bus to Butternut Creek for the craft show. That's all I remember. They tell me I was struck by a car—hit-and-run. I guess no one realized I had a child with me."

"They couldn't tell us your injuries," Adam said. "Privacy issues."

"Broken ribs, which punctured my lungs, broken leg plus a concussion. They're keeping an eye on my heart, but I don't know why or how long I'll be here." She waved toward Adam and Miss Birdie. "Thank you for taking care of Missy."

She smiled as she listened to her daughter chatter about day care and Miss Birdie and the cat and life in Butternut Creek, but after a few minutes she looked so tired Adam knew it was time to go.

"Here's my card." The minister placed it on the bedside table. "Call me for any reason. Would you like a prayer?"

Mrs. Smith nodded but was asleep before he said "Amen."

"Mommy's better now," Missy said on the drive back.

"Yes, she is, but she's not well enough to come home yet," Miss Birdie said. "Maybe in a few days."

Home to where? The house in San Saba without anyone to help? The care of Missy and an injured woman could wear Mrs. Smith's mother out. Maybe home health care could send a nurse out, but how long would it take to set up additional help? Could she get physical therapy there?

Maybe a nursing facility in the interim. There were several good ones in the area, but, again, what about Missy? If necessary, Miss Birdie would volunteer to continue caring for the child, but she looked worn out. Where else could Missy stay, and where could her mother recuperate without draining her own mother?

He'd think about that. A sketchy plan had formed, which he'd have to explore.

❧

Friday afternoon in the PT department of the hospital, Sam was acutely aware of the interest with which the general watched him go through his exercises with Mike, lifting weights to build up muscles lost during the long recovery.

For several repetitions, he pretended to jerk, to have trouble with the weights. Stupid, he knew, because this was easy stuff, but he had a lot he still needed to punish the general for, years of resentment.

That anger seemed weaker and more juvenile now than it had when it had kept him alive after the amputation. Back then, he wanted to wave the handicap in front of the general, flaunt it, make him suffer for all the man had done to Sam, the screwed-up thinking that had ended in his nearly bleeding out next to his best friend. His dead best friend who wanted to do whatever Sam did—and Sam had wanted to be exactly like the general.

They'd entered the marines together, he and Morty, to serve and honor. Morty hadn't come back and he'd come back without a leg. He needed revenge for those losses, but it didn't feel as good as he'd believed, as he'd hoped.

Not that he'd allow second thoughts to stop him. Could be the longer he made the general feel bad, the sooner Sam would feel better.

But he couldn't forget the tears on the general's face the other night and his words the next morning. They might not have been tears. Could have been a reflection. And the words? The general had to know how he'd warped his only son's beliefs and sent him off to war. How could he possibly expect Sam to call him "Dad"?

Now that he had something to fight the general with, he wasn't about to let go of it until the man suffered. One night of the general's regret did not make up for an entire childhood of neglect. Besides, people didn't change, not at his father's age. He'd go back to normal after the novelty of seeing his son with just one leg wore off, and Sam wasn't about to be made a fool of when he did. With that, he added more weight and struggled to lift it.

"Hey, that's enough, big guy," Willow said.

He turned to see her leaning against the wall only a few feet from him.

"What are you trying to prove?" she asked.

Couldn't tell her. His plan was neither sane nor admirable, but it kept him going.

The sight of her—so patient, so gorgeous, so tenacious—calmed him.

"Showing off?" she asked. "Save that for someone who'll appreciate it, Captain."

Those words were an ego buster.

"Not, of course, that all the women in the department don't enjoy the sight of your terrific shoulders and abs, but we're attempting to hold ourselves back."

The general laughed. Sam felt like an idiot.

"We want you to work on building up the muscles in your thighs, too, but first"—she nodded Christine, the PT assistant, away—"I need to talk to you."

When she settled on the bench only two feet from him, he could smell that vaguely citrus fragrance he thought of as Willow's. He took a deep breath. As Aunt Effie would've said, he was smitten.

Then he remembered the general and glanced at him. The

general looked back and forth between his son and Willow and nearly grinned. He appeared pleased, at least as much as the general indulged in such shallow emotions.

"General Peterson, why don't you come over here? Next to us?" Willow hesitated before she looked at Sam. "Do you mind if your father listens in?"

What could he say without sounding petty? Oh, he didn't mind *acting* petty, but preferred to behave like a better man around Willow.

"Whatever you think is best."

The general stood—straight and tall, the only way the man knew how to stand—and marched over to them.

She lifted Sam's leg, rested it on the bench, and gently turned it. "The prosthesis fits well. No bruising, no rubbing." She placed his foot on the floor. "How does it feel?"

"Fine."

The general patted Sam on the back, sort of like he was saying, *Good boy.*

Sam felt like a puppy.

Then Willow proceeded to study his thigh, pushing and prodding with a cool, professional demeanor. Finally satisfied, she said, "I'm releasing you from three-times-a-week physical therapy, Captain."

Stunned, Sam sat silently, mouth open. Would he see her again? He didn't believe they'd built enough together to cause her to stop by his house on her own. Maybe if he kidnapped her sons, she'd come over to ransom them.

Before he could say anything, she added, "But that doesn't mean you're free of this place." She lifted her arm and waved it inclusively around the area. "I have several new patients arriving next week for initial evaluation, so I'm turning you over to Mike and Christine and reducing your appointments to one every two weeks. We still need to keep an eye on your progress and add a few exercises as you build your strength." She glared at him. "I expect you to keep up the regimen at home."

"Oh, he will," the general stated.

Sam attempted a grin because he knew this should sound like good news. It probably would have been if he hadn't hoped to, somehow, make Willow fall in love with him right here, next to the physical therapy table.

The general patted him again.

"I've printed out your exercises." She held out a folder. "We'll send some weights home with you. All the instructions are in there."

"Great," he muttered.

"Mike and Christine'll take great care of you."

"Oh, sure." He drummed his fingers on the surface of the bench. "But what about you and me?" Sam asked, then slammed his lips shut as he remembered where they were and who was watching. "I mean, you're no longer my therapist," he added with a pathetic wink, as if he expected that to convey his meaning and interest in the new relationship. Yes, really pitiful.

"That's correct." She stood.

"Thank you." The general took her hand and shook it. "I appreciate all you've done for my son. Maybe you'd like to join us for dinner."

"Sir, I can ask her out on my own."

"Of course you can." He glanced at his son before turning the charm on Willow. "What I'm planning is a celebration of a milestone in Sam's recovery. You and your boys," the general continued. "And Sam and a lady friend of mine, Winnie Jenkins."

"Thank you for asking, but…," she began.

"Your boys love Sam. Maybe we could go to a movie they'd

enjoy." The general took her hand again and poured on the charm. "We'll have a great time together."

"Dad," Sam muttered, surprised that, because he'd slipped into his teenage years, he'd also slipped back into using that word.

When the general turned toward him with a grin—when had the man started grinning all the time?—Sam added, "Stop interfering." Then he turned to Willow, knowing what her response would be but hoping not. "Would you join us?"

"I can't, Captain." She grimaced. "You know why. I'm not ready. You're not ready."

"How ready do you have to be to go to a movie with my family?" the general argued.

"Dad." There, Sam said it again. Let that distract the old man. "She said no. Respect that."

"It's very nice of you, General." Willow held her hand out to shake his. "Thank you for the invitation, but no."

"Pick you up at six?" The general held on to her hand.

"No, but thank you again," Willow said.

"I'm not giving up." The general winked. Sam felt sure his father's wink was one of the signs of the apocalypse. On top of that, Willow must think they were the winkingest family in the state.

Then the thought hit him. As the general held Willow's hand and smiled at her and invited her to dinner with the family, Sam knew why. He realized what had happened.

The general had become one of the Widows.

Sam was doomed.

He sneaked a glance at Willow as she walked away and realized being doomed didn't sound bad at all. If he couldn't pull this off on his own—and he hadn't been notably successful—he shouldn't turn down help from anyone.

Chapter Eighteen

Hector tossed Adam the basketball. With a fake to the right, Adam drove toward the basket, leaped, and slammed the ball down for the last play in a close victory.

"Hey, Pops," shouted one of his teammates. "You've got hop."

Adam grinned. He had hop. What a great compliment.

"Pretty good for an old guy," Hector said.

Pops shook his head. He'd gone from a baller with hop to an old guy.

As the players began to pack up their belongings, Adam grabbed the ball and shrugged into his sweatshirt. The temperature in September fell once the sun disappeared.

"Hey, Pops." Hector ambled toward him. "Can we talk?"

"Sure. What's happening?"

The two never talked much, other than basketball. Adam knew Hector had a younger sister and life wasn't easy for them. He'd kept the door closed tightly on his life off the court, and Adam hadn't pried.

"It's about my sister...I wonder if..." He searched for

words. "I wouldn't ask if I could handle the situation myself, but I can't." He swallowed. "I've tried."

"Go ahead."

"Umm...my mother died five years ago and my dad...he isn't much of a father. He aims to be, but..." Hector shrugged.

Adam didn't say anything, afraid he'd cut off the words.

"He's an addict. Lost his job about a year ago. Got arrested two weeks ago. Possession with intent. Can't make bail."

Adam had read that in the "Arrests" column of the weekly newspaper. He hadn't been sure that Harold Firestone was Hector's father. He should have asked. His excuse? That hadn't been their relationship. Wrong decision for a minister— and yet it was because he was a minister that Adam had been careful not to push Hector away by intruding in his life.

"We don't have money to pay the rent next month. Do you know anyplace we could get assistance with some bills or a place we could live? Not for me." He pointed his thumb toward himself. "I can get along on my own, but I need a safe place for my sister."

Adam studied the kid who attempted to look cool and manly, to show no emotion, but he could see how tightly he clenched his jaw and looked away.

"You don't have money to pay the rent for October? Why didn't you talk to me about this?" Why hadn't Adam approached him? "Why didn't you ask earlier?"

Hector shrugged. "Not your problem, Pops."

"I'm a minister. I'm supposed to help people."

He bristled. "Don't need charity, Pops. Not for myself." He glared. "But I need help for Janey."

"Where are you living now?"

"We still have the apartment for a while."

Adam didn't push about how much longer they could live

there, especially without an adult. The whole situation seemed hard enough for Hector to bring up. The last thing Adam wanted was for him to pull away.

"How old is your sister?"

"She's eight." He glared at Adam. "I can take care of her in a lot of ways, just not this one." He shook his head. "She needs a place to sleep until I get things back together."

"You can't quit school."

Adam hadn't thought Hector could look more menacing, but his expression hardened.

"Don't lecture me, Pops."

"What about family? Can they pitch in?"

"After Mom died, we lost touch with her side. My father's family—I don't want Janey near any of them."

"Teachers or coaches?"

Hector stood. "If you don't want to help..."

Adam held up his hand. "I need to know the facts, Hector. That's it. Sit down and talk to me."

Slowly, he did.

"Why did you come to me?"

Hector took a deep breath and looked straight ahead. "It's not easy for me to talk about problems, but I need to, for my little sister." He turned to study Adam. "I trust you, Pops. You've always been straight, never cheated in basketball, and I like that. Yeah, I trust you and you've got that church with lots of people that might could help."

Adam nodded. "Okay, I'll check, see what I can find for Janey, but you stay in school, for now. All right? Until we—you and I—work this out. Then we can decide."

"Then *I'll* decide."

Adam watched as Hector turned and loped away. What in the world would he come up with? Not one seminary class had either covered the problem Hector faced or suggested a solution.

But that idea about the parsonage kept niggling at the back of his mind, a solution to two problems. That big old house with all those rooms and one man banging around in it, and those two bedrooms on the second floor with a bathroom between them and the double parlors on the first floor that stood empty except for the dining room furniture.

Adam's concern wasn't only Janey. He had to get Hector a place to stay as well, to make sure he got to school and had what he needed.

But what did that entail? Were there permits? Insurance? Should Adam look into being licensed as a foster parent? No doubt about it, he needed help.

❧

Saturday morning during football season wasn't a good time to meet, and this morning was worse than most. The football game Friday night had gone into triple overtime and the Lions had lost. Still, he had to call the Widows together for an emergency session.

He gazed around the circle: the pillar, Mercedes, and Winnie. "You may wonder why I've asked you to come," he began. Bad opening. Those stilted words showed a pretentiousness he disliked. Also, he could see that Miss Birdie's feathers had been ruffled, so to speak, by his tone or hint of condescension. "I have a problem. I'm asking you ladies to help with..." He stopped and considered his words. "To come up with a solution."

Feathers nicely arranged and unruffled after his retreat, the pillar nodded. Taking their cue from her, the other two Widows agreed.

First, he talked about Missy and her mother; then he explained Hector's situation. "If Mrs. Smith goes back to San Saba, she might not get the care she needs. I don't know about that for certain, but I do know taking care of Missy and Deanne would be hard on Deanne's mother, who's in poor health herself."

"I do worry about that," Miss Birdie said.

"With Hector and Janey," Adam continued, "there's no one, no family to watch over them."

All three women nodded in sympathy. Then he laid out the plan to have them all move into the parsonage. Looks of horror crossed the faces of the two original members of the group, but the provisional member smiled.

"How many people is that, Preacher?" Mercedes asked in a steady but unenthusiastic voice.

"Five." He counted them on his fingers. "Missy, her mother and grandmother, Hector, and Janey."

"I think that's a wonderful idea." Winnie looked toward the others and interpreted their glares. "Why not?" she asked, her voice filled with conviction.

"The parsonage is a home." The pillar nodded, only once but with so much emphasis Adam feared for the muscles of her neck. "For the preacher."

"And for his family," Mercedes added with a matching nod with even more conviction.

"Not," said Miss Birdie, emphasizing each word with a waggle of her index finger. "*Not* a boardinghouse."

"*Not* a bed-and-breakfast," Mercedes agreed.

With that, the two original Widows sat back, folded their arms, and glared at Adam.

"I like the idea," Winnie said. The other two turned toward her and glowered. Bless her, Winnie didn't back down. She looked back at them and nodded, then turned toward the minister. "I like the idea," she repeated. "It's what Christians do, provide for others in need."

Adam studied all three Widows for a few seconds, remembering the points he'd considered last night and this morning. At that time, he'd had them firmly in mind, but he should've written them on index cards. At the time, he'd forgotten how a glare from Miss Birdie could paralyze his thought process.

"The parsonage is for the minister and his family," the pillar stated.

"I'm not married," he said. "No family. You know that."

"Of course we do, Pastor." Mercedes's voice dripped with compassion. "We're doing our best to take care of that situation."

"Although you've done nothing to help us," the pillar added.

Inside Adam smiled. Yes, bless their hearts, they were. Despite the embarrassment it caused everyone involved, they wanted to find him a soul mate in a town not blessed with a surfeit of single women. If they couldn't find a soul mate for him, they'd settle for a woman he could live with in harmony, if not with passion, for fifty years; together, they'd raise a big family.

"Although I do appreciate your efforts"—Adam chose his words carefully—"I am *still* a bachelor. Even if I were somehow to stumble upon a charming young woman..."

Their expressions showed such obvious doubt this would happen that he forgot where his line of reasoning was heading.

Finally, nearly ten seconds into the silence, Winnie prompted, "Even if you did find a young woman yourself..."

"Even if I found a young woman to marry, it would take me a few months to court her..."

"Not if you got busy," Miss Birdie stated.

He ignored the words and pressed on. "It would take me a few months to court her…"

The three nodded, as if encouraging him—whether to finish his sentence or start courting, he didn't know.

"Then let's say an engagement period of six months or a year," he said.

"Six months," the pillar said as if this had been a multiple-choice quiz. "Plenty of time. You need to get the process moving. No namby-pambying."

"I don't think that's the word you want," Mercedes interrupted. "*Dilly-dallying* is what you're looking for."

"Or *shilly-shallying*," Winnie suggested.

"I don't care." The pillar glared at the two other Widows, then turned back to the minister.

"After the wedding," Adam said before any of the Widows could take a breath. "We'd need some time to get used to marriage…"

"Three months," Winnie recommended.

"You're not getting any younger," Mercedes said gently.

"I wouldn't even be close to thirty by that time," Adam objected. They didn't notice.

"As I add all those numbers up, there won't be a baby in the nursery until—best-case scenario—two years from now," Winnie said. "Only one baby, and that's only if the preacher moves fast. And at that rate"—Winnie showed the math abilities she'd used to run the asphalt company—"it would be four or five more years before that parsonage would be filled with children, assuming they popped out every year or two."

The prospect of his imaginary wife popping out children at that rate rendered Adam speechless. Even more stunning was their discussion of their imaginary sex life. Solely for the purpose of procreation, of course. He felt an incredible constriction in his chest as these three discussed the begetting process as calmly as they figured the proceeds from the spring bazaar.

"All of which means there's no reason to keep those rooms unused now," Winnie concluded. "It will be years before a family fills them. Even"—she turned to face Adam—"if you get busy this year. Right?"

Mercedes and the pillar watched the new Widow, their expressions softening little by little until they turned toward the minister.

He was so dumbfounded by what they might be thinking or what they might say next, his throat closed up.

"Guess she's right," the pillar mumbled.

"This would be a Christian way to use the space," Mercedes said.

Winnie asked, "How well do you know this Hector? Is he an honest young man? Does he attend church?"

"We play basketball together."

"Oh, yes. Basketball," the pillar said. "Odd activity for a minister."

"I've always heard Hector's a nice young man. Honest and hardworking," Mercedes said.

"Mercedes knows everyone," Miss Birdie told Winnie before she said to Adam, "From what my contacts in San Saba say, Mrs. Smith is a good, honest woman."

"Would they pay rent?" Mercedes tilted her head to consider that.

"I wouldn't think so," Winnie stated. "That would probably change our tax-free status."

"And we do want to help a young man and his sister in trouble," Mercedes added firmly. "Perhaps we could hire him to do some jobs, so he'd have some spending money."

Stepping back into the discussion, Adam asked, "What do we have to do to make this happen?"

Winnie pulled out her notepad and flipped it open. Pen in hand, she said, "I'll check about the insurance."

The Widows took over. Within fifteen minutes, they had considered all the tasks and assigned who would be in charge. Within a week, they'd have beds and curtains and other furnishings donated and the necessary paperwork taken care of. His only job was to call the plumber to check the leak he'd noted in that Jack-and-Jill bathroom.

❦

That evening, when Miss Birdie and Adam took Missy to see her mother, Mrs. Smith was again sitting up. Her face had lost the gray cast and her eyes held a hint of sparkle. Next to her sat an older but frailer version of Deanne.

"Grandma," Missy shouted and ran to the woman.

"This is my mother, Eleanor Peppers," Deanne said. "If you couldn't guess that."

He watched Mrs. Peppers cuddle Missy, then glanced over at Miss Birdie, who smiled broadly.

"We weren't expecting you for a few days," Adam said.

"My other daughter and the baby are doing fine, and I was so worried about Deanne and Missy that I jumped on an earlier plane." She turned to smile at her daughter. "She's doing well."

Yes, she was, but even with as much improvement as she showed, Deanne had a lot of recuperating ahead.

"I've been walking in the hallway to build up strength, but I'm still weak," Deanne said. "They say I may be able to go home soon, after a little more PT."

"Perhaps to a nursing facility," Mrs. Peppers said. "We don't know what's available in San Saba or what her insurance will cover."

"Where are you staying, Mrs. Peppers? Do you have a car?"

"I flew in this morning and grabbed a cab here. I'll be staying at the hotel next door." She glanced at her granddaughter. "I'll keep Missy with me at least overnight." Eleanor rubbed her granddaughter's back. "We'll go shopping this afternoon and to the park. We have a conference with Deanne's doctor tomorrow to work out a time line."

"If you need us to pitch in," Miss Birdie said, "let us know."

Deanne held out her hand and took Miss Birdie's. "Thank you so much. I'll never be able to repay you for your kindness."

After a few more minutes, Miss Birdie and Adam walked out. Odd to have only the two of them.

"I'm going to miss her," the pillar said. "But I'm so glad she has family." She sighed. "I'm even happier that I can get a good night's sleep."

After they got in the car, Miss Birdie said, "I was thinking about that parlor next to the front door. Maybe if we put a couple of beds there for Eleanor and her family. They can use the guest bathroom down there. You know, that's what a church does."

Then she fell asleep, her head against the headrest, soft snores escaping her mouth. Adam wouldn't mention that to her later, of course. He didn't dare. He'd never tease a snoring pillar.

❦

Wednesday morning, Adam checked his calendar. Winnie, the church treasurer, wanted to meet about the stewardship drive, and Howard had left a message about the next board meeting.

As he considered those appointments, the phone rang. He fought the urge to answer, because Maggie worked until eleven. As she'd often reminded him, *she* answered the phone when she was in the office.

After a few seconds, she knocked on the study door and came in.

A problem with her answering the phone was that the church had no intercom. Maggie had to come into the study to give him messages or tell him to pick up. Sometimes she just shouted. However, that was the way she wanted to do this, so Adam accepted.

"That was Rita Mae Parsons. She said Charley hasn't returned her calls."

Charley was the town handyman, a plumber and a good one. When business was slow, he did about anything anyone needed done.

"I let him in the parsonage about eight thirty and showed him the leak in that upstairs bathroom."

"Well, you know how Rita Mae worries," Maggie said.

She should. Charley was a good Presbyterian and the father of three small children. An enormous, woolly mammoth of a man, he stood six-three and weighed well over three hundred pounds. Everyone in town loved him and feared he'd have a heart attack before he was forty.

"His truck's in front of your house."

"Still? He got there two hours ago."

"Yes and Rita Mae wonders if you'd go over and check on him."

"Sure." Adam stood and headed off toward the parsonage.

Once inside the front door, he wandered through the first story, searching for a body. None there. He couldn't have missed Charley's body lying on the floor.

He called, "Charley?" No answer but he thought he heard a soft pounding from above. Adam moved toward the stairs, still looking around as if Charley could hide under the few furnishings gracing the house. As he climbed the steps, the pounding grew louder.

"Charley?" he shouted.

The sound increased and Adam heard a muffled "Help." He ran into the guest bedroom, through it, and to the bathroom. Charley's enormous denim-covered butt stuck out of the cabinet under the sink.

"I'm stuck," he said.

That much was obvious. Less clear was how to get him out. Adam started to ask, "How did this happen?" but that, too, seemed obvious. The cabinet had a sink on the top and, beneath that, two doors separated by a vertical strip of wood. Charley must have reached in the right side to check the leaking pipe, pulled himself too far in, and now, as far as the preacher could tell, couldn't get out.

"You're not laughing, are you?" Charley shouted, his voice slightly muffled.

"No, Charley." Although it was hard not to, Charley was such a nice guy that he couldn't. "Push," Adam suggested.

"I have been pushing." He gave a deep sigh, which made the cabinet vibrate.

"Okay." Adam studied the situation. "You push and I'll pull." The minister reached for the tool loops on Charley's overalls and attempted to tug him straight back. The plumber didn't move.

"Let's try again," Adam said. "On the count of three." He took a firmer hold of the loops, braced his feet, and counted, "One, two, three." Unfortunately, when he jerked back, the stitching didn't hold. The loops ripped off in his fingers and he stumbled backward. After a clumsy attempt to catch himself, Adam landed in the bathtub, his legs straight up. His head had narrowly missed hitting the hard enamel. Wouldn't that be great to have someone find them up there like this? Adam unconscious in the tub and Charley stuck?

By the time he figured out what had happened and got out of the tub, Adam realized Charley was laughing.

"You okay, Preacher?" he shouted between guffaws. The entire cabinet shook with his laughter.

Adam scrutinized Charley's position and that enormous rear end again. "Have you tried pushing against the back of the cabinet to work yourself out?" he asked.

"No, I'm enjoying the peace and quiet so much I decided to stay here the rest of the day and meditate," he said with a sarcasm Adam hadn't heard from him before. Of course, the preacher had never seen him in this...um...position before.

"Yes, Preacher, I've tried pushing myself out twenty different ways," Charley added long-sufferingly. "I'm scratched up and bruised but nothing's worked."

The idea of slathering the plumber with soap to pop him out didn't seem pleasant and probably wouldn't work because Adam couldn't reach the stuck areas. He bet Charley wouldn't cotton to the idea, either.

"Don't try to lather me up with butter," the plumber warned like a veteran of situations like this.

Adam didn't ask for details.

"What do you suggest?" They both paused to think. "Let's try that again, my pulling again and you pushing." This time Adam reached for the utility belt the plumber wore, which was firmly stuck between his body and the sides of the cabinet. It had the advantage that it wouldn't rip off. Probably.

"Okay."

"I'll count to three, then you push." Adam grabbed the belt and said, "One...two...three."

The minister could hear Charley straining inside the cabinet, using his knees—which were on the tile floor—to push against the wood surround as Adam pulled hard. For a moment, he thought they'd done it, that the plumber was free.

Instead, the shaking of the cabinet caused the toilet-paper holder on the side of the cabinet to pop off. It also made the pretty bowl of soaps the ladies had left next to the sink leap into the air. The yellow rose-shaped soaps scattered all over the room as the dish crashed to the floor and broke.

And when Adam's hands slipped off the utility belt, he flew back into the tub, banged his right arm against the spigot, and turned the shower on. For a moment, Adam sat there, a little dazed, attempting to figure out what had happened as cold water rained down on him. By the time he turned off the faucet, he was soaked.

"Pastor, you okay?"

Dripping, he struggled from the tub and surveyed the wreckage. "Fine. A little wet." Carefully Adam picked up the pieces of china on the floor because, the way this was going, he figured one of them would cut off an appendage if he didn't.

"I can't think of anything else to do." The minister studied the situation and shook his head. "Maybe I should call someone."

"No, Pastor, please don't," Charley begged. "I know I need to lose weight, but everyone will laugh if they know I got stuck here. Please keep this quiet."

"Okay," Adam agreed, guessing how mortified the plumber must feel. "But I can't think of anything unless I cut you out of there."

"Yeah, that's what it's going to take."

Adam could tell from the shaking of the vanity that Charley had sighed.

"I've got a saw in my tool kit and I've got a chain saw in the truck," he said.

"Charley, you don't want me using a chain saw anywhere near your body. I'd probably disembowel you or cut off some really important equipment." Adam pulled a small trimming saw from the plumber's toolbox. "Where should I start?" He studied the situation. "I'm not very good with tools."

"Start at the top."

From the empty left side of the cabinet, Adam glanced inside and discovered a good amount of room in there. He probably wouldn't take off Charley's ears. Kneeling, he started sawing. Fortunately, the piece was narrow. Unfortunately, it was made of some kind of wood harder than steel.

"Probably white oak," Charley mused as Adam sawed. "Used a lot in these older houses. You don't see it today on bathroom fixtures. Usually just laminate or veneer surfaces. This piece was made to last forever. Good craftsmanship."

Great. He was ripping up good craftsmanship with this saw. Of course if he didn't, Charley'd be stuck in this guest bath room until he lost enough weight to extract himself. It reminded Adam of a story from Winnie the-Pooh, one of his childhood favorites.

When at last Adam cut through the wood, he put the saw down, pulled on the work gloves he'd found in the toolbox, grabbed the lathe of wood, and pulled. It didn't break, but slowly the piece bent back against the nails that held it in place and came loose in his hands.

With that, Adam moved out of the way and Charley pushed himself from the opening. Once on his feet, the plumber took a deep breath and punched his body, looking for wounds. "I'll probably have a few good bruises," he said before scrutinizing the mangled cabinet. "I'll fix this. I'll use one big door so anyone can easily get in here to make repairs."

"Sounds good," Adam agreed.

Charley leaned down to study the plumbing inside. "The pipe's an easy fix. I need to replace this fitting here." He pointed. "See where that leak's coming from?" Then he looked at Adam. "You're not going to tell anyone, right?" Perspiration and supplication covered his round face.

"This is between a pastor and one of the flock," Adam responded.

"You're not going to tell Reverend Patillo, are you?"

"No, Charley—between you and me. No one else."

"Thanks. I'll call my wife then get right back to this. She worries." He pulled out his cell. "I'm going to tell her it was a bigger job than I thought." He looked at Adam, his eyes and voice filled with sincerity. "And I'll go on a diet tonight, I promise."

Chapter Nineteen

We're making cookies, Captain," Leo said.

"For Mr. Masterson," Nick added.

Sam gazed around the kitchen. He hadn't been gone for an hour, only enough time for a short walk and a visit to the library to pick up a couple of paperbacks. What did he find when he got home? The general sitting at the table while Winnie and Leo added ingredients to a bowl and Nick greased a cookie sheet.

Not being much of a cook, Sam knew he didn't have a single cookie sheet in the house. He didn't have a bowl or measuring cups or flour. He possessed nothing to use in baking because he and the boys had packed it up and Willow had taken it to the thrift shop. What he *did* have was a mess in his kitchen and two interfering busybodies—the general and Miss Winnie—who didn't know the difference between meddling and helping.

But he also had Leo and Nick there. That was good. That felt right. "Hey, guys, how are you?" Then he realized what Nick and Leo had said. "Cookies? For Mr. Masterson?"

"Yes, sir." Nick waved a napkin covered with shortening. "Your father, the general—" His voice filled with awe. "The general," he repeated and seemed to savor the words, "said a marine helps others."

"He said since Mr. Masterson baked that cake for you, we should return the favor," Leo said.

"Gosh, General." Sam infused every syllable with sarcasm. "What a nice thing to do. How are you helping in the effort?"

"I'm sampling."

"He's telling us what to do," Winnie said, but her words contained a spark of humor.

"He's good at that," Sam said. "He can command and *I'll* sample." Sam sat and placed his books on the table. "What kind are you making?"

"Snickerdoodles. Already in the oven." Nick nodded in that direction.

Aah, yes, the aroma of cinnamon filled the kitchen.

"And chocolate chip because the general likes those best." Leo attempted a surreptitious swipe of dough but Winnie spanked his hand.

"They'll be done soon," she warned.

"Then what?" Sam glanced back and forth among the four, certain something else was going on. He bet two of them had planned this and two of them were innocent pawns in the duplicitous scheme. But if so—he glanced around the kitchen— where was Willow?

"Mom's picking us up at five," Leo said.

Aha, the pieces were falling into place.

Leo glanced at the clock.

"The general says we're all—you, the four of us cooks, and Mom—going over to Mr. Masterson's house to give him the cookies."

"*Most* of the cookies, 'cause we want to eat a few, too," Nick said.

Sam glared at the general. "You've got to stop butting in."

The man smiled. Not an answer Sam trusted. Actually, not a response he'd ever seen before except way back when he'd been a little kid, before the general had become *the general*.

"Might as well give up on that," Winnie said. "I think that's how he got to be a general: butting in and ordering people around."

At five fifteen, before Willow even reached the porch, the boys had waylaid her and explained the plan. As they did, she glanced up as if looking for him. Then the boys came back inside for the wrapped cookies and hurried outside as the general grabbed Sam and hustled him out. Not that Sam really minded or protested too much.

"This isn't my idea," Sam said. Somehow—although Sam knew it had been part of the general's plan—he and Willow had ended up together several yards behind the others.

"You're moving well." Willow studied him professionally. "How's the pain?"

"Can't we just talk? I mean about something other than my leg or the pain?"

"Sure." She glanced up at him. "I left the hospital only a few minutes ago. I'm still in physical therapist mode. Let me switch that off." She blinked then smiled up at him. "There, I'm in person mode. What would you like to talk about?"

He had no idea because he'd been so distracted by that smile he'd barely heard what she said. He only knew what he didn't want to discuss: his leg and going to a movie with Winnie and the general and Willow and the boys, just the six of them. Instead he asked, "Would you go to a movie? With me?"

She stopped. "And your father and the boys in Winnie's car?"

He quit walking and stood next to her. "No, only the two of us." He wasn't exactly sure how he'd handle that. He would be able to drive his car, but he hadn't tried yet and he bet a Mustang wouldn't be the best vehicle for him now. Great car for a single man to show off his machismo. Horrible car for an amputee to try to get in and out of.

"I don' t think that's a good idea, Captain."

He held up his hand. "Please call me Sam. You're in person mode now."

"Okay, Sam, but I told you I'm not interested in a relationship and you said you weren't, so why?"

"I don't believe I said exactly that. I think I said I don't know where I'm going or what I'm doing with my life so probably I'm not in a place where I could pursue a relationship."

She shook her head. "No, that's not what you said. I would have remembered that."

He hunched his shoulders and stuck his hands in his pockets. "What's wrong with going to a movie? I don't know if you've noticed, but Winnie and the others are trying to get us together. It's not going to stop. If you think 'making cookies to repay Mr. Masterson's kindness' is the real reason for this outing, you're wrong. We've been set up."

She tilted her head and scrutinized him. "Are you saying we should give in without a fight?"

"I don't know what I'm saying. I want to take you to a movie. Why's that such a big thing? I haven't asked you to marry me or to sleep with me or to have a relationship *of any kind*. It's only a stupid movie."

She blinked but didn't say anything, only stared at him, her mouth slightly open.

Because she hadn't objected yet, he kept going. "I'm tired of staying home with the general. He's not a great deal of fun. And, yes, you attract me. And, yes, I want to kiss you again, but it's only a movie, not a commitment for eternity." He stopped when he realized he'd shouted the last few words. He took a deep breath before glancing ahead. The others had stopped in the middle of the sidewalk about twenty feet ahead of him to watch his tantrum with great interest.

"Oh," she said calmly. "Well, if it's only a stupid movie, fine. I'll get a sitter for tomorrow night. I'll pick you up at six thirty."

"I can…" Well, no, he couldn't drive but he hated that she assumed that.

"Don't get all macho on me." She glared at him. "I have your records. I know you haven't driven yet. Forgive my self-interest, but I prefer to get there and home alive. If we go out again, after you've practiced, you can drive."

He nodded and stayed on the sidewalk as she walked toward her sons. He watched her, thinking that that had gone a lot easier than he'd expected. On top of that, she'd said he could drive the next time they went out. Maybe not exactly those words, but that's how he interpreted them. They would go out again.

Of course, he still had no idea what to expect or what he wanted in the future, but one thing was sure. He felt good being with Willow. Cheerful. Even optimistic, a little, as much as he allowed himself to be.

The shouting had felt good, too. It had opened something inside he'd kept closed up. It had loosened his frustration. Maybe he should yell more often.

He watched Willow and her sons as the whole crowd went up the steps, rang the bell, and handed the box to Mr. Masterson. After a minute of chatting, the do-gooders turned and started back.

"Mr. Masterson really appreciated that." Nick hopped toward Sam. "He said we could come over and make a pie with him sometime."

"He said thank you and didn't even mention the time we were in his backyard," Leo said.

"Yeah, I know how he felt. I remember the time I found two short, redheaded, very noisy marines in *my* backyard."

"Captain." Nick ducked his head and laughed.

"But you like having us around and you *were* glad to see us," Leo said. "Once you got used to us and stopped drinking."

These were great kids. He hated that they knew, that they'd witnessed his worst traits. Maybe if he behaved really well, they'd forget that drinking-too-much part.

Maybe they could even accept him and their mother being together. He bet they'd like that. In fact, he knew they'd be on Sam's side.

Could he get them to influence her? He didn't think that would work. She didn't look ready for more, and she wouldn't like him using her sons to further a romance.

But at least he and Willow were going to that stupid movie together.

❧

"I need you to do two things for me." Sam hated to ask the general for help. Wouldn't have a few years ago.

The general stood by the stove, turning the bacon. With that idiotic pink towel hanging from his belt, he didn't look as imposing and inaccessible as Sam remembered him.

"What do you need, son?"

He'd never called him that, "son," when he'd wanted to

hear it. Not in high school when he'd won letters in football, track, and baseball and had gone to state in the hundred-meter. Not even when he'd gone to A&M on a football scholarship. The general hadn't paid him much notice at all until Sam had gotten his leg blown off, the biggest foul-up of his life.

"I need to practice driving my car. Would you help me?" The request hadn't hurt at all. "I'd thought about getting hand controls," Sam explained as if the general had asked that. "But they told me at Walter Reed I should be able to drive once I got used to this new prosthesis."

"Fine. When?"

"In an hour?"

The general nodded as he put a plate in front of Sam, and the few words of conversation ceased.

As he was shaving after breakfast, Sam considered his reflection. He looked a lot healthier. His face had filled out some, possibly due to the good cooking of the Widows and the big breakfasts the general served.

But his hair took more time to wash and dry than he wanted to spend. It took hours to groom the mess and a fortune on what they called "product" to tame it, but if his long hair didn't bug the general, what fun was that? It looked as if the general had won this fight without even fielding a platoon.

When they arrived at the high school parking lot, the general took out some books he'd stowed in the trunk and placed them on end to mark a course for Sam to maneuver through.

"You're doing fine, son," the general called out as Sam knocked down six books in a row. "Be patient. Give yourself time."

It wasn't that Sam couldn't steer; that was easy. It was controlling the speed that caused him problems. Alternating between the brake and accelerator felt as if he had to pull his foot from thick mud. He didn't have the motion down well, which meant he didn't slow as quickly as he'd like.

"You're getting better." Although he had paled when his son nearly mowed down a post near the entrance, he didn't cringe when Sam barely missed the chain-link fence surrounding the area. Of course the man had faced bombs, mortar, and grenades in battle.

The two near wrecks had taken place only moments after Sam had taken control of the car—or *not* taken control, because the vehicle had taken off on its own. After fifteen minutes of intense effort, Sam seldom headed toward total destruction of the Mustang or the fence or the general, who occasionally had to leap out of the way. Yes, his driving had improved but the pressure on his knee and the stress of attempting to drive perfectly had worn him out. Not that he'd tell his fa... Not that he'd tell the general. He stopped the car, got out, and walked around to settle into the passenger seat.

"We'll come back tomorrow," the general said as he strapped himself in the driver's side.

Sam nodded. "I want to get my hair cut."

Did he detect a grin on the general's face? A quick shimmer of gloating in his eyes? But all the man said was, "Okay, let's get to the barbershop."

"*Not* the barbershop. Aunt Effie used to take me there when I was a kid. They shaved me. Head for the strip mall on the highway east of town. I saw a place there."

They found themselves in a shop with neon pink chairs and curtains that he hadn't thought the general would enter. Now the man sat in the reception area on one of those feminine chairs and leafed through a book on hairstyles as if he planned to dye his hair blue or get a Mohawk.

When the stylist had completed the cut, Sam studied himself in the mirror.

"How do you like it?" the young woman asked, razor in hand.

He nodded. It looked better. He looked better. Nearly human again. Would Willow like it?

Crap. He hadn't done this for her. Maybe for the boys, so they wouldn't get the idea that long hair was masculine. For himself because it was easier, but not for Willow or the general or anyone else.

But the questions remained: Would she like it?

❧

"Nice cut." Willow admired the new Sam after he settled in the passenger seat. He'd been great looking before, but now he looked gorgeous and tough. She could barely drag her eyes away from him to watch the road.

Sam had pulled himself in and settled in the car without, of course, a smidgeon of help from her, thank you. As she pulled away from the curb, she asked, "What's the occasion? The long hair didn't bug your father enough?"

He laughed. "How'd you know?"

"Hey, I have two sons and I've worked with military men for years." She flipped on the blinker to turn onto the highway and toward Marble Falls. "I know 'tude and machismo."

From Sam's relaxed position, she guessed he didn't feel a bit emasculated with her driving. At least, he didn't hold on to the edge of the seat and point out oncoming cars. They talked comfortably about her life with two sons and his with a military father.

Later, during the movie, he did the stretch-and-drop maneuver to drape his arm over her shoulders. She hadn't had a man do that since she was a teenager, but it still worked and he had the maneuver down pat. She even put her head on his shoulder and he nuzzled her a little.

When they left the theater, she had no idea what to do next. She hadn't been the driver on a date before, if this was a date. She decided not to take him to a make-out place, although she remembered a few from her youth. They could go to his house, but the general was probably there with Winnie, which cut down on privacy. The boys would be at her apartment with a sitter, and she wanted to spend more time with Sam. Alone. Talking. Maybe more.

❧

As Mattie and Adam left the theater, he recognized the couple a few yards ahead of them and called, "Hey, Sam, Willow."

Adam was a little—okay, very—surprised to see the two of them. An odd pair, but they looked good together. When the couple stopped walking and waited for them, Adam asked Sam, "You get a haircut? I can tell you didn't go to my barber."

"I learned from your experience." Sam smiled.

"This is Mattie Patillo, minister at the Presbyterian Church." Adam nodded at her. "Mattie, I'd like you to meet Willow Thomas, a member of the Christian Church, and my friend Sam Peterson."

"Pleased to meet you." Mattie grinned.

"So how'd you like to get something to eat? There's a coffee shop just down the highway." Adam pointed. "Easy walk."

After he said that, Adam glanced at Sam. Could he walk that far? His gait looked good and comfortable now, but would it last?

"What do you think?" Willow asked Sam.

"I'm game," he said.

Then Sam took Willow's hand and gazed at her with an emotion Adam hadn't seen in his eyes before. Of course, the two men had only shared a few pizzas and watched some preseason football so he'd have been unlikely to see tenderness in the soldier's expression. Thank goodness.

"Sam's been so good with my sons." Willow turned toward Adam. "You know Leo and Nick are active kids."

The minister nodded, still keeping his eyes on Sam.

"I'm very grateful for all he's done."

To Adam, the words almost sounded as if the trip to Marble Falls were a debt she was repaying with her presence. Evidently Sam read it that way, too, because he kept his eyes on her face and all the tenderness the minister had glimpsed there seconds before drained away, replaced by a blank stare. When Sam looked away for only a second, Willow's expression held longing.

What was going on between these two? Would they be good for each other? Maybe. A current flowed between them even as they attempted to ignore it. What could he do to help?

Oh, good Lord, He sounded like Miss Birdie. Immediately he said, "Come on. Let's go. This place has great pie."

❧

Willow felt more and more nervous the closer the car got to Butternut Creek. Once or twice she glanced at Sam, then back toward the road.

Now that he was no longer her patient, she really wanted to kiss him again, but she had no idea how to put a move on a guy in the car. Her date had always done that. Was Sam as confused as she was? Probably he'd never put a move on the driver, but she didn't doubt he'd figure out how.

Maybe she should pull into a dark area, turn toward him, and let him take over, but that sounded passive and unlike her.

"Please don't let me out under the streetlight in front of my house, because I want to kiss you," he said, his voice seductive as well as holding a note of amusement.

She glanced at him, then quickly turned her head and kept her eyes on the road. Could she tell him she felt the same without the words catching in her throat?

"I want to kiss you, too." Yes, she could say that.

He grinned. "Could you find some place to pull over before we get to my house so my father and the neighbors aren't watching us?"

Life didn't get much better than that. Well, it would when she stopped but for now, that comment and his smile were enough.

"Especially not Mrs. Gohannon who lives across from you. Biggest gossip in town." She kept her eyes on the road and drove along the curving highway toward Butternut Creek. In fact, they were nearly to his house before she pulled off into a neighborhood park, turned off the lights and engine, and turned toward him. As he slid across the seat, she held up her hand.

"Not so fast. I have a question for you. "

He groaned. "You overthink everything."

"That's probably true, but I need to know this. Why are you interested in me? I'm not like the other women I imagine you've dated. I don't flirt. I'm not a bit girlie."

"You're right. You're nothing like the women I'm usually attracted to. Obviously I've been interested in the wrong kind of women."

Why did he have to be so darned charming? She steeled herself to say, "I'm divorced and have two kids and work long hours."

"Exactly the kind of woman I've been looking for."

"What? Why?"

He took her hand. That felt really good. How could only a touch fill her with so much pleasure?

"I have no idea," he said. "I knew you were the one when I first saw you. After I got acquainted with you, I was even more certain."

She considered that for a few seconds. "You're not saying it was love at first sight."

"Probably not. Maybe attraction at first sight or chemistry or a lightning strike, but you are the woman for me. I'm not going away until we can figure this out." He shrugged. "Maybe we can't. Maybe we have too many complications, but I want to try."

He drew his index finger down her cheek and gave her the smile she'd attempted to ignore. As if any woman could.

"You have no idea how beautiful you are, do you?"

How could she resist him?

"Okay." She nodded. "I need to point out that this is a local make out place so just one kiss. I don't want the cops to check on us. That would be embarrassing."

He placed his hand on her shoulder and moved it slowly to her neck.

She took off her seat belt and moved closer to him. "Only a kiss for now."

"But…"

"Hey." She held up her hand. "That's the deal. Take it or leave it." Oh, sure, as if she'd drive off now. "I want us to get to know each other better."

"Kissing is a great way..."

"For now I prefer the old-fashioned way. Conversation."

"You drive a hard bargain."

She grinned and nodded. Then Sam increased the pressure on her shoulder and she slid into his arms, at least as close as she could with the console between them. Since this was to be the only kiss tonight, she hoped it would be good and memorable.

And it was. Oh, Lord, it was.

❦

A few days later, the Widows met at the diner after the lunch rush to discuss the church and duties and who was sick and who needed help.

But they didn't mention Sam and Willow because they'd done everything they could and weren't prepared to admit failure or congratulate themselves for possible success. They'd just allow that relationship to simmer.

"What about the preacher?" Winnie asked. "Who else can we find for him?"

"How 'bout that new CEO at the asphalt company?" Mercedes suggested.

"Her husband died not too long ago. She's not ready."

"I'm fixin' to give up on him," Birdie said. "And you know how much I hate to concede defeat."

"I had hopes for Howard's niece," Mercedes said. "Too bad she was only visiting for a week."

Birdie shook her head. "Left before we could even introduce them."

"Not a spark between Pastor Adam and Reverend Patillo?" Winnie asked.

"None at all. Lost cause." Birdie shook her head. "All

right," she stated. "Let's get down to business. Winnie, take notes." Birdie didn't think of Winnie as the third Widow, not like Mercedes did. In Birdie's mind, Winnie was a provisional Widow. Maybe a Widow-in-waiting but not a full-fledged Widow, not yet. But she did take good notes.

When Winnie nodded, Mercedes, chair of the church elders, said, "Don't forget, there's an elders' meeting Wednesday evening. Will you both be there?"

The other two nodded.

"And we need to call a meeting of all the women of the church about the spring festival," Birdie said.

Before they could really get started—because Butch did make those nice apple coffee cakes for the diner and each had a healthy slice—Birdie's cell rang. After a short conversation, she turned it off and stood, fixing the other women with an unwavering gaze. "Ladies, we are needed."

Mercedes and Winnie leaped to their feet, gathered their purses and totes, and followed Birdie.

The Widows had accepted the mission.

❦

"Heaven help me," Adam murmured as he turned off the phone. In fact, heaven help all of them because the Widows were on the way.

Oh, he knew good and well the women were the best people to get the job done. They'd get the rooms in the parsonage fixed up in no time and do it right. But the whirlwind of the three of them—because Winnie had become an even greater force when triangulated with the other two—could rock the foundation of the house.

This was why Adam had started over to the church as soon as he called them, to get away. After a few steps, he paused beneath the huge oak tree that stood on the edge of the parking lot, midway between the parsonage and the church. He couldn't—could not—abandon the Smiths. Deanne had been discharged and would be arriving within the next hour. He'd called Howard to collect her, her mother, and Missy, and drive them here. No matter what the preacher might tell himself about all the work that awaited him at the church, he couldn't allow the family to walk unsuspectingly into a house filled with Widows.

Adam turned, slowly, and ambled back to the parsonage just as a pickup pulled into the parking lot and Jesse stepped out.

"Got a load of furniture from the thrift shop for you, Pastor." Jesse went to the back of the truck and opened the tailgate. "Give me a hand?"

Within minutes, they had beds set up in the previously unused parlor on the first floor. As they finished, the Widows bustled in with armloads of linens. Within a few more minutes, the parlor had been turned into a bedroom for Missy and her mother and grandmother. After another load arrived from the thrift shop, they put a bed in each of the two empty bedrooms on the second floor. The women made all the beds, tossing a colorful quilt on each.

Finished, Jesse, the Widows and the preacher stood in the hallway and looked into the larger parlor, admiring their work. Wall-to-wall beds, but the family didn't want to be separated.

"We fixed up the upstairs bedrooms," Mercedes said. "Just in case Hector and his sister do need a place to stay. And who knows? Maybe others will need a temporary shelter."

"It's truly a service to the community, Pastor," Winnie added.

Then Miss Birdie made a noise Adam hadn't heard before

and couldn't describe. It suggested possible agreement and maybe a bit of pleasure in the thought.

The pillar looked around the parlor and nodded. "Nicely done." She straightened the quilt a bit. She might have meant the remark as a compliment for her minister, but Adam wasn't sure. It could have meant she admired the pattern of the cover.

"I'll be back in a little bit, Pastor," Winnie said as she hustled out. "Have a few more errands to run."

"I have to get back to work." Miss Birdie took off after Winnie, and Jesse followed.

The departures left Adam alone with Mercedes, with whom he always felt comfortable.

"Preacher," she said. "I talked to my grandniece—she's a social worker for the state—about Hector. She made three suggestions. First, he could petition to be an emancipated minor and he'd be Janey's guardian. Second, she could be placed in foster care with you—or, third, both Firestones could be in foster care with you. If you plan to board youngsters here, you should be licensed as a provider, just to make sure it's all legal." She handed him some papers. "Fill these out and I'll take care of that."

Adam nodded. "Thanks for doing all this."

"You know, Deanne couldn't have taken care of herself in San Saba," Mercedes said. "Even with her mother there, she wouldn't have received the physical therapy and nursing care she needs. Taking care of both of them would have exhausted Mrs. Peppers. We've done a good thing, Preacher. I'm glad you and Winnie talked us into this."

Once she left, Adam put the laptop on the dining room table and started to work. He finished the bulletin and sent it to Maggie, filling the service with Miss Birdie's favorite hymns. She deserved a reward.

By noon, Winnie had returned with Sam's father and a dozen grocery sacks. The two stocked the cabinets and refrigerator with enough food to last if nuclear war broke out.

After they left, Howard pulled into the parking lot and helped Deanne inside. Missy and Eleanor followed her. Pale and tired, Deanne fell asleep as soon as she hit the bed. Missy curled up on the toddler-size bed and slept. Adam tugged the quilt over her as Howard brought in several plastic sacks of what Deanne had accumulated in the hospital.

"I have the key to my daughter's house," Eleanor said. "Howard's going to drive me to San Saba. I'll pick up some clothing and Deanne's car. Be back in a few hours." She glanced at the two sleepers.

"I'll stay here. Don't wear yourself out." As he watched them move down the sidewalk, Adam allowed pleasure to flood him and remembered his favorite verse from Micah: "…what does the Lord require of you but to do justice, and to love kindness and to walk humbly with your God?"

The church was doing the Lord's work, reaching out in kindness. He was blessed to reap the bonus of having company in the huge and previously echoingly lonely parsonage.

❧

Sam glanced at the clock. Seven thirty. In the morning.

How was he supposed to sleep with the general whistling—yes, whistling!—in the kitchen? The man had never whistled, at least not in the span of Sam's memory. Of course, for a lot of that time, the general hadn't been at home. He'd been overseas or transferred so Sam didn't know that the general *never* whistled, but whistling suggested happiness. The general had seldom showed any emotion, much less happiness.

Wondering why in the world he was considering this when

all he wanted to do was fall back to sleep, Sam pulled the pillow over his head. He hadn't noticed this before, but whistling has a particular pitch that is not at all moderated by the placement of a pillow over one's ear.

"What are you doing out there?" he shouted toward the kitchen. "Somebody's trying to sleep in here."

The whistling stopped abruptly, a realization that bothered Sam. The general had finally showed a positive emotion and Sam had told him to shut up. Amazingly, he had. Now Sam felt guilty.

He rolled to the edge of the bed, attached the prosthesis, and pushed himself up. By the time he reached the kitchen and could see the general standing at the stove with that stupid pink towel protecting his camo shorts, Sam regretted his outburst. He'd acted like a grunt.

"Sorry I woke you up, son."

"Sorry, Dad." The word and the apology slipped from his mouth without passing through the censor he usually kept on his statements to the general. Sam hoped maybe he wouldn't notice.

He noticed. His smile reached his eyes. "Oo-rah," he said.

Who says "Oo-rah" at seven thirty in the morning while preparing breakfast?

The general put the eggs and bacon on a plate and set it on the table. "Sit down, son. Have some breakfast."

"You didn't know I'd be up now." Sam scrutinized him. The general was smart, always prepared, but, "This is your breakfast, right?"

"Hey." He held his hand up. "I can always fix more. Why don't you sit down and enjoy?"

Rude to refuse. Besides, the stubborn man wouldn't eat the food after he'd offered it to Sam. It'd be stupid to turn it down.

If he did, no one would eat it. Sam sat, pulled the plate and fork in front of him, and dug in while the general put bread in the toaster and tossed a couple more slices of bacon in the pan.

"Winnie says I should cut down on bacon." The general looked into the skillet longingly before picking up the slices with a spatula and wrapping them back in the package, uncooked.

How serious was this relationship? The general had known her for only a few weeks and was giving up his beloved bacon? Sounded very serious.

"So," Sam said casually. "Are you going out with Miss Jenkins again?"

The general grabbed the toast when it popped up, smeared margarine and jelly on it, and brought it to the table. He placed one slice on Sam's plate, then sat down and tore the other piece in half. After he'd taken several bites, he swallowed and looked at Sam.

"You know how much I loved your mother."

"That's not what I mean."

"I know, I know. Maureen was very special. After she died, I never found another woman I liked to be with, one who was interesting and attractive. I enjoy being with Winnie."

Sam had always suspected the general had mourned his wife's death as much as Sam had grieved for his mother, but he'd never showed it. He'd stood stiff and emotionless at the cemetery during the interment. Sam had done exactly the same, a perfect little image of his father but feeling like a scared little boy inside. Not that he'd ever told the general that.

In fact, much of the problem was that neither of them knew how to share his feelings. He'd believed they still didn't, but the general sure seemed bent on trying.

"I didn't date much, even years after Maureen died. After all, I was trying to bring up a young son…"

"I was ten," Sam corrected.

"Yes, but that seemed really young to me. I had no experience with any kids but recruits." He shook his head. "Son, I apologize for my failures. I had no idea what to do with you."

So you sent me to stay with relatives or to boarding school during the academic year and to Texas or Ohio in the summer, Sam wanted to say, but he held the words back. For years he and the general had argued about the man's lack of interest and what Sam considered to be abandonment, but they'd never discussed emotion. Maybe Sam had grown and changed a little, because he didn't want to cover the same ground again.

Or maybe his tours of duty had made him realize how hard it would be for an officer to raise a child by himself.

"You and my career were my only priorities for years. You don't have any idea how much I regret not getting to see you grow up."

"You never told me." Sam attempted to control his reaction and not sound judgmental.

The general shook his head again. "Really messed up with you, son. Don't ever think I'll forgive myself for that but…" He caught Sam's eyes. "But I'd like to make up for it. I tried to be a good father but had no idea what to do. I treated you like a recruit because I didn't know how else to relate to a kid. It's what my father did."

"Hereditary?" Sam couldn't resist getting that dig in.

"Hope not. Hope you'll treat your sons differently. You've done well with Willow's boys. They respect and love you. Wish I'd done that well."

Hadn't he treated Nick and Leo like marines? Maybe it was a congenital problem. Not that they were his sons.

Sam shrugged. "I don't know. After all, I don't see them every day..." The general hadn't seen him every day, either, but Sam had to let go of that offense for now. "I'm not the one who has to take care of them or build their character. Being their friend is a lot easier."

"Maybe, but, son..." The general paused and seemed to search for words. "Son, please give me another chance. You're my only child. I miss you. I know your mother would've wanted us to get along, to be family."

"Hard for me to guess what a woman who's been dead nearly twenty years wants."

The old man's face hardened as if he were hurt that his son had rejected him. But what was Sam supposed to say? Or do? A lifetime of disappointment and anger, and the walls he'd built to contain it, would not evaporate because the general called him "son" and said "please." Even if Sam wanted to just let it all go, he still felt it, all of it. And he didn't know if he could survive without that core of fury.

"Yeah, sure," he said, pretty sure the general would pick up on the sarcasm. "Maybe we could go fishing sometime. Isn't that what fathers and sons do?"

"I'm not giving up," the general said.

Sam knew he wouldn't. The man never did. Unfortunately the general sounded wistful, an emotion much harder to ignore than his command voice.

"Changing the subject a little." The general stood and poured himself and Sam each a cup of hot coffee. "About Winnie. I think she's an attractive and intelligent woman. I enjoy being with her and see no reason to be alone the rest of my life."

Sam almost spilled his coffee on his lap. "Are you getting married?"

"Don't know."

Sam stared at the general. "You're serious?"

"Sure am."

"But you haven't known her for very long."

"You fell in love with Willow pretty quickly, didn't you?"

"We're not talking about me, sir."

"No, but there are times a man has to take action." The general smiled. "Of course, you have a lot of years ahead of you. I'm sixty-two and had a health scare. It hit me that I'm not going to live forever, and I have to take fast action to get what I want. You never know what's going to happen."

Sam could have died with Morty in Afghanistan. The sentence hung in the air between them as if the general had actually uttered the words.

Sam considered the general's statement as he finished breakfast. Did he want to spend the rest of his life alone because he didn't take action or plan or make decisions? But he didn't want to consider that now. Too intense. Too threatening.

"Were you serious about going fishing?" the general asked.

Stupid for Sam to have said that. He knew the general well enough to know that if he was determined to go fishing, they'd end up in a boat on the lake this afternoon.

When he scrutinized the general, though, Sam realized he'd spoken hesitantly, as if he were afraid of Sam's reaction. He didn't want his father, a respected officer and a proud, courageous man, to fear the reaction of his own son. What could Sam say to convey that?

"You know, there's a vets' group that meets at one of the churches on Wednesday evenings. I'm planning to go next week. Want to join me?" the general asked.

The suggestion shattered the tenuous communication. "Don't try to fix me, sir."

"I'm not, son." The general stopped and blinked. "But maybe when you're ready, we could go together." He glanced at the coffee cup then back up. "I attended a veterans' support group weekly in Ohio. Started..." He stopped and swallowed before continuing. "Started when you got hurt. I couldn't handle it."

Sam couldn't think of a sentence more unlikely to come from the general's mouth. "There's one at the Christian Church. Would you come with me?" he asked again as if Sam hadn't just shot down the request. *Dogged*, that word described the general perfectly.

"Why?" He'd never asked the general "Why" about anything. A strict do-as-I-say man, the general had never allowed it.

"Because I need it. Because I think you might, too."

"I'm not a wimp. I can handle this."

"I know you're not a wimp," the general stated. "But I've learned I can't handle what happens in battle alone. I found out I do a lot better in life when I can talk about what happened with vets who've been through the same thing." He scrutinized Sam's features. "I don't sound like the man you grew up with, do I? When you were wounded in Afghanistan, I felt so guilty I could barely function. Going to the group saved me. I discovered I can't do everything on my own."

Those words dropped inside Sam and burned. He had no idea what to say and, so filled with emotion, wasn't sure he could speak. The idea his father had been devastated by Sam's injury, that the amputation had changed the general's life, was something he'd never guessed and couldn't digest now.

He fell back to his default emotion: anger. "I thought you'd come down here to bully me into rehabbing."

"To bully you," the general repeated. "I'm sorry you expected that."

Who was this man who looked so much like the general but spoke like a concerned and loving father? Sam never could have imagined the words or the soft voice.

"Go ahead and get dressed." The general stood. "I'll clean up. If you want to, we can talk later."

With those words and the ones his father had spoken in the last few minutes, guilt began to eat at Sam. The realization surprised him. Had his feelings defrosted enough for him to regret his actions? To accept the general's concern? Must be all the warm bacon fat melting the cockles—whatever cockles were—of his heart.

There he went with his normal habit of defusing an emotion by making fun of it. Sometimes Sam was full of it. He just didn't know what to do about it. Change? Maybe. But how?

Chapter Twenty

Failure was not an option for Miss Birdie. She never fell short in anything if she could help it. And yet the minister stood there behind the pulpit and preached, looking almost handsome and much more confident than he had before she'd taken him in hand. Preached a pretty fair sermon now. Did good work, the evidence on display right there in the congregation.

Eleanor and Missy sat next to Bree. Mrs. Smith improved every day what with Mike, the PT from the hospital, dropping by every few days for exercises, the visiting nurse helping with medication, and the aide who came by to give Mrs. Smith baths.

Winnie and the general had arrived together and settled in a front pew, an unexpected and serendipitous success for the Widows that she and Mercedes didn't mind crowing about.

But the preacher stood up there alone. He deserved a woman, a wife, a soul mate. If they didn't find him someone, he'd probably go along happily playing basketball three or four times a week, welcoming people who needed a place to stay into the parsonage, going to football games, but never finding love.

Birdie studied the sanctuary. Attendance had grown some. A new couple—white-haired like the rest of the adults—sat on the side aisle. The Kowalski girls came with the preacher and went to children's church. But other than Willow, no single woman sat in the congregation, waiting for Birdie to introduce her to the preacher, waiting to fall in love with him and marry him.

Birdie closed her eyes and prayed for the Lord to get involved because she thought only through holy intervention would a mate be found for the preacher.

☙

"Pops?"

Adam looked up from the bench next to the basketball court where he sat to tie his shoes. Bobby Franklin, one of Hector's teammates on the high school team, stood next to him, silhouetted against the lights.

"What is it, Bobby? Sit down."

"You know about the problems Hector's having with the rent and all?"

Adam nodded.

"Him and his sister are sleeping in the park now."

"What?" He looked up at Hector, dribbling and shooting, then looked around the thick trees surrounding the court. "He and his sister are sleeping here? For how long?"

"She's waiting for him over there." He nodded toward a thin girl in pink overalls huddled on the bench next to the court. "Two nights. This will be the third."

"Why didn't he tell me? I'd have done something."

"He's ashamed. He figures he should be able to take care of the family. He's a man."

"Even men need help sometimes." Adam stood. "Thanks,

Bobby. I'll talk to him." When the young man started to say more, the minister said, "Don't worry. I won't mention you told me anything."

Adam picked up a ball and dribbled toward the basket where Hector practiced. "How's your sister? You guys still okay?"

Hector didn't turn toward him, just kept shooting.

"You want to play horse?" Adam asked. "Loser has to answer a question from the winner." Not subtle but he felt certain Hector wouldn't fill Adam in on his life without cover.

Hector glared at the minister, then nodded.

After a hard-fought game, which Adam won—actually, it was possible Hector threw it—the minister took the ball and held it. "How are you and your sister?" he repeated. "Where are you sleeping?"

"That's two questions."

"Okay, where are you sleeping?"

Hector didn't make eye contact, just jerked his head toward the trees.

"You're sleeping here? Out in the open? Is that good for you? Safe for your sister?"

The kid studied his feet. Finally, he looked at Adam and said, "I don't know what to do. We got evicted even though I had a week left on the lease."

Unbelievable anyone could do that to a couple of kids. "What now?" Adam asked. "What are your plans?"

Hector shrugged.

That was enough. "Go get your stuff. You're coming with me now. I have plenty of room at the parsonage."

He scowled. "We don't need charity."

"It's not charity. We have room. You may not think you need help, but Janey needs a safe place to live."

"Janey can go with you. I'll make my way."

"Buddy, your sister needs you."

"I'll visit her. I'll walk her to school."

When it became obvious that argument wasn't going to work, Adam came up with another one. "I don't know anything about taking care of a little girl." Adam pointed toward Janey. "All those cute little braids and barrettes in your sister's hair? I don't know how to do those."

"Yeah, that takes practice," Hector agreed.

"There are two empty bedrooms on the second floor. Right now, we have another family living in the parsonage, on the ground floor. She's just out of the hospital. I think..."

"You have other people living in that big, ugly house?" Hector interrupted.

The minister nodded.

"Oh." Hector considered that. "Then it would be okay. It wouldn't be like we were charity cases, right? Other people stay there, too."

"That's what churches are for."

"Not always, Pops. Not always." He glanced toward his sister. "I talked to the counselor at school. I want to be a legally emancipated minor and take care of Janey myself."

"Fine."

He examined Adam's expression for a few seconds, as if searching for clues about his feelings, as if Adam might have deeper motives for moving him and his sister into the parsonage. How sad he had to be suspicious, but Adam respected his caution.

"Okay, we'll come. Let me go get our stuff." He turned and took a step.

"I have a couple of rules," Adam said before Hector could move away.

He turned back and glared. "Yeah?" The kid's body stiffened, and his voice held a note of suspicion.

"First, you have to stay in school."

Hector nodded. "Plan to."

"And you have to be home by eleven on school nights. No drinking."

"No problem."

"And I'd like you to come to church on Sunday morning."

Hector's lips tightened.

"I'm not going to force you, don't plan to convert you, but I'd like you there. The parsonage belongs to the church. This would be giving back, thanking the congregation."

Hector nodded. "Okay, sure." He waved toward his sister. "Janey, come here. We're going to have beds tonight."

Adam watched them walk toward their campsite before realizing he should give them a hand. He ran behind the two. When he reached the clearing, Adam heard a low growling and something—a bear? a lion?—rushed toward him and leaped into the air. Before he could move, it landed on Adam's chest and knocked him to the ground. He looked into the face of a creature of some kind. It was enormous with a head the size of a pumpkin. A tongue lolled from its mouth, which made Adam believe the creature was friendly—just very drooly. His face got wetter with each passing second. The rhythmic pounding of the creature's tail against the ground implied the monster liked the minister.

"Chewy, come here," Janey said in a soft, high voice. The animal, who really did look like a Wookiee, pushed himself up and romped toward the girl, wagging its tail.

Adam stood slowly.

"That's Janey's dog Chewy," Hector said. "I didn't tell you about him, afraid you'd change your mind. Janey loves him."

Once on his feet, Adam could see exactly how massive the canine was. With the tawny coat, it resembled a lion, but the plumy tail and the darker patches on the side revealed that this dog had a long and varied ancestry. Afghan hound? Sheepdog of some sort? Perhaps even a little elephant in its genetic makeup?

"I have a fenced-in yard. He'll be fine."

"He won't like being out there all the time. He sleeps with her," Hector said. "She says he makes her feel safe."

This was not the time to debate Chewy's living conditions. Adam had to get these kids to the parsonage and security. "We'll work it out," he said to Janey, whom he could barely see over the huge dog. "Don't worry. But first, let's get you to bed, in a real bed."

Adam picked up a couple of sleeping bags and headed to the parsonage. Behind him, he could hear the dog crashing down the path. He sped up.

❦

Adam dreamed he was with Shadrach, Meshach, and Abed'nego in the fiery furnace. When he woke up, sweat poured down his body. He lay there wondering if the Hill Country had been hit by a heat wave overnight or if someone had, for some reason, turned up the parsonage furnace to one hundred.

As his brain slowly cleared, he realized a huge lump—a hot, breathing lump—lay next to him. Adam sat up. Chewy lifted his head and grinned. He hadn't known a dog could smile, but this one did, pleased to be here in bed next to Adam. Not that the bed belonged to the minister anymore, other than the narrow sliver he occupied. Chewy owned the rest. His tail hit the mattress as if he were a canine Ringo Starr.

How did he get in here? Adam took a few tissues from the box on the night table to wipe his face as he rolled off the bed and stood. The bedroom door was open. He knew he'd closed it; either Chewy could open doors or the catch hadn't held. He guessed the latter. Chewy didn't seem all that smart.

"Pops, breakfast," Hector shouted up the stairs.

Breakfast? Hector had prepared breakfast?

Knowing he'd have to shower later but also mindful that he now lived with five other people, Adam pulled on jeans and a T-shirt before heading quietly down the back stairs to the kitchen. Chewy bounced down behind him, occasionally nudging the back of his legs to hurry him along.

Although the signs of cooking lay all over the counter, no one was in the kitchen. He let Chewy out before searching.

"Pops, we're in here," Hector shouted from the dining room.

Adam had never used the dining room. Actually, with the furniture repositioned to accommodate the downstairs visitors, the table had ended up shoved in the smallest parlor, the one he used as an at-home office.

"Good morning." Deanne still wore her robe, but seeing her up and at the table pleased the minister. Hector sat at the end of the table, looking like the father of the family. Missy sat on a chair atop multiple pillows next to Eleanor.

In a bright pink shirt and overalls, her hair arranged in thirty or forty braids, Janey walked across the cramped space as carefully as if she were on a tightrope, balancing a cup of coffee for Adam.

Besides the necessities—plates, napkins, sugar, and milk—on the table were bowls of oatmeal, glasses of orange juice, and one plate piled high with toast. Hector grinned at Adam's surprise.

"Breakfast is my specialty."

"Great! Good morning." He settled in one of the heavy, formal chairs.

"Morning," Missy said through a mouthful of toast.

Hector pointed at an empty chair. "Sit down, sis, and eat fast. We need to get going."

"Thanks for the coffee, Janey."

She looked at Adam with eyes so big and dark and filled with uncertainty, it almost broke his heart. No child should look that lonely and scared.

"Thanks for breakfast, Hector," Deanne said. "It tastes really good. I love being up for breakfast."

"How are you two going to get to school? Do I need to drive you?" Adam hadn't thought about that before. Hadn't thought of a lot of stuff before he brought the kids home, but they could figure things out as they went.

"I can walk. Janey's school's on the way. I'll take her," Hector said.

"What about lunch?" Deanne asked. "Should I fix sack lunches for you?"

"It's okay." Hector swallowed hard as if he didn't want to say more.

Adam bet they had free lunch and he didn't want to admit it. The minister was glad they did, glad that during the tough times they'd had at least one good meal a day.

"What time do you eat dinner?" Adam shoved the bowl away and took half a piece of toast.

"Practice is over at six thirty, but I'm always ready to eat," Hector said. "Janey'll get home about four and likes a snack."

He turned to the child. "Janey, can you walk home all right?"

She nodded.

"It's only a few blocks," Hector said. "She can probably see the steeple from her school."

"The door's always open," Adam told her. "If I'm not here, come over to the church."

"I'll be here all day," Deanne said.

"I'll get home…" Hector stopped and grinned when he said the word *home*. "I'll be back about seven." He picked up his bowl and began to clear the table.

"Don't worry about that," Deanne said. "I'll take care of cleanup."

Before he left the dining room, Hector said, "You need to get a hoop, Pops. Right on the edge of the parking lot would work."

Hector and Janey grabbed their books and headed off to school. Eleanor washed and dressed Missy to take her to day care while Deanne cleaned up. Shortly after that, Chewy let Adam know he wanted inside, his deep, loud barks echoing through the neighborhood. As Adam let the dog in and started upstairs for a shower, he wondered: What in the world was he doing? He wasn't that much older than Hector, and certainly no wiser, and he had absolutely no experience with kids.

There hadn't seemed to be much of a choice. He'd do his best, try his hardest. Surely he'd do better than a drug-addicted criminal, right?

That afternoon Adam hadn't left himself enough time—not unusual—to visit the nursing homes and still get home to welcome Janey at four. While Deanne slept and her mother read in his television room, Janey sat at the kitchen table, copying words from a book. Still so serious for a child her age, she looked up and nodded before returning to her work.

The next night, Adam carefully closed his door, then tugged on the knob to make sure it was completely shut, that Chewy wouldn't be able to visit him. Satisfied, he turned off the light and got into bed. Before he could pull the sheet over him, he heard the *click, click, click* of dog paws. The sound stopped by his door. Then began what he guessed was the sound of a dog's muzzle hitting the door.

He smiled. Tonight he'd get a good night's sleep.

Of course, he didn't know Chewy well. After several thuds on the door, Adam heard the thud of Chewy's bottom against the floor. Before Adam could close his eyes, the sound of shrill howling filled the air.

Hound. There had to be hound somewhere in Chewy's genetic background, because the baying filled the parsonage.

"Shut up, Chewy," Hector yelled.

Didn't do a bit of good.

If he wanted to sleep, if he wanted the children to sleep, if he hoped Ouida and her family slept, Adam had to do something. He got up, walked to the door, and opened it. A thoroughly delighted Chewy pranced into the room and leaped onto the bed.

By the time Adam got back, Chewy had shoved the quilt into a gigantic lump and settled on it, smiling.

Adam studied the situation. Putting Chewy outside wasn't a solution, but he could prepare a pallet on the floor for the dog. Except he had a pretty good idea who'd end up sleeping there.

A few days later, the phone rang in Adam's study. Maggie had left, so he picked up.

"Pastor Adam," Mercedes said when he answered. "I wonder if you could drop by the diner after lunch, about three thirty. I have a problem I'd like to discuss."

"At the diner?" he asked. "Wouldn't you rather meet at the church?"

"No, n-no," Mercedes stammered.

Why not? As usual with the Widows, he suspected something, something he didn't look forward to. The suspicion scared him. In fact, the tone of Mercedes's voice frightened him. But he couldn't turn her down; the Widows were, after all, members of the church.

"I'd like to meet there because…um…I like their… um…chocolate pie. And raspberry tea. Delicious." She sounded pleased to have come up with not just one but two reasons.

After Adam agreed and hung up, he considered what had just happened. He didn't trust the invitation but couldn't figure out how to get out of it or why it had been tendered. He only knew the reason was much deeper and more devious than chocolate pie and raspberry tea.

Ten minutes later, the phone rang again. "Adam Jordan," he said as he picked up.

"Reverend Jordan, this is Pattie Malone calling from the high school. We have a faculty meeting so I won't be able to meet you this afternoon."

Won't be able to meet? Adam considered the words. Aha. Now he knew why Mercedes had called.

"Ms. Malone, I'm going to ask you some odd questions."

"Oh?" Her voice held a note of confusion and an entire concerto of apprehension.

"I'm assuming Mrs. MacDowell set this meeting up?"

"Yes. I'm Bree's volleyball coach. Her grandmother said you

wanted to meet about Bree's going to a church-related school like Texas Christian, maybe getting a scholarship for athletics because she belongs to a Christian church."

"Great idea," Adam said. "Are you married?"

"What?"

He could tell from her voice she thought he was nuts or scary. Didn't blame her. He did sound crazy, but Ms. Malone would understand if she really knew Miss Birdie. "Coach, I'm a bachelor...," Adam began.

"I can assure you...," she sputtered.

"Let me finish. Mrs. MacDowell wants to introduce me to unmarried women. She believes a minister should be married. I'm sorry she..."

But he couldn't finish because the coach started laughing. When she was done, she said, "My divorce was final only a few days ago. Almost no one knows that. How did she?"

Adam groaned. This was not the time to tell the coach about the Widows and their grapevine, which infiltrated every corner of Butternut Creek. Instead he said, "I'd be happy to meet with you about Bree. Maybe at the high school whenever it's convenient for you. And don't worry about being set up anymore. I'll take care of Mrs. MacDowell."

A promise he wasn't all that sure he could keep, but he'd try. Maybe having a wingman would help.

He called Sam.

"Do you know about the Widows and their reputation as matchmakers?" Adam asked.

"Do I! They've been trying to get Willow and me together since I got into town. Why?"

"I'm meeting them at three thirty at the diner. I don't want to face them alone. Want to join me? I'll pick you up a few minutes before then."

"I'm not convinced I want them to stop working on Willow," Sam said. "But I'll cover your back."

❧

When the two men strode—Sam had much improved his striding technique—into the diner at exactly three thirty, Miss Birdie looked up from the table she was clearing. Her eyes opened wide when she saw both of them, then she searched behind them. Looking for the coach?

For a moment he and Sam stood at the door, hands at their sides, and stared at her. Adam felt like Gary Cooper in *High Noon* but wasn't sure if he was the good guy or the bad. He almost expected Miss Birdie to say, *Draw, you dirty varmints*.

Of course, she didn't.

Instead she demanded, "Sam Peterson, what are you doing here?"

Both men took a few steps inside. In his head, Adam could hear the click of boots across a rough wood floor. In reality, his athletic shoes made almost no sound on the vinyl tile.

"Coach Malone isn't coming," he drawled.

She blinked. "Oh," she said in a voice filled with studied surprise. "Was she coming? Here? Today?"

Had he caught her off guard? If so, not for long.

"I asked you a question, Preacher." She put her hands on her hips and glared. Miss Birdie didn't need a gun. She could disarm dirty varmints by glowering at them.

"The preacher wants to talk to you about something," Sam said as he took a couple of steps backward.

"Lily-livered coward," Adam whispered to his friend, then turned to stare at the Matchmaker, a name that struck terror in his heart.

"Miss Birdie." He stood his ground and cleared his throat.

Refusing to give in to fear, he said more loudly, "Miss Birdie, you have to stop pushing me together with women."

"It's for your own good, Pastor Adam. You're not doing anything to find yourself a wife." She nodded decisively. "Someone's got to step in."

"You don't. And Mercedes and Winnie don't. When"—he paused to underline the word—"when I'm ready to get married, I'll take care of finding the bride myself."

"But...," she started.

His imaginary spurs jingling, Adam took a step forward and looked deeply into her eyes. She stopped talking.

"I appreciate your interest and efforts, but you need to leave me alone." There, he'd said it.

Of course, Miss Birdie didn't accept the ultimatum.

"And when is that going to be?" She took a step toward the minister, keeping her eyes on his, matching him glower for glower.

But he didn't retreat. With another step toward her, Adam lowered his head, glaring at her from under the rim of his nonexistent Stetson. "When I'm ready."

He didn't break eye contact. The Preacher and the Matchmaker stared at each other for what seemed like hours until Sam stepped between them. A dangerous tactic.

"Now, Miss Birdie," Sam said in a soothing tone, as if he spoke to a spooked horse. "All the preacher's asking for is time."

She considered his words for probably fifteen seconds before she nodded. "All right, Preacher, I'll give you time, but you'd better get the lead out."

As good as it was going to get. Adam stepped back and nodded. "Sam has something he'd like to say as well."

"You want me to leave you and Willow alone?" She squinted. "We've done a good job with the two of you."

"Yes, you have. But I can take over now."

She looked Sam up and down, then nodded.

Sam and Adam turned to leave, striding with pride.

They left the door swinging behind them.

❧

Sam had lived all over the world but had visited his aunt only during the summer, so he had never been to a high school football game in Texas. Adam had told him to prepare himself, but he didn't think anything could have equipped him for the crowd and the noise and the excitement. Even when he'd played college football in the packed Kyle Field with the fans and the corps shouting, he hadn't felt the energy that buzzed through this stadium.

The best part was sitting with Willow on his right and Leo and Nick on his left. Until nearly the end of the first quarter, the boys stayed with them, happy to attend the game with him. A few minutes into the second quarter, with the Lions ahead fourteen to three, Leo spotted some friends passing a football next to the bleachers and the boys ran off to join them, leaving Sam alone with their mother. Too bad, he'd just have to make the best of it.

Sam reached for Willow's hand and held it between them on the bleacher. She smiled at him, then leaned against him for quick second.

Could there be a better way to spend an evening?

Once they arrived back at Willow's apartment after the game and finally got the wound-up Leo and Nick settled in bed, Willow preceded him into the living room. For a moment Sam stood in the archway, feeling happy and comfortable. At peace, he realized. Life was good. Even when he started toward the sofa and a second of imbalance reminded him of the loss of his leg, he felt better than he had in months, possibly years.

Then he settled on the sofa next to Willow, put his arm around her, and kissed her.

The pleasant interval lasted for quite a while, until Sam pushed it. He should have—did—know better, but had given in to his baser urges.

Willow removed his hand and shoved him away. "That's enough. Don't forget I have two sons only a few feet away." She pointed down the hall.

"Let's go into your bedroom and shut the door." He reached out for her, but she scooted to the end of the sofa. The other end.

"Sam, not here." She shook her head but a smile softened her words.

"We could go to my house, but my father's there." He shook his head. "*That* would be uncomfortable." He thought for a moment. "We could find a motel."

"Sam." Her voice became very serious. "I'm not going to sleep with you." She held her hand up. "You may have gotten the idea I'd be willing."

He nodded.

"But I can't." She pointed down the hall again. "I have two little boys who lost their father and love you very much."

Sam swallowed. Did they really love him?

"For that reason, I have to protect them. Before I make any...umm..."

However she finished that sentence, he knew he wouldn't like it.

"Before I make a decision about you and me, Leo and Nick need to know they can count on you. They need to know that you're not going to run out on them if you find something better to do or another woman you like better."

"I'd never…"

"I need something, too. I refuse to fall in love with a man who can't make a commitment to me and to the boys."

"That's your problem. I didn't ask you to fall in love with me," he said, although he felt pretty sure he'd acted like he wanted exactly that. "Or to marry me, just, you know…"

"But I don't become intimate with a man unless I love him, unless there's a commitment between us."

"Commitment." He knew his voice reflected the absolute terror the word awakened. "I can't commit to anyone. I don't even know who I am and what I'm going to do with myself." He could feel sweat dripping down his neck.

"Then," she said in a soft, sad voice, "it might be time to figure that out."

The words burst from him. "Stop trying to fix me."

"For heaven's sake," she snapped. "I'm not trying to fix you. I'm trying *not* to fall in love with you."

He scrutinized her face. She looked sincere. She sounded angry. "How could you ever fall in love with me? I mean, possibly? I'm a mess. My life is a mess."

"You sell yourself short. You're handsome. Women fall at your feet."

"Not all of them," he said. Her, for example.

"There's more." She ticked off each point on her fingers. "I admire your courage and how you fight to get better and stronger. I appreciate how much you care about Leo and Nick. I like the way you make me feel. I thought for a while I'd never again feel this way with a man."

"That's good," he whispered as he attempted to close the small space between them.

She stood. "But I refuse to fall in love with you unless I trust you completely and until you can commit to us, at least try to. I will not have my sons hurt again. I will not make the mistake of loving a man who only wants my body. Not again."

"Hey, I want more than just your body, but that's a good place to start."

She made her feelings about his flip remark obvious with a glare. "One more thing," she started.

"One more thing? Don't you think you've dumped enough on me?"

"One more thing," she continued. "I will *not* commit to you until you can share all that anger and pain you keep inside you with me or with a therapist or your father. I don't care which, but if you don't get it out and talk to someone about it…well, you have to or you'll explode and the collateral damage from that could hurt me and the boys badly."

"Thank you for your opinion as a professional."

"Sam, it's for all of us. You *have* to work through what happened in Afghanistan."

There it was, all laid out for him, logically and honestly. At this moment, he hated honesty and logic because he wasn't nearly ready to face his feelings, his future, or, actually, anything.

Her words and expression summarized the whole predicament. His problems affected not just him, but Willow and her sons. He respected her for that, but did he want her enough to give in to those demands to communicate, to commit, to care?

Even more important, could he? His life would be less complicated if he'd been attracted to an accommodating woman.

"Does that mean Nick and Leo can't come over anymore?" Losing the boys would about tear him apart.

"Of course they can. They need a male friend." The expression in her eyes softened. "They admire you very much. You're good for them. What they don't need is the unrealistic hope that someday you'll be their father."

Crap. Not that he hadn't considered the possibility of having those kids for his sons, but he'd knocked it down every time it popped up, like a game of Whac-A-Mole.

Would having kids be so bad?

❦

Years earlier, when she was still a little naive and believed in true love, Willow had allowed herself to be taken in by a handsome charming man. How could she have been so gullible and trusting?

Despite all his good qualities, Willow knew one thing through her experience with wounded vets: A man who held in all that pain and anger would explode at some time. He could start drinking again or find relief with other women or just walk away. That would devastate Willow and her sons.

Not seeing him again outside the hospital, not having him look at her with longing while she both hoped and feared he'd kiss her, all of that she'd miss. The feel of his warmth next to her, of his touch and smile.

Oh, bother! She'd already fallen in love with Sam and would really miss him. She'd have to accept that and hope Sam figured things out, opened up, and included her in his life.

❦

"I want my old life back," Sam shouted. He wanted all the good stuff he'd lost. He wanted to be with his men in combat. He wanted his leg back. Most of all, he wanted to fight and to joke with Morty again.

None of that was going to happen, but that didn't mean he didn't want it.

He pulled the bottle from the dresser, a fifth of the best

Kentucky bourbon. He needed it. He deserved it. His life sucked. He'd screwed up with Willow because he couldn't give her what she needed and deserved. He'd screwed up because that was what Sam Peterson did best. Right now, he wished the general would leave—go home, move in with Winnie. He didn't care but he wanted to be alone to wallow.

He broke the seal and opened the bottle. No need for manners or a glass in the solitude of his room. He put the bottle to his lips, leaned his head back, and drank deeply. It tasted good. How long had it been since he'd had a drink of real liquor? Weeks, at least.

As the gulp went down, it warmed him inside. An artificial heat, not to be confused with any emotion. He knew that. Didn't mind. At this moment, he needed to feel something other than pain.

He sat on the edge of the bed and removed the prosthesis. He should wash it. He'd do that in the morning. Of course it wouldn't dry by the time he needed to wear it. So what? But he couldn't break the habit of checking his leg for redness and irritation. Everything looked fine. Willow and her prosthetist had done a good job on the fit.

He cursed. Everything, even the stupid leg, reminded him of Willow.

Settling the device against the head of the bed, he took another deep drink. The glow spread through him, down to his fingers and even the toes on his missing foot.

But the sensation filling his body didn't feel as good as he remembered. It deadened his brain and made him dizzy. He took another swig but still didn't feel any better. He couldn't even count on whiskey.

For a moment, he stared at the bottle before screwing the cap back it and shoving it under the bed to hide it. Last thing he needed was a lecture from the general about his drinking.

With that, he turned off the lamp on the bedside table, lifted his thigh to put it on the bed, and lay back on the pillow.

Rockets exploded around Sam Peterson. The acrid smell of ammo and war and the coppery stench of blood hung over the rocky hill.

Then his leg exploded with pain. He reached for it, felt nothing but blood and jagged bone.

"Morty!" he shouted and sat straight up.

In bed, he realized. In Aunt Effie's house. With tears running down his face he gasped for air.

"You're fine, son."

He swung his head to see the general, sitting in a chair only inches from the bed. Just like the last time. "I'm here."

Without even thinking—because if he had thought about it, Sam wouldn't have done it—he reached out for his father and pulled him to sit on the side of the bed next to him. Folded in his father's arms, he sobbed. His father patted him on the back. Neither said a word but for a moment, peace and acceptance filled him as his father wept with him.

"Son, I'm so sorry," his father kept repeating. "I'm so sorry."

After a few minutes, Sam struggled for control and pulled away. "Why?" He wiped his cheeks. "Why are *you* sorry?" He didn't think he'd ever heard the man say that word. No, that was wrong. He'd used it a while back, the first time Sam could remember hearing that word escaping from the general's usually tight lips.

But they weren't taut now. His face looked...droopy. Sad. And his lips, his whole expression looked soft as if he were begging, as if this moment were very important for him.

"Why?" Sam asked again.

The general returned to his chair. "I wasn't much of a father. I wasn't much of a husband, either." He shook his head. "Military families put up with a lot. I had the admirable excuse that I had to serve my country. I used it every chance I had."

"You did serve the country."

"Other parents in the military spent time with their families. Morty's dad—he went to every football game he could, every talent show."

"Morty's dad retired as a captain."

The general shrugged. "What's wrong with that?"

"You wanted to be a general. Morty's dad didn't."

"Morty's dad had better priorities than I did."

"Dad, I was a lot like you. I pushed and pushed and pretty soon I outranked Morty. That's what a Peterson does. It's what your father did, and his father."

"Generations of Petersons who taught their sons how to go off to war but never how to stay home and be a real parent." He shook his head. "I should have cared more about being your father than being a general."

Sam's thoughts flashed back to his grandfather, a three-star general who looked exactly like this general, who'd hit only two stars. Had he been a disappointment to *his* father as well? Sam hated to admit it, but perhaps he should or could be a little more understanding and less self-centered. The realization made him feel like a jerk.

"You weren't responsible for Morty's death," the general said after a long silence.

He could feel his body straighten and stiffen. "I don't want to talk about that."

"Morty didn't become a marine because of you." The general looked in Sam's eyes. "You know that, don't you? He was always crazy about the military, wanted to be a marine like his father, like me."

Sam couldn't form the words to answer. The general was right. Morty had been as crazy about being a marine as Sam had. Deep down, Sam knew that, but in his grief and guilt he'd denied it. Because he had lived, had come home. Morty hadn't.

"His death was a tragedy." The general shook his head and looked down at his folded hands. "But it was his choice to be in Afghanistan on that hillside. You never pushed him."

Sam closed his eyes to consider the general's words. The burden of sorrow lifted a little more.

As Sam reflected, the general stood. With that motion, he kicked the bottle Sam had shoved under the bed. He leaned down to pick it up. "Yours?"

Sam shook his head. "Take it back to the kitchen or pour it down the drain. I don't need it."

The general looked skeptical. "Not sure it'll be that easy, son."

"I know." He wished it were. "But it's a beginning, and I'm determined. I'll start meetings as soon as I find one."

The general looked almost victorious.

"I mean AA. I still won't go to the vets' group at the church," Sam said. "Not yet."

Once the general left, not quite closing the door behind him, Sam lay back against the headboard. He thought back twenty years, nearly twenty-five, to a memory of him and Morty shouting "Semper fi" and storming Guadalcanal or planting the flag on Iwo Jima. Even though they didn't know what the words meant, they'd sing, "From the halls of Montezuma to the shores to Tripoli," at the top of their lungs.

They'd been exactly like Leo and Nick, he realized. For the first time in over a year, he thought about Morty and smiled. Oh, not for long because it still hurt, but he felt hope. He closed his eyes as a tremendous burden began to fall from him. Maybe he'd started to heal.

Chapter Twenty-One

Saturday afternoon, Adam signed for the FedEx delivery and turned to carry the heavy box inside.

"Whatcha got, Pops?" Hector sat on the sofa and watched cartoons. The two males were alone. Five minutes earlier, Jancy had run off to play with Carol in the Kowalski backyard and the Smiths had taken a trip to San Saba to get ready to move back home.

"A package from my mother." He shook it as he walked to the kitchen. It sounded full. "She sends me stuff, mostly food, every now and then, to make up for the fact she and Dad live so far away." He dropped the carton on the table, picked up a knife, and began cutting through the tape, then opened the box and dumped the contents.

Hector watched as a shower of candy bars and packages labeled SHORTCAKE and BISCUITS and CRISPS cascaded out. "Man, she must feel real guilty."

"Can't get these in the United States." Adam held up one of the chocolate bars. "These are one of my favorites." He handed Hector a package of Turkish delight. "You're going to love these. Try one."

Settling at the table, Hector opened the package and scrutinized the square candy. He grinned and said, "Where do these come from?" before he popped the rest of the piece in his mouth.

"British Isles. My folks live in London."

"London?" He sat forward and took a box of cream crackers. "You mean, like, London in England?"

Adam nodded. Chewy sat next to them, his chin on the table.

"Don't give any of this to the dog." Adam reached to the counter for a box of doggy treats and tossed one into the other room.

"Why are your parents in England?"

"My dad sold his business a few years ago and they moved there."

He shook his head. "You must be really rich."

"My father is. I'm not."

"Bet you don't understand what it's like to grow up poor." He opened the box and took out a handful of crackers.

"No, I can't imagine, but I care."

"Yeah, Pops, I know you do." He tossed a handful of crackers in his mouth, chewed, and swallowed. "Why aren't you in London with them?"

"They like it. They travel a lot, go to Paris or Italy for a week or two. Mom likes the shopping. My father likes the theater." He shrugged. "I don't. I like Texas and the church and roundball."

"Man," Hector said through a mouthful of crackers, then chewed for a minute and swallowed. "Man, they're rich and you aren't? They live in London and you live here? You're really nuts, you know."

Adam grinned and sort of agreed. "But I'm happy."

"They ever coming to visit you?"

"Christmas, maybe."

"They're coming from London to Butternut Creek, Texas? How are they going to feel about that?"

They'd hate it. Adam knew that but wasn't about to tell Hector, who'd lived here all his life. Instead, he began to separate the goodies by category at the same time Hector attempted to sample one of everything.

"Hey, Pops, want to shoot some hoops?" Hector asked around a mouthful of shortbread.

"You're getting so good, I can't compete."

The kid grinned. Adam could still play him fairly even but not for much longer. By next year, when he was a senior, he'd beat Adam nine out of ten times. But there was still that tenth time to look forward to. When he got to college, Adam would be no match. Surely he'd have pity on an old man.

"We have a game Tuesday at Dripping Spring. You coming?" he asked.

"Where else would I be? If I didn't take your sister to watch you play, she'd hitch a ride." The change in Janey when she attended Hector's games amazed Adam. She shouted and cheered and jumped up and down for the entire time. When the final buzzer sounded, she again became the sweet but melancholy child.

But she seemed more comfortable with Adam, smiled at him a few times a week, allowed him to help her with her homework, and demanded to attend her brother's games.

"I know that's right," Hector mumbled as he savored a bite

of candy. "Save a couple of these bars for her. Janey loves chocolate."

🐾

Monday morning, Adam finished his morning meditation seated under the big oak with Chewy curled up at his side, his huge head on Adam's leg. The minister looked toward the parsonage. The lights in Hector's and Janey's rooms on the second floor glowed through the shades as the two got ready for school.

On the first floor, lights from the kitchen and the front hall reflected on the trees on the south side of the house and shone from the parlor where Deanne, Eleanor, and Missy had spent the last two and a half weeks.

That morning they had an event to celebrate. The three were going home.

As Adam walked toward the parsonage with Chewy prancing at his side, he watched Jesse make a trip between the parsonage and his truck, packing all they'd accumulated. Adam dropped Chewy's leash—the dog wouldn't run off—and hurried over to the porch to pick up a box filled with Missy's toys and clothing.

Deanne and Eleanor stood at the window, both smiling, but Deanne's lips quivered. Adam put the box down, went inside, and asked, "Are you okay?"

She nodded. "We're happy to be going home, to get back to our little house in our little town. I'll be able to start teaching in a week or two."

"That means you're happy?"

"Yes, but we'll miss you. You've been so good for us, so wonderful to care for Missy. If it hadn't been for your taking me in, I don't think I would have healed nearly as quickly. And I couldn't have cared for Missy, as sick as I was. The burden of the two of us—well, I know that would have worn my mother out. Thank you."

"Ready to go," Jesse shouted.

Adam picked up the box and took it to the truck. With that, the Smiths got into their car and took off while Jesse backed out. Adam waved until they turned onto the highway and disappeared.

When he could see them no longer, Adam heard the sound of someone running down the sidewalk. Turned out to be Miss Birdie.

"She's gone?" she asked.

"They just pulled out."

"Doggone, I thought I'd have enough time but we had a big crowd this morning and I couldn't leave." She reached into the pocket of her apron and took out a tissue to surreptitiously wipe her eyes.

He pretended not to notice. "How 'bout a cup of coffee?"

He and the pillar sat at the table and drank coffee in silence for a few minutes before she said, "Taking care of Missy was a nice experience for me. Sweet little girl, but I'm old to watch a little one." She reached in another pocket and pulled out a box. "I brought her a little present, seeing she's been brought up in the church. It's a cross, one my mother gave me when I was her age. I'd like her to have it."

"You could mail it. Or you could take it there."

She nodded. "Of course I could." Then she stopped absolutely still, as if something clicked in her head. "Mrs. Smith." She stopped to think about her words. "She's not married, is she?"

"You never give up, do you?" Adam shook his head. "You lost your chance. If you wanted to play matchmaker, you should have done that during the weeks Deanne was staying here."

"I can't believe I blew that opportunity." She looked at her cup then glanced up. "I'm losing my edge."

"Miss Birdie, a woman recovering from a terrible accident, who's in pain and worried about the future, is hardly the best candidate for a matchmaker." She looked so deflated, Adam added, "Besides, you'll never lose your edge. You'll remain sharp until you whip me into shape. I have faith you can do that."

For a moment, she grinned before becoming the pillar again. "Have to get back to work. No use diddle-daddling here." She stood. "Don't you have work to do?"

❦

Adam had just finished putting the last touches on the bulletin for Sunday when the phone rang. Because Maggie had left an hour earlier, he answered.

"Christian Church."

"Reverend Jordan, please."

"This is Reverend Jordan." A wave of pride washed over Adam every time he said that. Perhaps someday, answering the phone in the church he served would feel commonplace or even a bother. But not yet, not after only five months.

"This is Gussie Milton from the church in Roundville. I don't believe we've met. I coordinate youth events in the district."

Before he could answer, she continued in a voice filled with so much enthusiasm, he couldn't help but be drawn in. "In

February, the district high school kids have a winter retreat at the campground in Gonzales. Nice lodge, lots of fun. Great spiritual growth."

He remembered winter retreats from his youth—about ten years ago. They'd probably influenced his later decision to be a minister greatly, plus they'd been a lot of fun. "I..."

She kept on as if he hadn't spoken. He hadn't really, just one syllable, so he listened. "We have about fifty to seventy-five kids from all over Central Texas. Mac and Bree usually come, but we haven't received any registrations from Butternut Creek."

He glanced at the pile in his IN box. It neared a foot high and teetered. If he searched through the papers on the bottom, the entire structure would fall onto the floor, knocking over several other stacks.

Filing was his downfall. Maybe Maggie or Winnie would help. For a moment, he regretted not heeding Miss Birdie's advice about cleaning up the mess.

However, vowing to correct the deficiencies didn't help at this moment. "I don't know..."

"If you don't have them handy, I can email more," she said.

Aha! Not in a pile on the desk or the floor. In a very long list of unread email.

"Just a minute. Let me look—"

"My email is gussie@gussieM.org." She chattered on as Adam opened his email queue. "We have such a great time..."

"You sent it September fifteenth," he said once he'd located the folder. "I'm sorry I haven't gotten back to you."

"That's okay." She sounded as if his ignoring her email for seven weeks and her having to call him were not an inconvenience. "Hope you'll be able to bring some of the kids."

"I'll check with them."

"Great. Now, what will you volunteer to do here? We need leaders for small groups, song leaders, and a recreation chair."

Talking to Gussie Milton reminded Adam of being caught up in a tsunami. She made every opportunity sound exciting, like exactly what he wanted to join in on.

"Why don't we get together and discuss this? Meet me in Marble Falls for coffee?" she said. "It's halfway between Roundville and Butternut Creek. I'd like to meet you and discuss some ideas and get you signed up to help."

❦

"Son, I'm going to the vets' group meeting at church tonight." Wednesday evening, the general paused at the door and eyed Sam, who sat on the sofa with the remote in his hand. "Want to come with me?"

The general kept asking and Sam kept refusing, usually by telling the general he didn't need to be fixed.

But he did. Oh, maybe not like an outside force vacuuming out the old crap and forcing new crap on him, tightening the bolts, and whatever else *fixed* consisted of. But since he'd last seen Willow, his brokenness had become more and more obvious to him. He missed her. Not having her around was nearly as painful and incapacitating as not having his leg.

No, that was a bunch of bull. It wasn't nearly as bad, but she made him feel the loss less.

The boys came by once or twice a week. He liked that. But they'd looked so hopeful back when he and Willow had gone out, when they'd thought he and their mother would be together. Guess it was a good thing they hadn't raised the boys' hopes. Now they knew he'd never become their new father.

The realization of the lonely life ahead of him without those three would've about broken his heart if he weren't a marine. Marines didn't suffer from broken hearts and marines didn't give in to emotions.

Still, over the last few weeks the certainty had grown that he needed Leo and Nick and Willow in his life. Yet he had absolutely no idea what to do next.

"Son?" the general repeated.

How long had he been waiting for an answer while Sam's brain had wandered off?

"Not tonight," Sam said.

When his father left without another word, Sam flicked the set off, tossed the remote on the sofa, and glared at the dark screen.

Communication, that's what Willow had said. Get rid of the anger inside. Bring it into the open and face it, share it, stop allowing it to run and ruin his life.

He pushed himself to his feet, walked into the dining room, picked up a pen and several sheets of paper from the computer area his father had created in the corner, and sat down. For a few minutes, he just stared at the paper and drummed the pen on the table. Then he started to write.

Within minutes, the floor was covered with balls of wadded-up paper. On the table he'd amassed a pile of napkins he'd used to wipe his cheeks because every effort to write what had happened hurt so much tears ran down his face.

But he didn't stop. When he had one page pretty much the way he wanted it, he started on the next. It took fewer attempts to get this right because once he got going, the story flowed from him with the tears.

An hour later, the four-page letter completed, he wiped his

face one last time. He'd discovered there were times a marine needed to expose all the anger and pain, reaching down deep to haul it to the surface and expose it. Doing that wasn't a bit wimpy, especially the page about Morty. Unlike Morty, Sam had lived through the battle, had survived to relive and write about every bloody moment of it.

Finished, he folded the pages and stuck them in an envelope, not sure what he'd do with them. Probably should share everything with the general. Now that he'd started reliving the past, he probably should go to the meeting with him, maybe next week. If his father had made an effort to change, Sam could, too. He pushed up from the table and wandered into the living room with the envelope in his hand.

But he hadn't written the letter for the general, although he would give it to him to read later. It wasn't for the other vets, even though he knew he needed to attend a session or two, maybe more, as well as the AA meetings. No, he'd written the account of his experiences in Afghanistan for Willow, but he didn't know if he had the guts to share it with her. In fact, at this moment, he knew he didn't. He couldn't. Writing about the event had about killed him.

He tossed himself on the sofa and leaned back. If he didn't share with her, he'd lose her. He couldn't take that. He had to admit: He was in love with the woman, had been from the first time he saw her.

He loved her.

Holding the envelope in front of him, he studied it. Did he love her enough? Opening up to her would hurt both of them. He didn't know if he could bear to watch her read his words, but he did know he couldn't mail something like this to the woman he loved, couldn't expect her to read it alone.

"Preacher, it's four o'clock Friday afternoon. What are you still doing here?"

Without looking up from the surface of his desk, Adam knew who had entered, and not just from her voice. If he glanced up, he'd see the pillar standing at the door, tapping her foot.

He looked up. She was.

"Working on my sermon," he explained, knowing it would make no difference what he said. When Miss Birdie made the trip to the church and had fire in her eyes, Adam knew she owned him for the next hour.

"You can do that later." She attempted to stomp into the office, impossible to do in her rubber-soled shoes but she made a pretty good attempt.

"It's four o'clock," she said. Then, more loudly, she repeated, "Four o'clock on Friday."

What was she talking about?

"The parade." Her tone suggested he had the brain of a gnat.

When he heard the words, Adam realized he did have the brain of a gnat.

"The parade," he said as he jumped to his feet, grabbed a jacket, and struggled to stick his arms in the sleeves while running after the pillar. She moved faster than he'd thought she could, across the highway, down the block, and onto the square.

The square and Adam had a transitory relationship. Because he wasn't a tearoom-and-antiques sort of guy, his visits had been limited to renewing his driver's license at the courthouse annex and occasionally joining Mattie for lunch at Tea Time, a restaurant that served the quiche and sweet persimmon tea she loved, or grabbing a meal at the diner.

Now he was running through a mob of crazy football fans. Like there was another kind. As he joggled through them to the other side of the square, Adam greeted people he recognized from church and from games. He spied Mercedes about fifty feet away. Finally, Miss Birdie stopped on the edge of the curb next to her friend and motioned Adam to a place behind them.

"I saved your places," Mercedes said.

"This is the best side to view the parade from. That's the reviewing stand." The pillar pointed to a table only a few feet to the right. "The kids really strut their stuff as they pass here."

"Every high school class and some of the classes from the middle schools build a float." Mercedes stood on her toes to look across the square. "Should start any minute."

"The bands march and the teams and clubs ride on the back of trucks."

That riding in the bed of a pickup seemed dangerous to Adam but appeared to be an old Texas custom. Not that they'd be speeding through; the students should be safe.

Across the street, he spotted Willow and Nick and waved. Where was Leo? Maybe in the parade. Sam stood at the corner maybe twenty feet from Willow, keeping his eyes off her so carefully Adam guessed the romance wasn't going well. He needed to drop by with pizza soon because he knew Sam wouldn't call him.

"Can you hear them?" the pillar asked. "Look, you can see them."

Adam followed her pointing finger toward the first float of

the parade and heard the bands as the trucks moved forward. Leo marched with a group of kids behind a banner that proclaimed, YOUTH FOOTBALL. As the group went by, Nick kept up a relay, running to Sam then back to his mother at least five times since Adam had been watching, as well as jumping up and down and pointing toward his brother.

Sam waved at Leo, then looked past Nick to stare at Willow. His eyes showed so much longing Adam felt sorry for him but wanted to kick him at the same time. He guessed Sam was the problem in the relationship—but if he was so unhappy, why didn't he do something?

Nick did. He grabbed Sam's hand and tugged, not enough to make Sam lose his balance but enough to get him moving. The boy kept hold of Sam's hand and moved slowly but—as the cliché went—inexorably toward his mother. Expressions of panic and hope alternated across Sam's face, but he didn't stop. He didn't pull his hand from Nick's.

When the two reached Willow's side, she turned to look at Sam with a polite nod before she looked back to watch the parade.

Sam watched her profile for nearly a minute, yearning raw on his face. At least, that's what Adam thought it was. As with most facial expressions and body language, he wasn't always sure what they expressed, but even an illiterate like him could read Sam.

Fortunately, Miss Birdie had a master's degree. "Those two look miserable," the pillar said.

Sadly, they did agree on this one basic fact.

"Bird, we can't do anything more." Mercedes glanced across the street. "We've done everything we can to bring them together. The rest is up to them."

"Hrmph." Miss Birdie shook her head. "I know, I know, but someone ought to…" She stopped speaking as the notes of the "Lion Fight Song" filled the air. "That's Mac." Miss Birdie pointed toward the band, waved at her granddaughter, and began to sing along, "Go, Lions, win this game…"

Adam wouldn't have recognized Mac in her band uniform; the visor on the huge hat covered every recognizable feature. The chin straps made the faces of all the members look alike: chinless wonders with huge fuzzy heads and no other identifiable features.

Even though he didn't really know which one was Mac, Adam waved and shouted as well, then joined the fight song the second time through. "She's doing great," he said with relief.

Miss Birdie glared at him. "She's not going to lead the band into the fence, you know. They're just marching around the square."

After the band passed, a truck with Bree holding a sign that read VARSITY VOLLEYBALL drove by the reviewing stand.

"You have great girls," Adam said.

Without answering, the pillar elbowed him in the side.

"What was that for?" he asked, a little confused. He thought he'd been behaving well.

"Look over there." She moved her head in the direction of the northwest corner of the square. "Who's that man with Reverend Patillo?"

"I don't know." Tall and good-looking, but Adam didn't see evidence of an attraction between the two of them. Not like the chemistry Willow and Sam attempted to deny. "Do you want me to go ask?"

"Oh, for heaven's sake, Pastor Adam." She didn't have to

change expressions. The glare she'd used earlier still fit this occasion. "You might take some interest in your future. If you aren't going to allow the Widows to help—"

"Meddle," he corrected.

She ignored him, as he'd expected. "—then you're going to have to do some of this getting-married-and-raising-a-family business yourself." She shoved him. "Go over and introduce yourself to the competition."

With growing confidence in his ability to withstand the pillar's demands, Adam ignored her and watched the parade.

The day of his meeting with Gussie Milton, Adam arrived at the coffee shop in Marble Falls early and grabbed a table facing the door. How would he recognize her? He had no idea what she looked like. There was a woman in her fifties he thought might be her. She was a little plump and wore a camp shirt and athletic shoes. But she seemed to be there with her husband. Just as Adam was about to approach the couple, the bell on the door jingled.

For nearly a minute, Adam watched a woman of about thirty, pretty and slender in a charcoal-gray suit and high heels. She had dark curly hair tamed by a clasp at the nape of her neck. She stood at the door of the coffee shop and looked around. Then she spotted Adam and a brilliant smile broke out.

The smile said *Gussie*. The rest of her—the polish, the fashion sense—didn't. He feared his mouth had dropped open, but when he checked, it was closed.

"Hi." She reached out to grab his hand in a strong grip. "I'm Gussie. It's great to meet you."

Yes, it was Gussie. He recognized her voice.

"Let me get something to drink." She dropped a large canvas tote on the floor beside the table and walked away.

A few minutes later, she returned with two foaming cups, placing one in front of Adam while she sat. With an elegant motion, she dropped her big yellow purse on the floor and at the same time grabbed and placed the tote on the table. Then she pulled out a folder and flipped it open. Every movement done with the speed of a runner and the grace of a dancer.

"Where do you want to start?" she asked, smiling at Adam with an expression of pure delight.

He blinked. This woman was so full of energy and joie de vivre that she left him nearly breathless.

"Sometimes I move too fast. Sorry." She laughed, the sound he recognized from their phone conversations. Yes, this was Gussie. Whoever would name a girl Gussie?

"My father's favorite uncle, Augustus," she said as if she knew what he'd been thinking. "That's who I'm named for, but I'm only Gussie, not even Augusta or anything elegant or even normal." She smiled. "Everyone wonders so I always answer before they have to ask. And"—she shuffled through a few papers—"I'm a photographer and graphic designer."

"In Roundville?"

"Oh, no. In Austin. But my parents live in Roundville and I want to be close to them." For a moment, she lost the smile. "They're getting older. And I love the church there. I grew up in it. It's a short commute to town and worth it so I can live at home with my folks. I'm an only child."

Adam felt her warmth and happiness flow over him from across the table. He took it in until he realized she was watching him, a little perplexed, as if she'd said something and he hadn't responded.

"I'm sorry. What did you say?"

"That's okay. I often see that blank stare when I talk. Sometimes people can't take in everything I say at once, but that's how my brain works." She laughed. "Where do you come from?"

He gave her some quick background before he asked her to tell him about herself, adding, "And your family. You mentioned your parents. What about your husband and children?" Adam knew he'd never be subtle and suave, but she didn't seem to notice his stumbling curiosity.

"No husband. No children. No time." She shook her head. "My job and the church and my parents are all I can commit to now."

How had the Widows missed her? Had they thought she lived too far away? He couldn't imagine a small thing like a distance of fifty miles slowing Miss Birdie down.

By the time Gussie leaped to her feet—he was quickly discovering she never did anything slowly or quietly—ten minutes later, he'd studied the schedule she'd worked up for the retreat weekend. He wrote his name in a few slots while she brought a pot of coffee over and poured them each another cup.

"Those servers are always too slow," she explained as she sat down.

They chatted for a few more minutes. Once they concluded the business of the retreat, she grabbed her papers, stuffed them into the tote, waved, and dashed out the door. Her exit left Adam feeling as if a thoroughly enchanting hurricane had just passed through.

Feeling enchanted wasn't his goal. First, it would be stupid to be attracted to a woman who worked in South Austin, who lived an hour's drive away, a woman who cared for her parents and supervised the youth of her church in her bit of extra time. Second, if he didn't want an entanglement, he shouldn't be enchanted.

But Gussie was hard to resist.

❦

A few days later, Sam called Adam. He said he was on the way over to the church. Adam was terrified. Was Sam coming for counseling? He had known a day like this would come but hadn't expected it so soon.

Adam had taken courses about counseling in seminary, had even worked at a counseling center and as a hospital chaplain, but he'd never been on his own and certainly never with someone he knew. In all those sessions with strangers, there had always been someone—a faculty member or a psychologist or a supervising chaplain—looking over his shoulder, suggesting, helping, and telling him later both how to handle the situation and what to do as well as what not to do.

Today he'd be on his own.

What if he messed up?

What if he said the wrong thing and hurt the situation? Who in the world was he to help anyone else with their problems?

"Dear Lord, please help me." After a few seconds, he added, "Give me wisdom and compassion and a lot of help. And toss in whatever else You think I may need."

A knock interrupted the anxious prayer.

"Amen." He leaped to his feet and shouted, "Come in."

Leaning on his cane, Sam walked in.

"Bad day?" Adam asked, then kicked himself. Had that been the wrong response to the cane?

He nodded. "Sometimes I overdo, but I'm fine." He came

over to the desk without closing the door and lowered himself into the chair, leaning heavily on his left hand.

Should Adam close the door? Inside, he shook his head. He worried too much.

"How can I help you?" Were those the wrong words? "What can I do for you?" Again, had Adam insulted the marine and the handicap? This time his prayer consisted of, *Dear Lord, give me the right words and tell me when to shut up.* Then he moved a chair next to Sam's and sat.

"I was wondering what I could do for the church."

"What?"

"The church has been so good to me." Sam smiled and shook his head. "I really can't believe how good. The women have brought food. Howard Crampton came by the other day to fix the porch swing. You know, the one you broke."

Adam nodded.

"Did you know Jesse brings a horse by and takes me riding once a week?" Sam asked.

"He told me that. He really enjoys it."

"I appreciate all this. I'd like to do something in return, something that doesn't require actually attending worship."

"Sort of service in absentia?"

Sam nodded.

"Okay, what do you have in mind?"

"I'm not a handyman so carpentry and plumbing are beyond me, but I'm open to about anything else."

"A few of our people volunteer at the library, teaching English as a second language and literacy. They always need help." Adam thought for a few seconds. "They can always use extra hands at the food pantry on Tuesday and Thursday mornings."

"Teaching, huh?" He considered that. "I'll go to the library and ask about it."

Adam wrote a phone number on a piece of paper. "Call Ruth Cook. She's in charge of scheduling."

"Thanks, Adam."

The minister silently breathed a sigh of relief. That had been easy. But why had Sam come by the church? To the study? He could have asked that on the phone.

"Guess I'll head out." Sam stood, but turned at the door, scrutinized Adam for a moment, then shut the door without leaving. "There's something else I need to talk about." He took a few steps toward the desk. "I don't need a minister and I don't need some easy religious words or simplistic clichés to pacify me. Right now, I need to talk to a friend. You're the one I've chosen." He put his hand on the back of the chair. "Actually, you're my only friend in town other than two kids and the general, and he's the problem." He shrugged. "Are you willing?"

"Of course." The feeling of inadequacy melted away, as if God answered his prayer. Why in the world did he find it so difficult to accept the fact that God endowed him with certain gifts as well as the ability to use them? Why did he find it hard to believe that God had already answered his prayers by blessing him with talents to serve? "What can I do for you?" Adam asked pastorally as Sam dropped into the chair again.

He leaned his head on the high back of the chair and closed his eyes. "Do you get along with your father?"

"You mean other than his telling me going into the ministry was the waste of a good mind and an expensive education?"

Sam leaned forward and smiled. "Yeah, like that."

"My sister's a doctor who goes from refugee camp to refugee camp in Africa. We're both great disappointments to our father. Mom's pretty much okay with us. Don't know what he expected. We were raised in the church."

As the men discussed how to get along with a stifling parent, Sam and Adam became better friends. They tossed out ideas, joked and shared, even discovered that, at different times in their lives, when business or the military had called their fathers away, both had been sent to boarding schools.

But Sam didn't say a word about Willow.

"Thank for listening," Sam said after thirty minutes. "I don't think the general is a problem that can be solved."

"Maybe if you didn't call him 'the general,'" Adam suggested. "Have you thought about calling him 'Dad'?"

"Hey." He glared at the minister. "Don't try to..."

"I'm not trying to fix you."

"All right." Sam grinned and relaxed. "I've tried calling him 'Dad'—both to his face once or twice and in here." He tapped his head. "It doesn't feel right. At least, not yet."

"Maybe with practice."

"The really weird thing is the man never spent time with me when I was a kid. Now I wake up and find him sitting next to my bed. Crying." He shook his head. "Man, how am I supposed to deal with that?"

❧

"Pastor, we need to get to the bottom of this," the pillar said as she marched into the minister's study a few days after the meeting with Sam. She stopped in front of the desk and put her hands on her hips.

Adam quaked at the ominous words. Miss Birdie was in full *the-minister-has-done-something-so-foolish-I-cannot-believe-it* mode. "The community center is holding its craft fair the same Saturday as our spring bazaar." She bit the words off.

He relaxed. Not angry at her minister, at least not this time.

"Bird doesn't like anyone competing with the Widows for good deeds," Mercedes stated as she followed the pillar into the office.

"That's not the reason at all, Mercedes." She lifted her glare toward her friend. "You know that. It's just that..." She sat and leaned toward Adam. "It's just that we've always had our bazaar on that weekend. Everyone knows that. Competition won't be good for either group."

"Bird doesn't like to be left out," Mercedes stated. "She likes to know everything that's going on."

"No," Miss Birdie protested. " It's just that..." She sighed. "All right. That's true." She smiled ruefully. "I don't like to be left out. I do like to know who's doing what. I hate to be blind-sided."

Adam nodded solemnly. "I understand, but sometimes things happen."

"I know that very well, Preacher," Miss Birdie snapped. "Pushiness and impatience may not be attractive traits, but that's who I am and what I do best. I'm not fixin' to change at this time in my life."

"Bird's very proud of that," Mercedes stated.

"No, I'm not." The pillar shook her head. "Well, maybe a little, but I also know there are times I should step back and leave things in the Lord's hands." She sighed. "I'm not good at that, Pastor."

"Bird's not patient."

"Patience is a hard lesson to learn," Adam agreed.

"Especially if you don't want to." After receiving a glare

from the pillar, Mercedes added, "Like me. Hard lesson for me as well."

"For all of us," Adam agreed again.

Having exhausted that area of accord, the three glanced at one another, each waiting for someone else to begin a new topic. Adam hesitated because he had no idea why the women had come. They should have gone over to the community center to discuss the conflict.

But he'd learned it was never a good idea to make a suggestion to the pillar. If she liked it, she'd expect him to take care of it. If she didn't, she'd tut-tut and tsk-tsk and hrmph, generally making him feel like an idiot.

However, Adam felt that there was something else going on now. Although she was angry about the usurping of the date of the spring bazaar, the conflict didn't seem uppermost on the pillar's mind.

She knew she could wear Adam down with her glare. He held out for nearly a minute of scrutiny before he blurted out, "Anything else?"

"It's about the youth retreat," Mercedes said. "Bird's upset because you haven't done a thing about it."

"I can tell him—" the pillar began.

Before she could finish, Adam spoke quickly. The youth retreat seemed like a safe topic. "Yes, I have been late doing that. I have the forms. Gussie Milton called last week. I met her in Marble Falls to discuss scheduling."

When he mentioned Gussie's name, the two Widows glanced at each other, then—in unison—toward Adam and said, also in unison, "You met Gussie Milton?"

They beamed. Miss Birdie tilted her head up to look at the picture of Jesus knocking on a door, a gift from someone to a former minister that hung right behind the desk. "Dear Lord," she said to the figure on the canvas. "You do answer prayer. Thank You."

Adam recognized his error immediately. He should never have spoken Gussie's name. It was like tossing M&M's to a chocoholic. Forgetting anything else they might have wanted to say, both slid to the edges of their chairs, folded their hands in their laps, and watched Adam like cats watching a cricket, just waiting for it to move.

"What do you think of her?" Miss Birdie asked happily, as if she foresaw the restoration of her reputation as a matchmaker. Not that she'd introduced Adam to Gussie, but he bet she'd take credit for it.

"Very nice," he said hastily and pulled open a drawer to snatch up the registration forms Maggie had copied. He tossed them across the desk to the Widows in the hope of forestalling any more questions or considerations. "Here are the forms for Mac and Bree. Does anyone else need them?"

He'd also hoped Miss Birdie would pick up a couple of forms and they'd leave. Stupid of him.

Neither woman moved or said a word. Just grinned. He'd made them very happy.

The intensity of their reaction scared him to death.

Chapter Twenty-Two

Y̶ou can't park here."

Birdie turned to glare at Winnie, the bossiest woman she knew.

"It's reserved for tenants and guests only." Winnie pointed toward the sign.

She'd be so glad when Winnie married the general and they could kick her out of the Widows. "The lot's nearly empty. No one within thirty feet of us and it's convenient. After all, we're doing the Lord's work."

"That doesn't mean we can flout the rules. If we parked on the street…" Winnie stopped talking when Birdie turned off the engine, pressed the button that opened the back doors, and got out of the van.

Mercedes was supposed to have come, but she had an ailing uncle and that family was so close you couldn't separate them with WD-40. That meant today Birdie was alone with Winnie to deliver Thanksgiving baskets to shut-ins. The two of them occasionally didn't see eye-to-eye. The provisional Widow didn't respect seniority and was darned inflexible and pushy.

"Susan Pfannenstiel lives in the blue house…"

"Oh, for heaven's sake, Bird, don't you think I know where she lives? She's been in my Bunco group for years."

Had Winnie called her "Bird"? She only allowed Mercedes to do that. She'd need to take that up with Winnie sometime, set boundaries, but for now they had a mission that didn't include arguing in public.

"All right, let's visit her first, then we'll pick up the basket for…" Just as she started to wave toward the home of another shut-in, Birdie saw Sam slinking along behind several azalea bushes. Was he trying to hide from them?

"Isn't that Sam Peterson?" Winnie asked. "What's he doing?"

"Skulking," Birdie said. Then she grinned. "Right across from Willow Thomas's apartment. Don't that beat all?" But did he have the courage to go in? "I'm going to talk to him, make sure he's going inside to talk to her."

"That's not a good idea."

"She must be home because her car's right there." Stupid kind of car for a mother of two to have, but that wasn't the topic now.

"You can't do that," Winnie stated. "You have to let him alone, allow him to do what he needs to do."

"Haven't you learned?" Birdie turned back toward Winnie. "You can never be sure other people are going to do what they should do, not without some strong suggestions."

Winnie shook her head resolutely. "Leave Sam alone to make his decisions. That's what Mitchell said."

As if Birdie cared what Mitchell said. Well, she did, actually. He was Sam's father and might have more history and broader insight on his side than she did, but she remembered that look on Sam's face at the parade, the longing. "I want to do something. I can't just stand here…" When her voice broke, she cleared her throat before continuing. "I can't allow a person to ruin his own life, not without trying to point him in the right direction."

"Bird, we can't control everyone and everything. Sometimes you have to let go and trust people to take care of themselves."

"Hrmpp." She turned to glare at Winnie. What did the woman know? Where would the world be if everyone stepped back and didn't try, at least *try*, to set people on the right track? "There are times when people need direction." Darn, her voice broke again.

"Besides, what's your plan? Capture a marine and force him inside to talk to Willow?"

Yes, that had been her plan. Not a good one for a woman with a bad shoulder and an unwilling co-conspirator.

She turned to look toward the bushes that had barely covered Sam, but he was gone. "All right," she sighed. "I guess we'd better get on with delivering the baskets." She reached into the backseat, pulled out a basket, and handed it to Winnie to carry. The woman could do something more useful than issuing orders and disagreeing.

❧

He'd become a total idiot.

When Sam first saw the Widows in the parking lot, he dropped, totally by instinct, onto the ground behind a hedge as if hiding from enemy snipers instead of two elderly women.

But he knew how dangerous they could be.

Fortunately, the prosthetic joint held up well. It had folded easily and evenly at the same rate as the left leg. When he slid forward to peek through the branches, he realized Miss Birdie could see him and Miss Winnie had pointed at him.

Now he was stuck. He could hardly leap to his feet and pretend he hadn't been hiding—but he couldn't stay here, either, huddled like an idiot behind these shrubs. What was wrong with him? He'd fought in war, led his troops into combat, but now he hid from the Widows? They weren't even in full force and they scared him.

How could he ever explain this to his father?

Escape was the only answer. When he saw Miss Birdie turn to talk to the other Widow, he stood and ran faster than he'd thought he could toward the apartment building.

This was not the way he'd envisioned the morning. It had started out as a walk. As he strolled through the tree-lined streets, he'd reached into the pocket of his jeans to feel the crinkling of the envelope beneath his fingers. It had been on the dresser for several days. This morning he'd put it in his pocket, thinking if he saw Willow, by accident, he'd have it handy if the opportunity arose to share it with her. He didn't have the courage yet to share it on his own, directly. Only by accident.

How he'd do that he didn't know. See her at the H-E-B, shove the envelope at her, say, *Here. I thought you'd want to read about the horror that's been my life for the past year*, then smile and walk away? So far, that was the best plan he'd come up with.

But somehow as he walked he'd found himself across the street from Willow's—and the boys'—apartment building. He hadn't planned that, but his feet had brought him here. The place pulled at him like a huge electromagnet, and he possessed the resistance of a poached egg. Stupid analogy. Eggs aren't attracted to magnets, but the rest fit pretty well. He had no willpower when it came to the Thomas family.

What were the Widows doing in that parking lot? Were they setting something up between him and Willow? Not that he'd mind, but they couldn't have known he'd be coming this way.

Why were they in the parking lot of Willow's building?

Could be they weren't waiting for him, not matchmaking for him. Maybe they planned to fix Willow up with someone else.

Who?

He didn't know if there were more single men in town. Perhaps they'd decided to match Adam and Willow. The preacher was a good guy. They'd get along well. The minister would make a great father for the boys.

But not if Sam had anything to say about it. He made a decision without a second of thought: He had to reach Willow before the Widows did, before they found another man for her. Using the reconnaissance skills he'd learned as a marine, he started south, surreptitiously glancing toward the parking lot on his right every few seconds.

Nothing had changed. The women still chatted. Their presence had to be about Willow. Why else would they be here? Of course, fifty other people inhabited these apartments. Many more lived in the houses surrounding the complex. They could be sticking their noses into someone else's life. Maybe their appearance had nothing to do with him or Willow.

But if it did...He couldn't lose Willow and the boys.

He lost sight of the women as he dashed across the street. A few seconds later, he approached the building. Through a breezeway, he could see the Widows. As he watched, they broke formation and quick stepped across the asphalt, a movement that filled him with panic. Had he left things like telling Willow he loved her and sharing and communication until too late? Were the Widows marching in to correct that? Winnie held a basket, no doubt the pretense they'd use to get in the door. Willow would invite them to stay, and before she knew it she'd be matched up with some eligible Butternut Creek bachelor.

Not on his watch.

Boldly he entered the building and headed toward the Thomases' apartment at the end of the wing. He knocked. Then, afraid the Widows would stride into the building while he still stood out here, he knocked again, harder.

Willow looked out the window to see if the boys were coming home from practice. The apartment had a lovely view of the flat black asphalt parking lot and a few weary bushes. She waved when she recognized Miss Birdie and Winnie out there, but they couldn't see her. She watched as they walked off toward a house facing the parking lot, probably doing good deeds.

Then she saw Sam crossing the street.

What in the world was he doing out there?

She stepped back from the window, out of sight. Was he coming here? What would she do if he did? How would she handle it? She'd missed him, really, really missed him. When her sons talked about what they'd done with Sam, she'd actually been a little jealous of them.

Of course, he could be visiting someone else. But she didn't think so.

Before she could gather her thoughts, a knock sounded on the door and reverberated through the apartment. Or was that the rapid beat of her heart and the fear clenching at her throat?

Of course, maybe it wasn't Sam. Maybe he'd gone somewhere else. Could be a neighbor or a delivery person or the Widows. Who knew?

But she knew. Sam stood outside her door. He knocked again, actually hammering as if he didn't plan to go away. Slowly she turned and opened the last physical barrier between them. "Hello, Sam. This is a surprise." She flinched. What a cliché. Couldn't she come up with something clever?

"A pleasant one, I hope." He grimaced at his words and looked as uncomfortable as she felt.

She'd add another cliché to this soup of old chestnuts they both seemed to be swimming in, but her brain couldn't come up with a thought of any kind, trite or not. Still standing in the open doorway, she said, "The boys aren't home. They have flag-football practice this morning. They'd love for you to come to a game sometime."

"Sure." He nodded. "I didn't come to see them."

She tilted her head warily. "Oh?"

"Are you expecting anyone?"

Who? Like the Widows or all those eligible bachelors in Butternut Creek? "No."

"Can...may I come in?"

She studied him for a few seconds. "Okay."

"Would you like a cup of coffee?" she offered. That would slow things down, give her time to gain control of herself and find a few brain cells that Sam's sudden appearance hadn't fried.

"No, thanks." He walked around her and inside.

As she stepped back and closed the door, she glanced in the mirror. She wore tattered jeans and a burnt orange University of Texas T-shirt with matching socks but no shoes. She hadn't combed her hair so it stood out like a giant Brillo pad. No makeup. She looked terrible.

❦

"You look great," Sam said. He watched her, thinking she didn't look any more comfortable than he felt. Maybe he should accept the coffee. When they settled in the kitchen, he could tell her about how he'd started tutoring English as a second language at the library three mornings a week. He really enjoyed it, felt good to…

Good try, Peterson. Postpone whatever's hard to face; delay the difficult. He knew darned good and well why he wanted to chat about trivia. He didn't want to hand the letter to Willow, but putting this off was cowardly.

"I have something I want you to read." He handed her the envelope.

She glanced at it before she lifted her eyes toward him and frowned. "What's this? You want me to read it?"

"Yes."

"Now?" She took it from him.

"That would be good. If you don't mind." He leaned on the arm of the sofa to lower himself in the seat.

"Okay." She sat across from him on a rocking chair and opened the envelope. She lifted her gaze toward him, then began to read.

After a paragraph, she stopped and looked at him again. "Are you sure?"

He nodded, afraid to speak but also too choked up to say a word.

As she read, she began to cry. Reaching for tissues from the box on the end table next to her, she cried into them. As she read through the pages, she sobbed. "Oh, Sam," she said once. On the section about Morty, he thought.

By the time she finished the letter, he'd reached in the pocket of his jacket and pulled out a handful of tissues and wiped his own face.

For a moment, she stared at the end of the letter, then up at him before she stood, walked to the sofa, and sat on his lap. She put her head on his chest, pulling him close to sob against him. "Oh, Sam," she whispered. "I'm sorry. I'm so sorry."

He put his arms around her and enjoyed the moment, keeping her close and soft against him, feeling her concern and tenderness seep in and begin to warm those cold places inside, to heal the bleeding holes. After a minute or so, she turned and pulled his lips toward hers for a kiss that lasted for a more than satisfactory time, filled with much more than satisfactory emotion.

Then she scooted off his lap to sit next to him and took his hand. He'd prefer to have her in his arms, but this was okay.

"What does this mean, Sam? Is this a commitment?"

"I still want to sleep with you," he said. That wasn't what he'd meant to say.

She stilled for a moment, looking at him apprehensively. "I thought we'd..."

"But that's not all." He cleared his throat. "I also want to wake up with you every morning. I want to eat breakfast with you and Nick and Leo, to take the boys to school and to play football with them when they get home. I want to watch them grow up and visit them in college and hold their children, our grandchildren. But most of all—" Sam took his hand from her grasp and tilted her chin up so she had to look into his eyes. "Most of all, I want to sleep with you every night for the rest of our lives."

"Oh, Sam." She wiped her eyes again, then gave him a kiss that erased any doubt about how much the prospect of that future pleased her.

They'd just gotten to a really good part when she heard a key in the lock.

"Oh, dear." She attempted to arrange her hair while he smoothed her shirt.

The boys shoved into the apartment, laughing and pushing each other. When they saw Sam with his arm around their mother, they both stopped, stood completely still, and gawked at them. Then they shouted, "Sam!" and ran to him.

Juggling the boys, one on each arm, Sam grinned. How had life become so good?

But before he completed the thought, Leo stepped back, grabbing his brother's arm to pull him away as well.

"What are you doing with my mother?" Leo asked. Concern laced his voice as if he needed to protect her.

Sam grinned. "We were kissing." He glanced from Nick and Leo's scrutiny toward Willow, who looked as if she wanted to throw herself over the back of the sofa and hide from the questions she read in Leo's eyes.

Her older son glowered at Sam and put his thumbs in his belt. "What does this"—he pointed at his mother and Sam— "mean?"

Nick mimicked his brother's stance and facial expression although his glare came nowhere near the antagonism in Leo's.

"Nothing, boys," Willow said. "Sam and I were just talking about…oh, things."

He could read their expressions. Nick accepted her words. Leo didn't.

"My intentions are…"

Sam stumbled on the last word. He couldn't say *pure* because his intentions were hardly that. Still, he couldn't laugh, he had to complete the sentence, because Leo looked so serious.

"You hurt my mother," Leo said. "I hear her crying at night."

Sam closed his eyes and thought *Crap*, then turned toward Willow. "I'm sorry. I…I guess I knew, but I had to work this through, put my life in order."

She put her hand on his. "I know."

Both boys watched the two grown-ups. "Leo," she said to her very solemn son. "Don't worry. We're okay, Sam and I."

Sam nodded and stood to take a step toward what he hoped, if all went well, were his sons-to-be, the greatest kids in the world.

"Are you going to be our father?" Nick asked, cutting through the adult obfuscation.

Sam grinned and said, "Yes," before Willow could answer. "If we can convince your mother."

"Mom?" Nick's voice rose. "Mom, can we keep him? Please?"

"You make him sound like a puppy." Willow stood and grinned at all of them. "Give us a little time, guys. Okay? This is pretty new."

With that, Leo and Nick launched themselves toward Sam again. Careful not to knock him down, they stood one on each side and threw their arms around him. He reached out to Willow, put his arm on her shoulders to pull her into the group hug as the boys peppered them with questions.

"When are you getting married?" Leo tossed out.

"We haven't...," Willow began as Sam said, "As soon as we can talk her into it."

But the boys didn't hear either because Nick spoke over the words. "Are you going to have more kids?"

"Hope so," Sam said at the same time Willow said, "We have to discuss that."

"We probably should get married first," Sam added.

"Where are we going to live?" Nick jumped up and down as he threw the questions. "Are you going to paint the house in marine colors? Can we have a dog?"

For a moment, Sam felt as if he stood a few feet away from the group. From that distance, he could see himself with one arm around Willow and the other hand resting on Nick's shoulder and smiling like a fool.

But he wasn't a few feet away. He was inside the circle, part of the family. He could smell the apple scent of Willow's hair and the sweaty odor of the boys and feel the damp perspiration on Nick's neck.

And joy exploded around Sam Peterson.

❦

At twelve thirty, the fellowship hall of the Presbyterian Church looked full, wall-to-wall tables filled with the good citizens, and probably a liberal sprinkling of the sinners, of Butternut Creek. The churches had joined together for the community Thanksgiving dinner, free to everyone.

Behind Adam, the women of several churches prepared vegetables and mashed and sweet potatoes while men pulled turkeys from the ovens, set them on the woodblock counters, and carved them into huge slabs.

With the help of Ouida, his sweet next-door neighbor, Adam had contributed one. She'd prepared the dressing, stuffed the cavity, basted the bird, then put it in the oven of the parsonage. All he'd had to do was watch it and baste it and warm up gravy from a jar. In her solemn way, Janey had been a great help keeping him on schedule. The bird had turned out great. Amazing how his cooking skills had improved with Ouida living next door.

Adam stood third in the serving line, dropping globs of potatoes on a plate before handing it to Hector to pour gravy on everything. In the South, hard-boiled eggs were put in the gravy, an addition Adam neither understood nor enjoyed. Last Sunday at the church Thanksgiving dinner, he'd attempted to pick the pieces from the otherwise delicious dish. The pillar saw it and gave him her death glare, which always shriveled the recipient. Today he'd have to hide someplace in the back of the kitchen, maybe in a pantry, to pluck the rubbery egg whites out.

But that would come later, after they'd served everyone who dropped in for the meal. Across the counter, Mattie cleared and wiped tables. Janey, with her hair decorated in orange barrettes, stood by the desserts and smiled every now and then.

"She's a lot happier. Thanks, Preacher," Hector whispered. "She's feeling safe."

The high school basketball season had begun nearly six weeks earlier. Hector had a great start, leading the team in rebounds. A few scouts from small colleges had come to look over the senior center and had been impressed by Hector, only a junior. What would they do with Janey while he was in college? She could stay at the parsonage. Both she and Hector could call that home.

But Adam didn't need to consider that now. People were waiting for mashed potatoes.

"Pick up that nearly empty pan so I can exchange it." Mac shoved him aside. Sweat rolled down her forehead. The temperature today had reached eighty by noon and seemed about one hundred with the heat from the ovens. Finally, at two, the line closed and the servers fixed themselves plates.

After the volunteers cleaned up, Hector and Janey headed to the basketball coach's house for a get-together, so Adam was on his own. He wandered through town reflecting on how thankful he felt, how blessed he'd been to end up here. For a moment, Adam considered heading to Sam's house, but he was spending the day at Winnie's with his father and Willow and the boys. Nice for all of them.

After a few more blocks, he realized he was only a football field away from the pillar's house. She'd done so much today. With the bad shoulder she attempted to hide from everyone, Adam wondered how she felt. As her minister, he should check and thank her for her service. Adam wouldn't tell her he was concerned about her. She'd hate that.

Once in front of her neat little cottage, he took the steps to the porch with a leap and knocked at the front door.

"Have you swept off that porch?" Miss Birdie shouted from inside.

He looked around. A broom leaned against the wall next to the front door with a dustpan hooked onto it.

"I…" Adam attempted to speak, to identify himself and explain why he was on her porch.

"Don't backtalk me," she said firmly. "Get your south-forty in motion and sweep that porch."

What was a south-forty?

"And don't even try to get inside," the pillar continued, "until you complete that chore or I'll tan your hide."

Mystified but obedient, the minister picked up the broom and walked to the end of the porch. Maybe her shoulder was acting up and she felt grumpy and she couldn't do the task herself. More likely, she didn't realize it was him.

How carefully did this need to be done? Should Adam sweep between the rail supports? Knowing Miss Birdie, she'd expect that. If he didn't do it right, and she did know it was him, he bet she wouldn't really tan his hide—but he also knew how her words could take off a few inches of skin. Besides, he had nothing better to do.

Fortunately, the porch was small, maybe six by eight. He went over it once, grinning as he imagined her reaction. He swept the leaves and trash into the dustpan and scrutinized the area. A plastic bag was tied to the rail. He pulled it off and dumped the contents of the dustpan inside. After checking the porch again, Adam concluded that if he wanted to get inside the house, he'd better give it another sweep.

Finally satisfied, he tied the plastic sack, shook the broom over the railing to get rid of the dust, and turned toward the door.

"I'm finished," he shouted.

No response came from the house for nearly a minute. Absolute silence. Then the curtain across the window in the door was pushed aside. Miss Birdie stared out. She blinked and stood as if transfixed, her eyes still on Adam's face.

Suddenly the curtains dropped and the door opened.

"Oh, Preacher." Bright red suffused her face and covered her neck. "Oh, Preacher, I'm so sorry."

He glanced around the porch. "Did I miss a spot?"

"Come in, come in." She waved her hands toward the living room. "Please sit. Let me have that broom and the bag and the dustpan." As Adam entered, she pulled the items away and stood there, holding them, silent, in the middle of the room, her mouth a perfect O.

He hadn't thought a woman as commanding as the pillar could look mortified.

Adam smiled amicably, as if sweeping her porch was the exact thing he'd hoped to do that day. "I was in the area and stopped by to see if you've recovered from the dinner."

"Oh." She tossed the broom and other stuff in a corner. "Oh, Preacher, I'm so sorry. I thought you were Bree."

He didn't answer but felt sure confusion showed on his face as well as the desire for an explanation.

"She was supposed to help at the community dinner but didn't show up. For punishment, I planned to make her sweep the porch." She dropped in a chair. "I thought she'd knocked instead of coming right inside because she knew I'd be angry." Then she leaped to her feet. "Let me get you a slice of pie and some coffee." With a twirl, she left the room.

Having filled up on more pie at the dinner than one person should, he really didn't want more. His caffeine intake had reached a new high, so more would probably result in jitters. But he could not turn this down. He'd embarrassed the pillar and doubted her deep humiliation and sincere expressions of regret would be offered again. If she wanted to apologize, ply him with sweets and coffee, why should he refuse? Seemed the least a preacher could do. For her spiritual growth, of course.

They were both good. The pumpkin pie tasted spicy and delicious, but he enjoyed the humble pie even more.

❦

Traditionally, the church celebrated the Hanging of the Greens on the Sunday evening after Thanksgiving. With the service over, Adam looked around at the sanctuary beautifully prepared for Advent. Garlands framed the baptistery; wreaths hung on the fronts of the pulpit and lectern while a red bow marked each pew. A huge Christmas tree stood in the narthex—what the congregation called the lobby—its white ornaments glowing on the dark tree. The decorating finished, everyone had adjourned next door for more decorating and refreshments.

Adam strolled back toward the parsonage, again stopping under the big tree to contemplate the house and the church and the town and life in general. He zipped his jacket, pulled his hat from a pocket, and put it on, because November evenings in Texas did get chilly. After taking a deep breath of the crisp air, he blew it out, forming a cloud of moisture in front of his mouth, and listened to the hymn "Come, Oh Come, Emmanuel" ringing in the church steeple.

Through the big windows of the parsonage, he could see the activity inside. The ladies of the church—and a few gentlemen with carpentry skills who didn't mind being bossed around—bedecked the house. After all, who could expect a single male minister to decorate the way a minister's wife would?

On the porch railings and inside, up the staircase, they'd attached evergreen branches and bright red bows. In each front window, electric candles glowed. The parsonage looked beautiful and, he bet, smelled wonderful. He'd never be able to concentrate there.

As Adam blissfully watched, Miss Birdie strode out of the house with Chewy following at her heels. After attempting to shoo the dog away several times, unsuccessfully, the pillar ignored the creature and headed straight toward her minister, pointing toward the steeple from which the music emerged.

Her expression and stride warned him he was in trouble.

"What is that song?" she demanded when she was close enough for him to hear.

"It's an Advent hymn, Miss Birdie, because we're in Advent. In churches, the Christmas season doesn't start for four more weeks." He'd explained this over and over, but the information never sank in. Everyone wanted Christmas carols. "That's why we're playing 'Come, Oh Come, Emmanuel' instead of 'Silent Night.'"

She put her hand on her hips. "All of us"—she waved her arm toward those inside the parsonage and generally around town and the state and perhaps throughout the universe—"want Christmas music. You ministers can say anything you want, but for us, it's not Advent. It's almost Christmas. It's time for Christmas songs."

Adam glanced over her head toward the parsonage. The flickering glow of the candles and the light coming from Janey's and Hector's rooms on the second floor warmed him. In a few days, his parents would arrive to spend the holidays in Texas. They'd hate it, but they'd be here.

Thinking about the Firestones and the memory of the Smiths as well as wondering who might move in next, Adam was filled with joy. Add to that the bustle of church members inside and out, the scent of pine, and the sound of chattering and laughter, and the Victorian house was no longer the vacant building he'd moved into in June, no longer the echoingly empty residence of a single man.

He smiled. The choice of music—Advent hymns or Christmas carols—didn't seem important. "All right," he said, giving in.

Much to her surprise, Adam took the pillar's hand. "Deck the halls with boughs of holly...," he sang as the two of them strolled toward the parsonage. She joined in after a few notes. "'Tis the season to be jolly...," they sang together.

Taking care not to hurt her shoulder, Adam escorted the pillar up the front steps and onto the porch before he pulled her into a quick dance step as they sang, "Fa-la-la-la-la-la-la-la-la."

Wonder of all wonders, Miss Birdie laughed as they twirled inside.

The aroma of pine boughs mingled with the spicy scent of hot apple cider and surrounded them. In the hall, those church members who had gathered there joined in—"Don we now our gay apparel" —as Janey and Hector clattered down the stairs of the old Victorian house.

Adam was home.

Reading Group Guide

DISCUSSION QUESTIONS for
The Welcome Committee of
Butternut Creek

1. Adam heads out toward Butternut Creek in a car he's not sure will make it. How do you feel about his starting out so unprepared? Why did he do that? Have you or a loved one undertaken a task with no idea what lay ahead? If so, how did you or your loved one make it through the unexpected?

2. Do you know anyone like Miss Birdie? Does a person like her help or hurt a church? How do you feel Adam handled her? How would you deal with a church member or family member or acquaintance who's so certain he or she is right?

3. Adam dreads counseling Sam. Are there duties or responsibilities a minister has that may be difficult? How would a minister handle these? How do you cope with responsibilities you dread? Do you turn to prayer? How does God speak to you at that time?

4. Did Sam's reaction to loss seem realistic? Have you experienced a difficult loss? How did you handle that? Again, do you turn to prayer? How does God answer?

5. Willow refuses to become serious about Sam until he comes to grips with his anger. Do you agree with her decision? Why or why not?

6. How did the following help Sam to deal with his losses?

   • Adam and the church
   • Willow, Leo, and Nick
   • His father

7. Winnie Jenkins says that helping the Firestones is what the church does. Do you agree with their turning the parsonage into a shelter? Why or why not? What concerns did Miss Birdie and Mercedes express? Did they have valid points?

8. Hector says that, in his experience, churches don't always do good deeds. What do you think he might have experienced in his life that would make him believe that?

9. Adam tells Hector and Sam that his father, a very successful businessman, didn't like his choice to enter the ministry—even though he and his sister were raised in the church. Did this make sense to you? Why or why not?

10. How had the general become so demanding that Sam felt like a failure? What changed the general? Can you think of some examples of how tragedies change people, either good or bad?

11. Where can we find good in the midst of tragedy and loss? Does God cause those? Why do you believe this—or why not?

12. Have you experienced a loss that made you angry at God or left you doubting God's existence? What happened, and how did you recover your faith? Were you changed? How?